THE TAKER TRILOGY

is "a spellbinding journey through time"
(Danielle Trussoni, *New York Times* bestselling author)
from extraordinary new literary talent

ALMA KATSU

Critics and authors praise *The Taker* and *The Reckoning*,
Books One and Two in this "brilliant series" (*RT Book Reviews*),
while readers everywhere eagerly anticipate
the stunning third novel, *The Descent*.

THE RECKONING

"Beautiful, mesmerizing."

—*Library Journal*

"Picks up exactly where *The Taker* ended. . . . Grips you from start to finish. . . . Fascinating and thrilling. A unique, enduring story of the paranormal!"

—*Historical Novel Review*

"*The Reckoning* stays true to Alma Katsu's initial vision."

—*Publishers Weekly*

"It will utterly enchant you. A story told in such a distinctive voice, you won't be able to stop thinking about it."

—*RT Book Reviews*

"Gripping, pulse-pounding. . . . A whole new level of suspense [for] fans of Katsu's haunting novel *The Taker*."

—*Night Owl Reviews*

"Fast-paced. . . . [In] this supernatural drama . . . the heartbeat between love and obsession is very faint."

—*Genre Go Round Reviews*

The Taker

"Alma Katsu's searing tale of otherworldly lovers and eternal obsession will seduce you from page one. . . . *The Taker* is as irresistible as the hauntingly beautiful, pleasure-seeking immortals who scorch its pages. You have to experience it for yourself!"

—Kresley Cole, #1 *New York Times*
bestselling author of *Shadow's Claim*

"A frighteningly compelling story about those two most human monsters—desire and obsession. It will curl your hair and keep you up late at night."

—Keith Donohue, author of *Centuries of June*

"A rare and addictive treat."

—Danielle Trussoni, *New York Times*
bestselling author of *Angelology*

"This is a great book. And by great, I mean devastatingly so, like reading *The Scarlet Letter* while riding a roller coaster, on acid. Seductive, daring, soaring, and ultimately gut-wrenching. . . ."

—Jamie Ford, *New York Times* bestselling author of
Hotel on the Corner of Bitter and Sweet

"A sweeping story that transcends time. . . . A dark, gothic epic that moves effortlessly from the tempestuous past to the frightening present. . . . Enchanting and enthralling!"

—M. J. Rose, international bestselling author of
The Book of Lost Fragrances

"Sexy, dark romance. *The Taker* never strays from this question: What price are we willing to pay to completely possess another?"

—Alexi Zentner, author of *Touch*

"Marvelous. . . . *The Taker* will keep you turning pages all night."

—Scott Westerfeld, *New York Times* bestselling author of *Goliath*

"A haunting tale of passion, obsession, and immortal longing. . . . A gothic historical with a searing modern twist that will captivate your imagination."

—C. W. Gortner, author of *The Queen's Vow*

"Captivating. . . . Nearly impossible to put down. . . . [A] beautifully written, heartfelt narrative; compelling, unforgettable characters; and a mesmerizing blend of history, romance, and the supernatural."

—*Fantasy Book Critic*

"Like the hybrid love-child of a vampire novel and a historical classic, *The Taker* could be described as *Twilight* for grown-ups."

—Steph Zajkowski, TVNZ

"More than a wee bit dark, and super sexy. . . ."

—*Cosmopolitan UK*

"Full of suspense, twists and turns, and thrills."

—*Just Another Story*

"Every chapter pulls you deeper into its dark, luscious web of mystery and mythology. *The Taker* is at once gruesome and opulent, disturbing and enthralling, bitter and poignant. But most of all, it is utterly unforgettable."

—*Diary of an Anomaly*

THE
RECKONING

Book Two of THE TAKER TRILOGY

ALMA KATSU

GALLERY BOOKS

NEW YORK   LONDON   TORONTO   SYDNEY   NEW DELHI

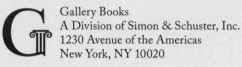

Gallery Books
A Division of Simon & Schuster, Inc.
1230 Avenue of the Americas
New York, NY 10020

First Gallery Books trade paperback edition January 2013

GALLERY BOOKS and colophon are registered trademarks
of Simon & Schuster, Inc.

For information about special discounts for bulk purchases,
please contact Simon & Schuster Special Sales at 1-866-506-1949
or business@simonandschuster.com.

The Simon & Schuster Speakers Bureau can bring authors to your
live event. For more information or to book an event, contact the
Simon & Schuster Speakers Bureau at 1-866-248-3049 or visit
our website at www.simonspeakers.com.

Manufactured in the United States of America

10 9 8 7 6 5 4 3 2 1

The Library of Congress has cataloged the hardcover edition as follows:

Katsu, Alma.
    The reckoning / by Alma Katsu.—1st Gallery Books hardcover ed.
        p. cm.—(The Taker trilogy; 2)
    1. Supernatural—Fiction. 2. Immortalism—Fiction. I. Title.
    PS3611.A7886R43 2012
    813'.6—dc23
                                                    2011052763

ISBN 978-1-4516-5180-5
ISBN 978-1-4516-5181-2 (pbk)
ISBN 978-1-4516-5184-3 (ebook)

For my mother and siblings, Linda, Diana and John

"You'll always be dear to me, Beast. I'm truly your friend. But I don't think I shall ever be able to marry you."

"You're my only joy," said Beast. "I'd die without you. Promise, at least, that you'll never leave."

—*Beauty and the Beast*, Madame Leprince de Beaumont

PART ONE

ONE

LONDON

We were nearly at the Victoria and Albert Museum when we saw the crowds spilling out of the entrance and across Cromwell Street, forcing our taxi to stop in the middle of the road. The driver turned to shrug at me and Luke as though to say we could go no farther as hundreds of people streamed toward the arched entry in a blur of color and movement like a school of fish. All there to see my exhibit.

I stepped from the cab, unable to wait a second more, and my eye was drawn immediately to the tall banner hanging overhead. *Lost Treasures of the Nineteenth Century,* it read, the dark print striking against the shimmering orange background. Beneath the words was an image of a lady's fan, extended to show the white satin stretched over whalebone ribs, its leash made of silk cord with a tassel curved upward like a tiger's tail. More treasured than the painted lilies and golden roses on the front of the fan were these words scrawled by hand on its lining:

Man's love is of man's life a thing apart, 'tis woman's whole existence.
—*Byron*

The museum had singled out this rather small and intimate object as the crown jewel of the collection and featured it on the banner and in advertisements, bypassing works by master craftsmen and artists, and rare ethnic antiques from the Silk Road. I could well imagine the excitement of the museum worker who found the words and signature of George Gordon Noel, Lord Byron on the back of this obscure little fan.

The fan was precious to me, and I'd never meant to part with it. But when we were packing up boxes to send anonymously to the V&A (shipped through my lawyer to make them untraceable back to me), I'd set it aside to return to its place on the mantel, and Luke boxed it up, thinking it a straggler from the dusty stacks of hoarded mementos to be cleared out. I wanted to get it back, but it was too late: we couldn't think of a way to ask the museum to return it without opening the door to questions.

That fan was one of the few gifts that Jonathan, my love of a lifetime, had ever given to me. After fleeing Boston, we wound up in Pisa. It was so hot that summer that Jonathan, tired of hearing me complain about the heat in our airless room at the inn, bought me the fan to cool myself. It was very fancy, meant for formal occasions, and not really suitable for my humble circumstances. But he had no idea about ladies' fashions and no experience courting, as he'd always been the one who was pursued, and so I treasured his gift all the more for being proof that he really did love me, for he had tried to please me.

As for the inscription on the back, Byron had written these words as secret solace to me, for the many times I had to hide behind my fan and say nothing as Italian ladies threw themselves at Jonathan right before my eyes. But that was in 1822, a long time ago. He was gone now and had been for three months.

I was still looking up at the banner when Luke finished paying and stepped from the cab. "Ready to go, Lanny?" he asked, sliding a hand confidently to the small of my back to steer me through the crowd. His eyes were glazed with excitement. "It's an amazing turnout. Who would've thought so many people would be interested in the stuff from your living room?" he joked, for he knew full well what marvels I'd kept to myself for so long.

We maneuvered our way through the crowd toward the first gallery, the hall reverberating with the buzz of many conversations. I wasn't entirely surprised that the exhibit, nicknamed "the mystery exhibit" by the press, was popular; there had been excitement in the city since the anonymous gift was announced in the papers. The Victoria and Albert wasn't the only museum to receive mysterious donations—museums in France, Italy, Russia, Turkey, Egypt, Morocco, and China also received shipments of mystery treasure—but the British institution had received the most, over three hundred pieces in all. The story, splashed on news programs around the world, had generated so much curiosity that the directors at the V&A decided to quickly assemble a small show to meet public demand.

Never before on public display, read the banner to our left as the queue shuffled forward. That was true: these items had spent the past century stockpiled in storage, having come into my possession as gifts or tributes or stolen outright in the case of pieces that were particularly tempting, the ones I hadn't been able to resist.

The entire divestment had come about due to Luke, really, because through him I saw my house with new eyes and realized that it had become a graveyard of keepsakes from my former lives, rooms filled to bursting with things that I'd been unable to let go. I'd accumulated and held on to these things with an irrational passion, but told myself that's what collectors did. I see now that I lied to myself to avoid the truth, which was that I collected madly to make up for the one thing I wanted and couldn't have: Jonathan.

We turned the corner into the exhibition hall, and the very first item on display, set on its own in a box on a pedestal, was the fan. It seemed to glow in the intense spotlight shining down on it, luminous as a ghost. People crowded around the pedestal, gently buffeting me as I stared at the once familiar object.

"Did Lord Byron really write that?" Luke asked me, forgetting for a moment that the people surrounding us did not know my secret.

I lifted my eyebrows. "Apparently. At least, that's what the description here says."

We were trapped in the crush of people shuffling through the gallery, forcing me to share a long, silent moment with each piece. It almost seemed as though the objects were reproaching me for upending our private life and casting them out into the world. I even felt guilt at the sight of some pieces, the most intimate ones, for having let them go like this. Mostly what I felt was panic, however, at seeing my life—a life spent entirely in secrecy—put on public display. *Nothing good can come of this betrayal,* the pieces seemed to warn me.

First was the urn that used to hold umbrellas in the entry hall of my Paris house, which my friend Savva had won from a pair of British explorers in a card game and turned out to be an Egyptian funerary urn they'd stolen from an archaeological site. Next was an Empire chair that occupied a spot on the third-floor landing: it had come from a little apartment in Helsinki where, for a brief time, I had been kept by a British officer as his mistress. As I gazed on each piece I recalled its provenance, and I should've been content with memories of my rich life, but I was not. I could not stop thinking about Jonathan. It was as though he were here beside me and not insensate and cold, buried in an unmarked grave in a faraway cemetery.

Jonathan had been absent from my life before, but this time was different, and I felt it to the marrow. Before, I had known he was out in the world somewhere, alive but happier without me, his choice for whatever hurtful reasons he felt were justified. Now his absence was permanent. I'd loved Jonathan my entire life, all 220-odd years of it.

And I was just coming to terms with the immutable fact that I would never see him again.

When Jonathan returned to me, briefly, at the end, I saw that he had changed in ways I'd never have guessed. He'd stopped being the self-absorbed adolescent I had known and had gone to work in aid camps, tending to the sick and displaced, whereas I, if I were to be honest, hadn't changed much at all. There was a part of me that believed I deserved my incurable immortal condition, a punishment meted out to me by an unspeakably cruel man. Adair had seen the bad in me, too, and known that I deserved punishment. I could only hope that I had been redeemed when I gave Jonathan oblivion, as he wished. I suspected, however, that whatever had attracted Adair had not been completely exorcised and was still inside me. I needed no more evidence than the fact that at the hospital I'd preyed on Luke, a man who'd been recently devastated by loss, to help me escape.

And, of course, there was the pain of being the one who took Jonathan's life, even if he had asked for it. That pain, I knew, would never go away. I shook my head to drive out the thought; today was about saying good-bye to the past and embracing the present.

"Are you okay?" Luke asked suddenly, snapping me out of my thoughts.

"I am. It's just . . ."

"Overwhelming. I understand." He touched my cheek; perhaps I looked flushed. "Maybe it wasn't a good idea to come. . . . Do you want to leave?"

"No, not yet." I squeezed his hand. He squeezed back.

We continued to inch along, and while Luke focused on the exhibit, I studied his features in profile. He was oblivious to my eyes on him, fixated instead on the pieces in the display cases. Luke didn't think of himself as good-looking, particularly in comparison to the perfect physical specimen that was Jonathan, whom Luke had seen for himself in the morgue. I tried to make him understand that he had his own kind of appeal.

We made a handsome couple, Luke and I, if lopsided in age. In public, he was likely taken for the father figure while I was cast as the infatuated girl. No one who saw us would suspect it was the other way around—that I was his senior by an impossibly wide margin. The truth was I was comfortable with a man at this stage of his life. So what if gray hairs had begun to mingle with the sandy-brown ones: young men were tiresome. I didn't want to endure the fits of impatience, jealousy, rage. I'd borne witness to a young man's maturation enough times to know that they'd resist any guidance from the women in their lives. No, I preferred Luke's steadiness, his good judgment.

Not only that, but I owed him. By helping me to escape, he had spared me the difficulty of standing trial for murder. A lesser man would've blinked when confronted with the impossible, would've pretended not to see the proof I'd given him that *I could not die,* would've handed me over to the sheriff and not thought twice. But Luke smuggled me out of Maine and across the border into Canada and wound up leaving his life behind and coming all the way to Paris, and now London, with me. How could I *not* love him, given everything he'd done for me?

It wasn't just the courage he'd shown that day that drew me to him. I *needed* Luke. He was my solace and support; he kept me from turning completely inward, crushed by the weight of what I had done. For the first time in a long while, I was with someone who took care of me, who cherished and protected me. It was incredibly appealing to be the object of his affection, to be foremost in his thoughts, and to be so desired that he couldn't keep his hands off me. His strong touch made me feel safe, and there was something about his manner—perhaps it was his physician's confidence—that made me feel capable of getting on with my life. Without him, I might have solidified into a pillar of grief.

Luke nudged me to point out a brick-red and gold silk carpet in the Hereke style, as supple as a handkerchief, acquired during a trip through Constantinople. I had been told it was a magical flying carpet (a time-honored Turkish sales pitch), although it never flew: its beauty was its own reward. "Wait—was I supposed to ship that to Turkey?" he whispered in my ear.

"No, it was meant to come here," I reassured him. In truth, it didn't matter which museum it ended up in. All that mattered was that the past was swept away and I was ready to move forward with my life.

Just then I noticed Luke's gaze fall on two little girls in line, staring at the tiny hands held in larger ones, their glowing faces tilted up at their father. Luke's expression grew wistful. He missed his daughters as surely as I missed Jonathan. His ex-wife, Tricia, had been unnerved to learn that her former husband had not only helped me escape but was living with me; she suspected that he'd lost not only his sense of judgment but quite possibly his mind. I hated that I was the reason he couldn't see his daughters. It was only after he'd exchanged a series of emails with Tricia that he was permitted to speak to them on the phone.

"Here," I said, positioning Luke so that he stood in front of one of the signs. I took his picture with my cell phone. "You can send it to the girls."

He squinted, not unkindly. "Is that a good idea? Tricia's still angry that I took off without a word. She says the sheriff in St. Andrew keeps calling to ask if she's heard from me. It might just piss her off to see a picture of me on vacation while she's dealing with my mess."

"Maybe. But at least the girls will know that no matter what you do or where you go, you're thinking of them—that you're always thinking of them."

Luke nodded and squeezed my arm as we continued to pick our way through the exhibit. Eventually, the crush of the crowd became too much for me. I tugged Luke's sleeve and said, "I have to get out of here," and without questioning he took my hand and we slipped out of the gallery.

Time to let go of the past.

We went up to the third floor and entered the long, darkened hall that held paintings of the nineteenth century, British and American, where the atmosphere was hushed, as if time held its breath. The rest of the museum was emptier than usual because of the opening of the special exhibit, and our footsteps cut through the silence and echoed through the hall like spirits rapping on the walls.

This hall, its walls crowded with oil paintings, had always beckoned to me, and I'd visited it on every trip to London without fail. I'd always loved the luminous Rossettis and Millaises, the rich paintings made even more beautiful by their melancholy. From the walls, the Burne-Joneses looked down on us, the Blakes, the Reynoldses. Lily-white women with long curled hair, faces heavy with maudlin expressions of love, clutching a bouquet of weeping roses, incongruously dressed as though in a classical Greek play. I think it was the models' air of sobriety that appealed to me: the sense that they knew love was fleeting and, at best, imperfect, but even so, its pursuit was no less worthy. They were doomed to try, and try again. Maybe I was drawn to this gallery because this was where I belonged, in a glass display case, kept with other things that were out of place in time. I would be a curiosity, like a mechanical fortune-teller or extinct bird, the oddities Victorians were so mad about, only I'd be a living artifact people could talk to and question.

I was squinting at a painting through the dimness—this hall was always so dark—when I felt a hum in the back of my head. At first, I thought it was only a headache from the excitement of the day, or from the claustrophobia of being swallowed up by a crowd (which I avoided whenever possible), or the dissonance of seeing my things in a strange setting . . . except that I never got headaches, just as I couldn't catch a cold or suffer a broken bone. The hum rattled, weak but not unfamiliar, at the base of the skull where it joined with the spinal column, and sent shivers chattering down my back like an old engine with a forgotten purpose being started up after a long time dormant. The hum was more than a sound: it seemed to convey emotion, the way a whiff of scent can carry memory. The hum was all these things. Once I was aware of it, it was all I could think about.

It was only then I understood that it was a signal, like the electric current that switches on a machine. I had been contacted, and a dread I'd carried for two centuries bloomed inside me, firing through every cell of my body. I could try to run from the past, but it seemed the past was not done with me yet.

I turned to Luke and reached for him; fear broke my vision into a pixelated landscape. My blood felt as though it had seized up in my veins.

"Lanny, what is it?" Luke asked, his voice filled with concern.

I clutched his lapel desperately. "It's Adair. He's free."

TWO

BOSTON

First came the noise outside his stone cell, louder than anything Adair had heard in a very long time. Then, as the noise grew closer, the shaking began, the ground reverberating underfoot as though someone were beating the skin of the earth with a big stick.

In his time, Adair had experienced avalanches and monstrous storms, lightning strikes that had shaken the ground, too, though not as steadily as this. He'd heard of volcanoes spewing hellfire and burning up villages as flammable as tinder, and earthquakes tearing the ground apart, forming great chasms and sucking houses into its maw. Maybe this was an earthquake he was experiencing now, he thought, a force of nature finally come to free him.

In this narrow niche in the wall in which he'd been sealed—his cell, as he'd come to think of it—Adair placed his hands on the thick stone walls that had not yielded in . . . how many years? He'd lost track, having no way to measure a day in constant darkness. He even tried to command fate to tear down the damnable wall to no avail.

But now, to his great surprise, fate, after being deaf to him for so long, obeyed and the hated stone wall fell away . . . only to reveal a second wall on the other side. Before Adair could bemoan his cursed luck, there was a horrendous tearing sound above, metal grinding on stone and timbers splitting as the ceiling started to crash down on top of him and the wall fell down around him: stone, lumber, brick, concrete—all.

When Adair regained consciousness, he found himself buried in a mound of rubble, grainy clumps of plaster strung together by tufts of horsehair, splintered lath, brick shattered into nuggets. The sunlight stabbed his eyes so painfully that he shut them again quickly to block out the sudden brightness. Once his eyes had adjusted to the light, he looked up through the tangle of what had been the exterior wall of the house and saw the sky, a vast welcome expanse of blue. The air on his face was like a fresh, cool kiss.

His senses were flooded at once after centuries of deprivation. He could smell plaster dust in his nostrils, taste sweet air on his tongue. Most glorious of all was the light. He'd been isolated in the dark, unable to move or feel anything except the ground under his feet and the bricks in front of his face. . . . It took only the slightest recollection and it was on him again, the smothering darkness and vast loneliness, threatening to overwhelm him. It was only with great effort that he managed to push it away. He was free now and would rejoin the living. He would be around people. He looked forward to conversation, to the sound of another person's voice in his ear, to jokes and whispered confidences, the humorous and the dour, all of it. He would feel the skin of another person again, sweet and smooth to the touch, damp from excitement or fear. He was free to pursue all the pleasures and peculiarities of the human experience he'd missed for an irretrievable length of time.

And the first thing he wanted to do—*had* to do—was get his hands on the woman who had taken this all away from him. Lanore.

Fury came over him swiftly and absolutely, decades of frustration finding release at last. He wanted to shout her name, to rattle the heavens with a demand for justice. *Bring the treacherous witch to me,* he thought, *so that she might suffer the special punishment reserved for traitors.* He wanted to wrap his hands around her throat—*now*—and throttle the life out of her. But this was impossible: he could sense that she was not nearby.

Still, the day would come and he would make her pay for her betrayal. He'd given her freedom above any of his other subjects because of his feelings for her, and she'd taken advantage of his generosity. And, more damning still, she'd betrayed him in favor of Jonathan, a man too self-absorbed to return her love. Adair had loved her, truly, but apparently *his* love had not been enough for her. For such a grave error in judgment, death did not seem an unreasonable punishment, and surely she had anticipated as much when she made her decision. But he wouldn't end her life immediately. Though the satisfaction he'd derive would be immense, it would be far too brief. He'd get greater satisfaction from extending her punishment, making her every day hellish and giving her plenty of time to regret her foolish decision.

As much as Adair wanted to rise up out of the rubble and leave his prison behind, the weight on top of him was too great. He had to wait to be dug out. He lay pinned by debris and listened to shouting voices and loud clinking in the distance, like a great many cannons being pulled into position. Perhaps there was a war on, and Boston was under attack.

Eventually, a lone man began picking through the rubble. He was dressed strangely, his head covered by an unusual helmet, plain as a mixing bowl, not like an infantryman's helmet at all. It seemed a wretched eternity before the man was close enough for Adair to call to him in a low tone so as not to draw anyone else in. The man followed Adair's voice until he found him amid the wreckage, and started pulling the rocks away quickly, shouting as he worked. "Holy cow! There's somebody in here! Hang tight, fella, I'm almost there.

I'll have you out in a minute." He was close, mere inches away, and was reaching for a small device hanging from his belt when Adair squeezed one arm free and grabbed the man by the collar. Holding on to him, Adair pulled himself out of the rubble.

"Jesus Christ, son, how did you survive having a house fall on you? It must weigh a ton." The helmeted man stopped speaking as he looked Adair over. It had to be due to the strangeness of his dress, Adair figured as he took in his rescuer's attire. The man's mouth hung open and his eyes widened behind dusty safety goggles while Adair brushed powder from his sleeves and his waistcoat and out of his long hair.

"What year is it?" Adair asked, his voice raspy.

"What do you mean, 'What year is it'? You musta gotten hit on the head pretty hard if you don't know what year it is." The construction worker reached for the handset hanging from his belt. "Look, you just sit tight, I gotta phone this in. . . . How did you get in here, anyway? We closed this site down a week ago. What are you, one of them actors they hire for the tour groups? Good thing you didn't lead one of your Freedom Trail tour groups here. . . ." He gestured to Adair's blousy shirt and shook his head.

Adair's hands found the man's throat and snapped his neck before he could finish his sentence. He felt a twinge of remorse for killing his rescuer, but circumstances called for it. He took the man's pants and shirt, since fashion obviously had changed since his imprisonment, and left his own tattered clothes behind. Then, lacing up the too-large boots he'd taken from the laborer, Adair ran from the half-destroyed house, completely overwhelmed by the change to his surroundings. First, there were the giant metal machines ringed around the mansion, tearing it apart like vultures with huge iron beaks. Then there were fast-moving carriages of some kind charging down the street, independent of any horses or oxen. The streets and sidewalks were hard and seamless underfoot. No mud, no cobblestones. And there was so much noise: horns honking, people shouting unintelligibly, and music, though not one musician was visible. To him, the jangle of the streets seemed to be pure bedlam. Adair fought his mounting panic and eventually came upon an empty building, where he found the quietest corner and sat on the floor, his back to the wall and his eyes closed.

He had to settle his mind before it was calm enough to latch onto the keening rising inside his brain, the signal that connected him to his creations. Early in his imprisonment, Adair had realized that the psychic bond he had with his minions was severed; he couldn't penetrate the thick walls of his cell to reach them. After that, he'd tried hard *not* to focus on the signal and made himself numb to it—it was either that or go crazy with frustration—but it came back to him now like a taste for sweets.

Adair squeezed his brain, working it like a fist in the hope of making it spark to life again. He sat for about an hour, struggling to grasp the signal. At first, the threads of his connection to his subjects were no more than an erratic niggling in the back of his mind that disintegrated like cobwebs at the touch. Eventually, the feeling became firm like a string, firm enough to follow, and he took its firmness to mean one of his people was close. Adair followed the string on foot, and miles later he knocked on the door of a house.

It was Jude who opened the door, the man who had masqueraded as a preacher in the Puritan settlements of the Northeast, espousing a lifestyle that both shocked and titillated the villagers. Now it was his turn to be shocked. His first reaction to Adair's return was not one of pleasure, Adair noticed, though Jude rearranged his expression to something more appropriate quickly. He stood aside as Adair stormed across the threshold. "Good God! It *is* you! I felt your presence this morning for the first time in . . . in millennia, it seems . . . but I didn't expect the honor of having you turn up on my doorstep."

That was understandable; his sudden arrival was bound to cause disruption. But, too, Adair knew insincerity when he heard it. Jude watched him intently and with slightly hostile curiosity, as though he was unwelcome. Of all the men and women Adair had bound to him over time, Jude was not one of his favorites. He wouldn't have picked Jude to be the one to help him now, but he had no control over the matter. Jude had always been an unrepentant schemer and untrustworthy. He still possessed a maniacal set to his eyes and a half-mad grin, and seemed every bit the calculating, self-absorbed man who'd attracted Adair's attention many lifetimes ago in Amsterdam.

Jude stood an arm's length away as Adair craned his neck to get a good look at the entry to Jude's home. Flawlessly smooth white walls swept up two stories, and suspended overhead was a strange sculpture that looked like a giant artichoke, with opaque white glass panels for its leaves. The floor was made of wide planks stained black. The overall effect was of power and austerity, with none of the gilt, the scrollwork, the opulence, of the age that he knew.

"Please, make yourself comfortable. Come upstairs. I'll draw you a bath and get you a change of clothes." Jude stretched his arms wide. "My home is your home."

Fighting back his uncertainties, Adair said nothing as he climbed the stairs. An hour later, after a sublime washing-up, and now dressed in Jude's ridiculous clothes, Adair rejoined his host in a large parlor at the front of the house.

Jude smiled solicitously at him. "I always wondered what happened to you. We all did. You just dropped off the radar—*poof.*" Jude made a gesture at the side of his head like the empty popping of a balloon.

"So you've seen some of the others?" Adair asked.

Jude shrugged noncommittally, but he recognized his mistake right away. He'd as good as admitted that he and the others had discussed Adair when he wasn't present, and discussing was a step away from *conspiring*, which was forbidden.

"You and the others talked about my disappearance, and yet you didn't look for me?" Adair snarled.

"Of course we tried, but there were no leads to follow. I couldn't feel your presence—none of us could. We didn't know where to start looking," Jude explained. "I went to the last address I had for you, the mansion on the other side of the Commons, but it was empty. It had been ransacked. Everyone had gone, except for that little sackcloth-and-ashes man—"

"Alejandro?" That was an apt description, Adair thought; Alejandro carried the guilt of his misdeeds with him like a defrocked priest, even if he was a Jew.

"Yes, the Spaniard. He said you had left for Philadelphia with your latest companions, that woman from the forest and her good-looking friend. Alejandro thought you had tired of him and Tilde and the Italian, and deserted them without a penny."

Adair squared his shoulders. "That man and woman were the ones who imprisoned me. Jonathan . . . and Lanore." Adair watched Jude twitch as a recollection from long ago flitted through his head. "You remember her, don't you? She insinuated herself into my graces, then tricked me. A most treacherous wench. And when I catch up to her, she'll truly see what it means to suffer. . . ." He let his threat hang in the air. He'd thought of revenge on and off over the decades, feeding his anger with short bursts of bitter memories the way one strokes an old scar to revisit the pain of its creation. But eventually his desire for revenge became so overwhelming that he had to put it out of his mind. Frustration nearly drove him insane, and teetering on the edge of that abyss was so frightening that he'd had to back away.

He'd hurled his considerable anger at the wall, over and over, and it had stood, leading him to believe that there might have been something supernatural about Lanore that enabled her to stop him. She *had* to be a witch; otherwise, how to explain his imprisonment? The wall had been nothing but a few layers of rock and brick. Over time, he'd almost convinced himself that Lanore must've put a spell on it to be able to keep him trapped inside.

Adair thought back to the moment he regained consciousness

and discovered that Lanore and that peacock Jonathan had walled him up. He remembered straining against the rope binding his hands, pulling his arms in opposite directions for what seemed like weeks until the rope stretched enough to slip off. Undoing the gag was easy then. He screamed and yelled and battered the wall with all his might, but no one heard him. No one came for him. No one knew he was there, or else, no one cared to search for him.

Inside his tomb, he'd listened to the world go on around him. Families moved in and out of the house. He heard sounds of construction, foundations of the house shaking. These times, he tried to will the wall to be taken down or the floor overhead to be torn up. But it never happened—until now.

"What year is it?" Adair asked.

"You're not going to believe it," Jude grinned insanely, like a Cheshire cat. "It's 2010, my man. Everything has changed. Everything. The world is an entirely different place now; it's going to blow your mind." The Cheshire cat's grin slipped into something more serious. "And you need me to show you what's up, because—believe me—you're not going to know how to do *anything*. Finances? No one carries money anymore. We use these." Jude fished in his pocket and pulled out a small rectangle of an unidentifiable hard substance, shiny and colorful. "Credit cards. A portable, personal system of letters of credit. Allows you to buy things anywhere in the world, immediately, no sending letters through banks and lawyers." He handed it to Adair, who examined it closely. It felt strange to the touch, and insubstantial.

"And you can go anywhere in the world in a matter of hours. You fly there in an airplane as big as a trading ship."

"How can anything as big as a two-masted sailing ship fly?" Adair scoffed, sure that Jude was making fun of him, and the crazy Dutchman had to know that was dangerous entertainment, to be sure.

"With big enough wings, anything can fly. But that's not the most astounding thing." Jude jumped up and walked over to an object on his table that Adair had mistaken for a pane of glass propped against an unusual easel. "Everything that was done before with paper and sent by courier or pigeon is now sent through the air, almost instantly, as if by magic. It's called a computer." He gestured grandly at the rather plain sheet of black glass framed with dull silver metal. Adair looked at it skeptically.

"Magic? So everything nowadays is done with magic?" Adair asked. Had magic become commonplace?

"No, no—it *seems* like magic because it's so easy. But it's all grounded in the physical world, I assure you. Sent around on waves of energy, directed by code." Jude waved his hands over the computer like a magician, as though he would conjure a dove out of thin air.

Adair was unimpressed. "It sounds very much like alchemy: using knowledge to control the forces contained within common elements." From what Jude had said, it seemed the same as knowing the right spells, the right way to reduce a thing to its most elemental state, how much energy to channel. It was the same magic, packaged differently for men who would not accept the existence of things that could not be quantified and captured in algorithms. But what was an algorithm but a recipe, a formula dictating the way to combine certain elements to get a particular outcome? Science was often indistinguishable from magic to the simpleminded. Did it matter what you called it? In the end, in its most basic state, it all came down to energy.

Jude shook his head, dismissing Adair's comparison of computers to alchemy with a brush of a hand. "Don't try to fit the new world into your old way of thinking. It won't work. You'll be better off if you just accept the new for what it is and say good-bye to the past."

"Then use your magic to bring Lanore to me," Adair demanded. "Now."

Jude settled back in his chair, casting a conciliatory look at Adair. "We will, we'll get to her. But . . . there are more pressing things that need to be settled first."

"Nothing is more important than finding her."

"In good time. Look, I don't want to rush you into dealing with this, but it must've crossed your mind. . . . Have you given much thought to your holdings? Everything you had at the time you . . . you were . . ."

"Imprisoned?" Adair finished the sentence for him. He was growing increasingly impatient with Jude, irritated by his hesitancy to take orders and by his smugness.

"Yes . . . we can look into the, uh, specifics once you've had time to recuperate, but I have to think that you lost everything." After the rush of words came out, Jude paused, blinking.

Everything lost . . . Adair recalled that he'd had quite a lot to his name: the old, large estate in Romania and another in the Black Forest. A house in London. Fortunes held in accounts in venerable old banks across Europe. He'd buried chests with treasure and left vital instruments with a trusted individual, one of his creations, for safekeeping. In all likelihood, those chests had been long discovered, and who knew what had happened to the trusted friend? Could it be true that his fortune was gone—that he was penniless and homeless?

"I'm sure, after all this time, the properties and bank accounts were forfeited," Jude explained as gently as he could. "Write down the locations, as best you can remember, and we'll investigate, but brace yourself for the inevitability that . . ."

That it would be gone, of course. Anger flooded through Adair again: that treacherous woman had stolen everything from him. . . . Of course, the others, realizing he was gone, might've been emboldened to try to find his fortune and claim it for their own as well. That might be why Jude thought it would be a waste of time to search for Adair's assets; perhaps he'd already tried to locate them and failed. Jude, as wily and greedy as a half-starved fox . . .

And then it occurred to him that the *contents* of the house had been lost, too, and among the contents were his books of recipes and spells. Panic stabbed his gut and heart, tightened his throat. Land and money he could lose and recover, in time, but if he lost the source of his power—the two books of spells—then he was helpless.

As he grasped the truth of his situation, Adair felt as though he were being pulled down to the ocean floor by an anchor tied to his waist. The collection of knowledge he'd amassed from the best practitioners of the dark arts, painstakingly gathered over lifetimes, *lost* . . . to say nothing of the blood he'd spilled to acquire such knowledge and power, all for naught. He had once been the most powerful man on earth, with abilities comparable to those of a god; and now— unless he could recall those spells from memory—he had to begin his quest all over again.

Then another thought occurred to him, one that made him sick to his stomach. Perhaps Lanny had figured out the books' value and kept them for herself. Perhaps that was how she was able to cast a spell on the wretched wall that had held him. If so, she might be a formidable opponent. He must not underestimate her.

"This is much worse than I thought," Adair said at last, struggling not to rail against this latest development, to howl at the cruelty of fate, to smash everything in his reach out of sheer black frustration and helplessness.

Jude put a hand on Adair's shoulder, the first sympathetic touch Adair had felt in a great long time. "I'm afraid so."

Adair let despair pass through him like a savage but swift illness; better to husband that rage, remember the galling impotence he felt, and save his anger for the day when he was face-to-face with Lanore again. This rage would fuel him on the difficult road that lay ahead—more difficult than he'd imagined, if what Jude said was accurate.

Jude patted Adair's shoulder again, more stiffly this time, and Adair couldn't tell if his awkwardness was due to nerves or insincerity. "Two hundred years alone . . . My God, it must have been hell. What was it like?"

To be shut up in a space no larger than a child's closet? How do you think it was? Adair wanted to shout at him, remembering the horror of being buried alive. Nothing he'd experienced had prepared him for that ordeal. After a long stretch of deprivation, the world he knew had faded away, the world of sun and plants and rich brown earth replaced by an endless black horizon. Sometimes in the blackness he knew where he was: trapped in a dank space deep in the ground, with only spiders for company. Other times, however, he felt transported to another place, a complete and utter void where he sometimes heard snatches of conversations in voices he recognized but could not place. And in those moments he was seized with indescribable feelings that he knew he'd felt before. It was far more frightening for him than he had thought possible, a man born with ice in his veins, though he'd sooner be tortured by a league of inquisitors than admit it. Especially to Jude. Adair looked away and said nothing as he moved to sit on the couch, letting his silence speak volumes.

"Your ordeal is over now, and somehow you survived," Jude said, bringing the matter to a close. "I don't know how in hell you did it, but you did, and that's saying a lot. A lesser man would've lost his mind."

Madness had been closer than Adair wanted to admit. There had been tricks he'd used to keep occupied: mentally, he traveled through his castle in Romania, pacing off the rooms, recalling his favorite appointments—the Flemish tapestry in the front hall, the heavy Bavarian chest used to hold the silver plate—and the views from certain windows. When he tired of that, he tried to recall the names and particulars of all his sexual conquests—the ones whose names he'd known—and then, exhausting that list, the names of all his horses. He picked through the rows of minerals and metals, the botanicals and organic matters stored in jars and bottles on the shelves of his laboratory, naming each in turn, forward and backward, the use and application of each. But eventually he ran out of diversions; he could think of only so many memory games, and not enough to last two hundred years.

And when his mind was unoccupied—when the wellspring of

his fury subsided and he gave in to exhaustion—he shivered to recall what came after that: the terrible visions that came out of the darkness to plague him, nightmares that needled him like aggrieved spirits . . .

Meanwhile, Jude was patting his shoulder, as he might do to cheer an old man. "I know it might seem impossible right now, but you'll get back on top. It'll just take time."

Is that what he had come to, Adair wondered, a man pitied by Jude? He rose from the chair, feeling strength rise in him at the same time. "Yes, I will gain back what I've lost, and it will happen more swiftly than you can imagine. In this, I have no doubt. And then we'll turn our attention to Lanore, and find her, and visit upon her the punishment she deserves."

THREE

LONDON

Adair freed. The day had come, as I'd always feared. I'd often thought about what I would do the day Adair escaped from the prison in which I'd entrapped him. Now that day was here, and I still didn't know what to do. Because nothing could be done: there was no way to stop the unstoppable.

I didn't realize I'd bolted from the museum until Luke caught up to me halfway down the block. I must have sprinted down the stairs, through the Chinese hall, and shoved my way through the crowds at the entrance on Cromwell. He took hold of my shoulders and spun me around to face him.

"What are you doing? You can't just go running off helter-skelter. What is it? Is he close by?" Luke's emergency-room training kicked in automatically. He looked into my pupils as he might those of a deranged person, searching for signs of trauma—not unlike the night we met, when I'd been brought in by the police.

"No, not real close. But I haven't felt him since . . . for so long. It scared me." I pressed a hand to my sternum in an effort to tamp down my wildly beating heart. "I'll be okay. Sorry for running out like that."

Luke held me tight, my face tucked against his chest, and I felt his heart pounding from having run after me. I hoped he remembered the stories I'd told him, the atrocities Adair was capable of; if so, Luke would be as frightened as I was. The very devil had broken out of hell, a devil who could be neither appeased nor thwarted and would soon be on our trail. A thought flicked through my mind: had I put Luke in grave danger? Without a doubt, Adair would stop at nothing to get revenge.

Luke ran his hand over my hair, a favorite gesture of his, as he tried to calm us both. "If you're sure that's what's going on, what do you suggest we do?"

I didn't know, but he was looking to me for an answer. "We have to run, Luke," was the best I could tell him. "We have to go somewhere he won't think to look for me."

We decided to check out of the fancy hotel near the museum. Having his presence in my head once again, I couldn't help but feel he was nearby, and this made me nervous about staying put. Once we were at the hotel, however, Luke dogged my heels, trying to change my mind as I flung clothing into suitcases we'd unpacked only a few hours earlier. "Lanny, be *logical*," he implored. "We don't know that there's any reason to panic. Please, be reasonable." *Logical, reasonable, no reason to panic*—now that the initial fright had worn off, I could see that Luke was reverting to his usual way of dealing with things. He was much more comfortable assessing everything methodically and dispassionately—choosing a beer at a pub could take half an hour—and became immediately suspicious whenever I became emotional. It had become a growing cause for friction between us.

Luke tried to pry a tank top from my hand as I stood over a suitcase. "I can understand why you're frightened. You feel his presence again," he continued. "But it just started again, right? Wouldn't that suggest that he has *just* escaped? If that's the case, he's on the other side of an ocean. And we don't know that he knows anything about you or how to find you. Maybe nothing's changed. You mustn't panic."

Except that everything had changed. And panic—justified panic—was exactly what I was feeling. Luke had never felt the air crackle with the electricity of Adair's presence. He'd never felt the chill from one of Adair's looks of displeasure, never had his marrow freeze in the bone in anticipation of one of Adair's soul-crushing punishments. Adair could swallow you up, pull you to him like a toy on a string, and once you were in his grasp, it was nearly impossible to escape. The force of his will was beyond charismatic: it was other-worldly. In two hundred years I'd met princes and generals, rebel leaders and movie stars, but Adair was the only man I'd ever met with a presence this fearsome.

Frustrated that I wasn't agreeing with him, Luke gripped my shoulders as he looked me in the eye. "He can't *possibly* know where you are if he doesn't know *who* you are. Think about it: even if he's been free for days, it would take him a long time to track you down. You have a new name, a new identity. It's a big world, and he hasn't lived in it for a couple hundred years. He has more than a little catching up to do, wouldn't you say?" There was an edge of irritation in his voice. "And logically"—there was that word again—"the thing you're feeling could be anything, right? I mean, it's been two hundred years; what are the odds that it's Adair? You could . . . have a migraine."

I pulled free and gave him a sharp look. "This isn't a headache. I *know*. Maybe I can't tell *where* he is, how far away or close, but I know what this feeling means. It's him." I might've been with Adair only a few years, but I'd felt this singular, intrusive presence the entire time, right until the day Jonathan and I walled him up. It was an electric current that cut through my mind like a wire, with no way to switch it off. There was no sensation like it.

"Can he use it to find you?"

"I don't know," I said quietly. The notion was terrifying—that this crackling in my head might allow him to follow it like a trail of bread crumbs—but I didn't think it was possible. After all, I'd felt Jonathan's presence the entire time we'd been apart but hadn't been able to tell whether he was in the next room or halfway around the world. Of course, Adair was much more powerful and undoubtedly knew how to read the nuances of the connection, knew what it meant when it warbled or stuttered, or when it was strong enough to block out any other thoughts. I had meant to ask Adair about it as I'd meant to ask him about many things, but was afraid of the answers and foolishly hoped that if I ignored my condition, it might go away. Once Adair was behind the wall, I waited to see if his spell would lose its potency and if my mortality would be returned to me, but I knew in my heart that was wishful thinking.

And now, standing here with Luke in a stalemate, I wondered again if I'd made a mistake. It had been selfish of me to take up with him—reckless, even—but I had been in a terrible frame of mind. I had lost the man who had been with me, in one way or another, for my whole life, and Luke—logical, steady—seemed like the perfect replacement. Unlike Jonathan, unlike the type of man to whom I was usually drawn, I knew I could depend on Luke. Now, with my head clearer, it was hard to imagine our relationship would last for more than just those practical considerations.

And, too, I was confronted by the flip side of Luke's virtues. Where I'd once seen him as steady and practical, he now seemed inflexible. By comparison, I was made to seem impetuous, to be the child to his parent. He didn't mean to bully me, but I had started to resent his corrections and coercions more and more. This friction seemed to be another sign that we were not meant to be together.

Also, I knew in my heart that being with Luke—being with *any* mortal, for that matter—was doomed to end badly for me. Even though I had promised Luke I would remain with him until the end—part of the bargain we'd struck when he helped me escape—I'd never found it easy watching the people in my life die. And—another sign that I'd acted recklessly in taking up with Luke—I'd promised myself I'd never seduce someone with children, and here I'd done it, forcing Luke to choose between me and his daughters. Of course, Luke had had equal part in every decision we made along the way, but I couldn't shake the feeling that I'd preyed on him in a vulnerable moment. I'd been wrong to pull Luke into my life, and now I was being confronted by my mistake.

"You think I'm overreacting," I said to him, throwing the last of my things into my suitcase. "But I assure you, I'm not." I looked at him with grim seriousness.

Luke took a deep breath before speaking. "I think it's important to remain calm until we know what we're facing."

"I won't feel safe if I stay here. You can follow me or not, but I'm leaving," I replied, and Luke gave in: he could tell I was not going to change my mind. Eventually, we found a cheap hotel on the rail line near Heathrow. For a bribe, the desk clerk kept our names and passport IDs off their books and we paid for a night's lodging in cash so there'd be no credit card record. The room was cramped, filled with mismatched furniture, the mattress unevenly soft from overuse. I find few things as depressing as a run-down hotel, perhaps because I'd spent more than my share of time in them. But it was just for one night, and in the morning we'd catch a flight to . . . somewhere. I hadn't made up my mind yet; I needed to find a place where I'd be safe from Adair. I only knew I'd feel better if we kept moving.

Luke and I made love quickly that night, in that tired old bed. I suspected he wanted us to have sex because he thought it might calm my nerves, but he was rather workmanlike about it and not reassuring at all. In any case, he fell asleep soon after we'd finished, but I was too edgy to do anything but try to ignore the painful keening in my head and all that it meant.

The longer I sat in the darkness watching Luke, the more I struggled with the urge to get out of bed and slip away. *He's going to leave you; it's inevitable,* the merciless voice in my head insisted. *He doesn't love you and he'll wake up to that one day. He'll want his old life back, the one he threw away to follow you. He's got children, after all. There is no happily-ever-after for someone like you; you're one of Adair's monsters and he* picked *you for a reason. Luke wouldn't love you if he really knew you— if he knew of all that you did to stave off loneliness and weaken the sting of Jonathan's rejection. He'd leave you if he knew half of your adventures and romances, because he thinks of himself as a good person, and good people don't take up with bad. Did you really think you deserved to be happy?*

I hated that voice. I heard it all too often. And behind it lurked the fear that I felt with every man, the same needle-sharp pain I'd felt when Jonathan had left me. That pain had been so bad, I swore I'd never allow myself to be hurt like that again. I resolved that, in all my relationships, if someone was going to leave, it would be me.

The truth was, too, that only one of us was in danger. Luke was only in harm's way because he was with me. If I left Luke, he would be safe. I was about to do something cruel and unforgivable, but I was doing it for his sake. I would break the promise I'd made to him when he helped me escape: that if he gave up everything to come with me, he'd never be alone again. He'd kept his end of the bargain, and now he would learn that he shouldn't have trusted me.

Quietly, I searched the writing desk until I found a forgotten sheet of hotel stationery. Luke deserved a note from me, even if I couldn't think coherently. I don't know exactly what I wrote that night; I think I thanked him for helping me at my time of greatest need and hoped he would be able to forgive me someday. I left all the money I had on me and suggested that he go back to America and see his daughters. I hoped that he would not be broken by my desertion, as I had been when Jonathan left me. But it was the only way.

I put the note on my empty pillow. *I have to go, I have to go, I have to go*—the words clamored in my head like the ringing of a bell as I gazed at Luke sleeping peacefully. Adair was coming for me and our

time together had run out. I had to take care of myself now and spare
Luke and his family. I would be alone again, but in the end, we are
all alone. How well I knew that lesson.

I hated to do it, but I slipped out of the room as quiet as a monk
at midnight vespers and refused to look back as I closed the door
behind me.

FOUR

The next morning, Adair rose early after a restless night. The darkness of evening wasn't nearly as complete as the darkness and quietude of his sealed tomb, and so he found it impossible not to waken at the minutest lightening of the sky or the slightest street noise. On the other hand, after just one night in a proper bed, he developed an appreciation for the ingenuity of modern mattresses and box springs. The bed in Jude's guest room might not be as decadent as the bower of pillows and sables on which he'd slept in the old mansion, but it was preferable by far to the hard-packed floor that had been his bed for so long.

Dawn had barely broken and Adair found Jude already up to his elbows in work in the only room in which he seemed to spend any time, the one he called his office. Jude always had been industrious—indeed, he first came to Adair's attention when he'd nearly brought down the Dutch gold merchants' guild with an ambitious scheme to break their monopoly—but today Adair was put off by his single-minded devotion to business. After all, his master had returned after an absence of two centuries; Jude should be happy to push aside his ledgers and accounting to celebrate Adair's return and wait on him as protocol decreed.

"Take me into this new world," Adair said, standing in front of Jude's desk, demanding his attention. "I want to see it for myself."

The Dutchman lifted his head from his work with forced patience. "It's a little early in the day to see much of anything. How about I set you up on the computer and let you—"

"No," Adair interrupted. "No more of your precious gadget. I'm tired of it." He suspected Jude was using it to keep Adair out of his hair. And besides, he didn't like the feel of it, the way it made his fingertips hum and set his teeth on edge.

Jude leaned back in his chair. "All right. Where do you propose we start?"

"I need clothing. We'll call on your tailor."

Jude had the audacity to smirk. "We don't have tailors make our clothes anymore. You can buy most things in stores. And you're right: you need clothing. My things don't really fit you, do they? Okay, once the stores open, we'll go shopping. In the meantime, you should get a sense of how men dress these days." He left the room to come back with bound stacks of glossy pages of images. "Magazines. Periodicals, like courants, but the modern equivalent," Jude said, dropping the pile in Adair's lap. "They're mostly advertisements, but that will give you an idea of what to expect." Thus directed, Adair took his time looking through the pictures, but they seemed like an endless repetition of insouciant and foppish young men, oversize illustrations of timepieces and variations of the mechanized carriages he'd seen on the street yesterday. He found the young men impossible to take seriously, and the other items held no appeal.

Shopping proved to be tedious and fascinating all at once. He'd secretly thought it would be his first pleasurable experience in the new world, since he had been fond of dressing up and, in his day, had indulged in the best cloth and finest tailors money could buy. Presently, however, the experience was much degraded.

First, Adair had to deal with the morbid sensation of making personal choices in front of strangers; he was used to dealing with tailors and clerks, but to make purchases under the curious eyes of other customers seemed too public. Then there were the clothes themselves, so thin and plain, devoid of lace and embroidery, piping, brass buttons, or frogs made of silk braid. Everything was dark and somber and devoid of self-expression, as though Quakers had taken over the clothing industry. And one wore so few layers that even fully dressed he felt scandalously loose and nearly naked. He felt especially unprotected at the throat, with no high collar and winding cravat, and Adair fingered silk neckties, but Jude assured him that he'd never need one. At the heart of his discontent, Adair recognized, was that he felt vulnerable in this clothing. One benefited from constriction in one's garb: you were sure of the boundary between your body and the rest of the world. You were held in check.

After spending nearly half the day in stores, he'd amassed an entire wardrobe, down to socks (fine as little gloves on the feet, he marveled, magically gripping the calf with no need for garters) and shoes, and a near-weightless wrap of clingy fabric at the groin instead of a saggy linen to hold one's testicles in place.

Next, Jude took Adair to a salon, which turned out to be a delightful experience. He sat in a chair while a fetching young woman ran her fingers through his curls, and a half dozen more hairdressers cooed as they passed by, commenting on his handsomeness, coming up with excuses to squeeze his biceps, telling him that he had sexy eyes. A young man trimmed Adair's facial hair in a style Adair would never have imagined, outlandish to the point of pretension, but it seemed to please the women.

That evening, Jude called for two high-priced escorts to entertain them. Adair sat on the low sofa and watched the two women dance together, studied the brazenness of their clothing, their hair, the precise makeup applied to their faces. Their limbs were sculpted, their eyes bright, their lips sultry, as though every aspect of their appearance had been calculated to make them as desirable as possible. The women he remembered, whether peasants working in the fields or courtesans to a king, would seem overfed and underpainted by comparison. Adair wondered for the hundredth time about the world he was thrown into, the sheer chaos of it, and how nearly unrecognizable it was from the one he'd known.

He and Jude took turns with the women and they seemed to make a game over which could come up with the most imaginatively obscene thing to do to Adair. They made a fuss over the sizable girth of his manhood and vied to make it rise again and again. They stroked and petted him, rubbed their pretty faces against his chest and backside and groin, worked their lips and tongues over his nipples and belly button and stomach, treating every inch of his skin to pleasures he'd not had for two centuries. He came so many times he wouldn't be surprised if he never climaxed again. One of the women slept in his bed that evening—Jude sent his away in a taxi—and Adair was surprised at how satisfying it was to have this stranger sleep beside him, like a kitten curled under his arm.

After she left in the morning, Adair wandered through the house until he found Jude again in the office. He leaned back in his desk chair upon seeing Adair. "Hope you enjoyed your treat last night." Jude smiled broadly. "I told the girls you'd just got out of prison for embezzlement: that's a high-class crime. They wanted to give you a warm welcome back to society."

Adair ignored him; discussing their activities of the night before seemed juvenile and ungallant. "So, what do you do now, Jude? No longer pretending to be a clergyman?"

Jude gestured at his cluttered desk, the stacks of papers and pieces of electronic gadgetry. "I'm a businessman."

"A businessman, huh? What line of business are you in, exactly?"

"The business of the day, my friend: making money. I have a partner in Hong Kong—we've never met face-to-face—and we speculate on the stock market. Essentially, we make money from nothing but intuition and timing. It's all very complicated. I'll explain it to you someday. Right now, though, I doubt it's the most pressing thing on your mind."

The condescension in Jude's tone made Adair seethe. He wanted to take him to task right then and there, but he held his temper, because he knew he needed Jude to find Lanore. Nothing could jeopardize his chances of finding her. "All I need to know is that you're very good at it and that it provides you with a considerable income, because I will be using *your* funds while I get back on my feet," Adair responded.

Jude's face fell in a way Adair found amusing. However, there was only one man to whom Jude owed everything and could deny nothing, and what would be the use of refusing? Adair would take what he wanted from him anyway. Jude sighed in resignation. "Of course. What's mine is yours. It's only money, right?"

"That has always been my belief. Money is only a means to what is truly important."

Jude hesitated before continuing. "Look, you need to understand, though, that while I have money, most of it is tied up in business ventures. It's not that I begrudge you any of it, but something tells me my little nest egg is not going to last the two of us very long. And as I explained already, you've been wiped out. I have an idea for a way to get you enough cash so that you'll never have to worry about it again. There are people who would pay a lot to live forever . . . if you would be willing to put this service up for sale."

Adair's first reaction was to refuse; indeed, even as the suggestion spilled from Jude's mouth, Adair felt uneasy. It would be an act of extreme desperation to sell such power. That was how he'd acquired the true elixir of life, the potion that granted immortality, in the first place: he'd found a penniless apprentice reduced to selling his master's potions to keep from starving while he waited for his master's return. Even then he'd resisted the temptation to use this power to get rich and sold only enough to meet his meager needs. And that transaction hadn't ended well for the apprentice: it only takes one wolf to show up at your door.

Still . . . he was no apprentice and this was an extraordinary situation. Adair felt the reasonableness of Jude's suggestion in his bones. *So be it.* "I might consider doing this once, and only once, Jude, so the recipient must be able to pay handsomely for the opportunity."

"Of course. . . . I'll find someone with the means to afford it."

"You're putting the cart before the horse. First, I need to find my books of spells." Adair had no illusions as to the difficulty of this task, however. Books were fragile things, easily hidden, easily destroyed. If he couldn't find the books, he'd need to go back to the old country and trace them back to their origins, as he had the first time. He looked down at Jude, who had no idea of the extent of the research it had taken to acquire all these powers in the first place, the years spent tracking down stories of Adepts, practitioners of alchemy who had developed spectacular powers, finding their adherents, convincing them to share the secrets. Convincing them by any means necessary . . .

"These books are quite singular, you see. There were two, a blue book of Venetian origin, and a much cruder one, no more than a collection of written recipes bound between wooden covers. It's the second, however, that is the more valuable."

Jude scratched his chin. "The books in the mansion—were those your only copies?"

"Of course not. I took precautions. I wrote out the most important recipes and hid them in a safe place."

"That's good. It might be easier to retrieve your copies than to try to find the originals. Where did you hide them?"

"A city in Saxony; a church in the city's center." He couldn't remember the year, but he'd stopped there for one season. He recalled falling in with a widow who owned a nice house in town, and she offered him companionship and a comfortable place in which to spend a wet winter. He used the gray afternoons to copy out his most important spells for safekeeping, wrapped them in a square of boar's hide, and hid the packet in the church's catacombs, among the priests' bones. He could picture the area in his mind very well, but the town's name eluded him, as did the year. Surely the town was unrecognizable by now, if it still existed at all. But a crypt would go unmolested. No one, not even in the modern age, would desecrate a crypt.

"Could you show me the location on a map?" Jude asked, though clearly reluctant to raise any hope as he spread an atlas in front of Adair. "Here's the region of Saxony. It's on the eastern side of a country called Germany now. See, right here where it comes up against the Czech Republic." When Adair didn't react beyond peering at the unfamiliar map, Jude flipped to another page, one that showed the area in topographical detail: greens and browns, with rivers in a meandering dark blue line. His finger circled aimlessly on the page. "Any of this look familiar?"

Adair's eyes picked over the place names . . . Königstein, Freital . . . the Elbe River, yes; he recalled that the town had stood on the south bank of the Elbe. And then his finger passed over the name, Dresden; yes, that had been the name of the town. It had been the seat of the margrave, as he recalled. He looked up at Jude, tapping the spot on the map.

"Are you sure that's the city?" Jude asked, but by his tone Adair could tell the news would be bad. "If that's the place, and you left your papers in the city center, then I'm sorry to tell you that they are probably gone. There's a chance that it might've been spared, if your memory is inaccurate and the place you remember wasn't exactly in the center but on the outskirts. But the city was destroyed by bombs and gutted by fire in a war." Adair felt his stomach tighten like a fist. "I'm sorry to have to tell you. We can go over there and search for ourselves, if you'd like. We can try."

Adair was very tired suddenly. The village he recalled had been a lovely place with verdant fields and forests running with deer and boar. The city had been lively and prosperous, and the young widow had been grateful for his company. Of course, he'd expected that the village as he knew it would be gone, the widow long dead, and yet . . . the news that it had been destroyed struck him like a blow to the head. He was disappointed, too, to hear that the package he'd tried to safeguard was gone. He rose, waving a hand at Jude. "No, let me think about it," he said as he retired to his room.

A few weeks passed, each filled with new milestones for Adair. A new identity was created for him, complete with documents of iden-tification, credit cards, and passports. Jude bought him a cell phone and showed him how to use it, though he had no one to telephone. He learned to drive, to use an ATM. Jude got a tablet computer for him, and grudgingly Adair spent a few hours a day laboring with it like a schoolboy over a slate in the old days, going through the exer-cises Jude laid out for him like a lesson plan.

Through all the learning and rehabilitation, the fits and starts, trying and failing and trying again, Adair fought to keep from pan-icking. Jumping into modernity was daunting, and the temptation to give up very strong. He'd observed over the centuries that what made people old was when they could no longer keep up with change. It's the beginning of the end, though few recognize it as such at the time. He'd seen it in his own companions, too: there came a time when they could no longer tolerate the press of *the new*. You might call yourself a traditionalist, pretend to see no value in new ways, or claim that you've earned the right to let progress pass you by, but the sad truth of the matter was that you were choosing obsolescence.

Being immortal meant never having the luxury of surrendering to change. That was its only imperative: you must keep changing forever. You might as well be trapped inside a wall or a cave or live at the bottom of the ocean if you couldn't keep pace with the world. And Adair refused to be made irrelevant. Besides, he had a mission to spur him on—finding the traitorous Lanore McIlvrae—and he knew to be grateful for such strong motivation. His hatred was a lifeline and he would use it to pull himself along, hand over hand, yard by arm-wrenching yard, until he reached the other end.

Although he noticed a strange change had taken place when he thought about Lanore (and he could not *stop* thinking of her). His stomach no longer churned, his guts no longer tightened in a lump. He no longer responded in the way he'd reacted to enemies in the past. The thought of her made his heart beat faster, but not from rage.

One afternoon, from down the hall, Adair heard Jude calling his name. Adair ignored him, appalled that one of his subjects had the impertinence to beckon him, as though the order of things had changed and Jude was the master and Adair his slave. But ignoring him had no effect—the man just continued to call for him, bleating like a sheep dumbly waiting for the shepherd—so Adair gave up and followed the voice to Jude's office.

As always, Jude was sitting in front of the computer. "I got something that's gonna make you happy, man. I found it. One of your books: the book of spells."

Adair looked over Jude's shoulder at the screen. "How did you find it?"

"The computer. I don't know how we ever got along without it." He rapped a finger against the image flickering on the monitor. "I think this is your book. Can't know for sure: there's no way to tell what was done to the contents of your house when you disappeared. The landlord probably presumed you'd abandoned it and auctioned off your possessions to pay whatever money was owed to the owner. So I did a little searching online: eBay, auction houses . . ." Jude prattled on, oblivious to whether Adair understood the terms he was using or not.

"I knew I would find it eventually, and I did. Voilà," Jude said proudly as he swiveled the monitor to give Adair a better view. But what had he found? All Adair saw was a photograph of an attractive building and a second picture of a shining hall of glass showcases. Words were scrawled across the top of the page, but the script was still unfamiliar and he had to fight to make out each word. "The Venetian manuscript, the one with the insignia branded onto the cover," Jude continued, "it's here in this building."

The Venetian manuscript was the lesser of the two major texts he'd owned. The book he desperately needed was the second book, a collection of alchemical recipes that he'd copied out from various tomes or captured by pen from the mouths of practitioners. It had been his life's work, painstakingly amassed over his travels, the loose and mismatched sheets bound by wooden covers and lashed with a leather thong. Perhaps the Venetian manuscript—the prettier of the two, with its blue linen cover, the gilt illustrations and meticulous calligraphy—would lead him to the more important book. He could only hope.

"Where is this place?"

"Not far. Marblehead. An hour north of here. 'North Shore Historical Society,'" Jude read, squinting through his eyeglasses at the screen.

"Write down the directions. I will pay them a visit."

The drive was quick enough, following Jude's directions, though he still had moments of unease alone in a car. (The contraption required you to do so many things at once and was so much less intuitive than a horse. He longed for a good horse.) He recognized the museum from its photograph on the website: a small brick building standing by itself on a narrow lot, surrounded by a grove of trees that filtered out most of the sound of highway traffic. It was not a popular establishment: there was only one car in the parking lot, and inside there were no visitors. Light filled the rooms from high windows, the kind that might be found in a church. Adair flinched at the echo of his own footfalls reverberating through the open space as he walked impatiently from display to display, searching for what he'd come for.

The majority of the items in the cases were unknown to him, having been invented after he was entombed. A large washbasin with a heavy iron mangle perched on top of it had a plaque that read "Clothes washer, 1907." There was a small collection of scrimshaw, which he recognized, having seen examples of the whaler's art from the sailors themselves, and a display of pistols and rifles, most from the late 1800s, looking handsome and well kept, gleaming with oil. Numerous photographs of Boston, aged when compared to the city today but more modern than the city Adair knew, hung on the walls.

He came at last to the book, lying in a display case in a narrow hall at the back of the building, sent to a lonesome corner like an unloved stepchild. "Book of magical spells, in Italian, ca. 1700, from the collection of Mrs. Brittany Leigh Hendrickx, Boston," read the small label affixed to the wall. Adair knew immediately that it was his book, the one he'd acquired as a young man studying medicine in Venice. He'd bought it in the late thirteenth century, not the seventeenth century, as the label said; obviously the fools had no idea what a rare find they had in their possession. His seal was branded into the cover, now faded blue linen stretched over a wooden board. The book was opened innocently to a ghastly spell that would make its victim break out in toadish warts, if someone could make sense of the old, formal Italian.

"May I help you?" Adair hadn't noticed a woman approach him. Middle-aged, she wore a knit vest and a wool skirt that hung almost to her ankles, and she held a pair of bifocals in one hand almost expectantly.

"This book—" Adair began, but she cut him off.

"It is a curiosity, isn't it?" she said, cocking her head like a bird. "It's part of the permanent collection. We're not sure if it's a reproduction, which is why we keep it in the back. Are you interested in old books?"

He ignored her question. "How did it come to be in your possession?"

"We'd like to know the provenance of all the items the museum owns, but often that's not possible." She smiled warily, as though unsure about engaging the visitor any further. "This piece was donated by a collector who moved to Marblehead from Boston. Mrs. Hendrickx, I recall, loved to collect things at estate sales. Couldn't bear to see really old things thrown away. I can check our records to see if there's any more information. . . ." She tilted her head in the other direction. "Is there a particular reason for your interest in the piece? Are you doing research, writing a paper?"

Because it belongs to me. The words floated through his head, but instead he said, "Yes. I am a collector myself, of such . . . oddities. I would be interested in purchasing this item, if you would be willing to sell it. It is, as you say, probably a reproduction and of dubious historical value. Hardly worth keeping in this noble institution."

She furrowed her brow, making a show of her attempt at concentration, or perhaps to indicate that he'd said something wrong. "That wouldn't be up to me. I'd have to ask the museum director. If he were to agree to your request, it would still have to go before the museum board of directors."

"I see," Adair answered, clasping his hands in front of him, trying to suppress the urge to simply snatch up the book and run, happy to have found even one of his treasures. "And . . . could you find out if you have similar items in storage? Perhaps more curiosities from Mrs. Hendrickx's collection?"

"We have a catalog of our entire inventory," she said with a hint of impatience, "but it will have to wait. I came over, actually, to tell you that the museum will be closing shortly." She gestured to the empty room. So that was why there were no other patrons. "If you give me your name and a way to contact you, I can call you once I've had a chance to do some research. But for now, if you don't mind . . ." She gestured in the direction of the door.

"Perhaps—since it appears there are no other patrons, and you are here alone—you would take the time to check your inventory *now*? I don't get out this way often. I would certainly appreciate your making this special effort on my behalf."

Adair saw his mistake right away, pointing out that the two of them were alone. She became nervous, glancing over her shoulder toward the office, perhaps thinking how she might trigger an alarm or summon help. She stepped away from him. "I'm afraid I couldn't take the time just now. . . . I have an appointment elsewhere soon, and they'll be worried if I don't show up. . . ." She was bluffing, Adair guessed, from her edgy tone.

He took her by the elbow—momentarily surprised by her fragility, her bones like dried twigs—nearly lifting her off the ground, and when she tried to pull away, he jerked her arm sharply enough to make her cry out in pain. "You will do as I asked." She opened her mouth to protest but the words evaporated as she began to understand that she was in trouble.

She first consulted a computer in the office, Adair standing at her side to monitor every keystroke to make sure she wasn't sending a warning, and then they went down a dark stairwell to the basement. Whimpering under her breath, she led him between rows of tall shelving, each shelf loaded with boxes or holding items draped in heavy plastic or shrouded with a drop cloth. She pointed to a stiff gray cardboard box on a high shelf. "That's the rest of the items from the Hendrickx collection," she said, drawing her arms across her chest and backing away from him, at once indignant and frightened.

Adair pushed the lid back and poked through the contents. If these paltry items represented the sum of this Hendrickx woman's life, it made for a poor showing. There were more books, though of worthless pedigree, and a few items whose purpose eluded him. The basement was dimly lit, and so he resorted to using his hands to feel his way through the assortment of bric-a-brac, but was rewarded when he touched an object made of moldering wood, bound with a cord of greasy leather.

He pulled out his ancient chapbook. It was reassuring to see the edges of various papers peeking out beyond the scarred wooden covers. He unlashed the leather and shifted through the pages; he couldn't be sure *everything* was there, but at least *most* of the recipes were, and that was more than he had dared hope to find.

He tucked the book under his arm and turned to the docent, who had backed to the very end of the aisle, as far as she could get from Adair. "This is exactly what I was looking for. I thank you for your assistance. Now, you're to stay here until I've left the building. . . . Wait at least fifteen minutes before you go upstairs. If I hear that door open before I've left, you'll leave me no choice but to do something you will find very unpleasant. I would prefer not to harm you, since you've been so very accommodating. Do we have an agreement?" She just stared at him, frightened and scornful, no doubt upset at being made to feel helpless. "Do we?" he asked, more menacing this time, and he only needed to take one step toward her for her to squeak out "Yes."

He was almost at the door when he remembered the Venetian manuscript, and doubled back to the rear of the building to fetch it. He tried to find a way into the display case, but there didn't seem to be one, not a hinge or lock to be seen, so he punched the box full force with his fist. Only, it didn't break. It wasn't made of glass. It splintered into a spiderweb of cracks under his knuckles. He punched it again, buckling the Plexiglas this time, so he could reach in and snatch up the book. Jagged edges cut into his hand and he spouted blood, but only for a minute, a few drops splattering against the white wall. Book in hand, he left through the main entrance and went straight to the car, waiting for him like a trusty horse.

FIVE

⚜⸺⸺⚜

OUTSKIRTS OF LONDON

Luke knew something was wrong even before he opened his eyes. He and Lanny were most connected when they were in bed: they'd slept together every night for the past three months, and took every opportunity to nap just for the excuse of nestling close to each other. He'd gotten used to the feel of her tucked next to him, of breathing in the scent of her shampoo from the crown of blond curls nestled right under his nose.

Now the covers hung too sharply from his shoulder, like a tent that had collapsed, and the sheets had gone cold around him. When he slept with Lanny, his troubles sloughed off and he was able to forget everything: the divorce, the monotony of his job, finding a buyer for his parents' house, missing his kids, the police back home waiting to talk to him. Yes, being with Lanny had been like living in a sweet narcotic dream with no responsibilities, no worries, no bad memories.

Luke sat up and rubbed his eyes awake. He ran his hand over the crater where Lanny's body had lain: cold; the bed had been empty for hours. He looked around the hotel room, quickly noticing that one of the suitcases was missing. His stomach dropped like an elevator in free fall. He jumped out of the bed, checked the closet and the dresser drawers even though he didn't need to; he knew all her stuff would be gone. Luke slammed his hand flat against the dresser and made everything jump: pocket change, passport, cell phone. He snatched up the phone and looked at the screen: no calls. She hadn't tried to reach him. Pride kept him from calling her immediately, but he knew that pride would give way to desperation before long.

It was then he noticed the small pile of things left on the bureau. A haystack of crumpled banknotes, all their cash. A bank card. Instinctively, he looked back at the bed and it was then he saw the envelope left on her pillow.

He pored over her note while standing up, one hand pressed against his stomach as he read it through twice, three times. *I'm sorry if I hurt you. It was selfish of me to ask you to come away with me. . . . You have children to think about. You should be with them. . . . You were kinder to me than I had any right to expect. I hope one day you can forget me.*

Luke felt his anger build. The letter immediately brought to mind the story Lanny had told him of Jonathan leaving her at a hotel in Fez: after all those years together, he fled under cover of night and left a cowardly note to make his apology. Luke recalled the emotion with which she recounted the centuries-old story and how it crippled her still. And yet, here she'd done the same thing to Luke, leaving nothing but destruction—to *his* life—in her wake. How could she do this to him? And how could he have been so naïve to believe that she wouldn't?

Then again, maybe these dramatic departures were a test; maybe he was supposed to run after her, find her, and tell her he loved her no matter what and he couldn't live without her. She needed reassurance and this was how she got it: by forcing a little drama. He resented the hell out of being made to play a role like some poor weak-kneed bastard in a play. Besides, he had a right to be angry: she'd left him, after the chance he'd taken by helping her escape, after he'd given up everything—his career, the home he'd grown up in, even regular contact with his children.

His ex-wife, Tricia, had flipped out when she found out about Lanny and the circumstances under which he had run away with her. She accused him of having the most predictable of midlife crises, falling for a woman so young, and then asked if he'd lost his mind in doing something so irresponsible and dangerous. She told him he was no role model for their daughters and she didn't want "that woman" anywhere near the kids. Luke tried to bring her around slowly, making weekly phone calls to show her what a devoted and patient father he was—and decidedly not crazy, just *living* for the first time in ages, and how could she begrudge him that?

Only he *was* crazy now, teetering on the verge of nausea . . . and why? Because she'd left him. He felt as though she'd gutted him and scooped out his vital organs. How foolish he'd been to trust her.

Luke packed his bag and stuffed himself into his clothes, then walked briskly to the front desk, which was manned by the same clerk as the night before. He tapped the counter for the clerk's attention. "The woman who was with me, did you see what time she left last night?"

"Left, sir?" By his expression, Luke saw that the clerk didn't know what he was talking about.

"Never mind," Luke muttered. "Checking out."

Luke hailed a cab out front. Nothing to do but head to the airport, though he wasn't sure where he'd go. Not back to St. Andrew, that was for sure: Joe Duchesne, the sheriff, would be waiting to question him and might even put Luke under arrest. He had family to the south of St. Andrew, but they'd probably heard what had happened, why he'd disappeared. They'd know the law was looking for him, and he couldn't in good conscience ask them to harbor a fugitive. Luke fingered his luggage tag, still brand-new, wondering:

When had his life become so small? When did he become such a loner that he didn't have a single friend to turn to for help?

It galled him that the only logical thing to do was to go to Tricia, just as Lanny had suggested . . . as though—ever the tactician—she had seen everything two jumps ahead. And yet, he had no choice. With his heart beaten to a pulp, he needed to see his daughters, needed the kind of unreserved love they would give him like a transfusion. Tricia, always practical, would let him hide out there and take care of him until he could think straight. He needed his family.

And who knew: maybe this was Lanny's way of telling him where to wait for her, like pointing to a map. Not promising that she'd come looking for him, but if she did, she expected him to be with his daughters in Marquette. She seemed to love his daughters sight unseen; wasn't she the one to bring them up at every opportunity, to ask if he'd contacted them recently, to find the perfect gift to show them he was thinking about them? It was as though that had been her chance to be a mother, to see what it was like to have that life of domesticity that had eluded her, and that had been Luke's private fantasy: that they'd settle into a house not far from the girls. That Lanny would've become a part of their lives. That he and Lanny would live cozily in Marquette when it suited them, then fly off for distant lands when it got to be too stifling. He'd wanted it and believed she had wanted it, too. Now he had evidence to the contrary.

No. He had to stop fantasizing about the life he could have had and focus on what lay ahead. Already he felt like a failure, skulking home to live in his parents' basement until he got his life back together—made worse by the fact that he wasn't even returning to his parents' house but to his ex-wife's. Meanwhile, Tricia's fiancé, Richard, was a really nice, laid-back guy, which made his mess of a life all the more humiliating.

Ironically, it hadn't been so long ago that Tricia had left him, and that had hurt like the devil, like he'd been kicked in the nuts over and over. The whole ordeal had leveled him, even briefly driven him to drink. There had been nights at the hospital when he contemplated getting into the pharmaceutical cabinet in the ER, the locked box that held the painkillers and sedatives. To escape. To rid his system of the residual traces of fear of being hurt like that again.

But Lanny was special and unique, irreplaceable. Not only had she reawakened him, made him feel strong again and needed in a way he'd never felt with Tricia, she had awakened his mind to an entirely new understanding of existence. Her very nature defied science. He'd felt the awe of the unknowable every time he touched her perfect skin.

As much as Luke hungered for Lanny as his partner and companion, he hungered for her knowledge. Lanny was the portal to this unseen world—a world that could change the way we thought about our lives, that changed the nature of how we lived and what we believed. A world that could be without worry, without pain, without fear. He was delirious with optimism and emotion.

Except that now Lanny was gone. Without her, the truth of the universe would be lost to him forever. And there was no way for Luke to mitigate *that* loss. No way at all.

SIX

BOSTON

"You mean there was no security at all at the museum?" Jude asked when Adair told him the story of his burglary upon his return. "No guard? No alarm went off when you broke the display case?"

Adair shook his head. The cuts on his hand had healed during the drive back.

"What about cameras? They might've gotten you on tape," Jude said, sober at the prospect. "Did you see any security cameras?"

"How should I know?" Adair snapped.

"They might have a picture of you," Jude warned. "We'll have to watch the news, check the internet, see if there's any coverage. We'll need to know if the authorities will be looking for you. You don't think they had a camera on the parking lot, do you? Any chance they could've gotten my tags?"

Adair left Jude to worry about these insignificant details and went up to his room with the books. Better to look them over in private, he decided, in case Jude had designs on them. Adair started with the older book, his hands shaking with anticipation as he turned each brittle page, his ancient Hungarian and Romanian coming back slowly as he studied the spells, recalling the ones he'd used and under what circumstances. The spells captured on these papers were the ones that conferred the strongest powers, including the one for immortality, copied from the original in Russian, stolen from an Adept's witless apprentice in St. Petersburg. . . . And then there was the crown jewel of his accumulated powers, a truly unique capability: the spell that enabled one to exchange his soul—or body—with another.

Now that Adair had his collection of recipes back in his possession, he felt a tremendous sense of relief. The source of his power was returned to him, and it was only a matter of time until he would be completely reestablished and independent from Jude.

Adair then looked over the Venetian manuscript with nostalgia, as though he were looking through an old photo album. Like a cookbook, the book held both favorites and useless recipes. (A poultice to induce euphoria? Why bother with a messy poultice when one could get pleasantly drunk?) One look at these pages—written in a meticulous hand, probably copied in secret from a master version by some monk—and he was transported back to his youth. He'd acquired this book when he was just beginning to study alchemy, a young man blessed with insatiable intellectual curiosity, though equally cursed with boundless arrogance.

He'd just left his family's estate to study medicine in Venice and become a doctor, as medicine would provide a plausible cover for his interest in alchemy and its attendant activities: purchasing materials, making inquiries after obscure texts, seeking out other men of science. Adair did not feel that he was called to spend his life attending to complaints of aches and pains from other nobles: it was just a convenient ruse. No, he had pledged his life to the pursuit of knowledge, the most holy calling as far as he was concerned, in an age where knowledge was power; it had been called the Dark Ages for good reason. It was this lust for knowledge—or power—that consumed him, driving him to uncover the forces at work beyond the physical world, and fueling his quest to harness their power.

VENICE, 1261

No good would come of it—that's what was said at the time of a young man's fascination with magic. And for most of the young men held in magic's thrall, nothing good did come of it: many were taken to the dungeon or the pyre, though Adair was saved by his family's high rank. A bad end came to his own tutor, the bedeviled old Prussian, Henrik, the one who had introduced Adair to the craft. Adair was too young at the time to do anything to save the old man when he was dragged off by the inquisitors, and his parents had made it clear that it was only with a lot of maneuvering that they'd kept this scandal from ruining Adair's life.

After Henrik was taken away, Adair did go to Venice to train as a doctor—that much was true. Given his peculiar leanings and the blight of association with the suspected heretic Henrik—black magician, alchemist, or wizard, depending on your disposition—young Adair declared that he would devote his life to medicine rather than to warfare or diplomacy or governance. His brothers and cousins had fulfilled those duties for the family, hadn't they? The physic's art— the blend of magic and alchemy, the natural and the supernatural— would be Adair's future.

Of course, his name was not Adair then. He'd nearly forgotten his real name, the one he'd been born with, his nearly unpronounceable given name and his illustrious and noble surname. He'd traveled in the peasant boy's body for so long that his old name eluded him, like trying to hold smoke in his hand. And when it finally came to him he wrote it down, because a secret name was a powerful talisman. According to the tenets of magic, if someone learned his secret name, that person would then have power over him, be able to command him like a puppet.

His family had tried to turn him away from magic when they learned of his interest, but nothing could stop him once he'd witnessed his first miracle—the one that proved to Adair that there was more to life than what he'd seen with his own two eyes. Old Henrik had used his bag of well-practiced tricks to impress his young wards, the special boys he'd already determined had the inclination or "the gift" or both, as Adair did. The tricks were minor manipulations: for example, combine a dram of a malleable solid with a drop of a liquid, work the two together and witness, the compound became hard and fast like a piece of iron. *Want to touch it, see for yourself?* Henrik had offered with a sneer of superiority to his awestruck charges. Such tricks passed for magic among the credulous. *Touch it if you dare.*

It wasn't until a few years later, when he and Henrik had done many experiments together in the old man's studio, that Henrik showed Adair the one impressive feat he *could* do. Henrik brought that baby bird back to life, though how he'd managed the feat had been as much a mystery to Henrik as it was to Adair. There was no disputing that the bird was dead to begin with: Adair had held its limp body in his hand, light and fuzzy as a dandelion head, loose bones in a thin sack of flesh. No, there was no question that Henrik had indeed brought the bird back from death, but it wasn't quite right the few days it lived, glassy-eyed and nearly inert, not a peep nor squawk from it.

Adair argued that they needed to try the spell on a man, because, once revived, a man would be able to tell them what it was like on the other side—whether there was a heaven and hell—but Henrik recoiled from the idea. That *was* heresy and possibly witchcraft, and even as he was seized with the idea, Adair had to agree.

The one thing Adair had not been able to determine, not in all his time and study, was *where* the powers came from. Changing the materials from liquid to solid, or bringing the baby bird back to life: had the power come from the materials themselves? Did it originate with God? Or could it be proof of the presence of the devil? After all these years, Adair was no closer to knowing, but he was beginning to believe it was pure energy, a certain rare, remote energy that existed in the ether. An energy you could generate with enough focus and determination if you knew how to harness it.

Many years of collecting recipes and perfecting spells elapsed before he acquired the crown jewel of his power: the alchemist's holy grail of immortality. Looking back, Adair saw that every experience he'd had—everything he'd learned and done in the past—had prepared him for acquiring that capability. By then, he'd been a practicing physic for decades. His title and family estate waited for him, a spit of land in the area that changed hands between Hungary and Romania. The duchy was his now, as his brothers were all dead, killed in battle or fallen to disease. He chose instead to work as a physician to royalty, traveling from court to court as cover for his real intention: to track down every major practitioner of alchemy and absorb their skills, learn their best recipes.

He'd heard rumors that there was an Adept in St. Petersburg, that glorious and wretched city, an alchemist with the strongest powers imaginable, much stronger than Adair's. He was an old man by then, very nearly blind, and even though he'd known of the elixir of immortality from his earliest days—even before he had left for Venice—it had eluded him his entire life.

When he was young, Adair had convinced himself that he wanted it only as a matter of professional interest. It seemed cowardly to chase immortality; only cowards were unable to face the end of their lives. But as the years passed and he grew more infirm, he felt desperation accumulate in his bones like silt dragged in on the tide. He lost sight in one eye and most in the other. His joints had stiffened so badly that he was continually uncomfortable, whether sitting, walking, or even lying in bed. And his hands had become so gnarled and numb that he couldn't hold a quill or carry a jar from his desk to his worktable. Yet, he wasn't finished living. He needed more time. There were too many mysteries that continued to elude him.

That was how he came to be shuffling down the alley in search of a certain man, dirty snow rising above his ankles and trickling into his boots. He cursed as he struggled on, searching for the address, but once he found it, he was sure he was in the wrong location. *How could this be the place where they were to meet?* the physic scoffed. It was a poor neighborhood, practically a ghetto. Any alchemist who could grant everlasting life would be an Adept indeed, and likely would have made himself wealthy with his talents, or at least be able to keep himself in a comfortable manner.

Full of suspicion, he finally found the correct doorway. Once inside, he saw that the place was beyond modest: it was the equivalent of a mouse's nest, tiny and squalid with one narrow bed, one small round table, and one candle burning on the mantel. The entire room was untidy at the edges, with dirt accumulated in the corners, and soot crawling up the wall over the fireplace.

The alchemist, too, was suspect—and slightly mad, judging from the way he gibbered under his breath and his eyes kept darting around the room, settling on Adair only when he thought he wasn't looking. He was short and stout and wore a heavy black tunic that swept to the floor, a full beard matted like sheep's wool, and hair tied back loosely. He seemed like a runaway from a sect, a dervish in hiding.

An intermediary had arranged the meeting for Adair, but now that the two were face-to-face, he realized he had no way to communicate with the other alchemist, for he knew no Russian, which he assumed was what the crazy little man was speaking. Adair tried to pantomime his intentions but, in the end, slapped a sack of heavy gold coins on the table and folded his arms over his chest, indicating that negotiations were over.

The alchemist peered into the sack, picked through the contents with a finger, grumbled and fussed, but eventually he went to a cupboard, unlocked it with a key that hung around his neck, and retrieved a small earthenware jar. He placed it on the table in front of Adair proudly and gravely, as though he had presented him with Holy Communion.

Adair peered into the wide-mouthed jar, skepticism curdling his face. First of all, it looked like no elixir he'd seen before; nearly every accomplished alchemist had an elixir of life in his repertoire, and this one resembled none that he'd ever come across. Then again, other alchemists' elixirs could do nothing more than extend life for a few years, and it occurred to Adair that perhaps *they* were the ones who'd gotten it wrong.

Adair scoffed. "What's this? I'm not buying the *potion*, you fool. I want the recipe, the knowledge. Do you understand?"

The alchemist stood adamant, unyielding as a boulder, his arms folded, and it was clear that he was not going to offer anything more than the elixir itself.

Eventually, Adair's desire won out, and he grasped the jar and brought it to his lips, then paused, looking the Adept in the eye. The alchemist nodded, maintaining an even stare as he regarded Adair expectantly, urging him to go on. Adair swallowed the viscous jelly dotted with specks of dirt in one long draft and immediately felt the inside of his mouth begin to burn as though coated with the most intense pepper. Bile began to back up in his throat, his eyes teared up, and his vision lightened, then blurred.

Adair fell to his bony knees, doubled over, and began retching violently. To this day, he still remembered the agony of that transformation, and he would see that same pain reflected in the face of every person he transformed. But at the time he was sure he'd been poisoned. Making one last lunge toward his killer, he reached for the alchemist—who merely took a step backward to evade Adair's grasp—before falling face-first on the floor.

Adair awoke on the alchemist's tiny bed, looking up at the low ceiling, dark like storm clouds hovering overhead. Still . . . despite being in a strange room under strange circumstances, he felt warm and safe in the alchemist's bed, like a child in a nursery.

It wasn't until his senses came back to him fully that he noticed the alchemist sat at his bedside, back upright, hands on his knees. Adair thought for a moment that this gnarled old man might be sleeping with his eyes open, he was so still; but after a moment he leaned close to the physic, studying him.

Adair tried to raise his head but the room began to tilt violently, so he lay back against the pillow. "How long have I been lying here?"

The alchemist remained as still as a hunter in the woods, and so Adair assumed he hadn't been heard, or that the alchemist ignored him since they didn't understand each other's language. But suddenly he said, "A day, no more" with an air of calm that struck Adair as deliberate.

Strangely, the alchemist's words fit in Adair's ear, making sense for the first time. "Aha," he said, thinking he had caught the other man in a deceit. "So you do speak Romanian after all."

The alchemist smiled in amusement. "No, I am speaking Russian. It is the only language I know. It is you who are conversing in Russian."

Adair rubbed his eyes and looked askance at the alchemist. "But I don't speak Russian. You must be mistaken," he retorted, but the other man offered no explanation for this seeming miracle, and just regarded him with distrust.

Adair pressed a hand to his clammy forehead and wondered if he had damaged his mind by ingesting the potion. He felt dazed as if in a thick opium haze. Indifferent to Adair's obvious state of shock and confusion, the alchemist pulled his chair closer to the bed and continued. "Listen to me. Since it seems we can now understand each other, I want to explain my actions. I have agreed to this deal with you because I trust the man who sent you here. He swears that you are a practitioner of great renown, and if this is the case, it stands to reason that you are then a man of integrity, too. But know this: if not for the dire situation that I am now in, I would never have agreed to sell the elixir for money, not even to a fellow practitioner.

"I am not the Adept who created the recipe for this elixir, you know; I am only his apprentice. That Adept is a very wise man—wise enough to unlock the mysteries of the world, but also wise enough to respect the limits of our earthly knowledge. My master has gone away on a pilgrimage and left me to care for his property and his recipes. If I did not require a little money to keep from starving and to buy enough firewood to keep from freezing, I would never share my master's elixir with anyone else. You should understand the tremendous responsibility that accompanies our work, and I trust you to use wisely the power you have now gained."

He scooted the stool closer to the bed so he could fix Adair with an ominous stare as he continued. "There are a few things you must know, now that you have taken the elixir of life. First, there is no going back. There is no antidote, as it were—no cure. You sought eternal life, for whatever reason, and now it is yours. God grant that you use this gift to better the lot of your fellow man and as proof of God's glory. Any other path will only bring misery."

"How do you know that God is behind this gift?" Adair asked in a tone so fierce and challenging that it seemed to give the alchemist pause.

The alchemist replied, "My answer to you is that we could not extend our lives without God's help, because God is the only creator of life, and the ultimate taker of life, too. We can do nothing without God's approval or his help. Do you not believe this to be so, or are you not a God-fearing man? I did not think anyone would have the clarity of mind to become an Adept if he did not believe in God."

As he was not interested in arguing with a zealot, Adair turned his attention to the new sensations he felt. He sat up in bed, aware of the miracle of his new circumstances. Sight had come back to his dead eye and the cloudy one was clear. His gnarled hands surged with dexterity, and his legs were strong. He felt as though he could leap out of bed and run through the square as swiftly as the strongest of horses.

By now, the room had ceased to spin, and Adair felt ready to start his new life. He stood without pain for the first time in decades. "So that is the only warning or advice you have for me: 'Go forth and do good in the name of God'?" he boomed at the little man.

The alchemist eyed him warily and, ignoring his tone, said, "There is one condition you must be aware of: you are impervious to all things but one. The maker of this potion saw fit to build in one fail-safe, the reason for such a caution unknown to me, for I am nothing but the humble caretaker of the elixir. As I have said, you are immortal now in all circumstances except for one: your life can be ended by the hand and with the intent of the one who gave you immortality."

Adair turned this twisted braid of words in his head. "The one who gave me immortality?" he repeated, raising his brows. "What does that mean, exactly? In this case, would that be you, since you gave me the elixir to drink? Or would it be your master, who made the brew in the first place?"

"As the one who gave you the potion, it is by my hand that you are now immortal." He pressed a hand to his chest and bowed slightly. "And it is by the strike of my hand alone that you can feel pain and by the strike of my sword that you will know death."

What a foolish man, Adair thought, to reveal such a thing to him. As long as the alchemist before him was alive, he was technically not immune to death. He would not truly feel immortal and he would never feel truly secure.

Adair gathered his cloak and walking stick from their perch beside the fireplace, taking his time as he thought about what he should do next. "So you lied to me. You have not given me what you promised. I paid for immortality—that was our arrangement. And yet . . . you can destroy me if you see fit."

The alchemist pulled his hands into his sleeves for warmth,

shaking his head. "I have given you my word. I have granted you eternity, for whatever reason you seek it. I am a God-fearing man of science, as are you. And you are the living, breathing proof of my master's work. I have no wish to destroy you—as long as you abide by the terms of our agreement and do not use this gift to harm others."

Adair nodded in assent. "Tell me, this elixir—surely you have tried it for yourself?"

The old man leaned away from Adair as though he were contagious. "No, I have no desire to live forever. I trust God to know the right time to call his servant home. I trust my God with my life."

A foolish pair, master and acolyte, Adair thought. He'd seen their type before: afraid of the capabilities they themselves had uncovered and now held at their command. Cowering at the edge of a great discovery, afraid to step into the glorious unknown. They used religion as a crutch and a shield. It was laughable, really: God wouldn't reveal such power to men if he didn't intend for them to use it, Adair figured. Men hid behind religion to keep others from seeing how frightened they were, how inept. They were weak vessels, to be trusted with such power.

"So this is all your master told you of the fail-safe? It seems a major provision, seeing that you can take my life at any time and for unknown reasons," Adair said, prodding the alchemist once more.

The alchemist pursed his lips, seeming to draw on the last reserves of his patience. "As I said, my master did not tell me why he built in this ability. It would seem to run counter to the very reason for the spell. But, knowing my master, I think it may be out of compassion."

"Compassion? Why would a man who cannot die—possibly the most powerful man on earth—require anyone's compassion?" Adair scoffed.

"Yes, compassion. For the day when a man says immortality is too much and asks for the cup to be taken away, for it is too full."

Adair grunted. Now he was certain this man and his master were addlepated.

The alchemist closed his eyes. "I think you can see that my master is a wise and compassionate man. God grant that I will live long enough to see him again. That is all I wish," he said, making the sign of the cross.

Adair saw his opportunity, and took it. "Alas, I am afraid your God turns away from you on this day," he said. As he approached the alchemist, Adair pulled a loop of braided leather, thin but wickedly strong, from his belt in one smooth motion. He garroted the old man before he could utter a word or slip even one finger between the cord and his throat.

Adair stepped over the body and began searching the room for the alchemist's recipes. He would have kept them close if he was in the acolyte's position; no one would risk leaving such valuable material beyond arm's reach. At last he found them: loose sheets of parchment kept in a leather pouch along with a rosary of lapis beads. He let the rosary fall next to the dead man and disappeared into the cold night with the pouch of recipes tucked close to his heart.

BOSTON, PRESENT DAY

Alone in the bedroom, Adair touched the pages of each book, re-reading words he'd once memorized but had now forgotten, and thought of his life's work: how he'd tracked down the recipes of all those Adepts, acquired an enviable collection of rare ingredients, and practiced and refined his alchemical skills. In time, with patience and sheer force of will, he'd surpassed every Adept he'd encountered and made himself the most powerful man who'd ever walked the earth, capable of performing feats to which no other could lay claim.

Now, once again in possession of these spells, he would become that man again. He would reclaim that power and rebuild his kingdom—for it had been as much a kingdom as his father's duchy, with castles and riches, and a retinue of courtiers, advisers, and jesters—and resume his conquests. Beginning with Lanore McIlvrae.

She had proven herself to be a cunning adversary, the only woman—the only person—ever to get the better of him, and for that he paid her a grudging respect. But Lanore also had stolen a part of his heart and buried him alive, and as Adair saw it, he had no choice but to become her master once again. It was the only way to restore peace in his breast and in his mind.

SEVEN

CASABLANCA

When I walked out of the hotel room, I didn't believe I'd actually left Luke. I kept thinking I'd turn around . . . while I waited for the elevator . . . as I crossed the lobby. . . . But I didn't stop, and before I knew it, I was in a taxi, crying, and headed for the airport. I was paralyzed by panic, knowing I was doing something irreparable. I'd taken similarly painful but necessary steps before: breaking a man's heart to keep him from wasting his one short, precious life; stepping aside so that someone I cared for would find a woman with whom he could have a family and a future. I knew this pain and was willing to endure it again for Luke's happiness.

There was only one place for me to go when I left the hotel room in London. Only someone who was privy to my condition and who understood what it meant to be at Adair's mercy would be able to help me, which meant it had to be another of Adair's creations. I knew of only one, Savva Egorovich Kononov, my oldest friend now that Jonathan was gone. He had saved me once and I could only hope that he could save me now.

I hadn't seen Savva in many years. The last I'd heard, he lived in Morocco. For a man who had been born to the snow and chill of St. Petersburg, Savva was drawn to the heat of the desert, and the fifty years we kept each other company were spent either in North Africa or along the Silk Road. I thought I would never return to Morocco because I had suffered one of the worst moments of my life there—one that hurt me in a way that I couldn't forget—and had no intention of ever going back. But I'd learned over time to never say never, not to anything, and so I returned to Morocco, preparing to confront my past.

I arrived in Casablanca in the late afternoon, just after the hottest part of the day, and took a taxi directly to the address Savva had given me over the phone. It turned out to be in a slum in an old section of town, away from the tourist hotels and attractions. The taxi let me out midway down a narrow street thick with locals. Hordes of young children ran between slower knots of distracted adults, old men smoked in doorways, young men rode by on bicycles. The ground floor of most every building was occupied by a tea shop or food stand or shallow storefront piled high with inexpensive necessities. The air was painted with smoke from food sellers' braziers and fragrant with a hundred different aromas.

I gave up trying to find street numbers on the buildings and went by Savva's description instead, looking for a mud-brick dwelling with an iron balcony that hung over the street and a red awning over the entrance. Every other building was faced with red clay, however, and they all had balconies, but it was the awning that led me to the right house. I passed through a set of double doors, emerging in a trash-strewn courtyard, and went up the interior staircase, hunting for the door to Savva's apartment on the third floor.

I wouldn't have recognized the man who answered the door if I didn't know whom to expect. He was frailer than the beautiful and impetuous man I'd traveled with for many years. He'd changed in ways I didn't think possible for those of us suffering Adair's curse. He'd once been a distractingly beautiful young man, a fair-skinned aristocratic Russian with features nearly as fine as a woman's, but somehow he had become as thin and leathery as a fakir, now nothing but sinew and bone. Savva's curly blond hair was the same, though it had grown into a long, unkempt ponytail, and his eyes were still blue but no longer crackled with vitality, as though the fire in his soul was nearly extinguished.

"Lanny! My dearest," he exclaimed as he wrapped his bony arms around me, frail as an old grandmother and as light as air. I didn't know what to say, so I stepped back, and cradled his face in my palms, to his embarrassment.

He ushered me inside. His apartment was as disheveled as his appearance, and nearly empty except for pieces of bruised furniture and discarded clothing. There were a few things I recognized from our travels together: a battered brass prayer bowl, a canopy of sari silk draped over a daybed. I knew he had some antiques that were worth a fortune—his share of the spoils we'd collected together—but they were mysteriously absent from view.

I suspected that something was very wrong with Savva. He had to be working hard to bring about this degree of deterioration, for it had always seemed that no matter how we abused ourselves, we'd never show the signs. Dona, the disagreeable Italian who had been part of Adair's entourage, used to cut himself with a kitchen knife in penance for deeds he would not admit; Adair smoked enough hashish to tar the wallpaper in his bedchamber with its resinous fumes. The sum of this abuse never showed on their handsome, melancholy faces, however. That was part of the curse, after all: break us and we heal good as new, ready to break again.

Savva welcomed me with a pot of mint tea, his hands trembling as he carried a round brass tray from the narrow kitchen to the parlor. I tried not to stare at the cracked glass cup he handed me, cloudy from use, something he might've gotten from a thrift shop. Gone was his gilt-edged tea service and gold-plated teaspoons, the fine, beautiful things he once surrounded himself with and could not live without. In a flash, I understood why the pretty possessions were gone: the man who lived here would have sold them all for ready cash.

The sounds that drifted up from the street and through open windows—children's taunts in an indecipherable language, the undulating melody of the muezzin's call to prayer—were not altogether unlike the sounds from our time together over a century ago. Savva reclined on a cushion, flicking a fan in front of his face, as there was no air-conditioning. I'd come here because I believed Savva was one of the few people in the world who could help me, but today he looked as though he couldn't help anyone. If anything, he seemed to be the one in need of saving.

"Don't take this the wrong way: it's not that I'm not pleased to see you, but this visit isn't purely social, is it?" he asked as he poured. "You had me worried when you wouldn't tell me over the phone why you were coming. . . . After all, it's been decades since we last saw each other. Whatever has sent you my way, it must be important. And while I would never turn you away, you know I'm not looking to complicate my life. It's complicated enough." His eyes searched my face warily for a second.

"I'll explain everything. But . . ." I was taken aback by Savva's condition and—unsure of what it meant—wasn't quite ready to tell him about Adair. "You don't mind if we *ease* into it, do you?"

An expression of curiosity flitted across his face—Savva never liked to be put off; he was an impatient man—but it passed. "Certainly. I understand. You've been traveling; you're tired." He sighed and settled against the cushions at his back. "You know, when I heard from you out of the blue and you said you needed my help, I was surprised. Happy to hear from you, of course, but . . . I almost told you not to come. I mean, look around," he said, gesturing to the threadbare room. "I can scarcely help *myself.* I appreciate that you haven't said anything about my reduced circumstances, but surely you've noticed. So I'm not sure there's anything I *can* do to help you, Lanny, with whatever situation you're in. But I am here for you and always will be."

I laid a hand over his. "What I will always remember is that you took care of me when I thought I couldn't go on anymore. You were a godsend." We both fell silent, thinking back to the afternoon we met several lifetimes earlier, when fate had sent Savva to save me.

FEZ, MOROCCO, 1830

After Jonathan and I left Boston, we decided it would be best if we went to Europe. We expected the false wall would be discovered after a few days at the most, and then Adair and his hellhounds would be after us. We went to Europe to make it harder for Adair to find us, never guessing that our precautions were completely unnecessary. It wasn't for a few more years that I would travel back to Boston to find out what had happened. And I would make that trip alone.

By the summer of 1830, Jonathan and I had ended up in Fez, taking a suite at a hotel frequented by Europeans and Americans doing what was known at the time as the Grand Tour, the trip taken by young adults from moneyed families to give them some knowledge of the world. The hotel was fancy enough to please wealthy clients but practical enough to maintain a row of rooms and suites along the back of the property for another class of travelers. These rooms were meant for the lost and the drifters, and that was where we found ourselves after wandering for seven years, little wiser and much poorer, still ill prepared for what lay ahead for us.

It was here that I awoke in a double bed with sheets that hadn't been changed in a week (we scrimped on maid service to save money) to find Jonathan's note telling me he'd gone. *Forgive me. This is for the best. Promise me you won't come looking for me. If I change my mind, I will find you. Please honor my wish. Your dearest, J.* I reread the note twenty, thirty times, the words making less sense with each reading, and remained in bed for another hour, uncomprehending. *He's mad at me for something,* I told myself. *He's upset over something I said or did, something I don't even remember, and has stormed out. He'll be back. If I wait here patiently, he'll be back.*

When I finally got to my feet, I found that his clothing was gone, along with his suitcase and the journal he'd gotten into the habit of keeping. He hadn't taken any of our money and could have no cash but whatever small amount he had on him. He'd also left behind the small pistol he carried, a sign that I was now responsible for my own protection.

He'll be back after sunset—that was the next thing I told myself, mostly in an attempt to remain calm. I sat in the shaded rooms, smoking cigarette after cigarette, wondering what had caused him to leave. Things had deteriorated between us, certainly, but every couple went through bad times, periods when they argued more and found less pleasure in each other's company. Arguments, sullen evenings . . . these things would pass. Jonathan had no choice but to return to me. In our peculiar situation, there was no one else he could trust. I started to wonder if there wasn't an outsider to blame, if perhaps Jonathan had been persuaded to take up with one of the adventurers who trekked through Morocco seemingly on a weekly basis—a strong-willed woman, one with a fortune and an independent streak. Maybe my worst fear had come to pass and he had finally fallen in love with someone else.

Nightfall came and went and still I was alone. It seemed impossible that Jonathan was gone, impossible that he would not come back. After all, we'd practically spent our entire lives in each other's presence. As far as I was concerned, there was air, water, sunshine, and Jonathan. Without him, the earth tipped on its axis and became strange and unfamiliar. I had the first of many panic attacks that day, locking the doors and shutters, crouching in a corner and wondering what would become of me. More than once I wished I had the option of suicide.

By the start of the third day, I was taking the edge off my despair with a constant supply of gin. I promised myself that as soon as I felt that I could leave the hotel room, I would seek out the stronger comfort of hashish and a water pipe. Now I understood why Adair had been addicted to his hookah: in the face of a destiny you cannot accept, how else could you tamp down panic and pain when it threatened to destroy you?

During those awful days, I thought of Adair, too. I appeased the dark, grinning demon that sat on my chest with thoughts of returning to Boston, of going to the mansion, tearing down the false wall with a sledgehammer, and prostrating myself before Adair. I would beseech him to take his revenge on me, for nothing could be worse than what I was going through, and I welcomed anything that would take my mind from the loss of Jonathan. Sometimes only pain can obliterate pain. The idea of Adair's punishment burned brightly in my mind, but deep in my cowardly heart I knew it was only brave talk from a woman who didn't even have the courage to leave her room.

After a week, I finally ventured out, mostly because I was out of gin and the front desk refused to send any more, fearing I was drinking myself to death. I made it as far as the hotel lobby and collapsed in a cane chair, fighting back tears as guests and poker-faced staff brushed by, ignoring my misery. Women walked by looking so composed in their fashionable dresses, with men on their arms, and the sight of them brought on fresh tears as I realized for the first time that I was truly alone. Like an animal separated from its pack, I feared I would not survive without Jonathan. I would go mad.

I soon realized I was being watched by a man I did not know, who had taken a chair opposite me. A guest in formal traveling clothes, he wore a full suit and hat despite the temperature. He was small and beautifully built, like an expensive doll meant for admiration but not play. He smiled uncertainly at me the way one smiles at a growling dog, wary but willing to risk being bitten in the cause of charity.

"I'm sorry if I'm intruding, miss, but . . ." He gave a little salute with his walking stick. "Have we met?"

"No, we haven't," I said warily.

"We have a friend in common, I'd wager. You know a man by the name of Adair, if I'm not mistaken." His expression lit up as I fell silent. "You *do*. I knew it. I can see his hand on you."

"See his hand on me?" I asked, shaken. "I don't know what you mean."

"That's just what I call it. I don't know what it is, rightly. It's just an aura, a stillness, you might say. It's not something anyone would notice; you have to know to look for it. Go on, try it for yourself. Look at me; really concentrate. Don't let your eye wander. Do you see?" He held his pose, willing me on with his eyes.

I held my breath and tried to hold absolutely still, and slowly I saw what he meant. It was almost as though he were flattened a bit, made to look like an image of his own self. "I—I think I see it."

"There, you see: his hand is on me, too," he said brightly, as though we were comparing something as benign as birthmarks or childhood scars.

We went to my suite with a fresh bottle of gin. He insisted on throwing back the shutters to let air and light drive the stink of fear from the room. He sank into a deep chair as I spoke, telling him first about my present predicament before going on to the story of my life. His deep-blue eyes never left my face as he poured thimble-size sips of gin for me until my tale was finished.

I was exhausted from speaking, but so much calmer: the trembling and tears subsided. We were now sitting next to each other on a fainting couch that had seen better days. With the frame seemingly ready to break apart in the center, there was no way for two people to sit on it without rolling against each other, so there we were, having known each other for barely half a day, and we were already leaning against each other for support, as cozy as twins. It was all I could do not to hug him to my breast, so grateful was I to have someone to stave off the absolute emptiness of being alone. There seemed to be no question that we would remain together for some time.

Born in 1705, Savva was from St. Petersburg, and though he was there for only the first twenty years of his life, St. Petersburg was burned into his soul. He claimed to owe his sense of style, his fine manners, and his snobbery to his birthplace, for the city was the crown jewel of the Russian empire, and those who lived there believed themselves superior to the rest of their countrymen. St. Petersburg was very cosmopolitan, filled with all the foreign representatives to the Russian court, but with a fierce Russian pride at the same time. There was no better place to come from and no better place to be raised, as far as Savva was concerned. If he loved it so much, why wasn't he in St. Petersburg at that very moment? I had wanted to know, and at that, my new friend grew wistful and took a slug of gin before replying that, as another of Adair's companions, I already knew the answer. As one of Adair's creatures, he, too, was an outcast from humanity. Like me, he could never go home.

In the closeness of my hotel room, Savva explained that his troubles had started many decades earlier when, as a young man, he confessed to his father, a minor official in the royal court, that he had fallen in love with a young Hussar officer. His father's response was to throw Savva out on the street, where he wandered for hours in an icy rain as he tried to figure out what to do next. The Hussar officer was quartered with his regiment and would not be able to take Savva in. Besides, Savva suspected his lover wouldn't help him anyway: affairs such as this, between young men, tended to be fleeting.

Savva wandered through town in shock and indecision until he collapsed by the side of the road. By then he was soaked to the skin; his teeth were chattering violently and his head was swimming. As he lay in the gutter, he prayed unconsciousness would set in and that he'd be dead by morning from pneumonia. He was just tumbling into darkness when a carriage pulled up beside him and the door swung open. . . .

Savva awoke in an unfamiliar room. He had been tucked into a bed made cozy with layers of blankets and a firm feather pillow. His clothes, brushed and neatly folded, hung over the back of a wooden chair set before the fire. Likewise, his boots stood drying on the hearth. The room and the house were quiet. It was like waking up in a fairy tale after having been scooped up by unseen hands: everything smoothed and righted by fairies while he slept.

And then Adair appeared "with those amazing eyes." Savva smiled at me conspiratorially. "One look at him, so dashing and mysterious, and I almost forgot my troubles. He reminded me of the Cossacks who ruled the steppes. You could still see them at the time, roaming the plains on horseback, their families in caravans. . . . Adair had the same coloring, the same rough hair, the same animal ferocity. The same cunning. His wild beauty appealed to my Russian soul."

Adair introduced himself as a recent arrival to the city and admitted to being a Hungarian noble but made it clear that he was not there as an emissary of the Hungarian emperor, sent to join the court. "'No, no . . . I represent only myself,' he said. 'I'm here to see the marvels of the Great Peter's empire, to see for myself his wondrous accomplishments,'" Savva recounted. Adair acted humbly that first night—Savva would later learn how much of an act it was—and charmed his guest with his attentiveness. For the heartbroken, confused boy, warm soup, brandy, and a bright fire were enough to win his affection.

And there was one aspect of Adair's behavior that Savva understood clearly. There was no mistaking the glimmer in his eye. By twenty years of age, Savva had already seen the surreptitious inquiry made by one man of another with a glance held a second too long, the silent begging by a man of a certain temperament. And Savva was inclined to respond, despite his feelings for the Hussar officer (whom, as it would turn out, he'd never see again). The two men were alone for the night, the servant sent away, heavy curtains drawn over the windows, stout locks on the door. Savva succumbed to the temptation. "The most serious mistake of my life," he lamented to me that day, tipping back the last silvery drops of gin.

I wouldn't hear the rest of the story of Savva's short time with Adair until many years later, and what a sad story it was. I thought Savva lucky in one respect, however: Adair didn't keep him for very long. Adair needed Savva to introduce him to the Russian aristocracy, and once Savva had served his purpose, Adair let him go. He was one of the few chosen whom Adair set free, but Savva took a pessimistic view of even this good fortune, believing that he had simply failed to be of much use.

CASABLANCA, PRESENT DAY

By the time the sun had set, the air in Savva's front room was blue with smoke. He'd brought out gin and cigarettes, a tin box, and a hookah. The water pipe, though prettily ornate, was old and not well maintained, the ivory mouthpiece as stained as an old set of dentures. But Savva was a good host, peeling open a much-worked packet of foil to reveal a half brick of hashish, and he doled out generous dabs throughout the afternoon so we could smoke our inhibitions away.

In Savva's company I felt a peace I hadn't known in a long time, strong enough to suppress the last of my jitters after having left Luke. This calm came from being with someone who had been through what I had been through with Adair. No matter how close we might get to a normal person, there was always a barrier, a final veil, that couldn't be pierced, and that apartness from the rest of humanity took a toll. Ours was a terribly lonely existence. The only time we could lift the weight of a thousand sins off our shoulders was in the company of someone with his own thousand sins on his conscience. Adair used to chide me for being aloof with Dona, Tilde, and Alejandro, explaining that we might not like one another but we would always need one another—because, like any family, no one else would truly understand us. At the time, I didn't want to be like them, and so I resisted. Now I had come to see what Adair meant. It was the only gift he gave us.

"Better?" Savva asked as he playfully blew gray-blue smoke rings in my direction. He used to do that when we overnighted with tribesmen—whether we were with Tuareg in the Sahara or Kurds in the Taurus Mountains—to amuse their children.

"Yes, better. Thank you," I replied, though it bothered me to encourage his drug use. Still, I imagined he would imbibe whether I was there or not. I continued cautiously, "Perhaps tomorrow, when we're more clearheaded, I can tell you why I've come here. You see, I've come for your help, Savva."

He took another long draw on the mouthpiece, and the sound of gurgling water filled the emptiness between us for a moment. Then, after holding the smoke in his lungs for a good while, he exhaled with deep satisfaction. "All right," he said hoarsely as he passed the mouthpiece to me. His gaze was coquettish. "Is it possible to persuade you to indulge me for a moment? I can't help but wonder, though, if the reason you're here has something to do with Adair's presence. I felt it return yesterday for the first time, after being dormant for two hundred years. That wouldn't be a coincidence, would it?"

EIGHT

BOSTON

Adair spent the next few days getting further reacquainted with the contents of his two treasured books, and specifically with the recipe for the elixir of life. For such a specific potion, it didn't call for exotic ingredients, or even that many. The challenge seemed to be in its preparation. Certain elements needed to be purified to an exacting degree, and that called for equipment not found in an average household, let alone that of a bachelor. He gave Jude a list of the things he needed—cauldrons and beakers and pipettes, a scale—to do the refinements necessary to complete the elixir.

Jude glanced over the list before handing it back. "Adair, honestly, where do you expect me to find this stuff? Half of it is arcane. You should've picked it up while you were at the museum."

"And a furnace," Adair said, ignoring Jude's obstinacy. "I need a fire capable of producing a very hot flame."

"I don't have that kind of furnace—not something that makes actual fire. We use electricity to heat this house."

Adair pointed to the fireplace. "What about that?"

"It's a gas insert. You can't cook anything with that."

"How can you live like this?" Adair said in disgust. The wish to return to the past shot through him like an arrow, and he knew to let it pass. "You act as though you live in a castle, but it's a hovel. It's not properly outfitted at all."

"Take it easy," Jude said soothingly. "In this day and age, there's got to be some piece of equipment that runs on electricity that can do this kind of work. I'll look into it. . . . Oh—and I've got a lead on someone we can sell the elixir to. He's one of these high-tech gazillionaires and he's on death's door. He's always been a real ruthless bastard, but now that his cancer's metastasized, he's not so tough. The only problem is that it's hard to get an appointment to see him. I'm trying to get him on the phone but not having much luck. . . , Anyway, I'll let you know in a few days."

Adair heard the crackle of greed beneath Jude's words, a reminder of their shared past. Jude's love of wealth had been his downfall. It had fooled him into believing he could break the Dutch guild's hold on the gold market, but Adair found him hanging from a rope in a warehouse and left to die by an assassin hired by the merchants' guild. Adair heard this same rasp of greed as Jude told him about the man he'd selected as a candidate. He must want very badly to get his hands on the man's fortune, and Adair had to remember not to let Jude's greed put him in a bad position. He'd go ahead and prepare the elixir for sale, but he'd judge this man's suitability for himself.

Adair hadn't realized how much he would enjoy making the elixir, deriving no small amount of pleasure from practicing an old skill at which he'd once been expert. So much of alchemical practice was done by feel and experience: knowing how hot to cook the ingredients without scorching or altering the composition too quickly, finding the right consistency of a compound, or measuring components without conventional volume or weight (how to measure an ounce of sighs, for instance, or a quintuple of broken dreams?). He was delighted to see it come back to him as though he'd never stopped practicing at all. The elixir came out perfectly: the liquid was so clear you could barely see the meniscus in the glass jar, and it had eddies in it like air currents swirling and colliding, and flecks of gold dancing within like snow caught up on the wind. It was beautiful in this state, though with time it would age gracelessly, turning an ugly brown while the gold flakes would darken until they appeared to be specks of dirt.

On the same day the elixir was ready, Jude told Adair he'd finally managed to speak to the investor he'd mentioned and persuade him to allow them to come to his house. "He made his fortune with a dot-com start-up about fifteen years ago," Jude told Adair, to put him at ease with his choice. He didn't bother to explain to Adair what a dot-com start-up was: he had fallen back into using strange shorthand for modern things, and Adair had grown so accustomed to his arrogance that he no longer bothered to ask Jude to explain. Not that Jude's arrogance was accepted: Adair just figured he would deal with it one day, when he could abide it no more.

Jude continued, "He sold his shares at the peak of the internet boom, but instead of spending it on yachts and blow, like everyone else, he started some new companies, all business-to-business. Nobody cared about this stuff at the time, so he managed to corner the market on some key services, like data forensics and security. So now he's the guy who knows where all the secrets are buried on the web. If his code monkeys can't find it, it can't be found. All those Fortune 500 companies—banks, insurance agencies, health care providers—line up to hire him. That's one reason I chose him: he'll be useful to you in other ways. Finding Lanore, for instance." Jude paused and studied Adair for a reaction to her name—but there was no outburst, and Adair allowed only a wrinkle to pass over his brow—and so Jude continued.

"He and I both invested in a new tech start-up once upon a time; that's how I got to know him. To set up this meeting, I told him you had a really good investment for him. . . ." Then he paused, concern quieting his normally irksome face. "You know, it was sad. . . . He asked me what good are investments to him now. They stopped the chemo; there's nothing more they can do for him except try to manage his pain. The doctor told him he has weeks to live. He looks like an old man, but he just turned thirty-eight last summer. You'll be shocked when you see him."

Jude's subdued air didn't escape Adair's notice. "This dying man—he is your friend?"

"No, not really," Jude replied.

"Good. For what we are about to do, there is no room for sentiment."

Adair had spent the hours before the meeting deciding how exactly to put this proposition to the dying man. He'd never *offered* this gift to anyone before: he'd always chosen his recipients and given it to them only as they were dying, like last rites. And his choices had always been instinctual, as though he followed a voice that guided him to his next companion, the chosen individual preordained. He was uncomfortable with the prospect of selling what should be beyond price, but Lanore had forced his hand, and the sooner he got this transaction out of the way, the sooner he could pursue her and make her pay for her betrayal.

According to Jude, the ailing businessman he'd selected was worth an unimaginable sum, in the hundreds of millions. He was a very sick man who wasn't used to losing and wouldn't give up on his life without a fight. And although Adair recognized the necessity of acquiring the resources, financial and investigative, to rebuild his life from scratch, he still had reservations. He was particularly conflicted about granting immortality to a stranger who'd then have to become part of his inner circle. Adair wasn't optimistic that it would work out; after all, few of the people he'd transformed had been worth the trouble. Many had been too weak to endure eternity. The stress could shatter one's mind and leave one as vulnerable as a newborn—or as dangerous as a psychotic.

Then there was the question of loyalty: he'd been looking for people he could depend on as though they were family, but the result had been disappointing. His minions lacked the fanatical devotion he'd hoped for, as evidenced by the fact that they managed to go on with their lives—quite happily, in Jude's case—after he'd disappeared. It seemed especially risky to transform someone he hadn't chosen himself, though it seemed he had no alternative and he could only hope Jude had used his not-inconsiderable cunning well.

Adair and Jude drove to a stony mansion in the Boston suburbs. Nearly every window was dark in the large house, and it was cloaked in such complete stillness that it seemed as though the owner was already dead. An old man in a dark jacket answered the door. "Mr. Kingsley is expecting you," he said almost too softly to be heard, and he shuffled down a hall with a sad air, as though he half expected they wouldn't follow.

"There's someone I'd like you to meet," Jude said to Adair, gesturing toward a man collapsed behind a huge desk at the far end of the room. Adair realized right away that Jude hadn't exaggerated: the man looked as though his end could come at any moment. He was little more than a skeleton wearing his jaundiced skin like a suit of clothes. His hair was nearly gone, and what was left of it was graying, revealing an eggshell-thin skull. The only part of him that seemed alive was his eyes, and they followed Adair with savage intensity. He was sizing Adair up, to be sure; he seemed the calculating type—one who always wanted the odds to be in his favor—and much too arrogant for a man about to die. *If you must die, face death with humility; there is no other way to go through that door,* Adair wanted to advise him, but there were some people who would not be advised, no matter the circumstances.

"Adair, this is Pendleton Kingsley," Jude said.

Pendleton didn't even extend his hand, instead holding the mask of a respirator to his face while staring them down. In the background, Adair heard air escaping faintly from an oxygen tank like the hiss of a snake. The sick man took a deep breath before speaking. "'Adair'—that's an unusual name."

"So is 'Pendleton.'"

"Isn't it, though? It's actually my middle name. My parents named me Jack—nice and folksy—but I never cared for it. Don't like people to be too familiar, if you know what I mean. 'Pendleton' is better for business." He set the mask on the desk in front of him and turned to Jude. "So, Judah, what's so important you need to see me at a time like this? It better be good."

For a man in such fragile condition, Pendleton was as vitriolic as a scorpion, but strangely, Adair found his repugnancy impossible to ignore. There was something poisonous about him that made him almost alluring, as though he exuded a pheromone to which Adair was programmed to respond. Pendleton's natural aggression, even his simmering anger at dying, was blood in the water to Adair. This feeling came over him whenever he met someone he was meant to bind to him, and it was the sign Adair had been hoping for.

Over the course of an hour, Adair probed Pendleton for weaknesses. It turned out there was little to admire about the man: he'd gotten rid of two wives through vicious divorces that forced them to walk away with no compensation for their loyalty or love. His one child, a daughter, no longer spoke to him. He'd acquired companies and pushed out the men who'd built them from nothing, bought intellectual property from desperate inventors for pennies on the

dollar. He made his employees work slaves' hours with the promise
of recompense that never came through. Meanwhile, he'd amassed a
fortune that dwarfed the treasuries of small nations. And he sneered
at everyone he'd left ruined in his wake, confident that they'd gotten
only what they deserved.

When Pendleton had tired of talking about himself, he looked at
Adair disapprovingly. "So, what is this about? Did you come over to
waste a dying man's time, or are you going to tell me why you wanted
to see me?"

Adair rolled alcohol—an inferior whiskey served to guests;
Pendleton himself had none—around in his glass. "First, you must
tell me how much you are worth."

The man guffawed to cover his surprise. "It always comes down
to money, doesn't it? Well, you get right to the point, Adair, I'll give
you that. Not much for manners, but you *are* direct."

Adair fixed him with a stare. "Naturally I'm interested in your
money. Apart from your business acumen, you have little to recom-
mend you, and I certainly didn't come here for your company. But
in exchange for your fortune, I have something to offer you—something I know you want with all your heart. You're clearly a man of
means, but what I've come to sell is very expensive indeed. So I need
to know that you have the funds to pay for this—your dying wish."

"So, you want to know if I'm rich enough for whatever scheme
you're peddling? Am I rich enough?" Pendleton's small, bright eyes
shifted from Adair to Jude. "Is this a joke? You know I've got means,
Jude. I've got the means to buy and sell you *both*."

Jude shook his head, meaning to defuse the dying man's anger,
and looked down at the floor. "Take it easy. I think you'll be interested in what my friend has to say, or I wouldn't have asked for your
time. But I advise you to listen to him closely. *Closely.* The devil is
always in the details."

Adair snapped his fingers to draw Pendleton's attention back to
him. "You are not a *well* man, Pendleton."

The sick man looked as though he'd spit at him. "You think that's *funny?*"

"Your doctor may have told you that you could count on four more months, maybe six at the outside, but I am here to tell you that you have only three weeks left to live. No more."

The big man went white, but he managed to curl his lips. "How dare you say that to me? Are you trying to give me a heart attack? What makes you think you know more than my doctor—"

Adair pressed on. "The men in your family have never been long-lived. Men in your family seem to be born under a curse. Your father was in high school when your grandfather died. And you were only five when your father was taken from you."

Pendleton snorted. "You could've read that in *Newsweek*."

"You think I know this because I've studied up on you? I know what is wrong with you by looking at you. I can see where the disease eats away at you, and what's more, I can see the fears you tell no one," Adair said. "Every man in your father's line has died young from a heart attack. What's killing you, ironically, is not your heart. You had several heart surgeries by the time you were thirty-five, and just when they got your heart back to sixty, seventy percent capacity, your doctors found tumors. The cancer's spread to nearly every organ in your body, your brain, even into your bones."

Pendleton said nothing, but his hand scrabbled for his oxygen mask. He had a look of defeat in his eyes as Adair delivered the news he knew to be true, despite his well-paid physician's slightly more optimistic prognosis.

Adair leaned toward Pendleton, who breathed hotly into his mask. "You've looked in a mirror. You know that Death is readying you for his arrival. You know his handiwork, the pain that can hardly be controlled by medication. You've felt Death coming, and you gnash your teeth at the unfairness of your situation. Why should you have to die, you think? Why doesn't Death take some lesser person with fewer achievements? Death should spare you, a captain of industry and a philanthropist, someone who has done so much to benefit his fellow man. It's not fair. But life is not fair. You know that, too."

Pendleton was contemplative, as though he'd had these same thoughts, but he was too self-possessed to acknowledge them out loud. The moment passed, and he swung his fragile head in Adair's direction. "Life is unfair; yes, I've known that for a long time," he sneered impatiently. "Let's get down to business, shall we? As you so graciously reminded me, I don't have a lot of time."

Adair smirked at the dying man. "Fear not, for time is exactly what I have come to offer you. What if I told you that I could rid your body of pain? That I have the ability to eradicate the nausea and headaches, the chills and sweats you suffer from sunrise to sunset? What would you give to be well again, Pendleton?" He stood with arms folded across his chest, looking down on the shriveled man, who seemed to shrink even farther into his seat. "What would you say if I could give you the ability to live forever?"

Pendleton hesitated a second before letting out a humorless laugh. "I'd say you're out of your fucking mind. What are you, some kind of quack Jude found on Craigslist? You want me to throw my fortune away on some miracle cure when I know it's hopeless? Do I look that gullible? I already have the best doctors in the world." His voice receded at those words—"best doctors in the world"—knowing the little good they did him now.

"Don't pretend you're not interested. You say you know your situation is hopeless, and yet, there is hope in your voice, hope shining in your eyes. Of course you want to know more; I can keep you alive, and what's more, you will live forever. Imagine how it will feel not to fear the tumors inside you, your failing heart. You've been sickly and cautious your entire life: imagine what it would be like to have no concern about what the future holds. It's complete freedom, that's what it is. Your life will never be the same."

Perspiration broke out on Pendleton's upper lip and he wiped at it nervously. He whirled on Jude as though he might strike him. "What the hell is this, Judah, some kind of tasteless practical joke?"

"He's not joking. It's the truth."

"Are you intrigued?" Adair interrupted. "There's no reason to take me merely at my word. I can prove it to you." Blood thrummed in Adair's ears, as he reached into the breast pocket of his jacket and pulled out a snub-nosed .22 pistol.

Pendleton sucked in a breath at the sight of it. "Now wait a minute. There's no need for *that*. Let's not get carried away—"

Adair interrupted, "Write your worth on that piece of paper."

Pendleton looked from the pistol, to Adair, to Jude's pinched face for reassurance—there was none—then reluctantly scribbled something down. Jude craned over the desk to read it. "That sounds about right," he said to Adair.

"Good. So, what would it be worth to you to live forever? We are talking more than just cheating death, cheating your destiny. You will be a god among men, impervious to any harm. Money is nothing in comparison. Would you give up 70 percent of that?" He tapped the paper. "Eighty?"

Pendleton had softened, wanting to believe what he was being told, but at the mention of money he stiffened, resisting. "Are you out of your mind? That's a lot of cash, and for what? What are we talking about?"

"You will live to see the end of time. The end of time! Can you imagine it? Of course you cannot. You can barely remember things that happened to you a decade ago, isn't that true? Think of your fragile body—and then think of what I am offering. . . . You want to know exactly what you will be buying? That seems a fair request. Let me demonstrate." To Pendleton's surprise, Adair walked around the desk and pressed the gun in his hand, wrapping his fingers around the grip and holding them fast.

"What—what are you doing?" the sick man asked in alarm.

"I require your assistance. Only for a moment." He stretched

Pendleton's arm to its full length, the nose of the gun inches from Jude's chest, and squeezed the finger over the trigger. The noise ricocheted around the hard white box of a room, and Pendleton leapt from his chair as though he'd just been struck with a cattle prod. There was smoke, choking and acrid, and in the middle of all this, Jude fell to the floor. Pendleton dropped the gun and bolted to his feet, but Adair pressed a hand to his chest to freeze him where he stood. "Stay where you are. Wait. Watch, and you will see."

They leaned over the desk, staring down at Jude and the crimson circle on his chest with a neat bullet hole at its center, the circle spreading across his shirtfront.

Running was heard outside the door, then a knock.

"Tell your man that you're okay," Adair ordered.

Pendleton obeyed, wide-eyed. "Go away, Carlos. It's nothing," he called out.

Both men held their breath, Adair in amusement and Pendleton in dumbstruck horror until, after a moment of absolute stillness, Jude shuddered back to life. Moaning, he pressed a hand to his wound. "A little warning first, next time?" he said weakly to Adair as he staggered to his feet.

"What the hell—" Pendleton started backing away.

"It's a miracle, isn't that what you would call it? A dead man brought back to life like Lazarus? This is what you are buying—a new destiny," Adair said, picking up the gun. "You pride yourself on being a shrewd man; you are probably thinking it is a trick of some kind. Let us not have any lingering doubts. Go on, check the wound. Prove it to yourself."

But Pendleton stood frozen on his side of the desk. "I don't need to see anything more. It's *got* to be a trick, like what those magicians do on television. . . . And it's a pretty good one, I'll give you that. But there's no way he was really shot, not if he can get up like that. . . ."

"It's no trick." Adair grabbed Pendleton's hand, crushing it as he led him over to Jude and pressed his hand into the wound. "Touch it. Go on, don't be a coward. What do you feel? It's healing already, isn't it? Can *you* explain what is happening? Of course you can't; it's like nothing you've ever heard of." Adair released his hand and pushed it aside. "Listen to me, and pay attention. I don't make my secret known to everyone, Pendleton. I'm only giving you this opportunity because I am experiencing pecuniary difficulties. Because of my unfortunate situation, I am making you the offer of a lifetime. In all the world there are only a handful of people like me and Jude. I'm offering you the chance to join us."

Pale and shaken, Pendleton staggered to the side table and poured himself a drink. "Is this true, Judah? Are you immortal, too?"

"Obviously," Jude replied.

Pendleton pointed a trembling finger at Adair. "Who—what *are* you? The devil?"

"For a man who prides himself on his reason and intellect, you revert to superstition rather quickly," Adair chided him. "If I were the devil, would I need your money? I am, however, a very powerful man, in ways that you are not ready to understand. Transfer 80 percent of your worth to me—Jude will handle the transaction—and you will not die in three weeks' time. The cancer that has spread throughout your body will disappear and you will live forever. But if you wish to accept this offer, you must prepare a document for your attorney in advance, naming Jude as the executor of your affairs, authorizing cremation of your body, asking that no funeral service be held."

At the latter, Pendleton darted a suspicious look at him but held his tongue.

"It's a lie, a diversion. To keep people from looking too closely at the miracle that will be your recovery," Adair explained. "You will be alive, trust me, and we will make sure you are fully prepared for your new life."

"My new life?"

"Your new, *healthy* life," Jude interjected, gesturing to the spot where the wound had been.

"What do you say?" asked Adair.

Pendleton's eyes were blank and unseeing but started to fill with a mixture of hope and growing certainty. "I—I can't make a decision this big so quickly. I'll have to get back to you."

"Don't wait too long," Adair warned as he put the gun back in his pocket. "Remember what I said: you have three weeks. If you find you are on the verge of dying and want to accept my offer, don't send for an ambulance. Call us instead. There's not much I can do for you once you're in a hospital, surrounded by people. And, needless to say, you are not to share what we've told you with anyone. If I hear you've told anyone about me, I disappear and your only chance to live disappears with me."

The call came exactly twenty-one days later, early in the morning. Jude drove in Boston's infernal morning traffic, zigzagging through cars like a reckless skier down an icy slalom run to get to Pendleton's estate. They found him pale and sweating in his bed, his face a mask of terror as he gulped for every breath. His attendant stood by, looking sideways at the telephone on the nightstand, anxious to call for an ambulance. Also on the nightstand was a document, folded in thirds. "You asked for this," Pendleton rasped as he pointed to it.

Adair looked deeply into Pendleton's face for the telltale signs of death. "We cannot perform the service here. We must move you. We are going to carry you down to the car." At those words, the servant started toward them in protest, but the dying man raised a hand weakly to wave him off. Adair lifted him, and he felt as light as a scarecrow made of straw.

"Don't let me die," Pendleton whispered as he held Adair's hand, the arrogance squeezed out of him now like toothpaste from a tube. "I'm not ready to be judged."

Neither am I, Adair thought, with a rare flash of compassion.

Once they'd arrived at Jude's town house, Adair carried Pendleton's nearly inert body up two flights of stairs to a guest room. After he had deposited Pendleton on the bed, Adair's hand settled on the flask in his pocket holding the elixir of life. "Just relax. The process is not painless, but nothing worthwhile comes without a price. Do not fight it." He tipped the flask toward Pendleton's mouth, though he felt that it was almost unnecessary. It was as though this man's soul, gray and threadbare as an old handkerchief, was already in his hands. Still, he placed a few drops on the man's tongue, said a few words over him, and waited.

It had been so long since he'd done this that he almost forgot what to do. He felt a force bear down with amazing speed, and prepared for this energy to funnel through him into the other man. The feeling swept through Adair like a thunderstorm, as if all the power of the wind were captured and twisted tightly together until it could pass through him, as though he was a portal. All this energy did not go to Pendleton. This feeling fed Adair, too, renewing him in a way that nothing else did. Right now, he was alive in a way he hadn't been since the last transformation. Since Lanore. That was why he did it, Adair realized. Plucking up these rotted souls was something he was meant to do.

If only he knew *why.*

At the last moment, he remembered to say the words that would bind Pendleton to him. "Your life and your health will be restored to you, but all that you have now belongs to me. Your soul is mine, to do with as I please. This shall be done by my hand and intent."

Once Pendleton's exhausted body had given in to sleep, Adair and Jude stood at the door.

"You don't have his money yet," Jude reminded Adair. "It'll take time to shake it loose from all its hiding places. I'm sure Pendleton uses offshore banks and brokerages, shell accounts, to evade tax collectors. It'll be very complicated, getting it out."

Adair clapped a hand on Jude's back, trying to bolster his confidence. "If anyone can find the money, it's you. Talk to him. And make him understand: he has no choice now."

Hours later, when the body had shut down and come back to life, Adair went to see Pendleton in the darkened room. Even in the dimness he saw that the change was nearly complete. The man on the bed looked his age again, his skin fresh and supple, his hair darkening and thickening. He was thin still, but the muscle was rejuvenated and, with time, would become normal again. It was a promising body—not a god-like specimen as Jonathan had been, but you could tell he'd been fit once, as much as his weak heart had allowed. He would be pleasant enough to have around. Adair sat on the edge of the bed and looked into the frightened eyes.

"How do you feel?"

Pendleton's tongue ran over his cracked lips. "Shitty. But different. Changed."

"I restored your health, as I promised. You may not feel it yet, but as you will see in the mirror, you are as you were before the illness. Do you want me to prove it to you?"

Pendleton's eyes reflected memories of the gun, and Jude on the floor. He shuddered. "No. No, I believe you. I can tell. Even now, I feel better than I have in months. I just want to get out of here. I want to get on with my life."

"And so you shall."

Pendleton steadied himself against the bed. "So . . . what happens next? Do I get some kind of training? There must be things I need to know, like how to go undetected in the normal world. And you're going to explain it all to me, right? Where this power came from? What it all means?"

"In a sense, yes. But you have plenty of time to learn. You will move in here with me and Jude. You will become part of my household . . . like a servant, really. You will do everything I say—*everything*. Because if you don't obey me, I will kill you."

Pendleton struggled to his elbows, despite the spinning in his head and the cold sweat blooming across his back. "What do you mean, 'kill' me? You said I would be immortal—"

Adair shook his head. "When we met, you seemed to pride yourself on being clever, but for a shrewd man, you didn't ask very many questions when it came to our deal. Jude warned you to pay attention to the details of my offer, but alas, you did not. If you had, I would have explained that while you *are* immortal, there is one exception, one little chink in your armor of invincibility. And that one exception is *me*."

Pendleton, graying around the eyes, squinted at Adair.

"Nothing in this world is absolute. Haven't you learned that already? I would imagine that, given your life, your business and personal dealings, you'd know this was true. There is always a . . . *provision*, I guess you would say. Checks and balances. That is how the world is made to function, it is inescapable. I am the check on your power. Do you remember when you first met me, the demonstration with the gun—how I put it in your hand and made you shoot Jude? That's because if I had shot him, he would have died. Only *I* can end your life, just as only I can make you feel pain, and you should know that I am not hesitant to exercise either power when I see fit. You may have cheated people in life, but you will never cheat me. Never."

"Th-this isn't what I paid you for. . . . This wasn't our bargain," Pendleton sputtered as he tried to rise from the bed, but, still weak, he collapsed on the floor at Adair's feet.

"Not our bargain? Can you explain, then, exactly what it was we agreed on? Show me where it's written, present to me a contract? Of course, there *is* no contract. There is only one path to immortality that I know of, only one way to be given eternal life, and that is from me. I *know* my terms, Pendleton. I have lived up to my half of the bargain. Now would be a good time for your first lesson, I think."

Jude stepped into the room holding a large kitchen knife, thumbing the blade nervously. Pendleton looked from the knife to Adair, fear mounting in his eyes.

"This is a step we all go through—Jude, the others I have brought to my side—to prove that I am telling you the truth. So you'll never test me again." He nodded at Jude, who crouched next to Pendleton. He held on to Pendleton's shoulder to steady himself, turned his face away, and drove the blade into the man's soft belly.

Pendleton cringed and opened his mouth to howl, but no sound came forth. His eyes popped open in surprise. He took the knife from Jude and stared at the bloody blade. "What the . . . I didn't feel anything. Nothing. How did you do that?"

Adair laughed darkly. "You are no longer made of the stuff of mortals. Your body is just a vessel now. No knife can harm you, nor any bullet. Not fire, not water. Not heat, not cold, thirst nor hunger. You will note that it was Jude's hand that held the knife, which is why you felt nothing. It is exactly as I told you: you have nothing to fear from any man. Except me."

Before Pendleton could complete the equation in his mind and see what was coming, Adair reached out and snapped Pendleton's wrist back, the crack of his bones echoing through the room. The knife clattered to the floor. "Goddamn!" Pendleton bellowed, clutching his forearm. "You broke my wrist! You broke my fucking wrist!"

Adair stood, rolling back his sleeves as Jude hurried out of the room. "Yes, I did. You see, we have come to the second part of the lesson, a painful but necessary lesson. Because very soon you will start to enjoy the gift that I have given you. You will feel powerful and free to do anything you want. But you must always remember, Pendleton, that ultimately you are *not* free. You are beholden to me for the rest of time. Sadly, it has been my experience that mere words will not be enough to make you remember. I must make it clear to you in a way you will never forget, so that you will always fear me. Fear and obey me." He reached down and stroked the side of Pendleton's face, drawing two fingers from his sideburn across the ridge of his cheekbone, the man shivering at his touch.

Then he drove his fist into the same spot he had just stroked, a punishing blow that left Pendleton seeing flashes of white and grinding his teeth in pain. Pendleton hadn't been in a fight since prep school, one of those little outbreaks between boys, as combustible as a match and about as long-lasting. This was different: pain traveled up his jaw and through his skull as though he'd been hit with a plumber's wrench. That was from one punch; he couldn't imagine he would survive a second.

He fell at Adair's feet momentarily, then rose woozily to his knees. "I get it. You're the boss. You can stop now," he said, struggling to get away from him, too late.

Adair held Pendleton's jaw in a crushing grip and drove a fist into his face again, into the same tender spot. "Think of this as a necessary exercise in obedience. You are like an untrained dog, you see, but by the time I am finished with you, you will be attentive as the most devoted hound. And, like any pack animal, you will learn to take comfort in discipline, in knowing your place in our family, and in doing as your master tells you. For I am your master now: the master you cannot cheat or deceive, the master from whom you can never escape. From now until the end of time, you and all you possess are mine. I am your life now; I am your god."

NINE

Adusty darkness had fallen over the city. The street below was quiet, the bustle of the day replaced by the murmurs of the evening crowd, families sitting down to dinner in the cool of a courtyard.

Savva and I sat on the floor in his apartment with his paraphernalia scattered around us, the water pipe silent and hashish gone, only flecks and smears left clinging to the crumpled tinfoil. He was in that temporary peace that came from narcotics and wine. Savva's wise blue eyes watched me closely as he questioned me again.

"This wouldn't have anything to do with Adair, would it? As incapacitated as I am, even I can put the clues together, Lanny dear. His presence had been missing for almost ten years when we first met. It comes back after two centuries, and the very next day you show up on my doorstep. That's too much of a coincidence for me. I can't help but wonder if you have something to tell me."

I was flooded with a tremendous sense of relief to finally be able to share my secret with someone who would understand as only those who'd lived under Adair's spell could. But I was ashamed, too, because I hadn't told Savva earlier. We'd lived together for decades and swapped stories about Adair, yes, but there'd always been a line I wouldn't cross. No one could know about the wall. I hadn't kept this secret from Savva because I thought he'd release Adair, but I knew he was in contact with the others and was afraid he might inadvertently let it slip when he was drunk or under the influence of one drug or another.

With no reason to be cautious any longer, I confessed the entire story. I told him that Adair was more powerful and crueler than we had been led to believe, and how he'd deceived us all. I told him how I'd pretended to love Adair in order to trap him. His eyes grew wider as my story spilled out in a tumult of words, for once I'd started, I couldn't stop for the sheer relief of confessing.

"Where did you find the nerve to take on Adair? It's like facing down the devil himself," he said, incredulous. "I don't think anyone else would have dared to do what you did. You have more balls than any of the rest of us, my dear, and when you think of the cutthroats and villains Adair has gathered to serve him, that's saying a lot."

At the time, I'd felt more foolhardy than brave. I'd acted out of panic, not courage. Admiration alone wouldn't help me; I'd seen more than one condemned man cheered by the mob for his moxie—all the way to the gallows. "I've come to you for help," I said. "I didn't live with Adair long enough to learn anything about the source or extent of his powers. I don't know what he's capable of. I need your advice."

Savva turned grimly from me and began tidying to distract himself, sweeping the utensils into the tin box. "I won't be of much use, I'm afraid. I wasn't with Adair for very long, either. A couple years more than you, at the most."

"But you got to know his other companions. You must've heard stories of his exploits, his adventures, of the things he could and could *not* do. . . ."

"What is it you want me to say?" he asked, turning on me sharply. "If there's sanctuary, I haven't heard of it. If there's a way to stop him, none of us have been able to figure it out." His shoulders slumped and he sighed apologetically. "I would like to offer you hope, but I don't see the point in lying to you, either."

Fear bloomed inside me again, a creeping coldness that I had been trying to suppress. "Please, Savva. Help me. I don't want to end up . . ." I shivered from head to foot. "I don't want to end up like Uzra," I admitted. "The poor woman, forced to stay with Adair, to endure his sick fancies and his bad temper. And for what reason? Her only crime, if it can be called that, was that she was too beautiful for him to resist."

"Is that what you thought?" Savva gave me a sidelong look. "Did we never talk about Uzra, not in any depth? My dear, you are wrong. Uzra was not an innocent. She was no different from Dona or Tilde, me or . . ." He trailed off before he came to the last word: *you.* "She was a murderess."

I thought of the odalisque. Surely she was too slight to be dangerous, let alone kill anyone. She'd had a fierce nature, however, and there was no denying that something had burned in her heart. Although Adair had kept her prisoner for centuries, you could see by the determined, defiant look on her face that she would never stop trying to escape. "A murderess? Her father, you mean—she killed her father, that terrible man."

"More than just her father. Her brothers, her uncles . . . every last man in her tribe. She betrayed them to a rival group by smuggling the assassins right into their midst. Supposedly she helped them on the condition that they'd leave no males alive. She wanted her family's bloodline wiped out. It was a terrible crime, like genocide. The women who survived brought her to the sultan for judgment, and that's when Adair found her and stole her away."

I had the sensation of the world being turned upside down and shaken like a snow globe, the landscape obscured by the swirling flakes, my way lost again. When it came to Adair, you could not be sure of anything. The past was not set in stone. Here, with only a few words, Savva had unraveled what I thought I knew about Uzra. I groped for steady ground. "That's not what Adair told me—"

"Haven't you learned yet not to trust Adair's stories?" He laughed meanly.

"Adair told me that her father killed her mother because he suspected a foreigner was Uzra's true father. And then he made her take her mother's place—in his bed."

"Well, that might be true. It would explain why she hated her father and wanted revenge on her family. Why not wipe out the entire clan if they let him kill Uzra's mother, and then stood by as he raped a girl who thought of him as her father. Oh no—if you ask me, they only got what they deserved. Though . . . I'm sure there are some people who would disagree. Was it fair to kill her brothers, poor little boys who had no say in their father's insanity?" Savva rose from the floor, a box of drug paraphernalia tucked under his arm. "That's the trouble when you look to apportion blame: it rarely falls into neat little piles. Does it matter whether she cut one man's throat or dozens? Was she entitled to revenge—are any of us? I don't know how to make sense of it. I only know that Uzra did *something* bad all those years ago to bring her to Adair's attention, just like the rest of us."

My heart beat faster at Savva's words, and my throat tightened. I didn't want to discuss it with Savva, but the distinction was important to me. I'd always looked to Uzra as proof that Adair did not *only* gather monsters to him. If she had been innocent, there was a chance that maybe I was innocent, too, and had come to Adair's attention by mistake. Now, Savva was telling me there was no hope.

"Why would he lie? Why didn't he tell me the truth about Uzra?"

Savva snorted. "Come now, Lanny, you know as well as I that Adair lied all the time. He lied to suit his purposes and to cover his tracks." He closed his hand around the emptied foil packet, crushing

it into a ball. "Or perhaps he got her story mixed up in his head, and
it seemed like the truth to him. What is truth, anyway? It's just one
person's side of the story."

That sounded like a junkie's logic to me. "You don't really believe
that, do you?" I asked Savva, prodding. "Surely you believe that some
truths are absolutes. A fact is a fact."

He laughed darkly, under his breath. "Oh my dear Lanny, after
everything you've been through, you can't possibly believe in anything as quaint as a *fact*. . . ." He swept a hand grandly from head to
foot. "I have no explanation for what happened to us—do you?

"Let me tell you about the incident that brought this home to
me," he continued, speaking over his shoulder as he went to put the
tin box away in a chest. "I'd been seeing a man named Daniel, a
lovely man but nonetheless I decided to break it off with him. I felt
terribly guilty, you see. He'd never been with a man before me—
didn't even know this was what he wanted. Once we were together,
he walked away from his wife, his family. Even a selfish old thing
like me is capable of feeling guilt. I felt as though I'd ruined his life,
so I left him. Years later, I heard he was dying. AIDS. I decided to
go see him; it's the least I could do. I still felt terrible for what I'd
done to him and now this, too, he's dying and it never would have
happened if not for me . . ." He choked, bringing a hand to his
mouth, momentarily.

"Anyway, I went to his apartment, feeling like the angel of death.
He's dying and yet, look at me, not changed a day since he last saw
me. Where is the justice, another man might ask. Yet he wasn't
angry; he didn't blame me. He told me he was grateful that I'd come
into his life. That if not for me, he wouldn't have been the man he
was supposed to be. Do you see? One incident, two views. Which is
the truth? Can't they both be the truth?"

I opened my mouth but didn't have a response.

"I've thought about this a lot," he said, suddenly vehement. "It's
important to me, too. You're not the only one to wonder why you'd

been chosen by Adair. We all do, every damned one of us. I always thought he chose me because I'd ruined all these men's lives, because I was so selfish and had gone after any man I pleased. That was my sin, and Adair was my punishment. But if Daniel could forgive me, didn't that mean that what I'd done wasn't so bad after all?" He took a deep breath. "If we come to see our faults and learn to change, shouldn't that be all that matters? Shouldn't that make us deserving of absolution? I keep hoping that maybe, one day, it will."

The hashish should've made me sleep like an infant, but I lay on the sticky sheets through the humid night, thinking about what Savva had said. He seemed so sure of what he knew of Uzra's story, but how could that be? He hadn't heard it from the odalisque—during the time they lived under the same roof, he didn't yet speak Arabic—and now that she was gone, there was no way to corroborate the story.

If Savva's story was the truth, I couldn't figure out why Adair had lied about her past to me. He'd told me the others' sordid stories—Dona, Tilde, Alejandro—so why not Uzra, too? I thought about my early encounters with Uzra, the ones that had taken place before my transformation, and all the time we spent together once I had been made a member of the household. I was the only one whose company she sought; could that be why I tended to identify with her in my mind, because she had accepted me?

I had seen her only once before I was transformed: the night I tried to escape from Adair's house. Sick, dying (as it turned out), I encountered her on the stairs in the mansion and fainted at her feet. The next thing I recalled was lying in bed, with Adair and Alejandro standing over me, Adair deciding whether to let me die—or live with him forever. I could still picture his face, tense from indecision. What had made him keep me? Was there some dark mark on my soul that only he could see?

And then I remembered something totally new: Uzra had been

there, too, crouched at the foot of the bed like a cat, her eyes glowing. While the men stood over me, she had pressed up against Adair for his attention, stood on tiptoes and said something to him in that tongue I didn't understand. He understood her, though; he knew that she wanted him to save me.

Had she really been there? This wasn't how I'd recalled the scene before, but now it was impossible to see it any other way. Uzra had been in my room, watching over me. She asked Adair to save me. Later, we were friends: I was her *only* friend. And Adair didn't tell me Uzra's story until much later, after Jonathan had joined us—as though he didn't want me to know.

I wanted to blame the narcotic for clouding my head and leaving me strangely restless. Fragments of the past moved above me like stars in a constellation; perhaps our destinies are not so fixed, after all. By hiding her story from me, could Adair have been trying to spare me? Did he want me not to think *badly* of her? Maybe I was remembering it all wrong. What was memory and how could it be trusted, when it could be altered so easily? Maybe it was all because of Savva and the bloody theory he'd planted in my head, that there was no truth. It seemed blasphemous to consider even for a moment that there was no such thing as truth: you might as well say there were no such things as gravity, or day or night. Or that time would run out one day, that we'd all grow old and die. Despite the evidence, I clung to the promise that there were *some* truths we could depend on, truths like a brick wall that stood solidly at our backs. I didn't want to be left adrift in an unexplained cosmos. My head swam, my heart ached. I wanted my punishment to be over.

TEN

BOSTON

Adair stood in the front room of Jude's town house and stared down on the street. He'd grown to hate this house in the weeks he'd lived there, hated its pristine plainness, its monumental emptiness. Hated these oversize windows; it was like living in a glass box. He watched people scuttle up and down the sidewalk, oblivious to him—as they should be—and yet, he simmered with a nameless rage at the sight of them. He was angry all the time. Jude said it was natural, given what he'd gone through. Gave it some fancy name: post-traumatic stress disorder. *I don't believe in it,* Adair had snapped. *I don't believe in any of your nonsense.*

He was beginning to realize that there might be something to this stress disorder. Even with all he'd accomplished in the days since his escape, he was disappointed and restless. His eye was forever on the next prize. Desire, he mused, seemed to be a constant force of the universe, a basic condition of man, even if the ability to satisfy that want—more often than not—was lacking.

He had emerged from his basement prison with nothing, not so much as a penny in his pocket; and yet, a few weeks later, he had secured enough money to put him back on his feet, and reacquired the two books of secret knowledge, the source of his power. He should've been pleased to have accomplished this much in so little time, but that was not the case. He sat in Jude's house, wondering how he might find Lanore. Jude hadn't been able to find the least little bit about her. Until she was in his possession, to do with as he pleased, he could not rest.

Lanny's whereabouts weren't the only thing bothering Adair. He didn't want to admit it, but he was beginning to feel a lack of confidence. Returning to find the world so completely changed, he began to doubt himself. Everything moved in fast motion and the thought of trying to keep apace paralyzed him. How would he ever catch up to Lanore when there were so many more people in the world, more cities and villages, more remote outposts—more places where she could be hiding.

All he *did* know was that she was far away enough that he barely felt her presence.

Watching pedestrians from an obscured chair in the sitting room, Adair noticed that everyone was glued to their devices—computers, cell phones, tablets—as Jude was. Apparently this complicated equipment was the only way to know what was going on around you, your eyes and ears having been made inferior. And it was certainly how people kept tabs on one another. In the old days, it was easy enough to find a man, and Adair had been as skilled as anyone at tracking an adult or child, whether following footprints and trampled grass through field and forest, or in cities and towns, where you might make sly inquiries of prostitutes and shopkeepers. But he suspected such skills wouldn't get him far today when all the footprints were electronic.

He sat in the front room of Jude's stark home, turning the problem over in his mind. It wasn't long before Jude joined him—as he always did, anxious about leaving Adair on his own for long, as though he were a feeble old man or half-wit child who would get into trouble—and Pendleton scurried in behind him. The once powerful industrialist wasn't doing well since his transformation, Adair had noticed. Fitful and twitchy, he was still in shock and overwhelmed. He had taken to watching Adair constantly, and followed him like an anxious dog. He hovered in the corner, seeming less a man than a spare shadow. Of all the people he'd transformed, Pendleton seemed to be having the most difficult adjustment. Adair wondered if this had something to do with the modern age, if something about the times made it harder to accept the supernatural.

"What's wrong, Adair?" Jude asked as he dropped into a seat. "You should be happy. Aren't things going exactly the way you wanted?"

Adair lifted an eyebrow before speaking. "We have made no progress in finding Lanore."

"I've been thinking about that," Jude said, cloyingly upbeat. Whenever Jude was like this, falsely optimistic, Adair knew not to trust him. His enthusiasm was his greatest tell. "The question at hand is how best to trace Lanore's whereabouts from when she left Boston, in the early 1800s, to the present day. We could hire a private investigator . . . you know, like a detective," Jude offered.

"Do you know an investigator who would take on a two-hundred-year-old mystery?" Adair asked scornfully.

A low voice came from the back of the room: "I do."

Adair swiveled around. He'd nearly forgotten Pendleton was there. With eyes shrunken to red pinpoints and the tip of his nose twitching in distress, he reminded Adair of a worried animal hovering at the edge of a field.

"What did you say?" Adair snarled.

The man shut his mouth tightly, seeming to weigh whether he should speak again, but when one minute passed, and then another, and his head had not been taken off, he finally ventured, "It might be nothing, but I know someone who might be able to help you. I've used him in the past when I needed to find corporate data to, uh, *nudge* a deal along." Pendleton paused, as though considering the legality of what he'd just revealed. "He can find anything, if it has to do with the internet."

Again—no surprise—the answer was to turn to the internet. Adair was rather tired of the way people talked about the damn thing, the magic box with fantastical tentacles apparently connected to every piece of information in the universe. Yet, so far, all Adair could see was a rabbit hole designed by the devil to waste men's time and raise their hopes.

Jude leaned toward Adair with a confidential air. "This is his area of expertise; you'd do well to take his advice. Jack's people were able to solve some pretty spectacular cases of data theft. A few required inside knowledge so privileged and compartmentalized that people swore it had to come from the chief accountant or head of data management. It was like he could spirit this stuff out of thin air."

Spirit stuff out of thin air—isn't that what he himself had done, before? Adair thought wistfully. Make the impossible happen with nothing more than a couple of grams of minerals and a few words? The meaning of the phrase had changed. It also served to warn Adair about relying too much on the computer to communicate with the others if it could give up its secrets that easily. He still had information he wished to protect, a string of confidants he'd planted in specific locations, fail-safes to whom he could turn in the most desperate of emergencies. It was information committed to memory, and he vowed then not to trust these details to the computer.

He looked back at Pendleton. "This man, does he come from around here? Can you arrange a meeting?"

Pendleton nodded hesitantly, as though starting to wonder if he'd been wise to offer the suggestion; after all, if it didn't work, there would surely be repercussions.

"Then do so. Set it up right away." Perhaps Pendleton would turn out to be more useful to him than Jude, who wouldn't lift a finger unless it was to line his own pockets, all the while feigning devoted service to his maker. Adair found Jude's transparency almost charming—it certainly was predictable—but as a servant he had limitations. Pendleton might turn out to be a good addition after all.

Pendleton's contact came the next evening. He was a short man of dark and indeterminate complexion, dressed in layers of rumpled clothing. His hair, which looked as though it had gone unwashed for days, laid flat against his skull, complementing the greasy lenses of his black-framed eyeglasses. He smoked a crumpled cigarette, broken in the middle, and his gaze darted shiftily from Adair to Jude and back as they walked to the dimly lit dining room.

"What is your name?" Adair asked the stranger.

The visitor thought about his response for a moment. "You can call me Maurice. I'm a grad student at MIT, working on my PhD."

Jude cut in. "PhD at MIT. That's all well and good, but you know the kind of work we're offering. Pendleton always said you were the best, and that's why I called you. All we care about is whether you can do the job and whether you can keep a secret. How much do you usually charge for your services?"

Maurice shrugged, sending ash tumbling from the tip of his cigarette. "Depends on what you want. But for a big job of a *confidential* nature, could be as high as"—his gaze shifted between the two men facing him, and his breath quickened as he calculated how much of a risk to take—"maybe $50,000?" Then he swallowed, and waited.

"This will be a highly unusual case." Adair fixed his gaze on him as he spoke. "I think you'll find it enormously challenging, and for this reason I'll pay you $250,000," Adair said, aware that Jude turned toward him abruptly in surprise. "For that, I expect you to listen to every bit of direction you are given. No questions. And absolute secrecy. You can tell no one of your task. Absolutely no details can be revealed. But if you find what I'm looking for within two weeks, I'll double your fee." Jude cleared his throat, unhappy at how free Adair was with their money.

Maurice looked back at Adair in astonishment, a sheen of sweat coating his face. "How could I say no to that? You got a deal."

"Listen closely," Adair continued, leaning toward him. He'd thought hard about what could be done to trace Lanore to the present day and had come to the conclusion that, as a woman alive in the early 1800s, few records would be kept in her name. She'd be hidden in the shadow of whichever man to whom she'd attached herself—and she was good at that, he knew. The one man she'd never let too far out of her sight was Jonathan. Fortuitously, as he'd decided to take Jonathan's perfect body for his own shortly after meeting him, Adair had already set up a new identity for Jonathan under the name Jacob Moore. The account he'd set up in Jacob Moore's name would leave the trail needed to trace Jonathan's whereabouts, which should lead back to her.

"In 1823, a sum of money was transferred within the First Bank of Boston, from the account of a Count Adair cel Rau, to set up an account for a Jacob Moore. Moore's Boston account was credited with transfers from banks in St. Petersburg, Paris, and elsewhere, all from the same count's bank accounts. The lawyer in Boston who managed the transfers was named Pinnerly. At some point, Moore's money would have been transferred to the account of someone else. I want you to find out who was the beneficiary of Moore's estate."

The hacker coughed and raised both eyebrows as he scribbled everything on a scrap of paper.

"And then you are to find the beneficiary of *that* man's estate, and so on and so on, up to the present day," Adair finished, sitting back in his chair. "In other words, I want you to find out who is in possession of Jacob Moore's money *today*."

"Sounds like some kind of word problem out of a math textbook," Maurice joked, but when neither man facing him so much as blinked, he dropped his nervous smile. "Let me get this straight: you want me to find a money trail from two hundred years ago and follow it to the present day?" Bewildered, he looked from Adair to Jude. "Did banks even keep records back then?"

"They most certainly did," Adair replied. "I've been told you are capable of finding the most obscure piece of financial information, no matter how well it's hidden. If you can't find the answer, then no one can. That's why I've come to you, and that's why I'm offering such generous compensation."

"I'm not a historian," he said sheepishly. "I find hidden money, but *today's* money. I can't find it if it's sitting in a ledger somewhere."

"Then hire specialists—historians. Or bribe people inside the Bank of Boston, or the Federal Reserve, or whatever you need to do," Jude snapped. "I take it that *is* what you do: bribe insiders."

Maurice colored. "Let's say I end up needing to hire consultants. You just told me I can't divulge anything about this job. . . ."

"Don't be cute," Jude said. "Give them only a part of the task, or hide what it is you're *really* after. You know how to do this."

"You'll figure it out," Adair took over. "Do whatever it takes to get the answer to me as quickly as possible. I'll pay you $50,000 if you fail, $250,000 if you succeed, and half a million dollars if you bring me the answer within two weeks."

"Only $50,000 if I fail?" Maurice frowned. His cigarette was now burnt to ash and scattered, forgotten, over the fine table. "I'll be spending the same amount of time and money whether I get you the answer or not."

"I'm not going to pay you the same whether you succeed or fail. I've found that a little extra incentive makes all the difference between success and failure," Adair said, pushing back from the table. "If you want a big payday, my advice is to find what I want."

The hacker's nerve apparently failed him at this point, and he stared into his lap rather than address his employers. "I have to say, this is a really strange request. Can I ask why you're doing this? If I know what it is you're looking for—*really* looking for—I'll have a better chance of finding it."

"You've been told all you need to know. The information you've been given should take you on a journey. I want you to tell me where it leads you," Adair said.

But that had been no help at all; if anything, the hacker looked more dispirited. Adair stopped in his tracks, realizing that this was no time to hold back any information. All his efforts had led him to this crumpled mess of a man sitting at the table in front of him. This man was his best chance at finding Lanore, and it would be futile to take half-measures now.

"Wait, there is one detail that may prove helpful. . . ." He glanced at Jude, anticipating an objection, before continuing. "Pretend Jacob Moore has never gone away; pretend he has been alive for more than two hundred years and follow the transfer of funds. Lastly, the most important detail . . . this Jacob Moore: he was said to be uncommonly handsome—the kind of looks that defy time, so burned are they in the memory of the beholder."

The kind of looks that inspire love at first sight, thought Adair with a touch of bitterness. He'd come so close to taking Jonathan as his vessel, and the sole reason—he laughed at his naïveté now—had been to please Lanore. He had been resigned to the fact that she would always love Jonathan more, and had thought that by taking on Jonathan's form, he could give her the greatest gift of all: the experience of feeling real love, at the self-assured hands of a real man, in the body of her first love. When Lanny discovered his plan, though, she'd meted out a punishment of her own: two hundred years behind the wall. It was time to pay her back . . . and yet, Adair felt something tugging for consideration at the back of his mind, like a street urchin pulling on his sleeve. Distracted, he walked out on the meeting and left Jude to see the visitor out.

He wandered to a corner, led by a voice cutting through his fury and anticipation of revenge. A plaintive voice reminded him that he *missed* Lanore. He still remembered how she, and she alone, could make him feel. Why this one woman? It wasn't that he lacked for choice. There were women everywhere he turned, of every size, shape, coloring, age, temperament, and yet none interested him. His eye would pass over each one and wander to the crowd, continuing to search for Lanore. He was alarmed to realize that only she would satisfy his restlessness.

After escorting Maurice to the front door, Jude sought out Adair. "What's wrong with you?" he demanded.

Did his melancholy show on his face? Adair wondered, touching his cheek. He would sooner die than admit the truth to Jude. "What are you talking about?"

"Why did you offer him so much money to do the job? He would've been happy with fifty thousand. You could've offered him seventy-five, even a hundred thou. You offered him so much, it'll make him wonder *why*."

So, Jude had no idea what was troubling him and, as usual, was focused on money, Adair was pleased to see. He had a ready answer at hand. "To impress upon him the importance of finding the answer. It's simple: if he knows he'll be well rewarded, he'll try harder to find the answers sooner. I'm weary of waiting; it's time to find Lanore."

The hacker called nine days later to set up a meeting. He sounded exhausted and slightly deranged, refusing to hand over his findings and insisting that he needed to explain how he'd pieced the entire chain of data together for Adair to have any faith in the result. When Maurice arrived that evening, he looked even worse than expected. He appeared not to have slept since their last meeting; his skin was puffy and bloated, as though he had been living off salty snack foods and caffeine. His hair was even greasier, if that was possible, and he bore the rank odor of the unwashed. He might've even been wearing the same clothes. He went straight to the same place at the dining table and pulled a small notebook from his pocket, drawing attention to the nicotine burns on his fingers.

He seemed triumphant, if a bit defiant, as he stared at Adair. "I have to admit, when I walked out of here the other night, I thought maybe you were . . . eccentric," he said, choosing his words carefully. "No one's ever given me a case like this. It sounded like a stunt of some kind. But then I started thinking about it, and I decided, what the hell? I like a challenge.

"So, I caught one lucky break right up front: the First Bank of Boston is still around. It's gone through mergers over the years, but the fact that it never went out of business meant there was a good chance that its records were still intact. I won't go into the details, but suffice it to say that I found someone who could access the bank's historical records and you were absolutely right: there was an account for this Jacob Moore guy." Maurice poured himself a glass of water from the pitcher on the tray in front of him and gulped it down before continuing. "My associate was able to find out that all of Jacob Moore's money was transferred a couple years later to an account in his name with an Italian bank.

"It went on like this every decade or so, all over Europe. Then, in the early twentieth century, which would make Jacob Moore *at least* a hundred years old, he transferred all his money into an account for"—he consulted his notebook—"a Rolf Schneider, in Berlin. This happened right before World War I. And here's where we run into a problem: bank records in Europe got messed up after the war, especially in Germany, because of the political turmoil. People started keeping their money close, in shoeboxes and such. . . . There were no further bank records for Mr. Schneider."

He fiddled with his notebook again, nervously. "So I leave the financial records and look elsewhere: marriage licenses, property records . . . One of my associates finds a record of a Rolf Schneider enrolled in a doctors' college in Heidelberg. I'm wondering: could it be the same man? That's when I remembered your advice." The hacker looked Adair squarely in the eye. "So I hire a German speaker to look through microfiche of old newspapers, society pages, anything and everything we can think of, and sure enough, she finds these mentions of a good-looking medical student, Rolf Schneider, at these society parties."

Adair nearly lunged across the table. "Do you have a picture of this man, Schneider?"

Maurice fumbled in his pocket and drew out a much-folded sheet of paper. He smoothed it with his palms before sliding it across the table.

It was less like a photograph and more of a gesture drawing, a charcoal sketch of human forms—blobs of black on a white background—the image as vague as a brass rubbing of a weather-worn headstone. Adair could make out some of the room where the figures were gathered in the photograph, but he searched the indistinct faces with an air of futility, doubtful of seeing anything clearly through the graininess. . . . But no, there was no mistaking *that* face, even if it was just the shadow of a cheekbone and the arch of an eye socket on a half-turned face, graced by a fallen lock of dark hair. It was Jonathan.

Adair sat back and let out the breath he'd been holding.

The hacker continued. "So we kept looking for mentions of Rolf Schneider in the German records. We find him on the roster at one hospital, then another. . . . And then he disappears for a while. It's not uncommon. Lots of records were lost in Germany after the war. But I tried everything. I even had a guy inside the Defense Department look up the records from the occupation. Still, the trail ran cold and I thought I'd lost him. Then, for grins, I try searching for Rolf Schneider in all the databases I can get into. There are a lot of databases out there. That's why companies are putting everything they have into data warehouses right now, because there's money in it. Airline ticket sales, credit ratings, insurance records, school records, voting records—you'd be surprised.

"Anyway, I find a match, but it's now decades after the end of the war. Some doctor by the name of Rolf Schneider is working for an aid organization, the kind of place that sends medical teams into war zones or where there's an outbreak of some disease, you know? Anyway, I found a picture of the guy in one of their newsletters." Hands shaking, the hacker reached into another pocket and pulled out a second piece of paper, which he slid over to Adair with an air of satisfaction.

This photograph was much sharper than the first. It was a group shot of people lined up behind a table outdoors, someplace where it was very sunny. Adair saw three white people and five Moors, the white people looking depleted by the heat, the Moors smiling or affecting serious expressions. The tall, dark-haired man on the end of the row had his head turned, trying to cheat the camera and blur his image. But there was no mistaking the man for anyone *but* Jonathan: there could not be two sun gods in all of history. The caption underneath read "Mercy for Peace International team vaccinates two thousand against measles, Serrat refugee camp, Chad." The date given was from the year before.

"It's *got* to be the guy's descendant. I mean, he's the spitting image. . . ." The hacker motioned to the first photograph. By the tone of his voice, a mix of awe and fear, he wanted to be reassured.

Over the years, Adair had discovered that whenever someone stumbled too closely to his secret, that person could usually be dissuaded from pushing the matter any further: the idea that someone might live forever was too fantastical, too heretical. Ordinary men were afraid to pursue this line of questioning to its end, no matter how strong the evidence; it seemed to lead to madness. The hacker didn't want to be told that Jacob Moore had indeed lived for centuries; he wanted to be given a logical explanation. "Of course it's his descendant," Adair said back to him. "Who else could he be?"

Maurice looked from Jude to Adair and then lowered his eyes, relieved.

Adair turned to him. "So, where's Moore's descendant now? Is he still in . . . Chad?"

Maurice shrugged. "I don't know. You said to follow the money.

The trail went cold in 1914. I have yet to verify his whereabouts or his demise, but I still have five days left on the clock," he said quickly.

Adair couldn't help but smile as he turned to Jude. "Pay him. Five hundred thousand dollars. I value good work, and you've done a very good job," he said to Maurice, who quivered in disbelief. "But do not forget, you're not to say a word of this to anyone. If I find out you've talked about this, piqued anyone's interest in Rolf Schneider, alerted any authorities . . ."

"Hey, don't worry about it. I know that you expect discretion."

Adair took the two photographs, leaving Jude to wrap things up, and went to Jude's office. He tried to ignore the feelings of triumph rising inside him, tried not to let his mind race ahead optimistically. He was a step closer to capturing his quarry but knew to expect more obstacles lying in wait, ones that he couldn't begin to imagine.

But first he had to find Jonathan. He closed the door behind him and went to the computer to search for Mercy for Peace International, then dialed the phone number given on the website.

"Hello? I'm trying to find an old friend who works for you. . . . Yes, I'll hold. . . ." He swiveled in the chair as he held the cell phone to his ear. (Unlike computers, he had instantly seen the utility of cell phones, a magic he would never have dreamed possible.) "Hello? Yes, I'm looking for a friend who works for your organization and I was told you might be able to help me. His name is—" Adair said the name carefully and precisely, then listened as the woman on the other end explained that it was their policy not to give out information on their employees.

As easily as that, yet another obstacle was thrown in his path. He was tired of being frustrated. In pursuit of Lanny, he'd risen to every challenge—witness the lengths this Maurice, this clever thief of information, had gone to to bring Adair this much further—only to be stymied now by an insignificant clerk. To be tripped up in this way made him mad. Anger rippled under his skin as faintly but unmistakably as thunder on the horizon. He would almost swear that he felt sparks ignite in the air, and the connection between him and the voice on the line lit up as though on fire.

And suddenly, unbidden, the woman continued, saying that the doctor had taken an extended leave and couldn't be reached, but he had mentioned to a colleague that he was visiting an old friend in the town they'd grown up in. Barely remembering to thank her, Adair put the phone down, amazed by his luck. Had he been able to make her do his bidding merely by wishing, or had it been a slip of the mind? Or was she perhaps a gossip? He thought of the feeling that went through him and the electricity in the air, and resolved to think more on it later.

Because now he had a trip to make. Lanny's childhood home—why hadn't he thought of that earlier? He'd seen this so many times before in those he'd transformed: the impulse to return from whence you came and feel the comfort of home again, even if you know it will only be a shadow of the way it used to be. All of his subjects felt it at one time or another; some, overwhelmed by the wider world, had been unable to leave the embrace of the past, and he had been forced to kill them for their own good.

He was disappointed that the woman he'd always found so unpredictable had resorted to such predictable behavior. But then, Adair could understand the appeal for Lanore of going home with Jonathan on a cozy trip. He pictured them returning to the places they used to go as teenage lovers and re-creating those impassioned moments, and the thought made him briefly upset.

On his way to bed, Adair told Jude to book him passage to St. Andrew, Maine.

ELEVEN

CASABLANCA

By the end of my third week in Casablanca, I was ready to leave. The idea of traveling made me nervous, as if any movement would draw Adair's attention and put him on my scent, but living with Savva had become unnerving enough to make me want to risk it. I didn't mean to be cruel or ungrateful, but I think I'd forgotten what it had been like to deal with him on a daily basis, or perhaps I'd idealized our time together.

The truth was he had been difficult to live with even then, frequently getting us in trouble with his mercurial temper. He would make snap judgments when he met strangers, either loving them as though they were long-lost brothers or hating them as intensely as he would a sworn enemy. He could go on manic sprees for days before crashing in exhaustion. He spent our money impetuously, without a care as to how we'd find more, and I would become exasperated with him, thinking it was within his power to change. I should've known there was more than recklessness to his behavior, for the signs were all there. Back then, though, we didn't understand bipolar disorder.

Instead, we let people like Savva run to physical or emotional exhaustion, dosing themselves with laudanum or alcohol, until they committed suicide or were locked up in prison or an asylum.

Savva was much worse now. He was clearly too much of an addict to medicate responsibly; he had worse demons to fight than his chemical imbalance, and very little willpower to draw upon. His mood swung unpredictably, and he was often angry and unreasonable and paranoid, though he was slightly less hostile when he was high. He shot up so frequently that he was more efficient with a needle than any nurse. He ate whatever pills he could get his hands on and alcohol was the only liquid he'd ingest. It was frightening to be around him and yet hard to leave him in this condition. Drug therapy might've been able to help whatever disorder he had, but I couldn't see a way to get him under a doctor's care. It made me angry to think Adair might have seen this weakness in Savva and chosen him anyway, condemning him to an eternity of suffering for the sake of a few introductions to Russian aristocrats.

After these weeks in Savva's presence, I now understood why he lived the way he did. We rarely left the apartment. He slipped out when he needed to score, though occasionally we were visited by a young man with dark, suspicious eyes, and the two would go into the hall to conduct their transaction in mumbled Arabic. Sometimes a friend would come by, a pretty young man or a thuggish older one, and I'd leave to give them privacy. When I got back, he'd be asleep on the sour mattress that served as his bed.

It was understandable, then, why I was relieved when Savva came to me one day to tell me that he thought he had the answer to my situation. He'd come to the conclusion that if I wanted help, I had no choice but to turn to the ones who had served as Adair's minions. "You need a better adviser than me, Lanny. Adair never loved me enough to bring me close—not *really* close," he explained. "He never told me his secrets. You need someone who spent a good deal more time with him. I think you should go see Alejandro."

My heart sank at his recommendation. "Alejandro? I don't think he'll talk to me. He thinks Jonathan and I took Adair away from him."

"Well, you've no choice but to tell him the truth and convince him to help you. Would you rather go to Dona? Alej's the only one you'll stand a chance with. Besides, of all of us, Alej has always been the most conciliatory, the one to smooth over any conflict in the group. He knew best how to handle Adair."

I thought of Alejandro. He'd been the kindest to me of all the members of Adair's household, that was true. But the sin that had damned him was betrayal: he had given over his sister to the inquisitors to save himself. I hoped for his sake that he had changed, and maybe even found redemption. In my heart, rightly or wrongly, I distrusted him.

"I don't know, Savva. I never really knew what to think about Alej. At least I always knew where I stood with Tilde and Dona. Alej kept his true intentions to himself. I'm not sure if he'll help me once he finds out I was responsible for Adair's disappearance. He worshipped Adair."

Savva was firm. "I wouldn't assume he feels the same way now. You remember what it was like living with Adair: it was like being a kidnap victim, always tense, always afraid. You would do whatever it took to avoid being the object of his attention or bringing his wrath down on you. Alejandro has had a long time to heal, to put that time in perspective. He's a different person now." Savva kissed my hand and gave it a pat. "I'm no use to you. Not in my condition. Go see Alejandro. I know where he lives; I'll tell him you're coming to see him. We'll have to go into town, though, for me to do that: there's no cell phone reception here, none at all. We'll need to go to the hotel where the tourists stay."

The hotel turned out to be very exclusive, the sort of place where rock stars and the jaded rich stay while taking in the city. I regret to say I felt conspicuous there with Savva, who looked odd in his hodgepodge of make-do clothes. I was afraid they wouldn't allow us to stay—the hawkeyed attendants rushed to shoo us out as we attempted to settle in the lobby—but I asked to have some very pricey tea and cookies brought to us and that seemed to assure them that we fit in, that Savva was merely eccentric and not a derelict.

Savva went off by himself to make his call, while I checked email. I was waiting for my computer to boot up after its long dormancy, when my cell phone leapt to life, buzzing and vibrating for attention. I checked the tiny screen to see twenty voice mails from Luke in the queue. Warily, I pressed the phone to my ear and listened to the first message.

"For God's sake, where are you? Why aren't you answering?" It was his voice, but vulnerable in a way I hadn't heard before, and it hit me like a baseball bat to the stomach.

"Pick up, Lanny. Don't play games with me. . . ."

"I didn't mean to lose my temper. . . ."

"Call me. At least let me know that you're safe, that nothing has happened to you. . . ." And his voice choked to silence, as though he was remembering what I'd told him about Adair and wondering if my fears had been realized. That sickening pause was almost enough to make me dial his number, to reassure him and apologize for causing him worry. *Almost.*

There were emails, too. One long one in particular struck me, obviously written after the barrage of phone calls, when he'd had time to think about how to persuade me to return to him. It was clinical, as though his professional self—Dr. Findley—had evaluated me and was ready to give his diagnosis. He laid out my psychological motivation for leaving him, explaining that I was acting out of fear and had run away because, subconsciously, I was afraid he was going to leave me as Jonathan had. By leaving, he wrote, I was testing him, but I had to realize that he wasn't Jonathan and he'd never do that to me. We could disagree and argue, but if I trusted him, I would come back and we'd work through our differences. It read strangely for a love letter, lacking passion.

I saw in that instant that he was, like so many men, removed from his emotions. He was unable to abandon himself to passion, as though he'd given up on it a long time ago. The closest he had come was when he'd run away with me, but that dangerous anomaly had been corrected and the old Luke had crept back in place. He wasn't perfect, as I'd thought at first: he was damaged in his way, a part of his psyche amputated, and that might've been why I had been drawn to him. Not for his steadfastness, but because he was broken and I wanted to protect him.

By now I was crying and reached for a napkin from the tea tray to wipe my tears. Yet, I did not dial his phone number or reply to his email.

"What's wrong?" Savva asked as he came back from his corner of the lobby, pocketing his cell phone.

"There's a man," I sniffed, too weary to fully explain and half-afraid of what Savva would say anyway. "I left him as soon as I felt Adair's presence, as soon as I knew Adair was free."

Savva listened as I read Luke's email to him. "How very romantic of him." His tone was droll, as though he found Luke's analysis anything but romantic. "You are right, however: with Adair coming for you, you can't afford to keep him around just for the solace of his company. You need to travel light. He'll only slow you down. It's all part of the curse: we're doomed to be alone."

I scrubbed under my eyes with the disintegrating napkin, though my tears had stopped as the reality of what he was saying began to sink in. I couldn't hide forever and couldn't bear to live in a perpetual state of fear—on the lam for life—while Adair located everyone important to me and made our lives a living hell until he got what he wanted. Me.

"Face it, we're damned to unhappiness," Savva said, leaning toward me. "Of course we want to have someone with us, to drive away the loneliness. For us, it might even be necessary, since we're locked in these ageless *containers*"—vessels, Adair called them—

"with the memories of the horrible things we've done. Having some-one else to live for might be the only way to go on."

He was right: that was how I got through all those years without Jonathan. It was only the hope of seeing him again that kept me from losing my mind. "If that's the way you feel, then why don't you find someone to live for?" I asked. "Why don't you do that instead of living by yourself and taking all these drugs to get you through your days?"

"Love has never worked out for me." He picked up my cup of tea and drank from it. "I can find someone to love me; that's never been a problem. I just can't seem to love them back. I can't seem to keep from hurting them. I've always thought of myself as the scorpion in that children's story—you know the one?" A sad smile flickered across his face. "A scorpion asks a frog to carry it on its back across the river. The frog refuses, saying that the scorpion will sting him and kill him. The scorpion argues that this would be preposterous: if he kills the frog, the scorpion would drown and die as well. You know the ending, of course: the scorpion stings the frog, and as they both sink into the water, the frog asks the scorpion why he killed them both. And the scorpion replies that he *had* to. It was in his nature." Savva held me in his cold blue gaze. "It's in my nature, too. It's what Adair looks for, I think. It's in your nature, Lanny, or he never would've been drawn to you."

His words settled in my chest like shots of lead. I didn't want to believe Savva, but of course he was right. I preferred to believe we had a chance at salvation if we fought our natures with all our might, and that the truly worthy would be rewarded with a perfect love. Savva would scorn this as sentimental hogwash, a pretty thought that was impossible to put into practice. It mattered little now what I wanted to believe in anyway: with Adair released, it was unlikely that I'd have the chance to love anyone ever again.

Savva helped me up from the chair and tucked my arm under his, and we left the comfort and security of the hotel, its air-conditioning and Wi-Fi, for the gritty reality of the Moroccan street. As we stood on the curb, waiting for traffic to pass, he said, "Alejandro has agreed to meet with you, by the way. We should stop by the travel agency and book you on a flight to Spain."

"All right." It was frightening, suddenly, to think of leaving Casablanca. Travel meant making myself vulnerable, like a rabbit popping its head out of the warren when it knows a hawk is circling overhead. I wasn't sure I was ready for this.

"There is something I need to ask of you, Lanny," Savva continued, leading me down the street and refusing to look at me. "I want you to promise that if Adair *does* catch you that—when the opportunity presents itself—you'll send him to me. I want to end my existence. For obvious reasons." I opened my mouth to object, but he jerked on my arm to silence me. "Don't argue; you did the same for Jonathan, so I know you understand. It would be a mercy. Please, Lanny. Promise you'll do this for me, if you have the chance. Promise me."

With reservations made to travel to Barcelona in the morning, I had just one more night in Casablanca to get through. I longed to sit on the balcony and chain-smoke until dawn, but a voice in the back of my head reminded me that I'd given up smoking to please Luke. I had to laugh at myself: if I couldn't bring myself to light up, then clearly I wasn't really free from him, not in my heart.

I was sick to my stomach over what I'd done to him. Like Savva, I seemed destined to hurt those who loved me. Every time I've been in some kind of bad emotional situation, I've tried to outrun the hurt. Two centuries ago, I fled rather than be sent to a convent to give up Jonathan's baby. I'd run from Adair and, over the years, left other men, too, for all sorts of reasons; and now, in the middle of an argument with Luke, I had panicked and fled.

I hoped I was doing the right thing by giving him up. I wanted to think that we weren't meant for each other, and I would have left him eventually anyway. And since he protected himself from feeling true passion, from wanting anything too badly, it wasn't as though my leaving would devastate him. Better to leave now when it would hurt less . . . although did it ever hurt less?

And, most important, there were Luke's children to consider. For two hundred years I'd avoided getting involved with a man who had children. Breaking a man's heart was one thing; removing yourself from a child's life was quite another. Because of me, it was hard for Luke to see his children, as his former wife, Tricia, was understandably reluctant for them to learn that their father was living with a fugitive murderess. Even if Tricia's misgivings could be overcome, there would be a day when their father would be very old and I would still appear to be very young—younger than his children—and there would be nothing left to do but disappear. I had told Luke about my immortal condition, but knew I couldn't share my secret with his daughters and ex-wife. And God forbid what would happen if Adair ever found out that Luke knew our secret. No, I couldn't put him or his daughters in that kind of danger.

For our last night, Savva insisted on taking me to a café, where we had a marvelous lamb tagine, savory with ginger and saffron and coriander, and we reminisced about our travels together through northern Africa and central Asia. At the time, we'd chosen this area of the world because much of it was still run by tribes and local strongmen, and it was easier to keep a low profile without a government breathing down your neck. In such a freewheeling environment, we also found ways to make money without the hassle of finding legitimate work, which would require names and histories, the kind of things that could trip us up.

At dinner, Savva reminded me of the time we sold guns we'd stolen from the British garrison to the very Afghan rebels they were fighting: typical of Savva, to line his pockets while thumbing his nose at those in authority. Our adventure took an unexpected turn, but Savva stood by me loyally and, in the end, took care of me as only a true friend would.

Unsurprisingly, when I fell asleep that evening, I dreamed about that incident, and the dream led me to an epiphany I would wish had remained hidden from me forever.

Afghan Territory, 1841

The winds that day coming up the Khyber Pass were unlike anything I had experienced before, I recall, harsher than the dry, hot winds off the Sahara. I remembered standing in full sun, in layers of men's clothing, breeches and a cloth like a keffiyeh, the headdress that Arab men wore, pulled over my nose and mouth to keep the sand out. I kept my long rifle pointed in the direction of the men with whom we'd come to barter.

Savva was down in the valley basin bargaining with a Pashtun warlord, our interpreter at his side. He wore white men's clothes with his head wrapped in a thick cloth the same as I, so we looked like Englishmen rolled in rags. Underneath it all, I was wet to the skin and tried not to let the sweating trigger a bout of nerves; I kept my hands steady on the rifle and tried to keep my squinting, sweat-stung eyes on the twenty tribesmen surrounding Savva and the warlord.

The Pashtun were known to be excellent on horseback, filthy as dirt itself, near toothless, and violent in the extreme. They wouldn't be pleased to know that I was a woman. Not unexpectedly, there wasn't one woman among the group that had come to bargain with us. Apparently, men and women didn't mingle unless they were family. Once, on a visit to an Afghan village, I managed to catch a fleeting glimpse of a black-clad figure scurrying between mud huts whose diaphanous garment reminded me of Uzra, who used to wrap herself from head to toe in a long, winding cloth. It reminded me of my own village, not so long ago, and how we women were weighed down with layers and layers of skirts and petticoats, tuckers and kerchiefs and all manner of garb, to protect our modesty. Of how, too, we were commonly separated from the men. We were not so different, once upon a time.

Negotiations had begun in earnest, I was glad to see. Savva had unfurled a blanket on the ground and placed a few rifles on display. The young warlord hefted an unloaded rifle and began investigating its mechanisms, asking if the rifles were as good as those of the British military, his pinpoint black eyes trained first on the translator, then on Savva. "Of course," Savva laughed. "Who do you think I got them from?" It was brazen of us to sell guns stolen from the British to their foes, but Savva thought it practically patriotic of him as a Russian to undermine the British attempt to colonize Afghanistan, given that the Russians had designs on the area, too. Nevertheless, our primary reason for running stolen guns was profit.

As I stood under the cloudless sky, repositioning the rifle to relieve my now aching shoulders, I couldn't help but wonder why these fearsome men didn't just overpower us and take the weapons. Both Savva and I were tiny compared to even the youngest among the Afghans and certainly no fiercer than the oldest members, who, though wizened and gray, looked capable of tearing apart wild beasts with their bare hands. Their warlord leader, conferring with Savva at that moment, cut a particularly impressive figure. He stood a foot taller than my friend and was broad-backed and long-legged, and I could easily picture him as one of those Greek athletes the old tutor back in St. Andrew used to rhapsodize about.

As I watched him, the man impatiently jerked the cloth away to drink from his goatskin, revealing a dark, handsome face. He reminded me immediately of Adair, due in no small part to the mix of savagery and intellect in his expression and the long curls of dark hair that fell over his shoulders.

Farrar, the interpreter, head down in a show of deference, had been leading the discussion with the Afghans, but at that point he became so animated that it was apparent things were not going well. The locals began to pass one another guarded looks.

"A box of rocks?" Savva's voice floated across the hard ground to where I stood. "He wants to give us a box of rocks for good British rifles?"

The interpreter gestured vigorously at the battered tin chest at their feet. "Not rocks: these stones are lapis. Very precious to these people. They are offering you a fortune."

Savva crouched next to the box and pulled out one of the rocks. He spit on his hand and tried to rub off the crusted dirt, but it looked like nothing more than a piece of stone chiseled straight from the earth. When he turned it a certain way, however, the sun lit up a vein of blue.

"You can sell it in Kabul. I know people who will give you a good price," the interpreter said to Savva while nodding assurances at the blank-faced tribesmen.

"This is ridiculous, expecting to trade rocks for guns. They are playing us for fools. I want gold. Don't these people have any gold?" Savva roared. I repositioned my damp hands on the rifle but felt my arms droop.

"No gold. They do, however, hold our lives in their hands," the interpreter warned, drawing Savva close. "Trust me, you will be amply compensated in the city."

Savva threw his hands up and tucked the box under his arm as he climbed the hill toward me. "Very well . . . if this is the best we can get. . . . Tell them it's a deal. C'mon, Lanny, let's show them how to use these bloody rifles and fulfill our end of the bargain, and get out of here."

We used anything at hand as a target—native melons, gourds, a goat carcass—set on rocks in the distance, and then we demonstrated how to aim and shoot. Of the two of us, Savva was by far the better marksman, and most of the men gathered around him; but the warlord I'd noticed earlier came over and watched me, his arms folded. Again, his prepossessing demeanor made me a bit giddy, and I fought my nerves as I raised the rifle, closed one eye into a squint, and stared down the long barrel at the melon in the distance, nearly the exact color of the rock it sat upon. I drew in a breath, held it, and pulled back on the trigger as smoothly as I could. Amid a plume of smoke and a wicked crack of thunder, the melon burst almost instantaneously, pulp hurtling into the air. I couldn't help but smile in relief beneath my scarf that I hadn't missed, and when I looked over at the leader, he was smiling, too.

It was no use trying to show him how to hold the rifle correctly, as he was so much taller than me and I had to reach over my head to position his arms. So I did my best by taking up my rifle, standing next to him, and pantomiming the steps. Several of the other men came over to watch and clap the fellow on the back when, after the first few shots, he sent one of the hard gourds skittering off its rock like a scalded cat.

By the time they finished up, the sky had shifted from a watery blue to an indigo band falling over the mountaintops, and as both sides packed, the interpreter came over.

"Owing to the late hour, the warlord has invited you to their camp for dinner and to spend the night with them," he said, glancing once over his shoulder back at the Afghans.

"It's out of the question," Savva replied.

"You don't understand: it would be an insult not to accept."

"First you have us trade good arms for a pile of rocks, and now you want us to spend the night in their tents so they can murder us in our sleep. No," Savva said. I knew what caused him to be so peevish: his ego had been bruised because he had been forced to accept what he saw as a lesser payment for our cache of prized British arms. Savva would chafe each minute in the Afghans' company.

"According to our customs, he is bound to offer you his hospitality." There was a pleading look in the man's eyes.

"That's all well and good to talk about honor and custom, but we're dealing with a bunch of savages here. I, for one, am not spending the night in their camp. You can do whatever you want. We're leaving."

I'd seen that look on Savva's face before: he could be foolhardy and stubborn when he felt he'd been taken advantage of. It was impossible to force him to do anything once he'd set his mind against it, and it seemed the more he was pressed, the more he resisted.

"And if we decline?" I asked, checking the pistol I had tucked in my waistband.

The interpreter shrugged. "The mountain pass is difficult—you've seen that for yourself—and it is even more difficult in the dark."

"I don't know," I said, hands on hips. "I'll do whatever you decide, Savva, but I think we ought to listen to Farrar. What's one night?"

Savva rubbed his chin. "It's one more night around *them*. If we leave, we're free of them, and I don't know about you two, but I would feel infinitely better." Resolved, he clapped a hand on Farrar's shoulder. "Tell them we appreciate the invitation and we don't mean any disrespect, but we will have to turn down their hospitality," he said. Savva and I left on horseback, the box of lapis tethered to his saddle, under the intense stares of the tribesmen. I knew that no good would come of this.

We'd been riding an hour when we heard the rapid thudding of hooves on the trail behind us, punctuated by the snap of a leather switch on a horse's flank. Savva, having the hearing of a fox, put spurs to his horse's side immediately, the prickly gelding almost leaping out from underneath him and tearing down the near invisible trail at a gallop. I held the pommel for dear life as my horse shot after his, lying flat against the horse's neck and spurring for all I was worth.

The Pashtun were excellent horsemen, and they were very familiar with these passes, knowing all the shortcuts and which trails dead-ended onto a steep drop. With blackness rushing up to them, I wondered when the road would suddenly disappear underneath my horse and I'd leap into emptiness on a flightless Pegasus.

The trail began to cut through passes, twisting blindly left, then right, and I could see neither Savva in front of me nor the horsemen behind, though I could hear the thunder of them over the sound of my own mount's hooves. Just as the trail emerged into a clearing and I could see Savva once more in front, two figures on horseback suddenly cut in from the left, steering Savva off the trail with them. The riders had apparently taken a shortcut and were able to catch up to us, and just as I thought about ducking off the path and hiding in the brush, I was tackled from behind.

I rolled over and over in a flurry of flapping scarves and dust clouds on the ground with my attacker, and scrambled away from him before he got to his feet and chased me. Several more horses rushed by in the darkness as my pursuer made a second leap, knocking me to the ground again, but this time he pinned me flat and reached up to pull off my scarf. A gasp of surprise escaped him as my long blond hair tumbled out, and he relaxed the grasp on my arm the slightest bit, allowing me to pull the pistol from my waistband and press the nose of it to the underside of his jaw.

We remained frozen in place as I tried to calculate quickly whether any more horses were coming up the trail or if the rest of the men had gone off in pursuit of Savva. At the same time the man released me and held his hands away from his body, seeming to indicate that he was giving up his claim. As he backed away, I saw that it was the warlord I'd taught to shoot, a half-suppressed smile on his face.

We were still standing that way, neither making any overture, when the rest of the riders emerged together out of the darkness at a slow trot. Savva was in the midst of them, led by a rope around his neck and his hands tied behind his back, looking as though he'd been through a struggle.

"Now what?" I called to Savva, my pistol still pointed at the warlord.

"They might swap him for me, but I'm afraid we'll never know, because they don't speak English and we don't know their blasted

tongue." The group came to a stop when they saw a woman pointing a gun at their leader's chest. "I'd give up," Savva called out. "You
can't shoot all of them."

"Maybe if I shoot a couple of them, the rest will let us go."

"Or they'll shoot us and take their rocks back."

I cocked the trigger for good measure. I didn't want to shoot the
man, but he was the only one I knew I'd be able to hit cleanly, given
the darkness. At this moment the rest of the band came up on a trail
from the other direction, a couple of brigands leading Farrar with his
hands bound by rope.

"Farrar!" Savva called out loudly. "Tell these devils to let Lanny
go!"

The interpreter barked a few words at the warlord at whom the
gun was pointed, but before he could say anything, one of the elders
spat out a few harsh words at the warlord and then at Farrar.

"The elder says no. He doesn't like the way you disrespected their
payment. They feel you voided their relationship when you refused
their hospitality," the interpreter explained glumly.

"They can have the blasted rocks; just let us go," Savva called out.

"I suggest, Miss Lanore, that you hand over your pistol. It will
only be worse for us if you persist in defying them," Farrar said. As
though to make a point, the man holding the rope tied to Savva's
neck gave it a vicious yank and he fell to his knees.

I cocked the pistol upright, nose in the air, and raised my hands
in surrender.

Back at the Pashtun camp, we were put into one of the few tents, a
guard posted outside to watch. I heard voices outside the tent, which
had been constructed from kilims stretched over sticks pitched low
in the ground. I also smelled smoke from a fire and the savory aroma
of meat cooking. "Can you hear what they're saying?" I asked Farrar.

"I can only think they are deciding what to do with us," the interpreter answered. "They have no love of foreigners, even if you brought them weapons to use against the British. They've learned not to trust outsiders. I'm afraid it probably will not go well for us."

"They've got their treasure back and the guns, so why should they be vindictive? They should let us go if they're so concerned about honor," Savva said.

"You don't understand their view of honor. As you see, these people are nomads, and poor, and yet they offered you what little they had, which is their obligation as hosts, and you refused them."

"If you'd explained it to me like that," Savva replied, a bit defensively, "I wouldn't have turned them down."

"That is very bad." Farrar hung his head.

We were silent for a moment. Savva, sitting cross-legged on the ground, slumped against his bindings, demoralized. "What about . . . Lanny's honor? Will they harm her?"

Farrar looked puzzled for a second and then seemed to follow Savva's meaning. "I don't know. It's possible. Generally, such acts are against our customs. We respect women, but she is a foreigner. . . . The elder of this group, he is known as a devout man, so she may be safe. We will see."

"Tell them to leave her alone, for God's sake. Tell them she's diseased, that their cocks will fall off if they touch her. . . ."

"Savva!" I wanted to hear no more from him. It was his fault that we were in this terrible situation, as far as I was concerned. I didn't want to contemplate what might happen to me that evening. I'd been treated brutally by Adair and thought I could endure anything, but I had no idea what these men might have in mind.

It had grown quiet outside. Presently, the front of the tent was drawn back and the young warlord entered, crouching on the balls of his feet. He said a few words gently to Farrar.

"He is going to take you to his tent," Farrar explained to me. "He says you will be safe with him. He's afraid one of the men may come for you if you remain here."

Savva sniffed. "A gentleman savage. How refreshing."

"Savva, enough. I'll take my chances." I felt by then that the warlord was a gentleman: he hadn't tried to overpower me when we struggled on the trail, although he had certainly stood a good chance of getting the better of me. He'd let me hold him at gunpoint, despite the affront to his dignity. So I struggled to my feet, holding my bound hands out for balance, but the warlord reached under my elbow to help me up.

Savva called out, "Be careful, Lanny. I don't like the idea of us being split up." Even if I'd had enough of him, it was gratifying to hear that he still worried for me.

The warlord's tent was no different from the others, except that it had a bed made of a stack of kilims and the blanket from his horse's back. He gestured to the bed and untied my hands. He left the tent and came back with a skewer of meat, the fat on its surface still spitting and crackling from the fire. After I'd eaten, I braced myself, expecting him to lie next to me on the bed, but he didn't. He took one of the blankets and spread it on the ground before the tent's opening, then lay with his back to me. I was relieved by his consideration.

I remained awake for a while, wondering how Savva and Farrar were faring and what would happen to us come the next day, but eventually my gaze fell on the warlord, watching the rise and fall of his chest. It was as natural as anything to watch him sleep—why was that?—as though I'd done this very thing before. My eye traced the high ridge of his cheekbone, then the curve of his upper lip, which suddenly looked very inviting in the moonlight. I pulled myself from this reverie before I gave in to temptation, rolled off the kilims, and climbed on top of him in his sleep. I turned away from him, resolved to remain where I was until morning.

The next morning I waited until the warlord awoke and then followed him outside. When I looked over to where the other tent had stood, I was startled to see that it was gone, already struck, the sticks upended and lying on the ground. "Where's Savva?" I demanded, even though I knew he couldn't understand.

"Miss Lanore! Here!" Farrar's voice called from beyond a rise, and both the warlord and I walked over to find the interpreter sitting on a rock under a tree, looking off to a distant plain. Several streaks of dust rose in the air. Through the dust clouds I could make out the figures of several men racing on horseback at a flat-out gallop, performing tricks. One of them had to be Savva: he could ride like a Cossack.

"What's going on?" I asked Farrar, who grinned with glee at the display of horsemanship.

"Mister Savva challenged these men to a contest on horseback. If he can do everything they do, they will let us go."

"And?"

"So far, they haven't been able to outdo him," Farrar said.

"And do you think they will let us go?"

Farrar tilted his head to one side, squinting against the sun. "Of course. They are men of honor."

We watched the antics on horseback for a while longer, Savva playing follow-the-leader with the Afghans, leaning far over at a dead gallop to tear a handful of grass from the ground, standing on his horse's back while holding the reins all the way to the very tip. And then, gesturing to the warlord, I asked Farrar, "Do you know this man's name?"

"Yes—it's Abdul." At hearing his name, the warlord turned toward us expectantly.

"And could you ask him, please, if he is married?"

A short, pleasant exchange took place between the two men, and I tried to hold on to the sounds of some of the words, but they were too foreign, too unlike English. Farrar turned to me. "No, he does not have a wife. Do you have something in mind, Miss Lanore?"

I looked over at Abdul again. There was something about him that I found desirable. Perhaps it was that he reminded me of Adair, handsome if savage. Perhaps it was that I'd been traveling with Savva for years now, which meant the men I'd taken to my bed were few and far between, since most assumed Savva was my lover if not my husband, and for Savva's safety I rarely disabused them of this notion.

"Please tell Abdul I would like to thank him for his hospitality," I said to Farrar before taking Abdul's hand. He looked in surprise from my hand to my face, but he didn't resist in the least when I led him back to the tent.

We lay on the kilims together this time. He was hesitant to undress me, so I began, hurriedly slipping buttons free on my jacket until Abdul took over, and there was something thrilling about seeing the trembling in those strong, confident hands. He was enthralled with my body, anxious to explore tender feminine skin, raising goose bumps on my arms and the back of my neck. He helped me shift through the layers of his clothing until I uncovered his cock, swollen and seemingly ready to burst at the touch with a luscious pearl of his fluid waiting to be tasted.

I took him in my mouth, which surprised him at first but soon had him moaning low and guttural animal noises of pleasure. He came very quickly and so I lovingly took his head and guided him down to a place on a woman's body he'd probably never seen before. Again he seemed startled by the suggestion, but having no doubt of my meaning, he plunged in hungrily and had me spent and quivering in no time. By then he was aroused again, hard as petrified wood, and, now in more familiar territory, he climbed confidently on top of me and drew me close so that we could enjoy each other at a more leisurely pace.

I thought at the time that I'd have one morning in Abdul's arms—that I'd indulge my curiosity and hunger and make a gift to him of my gratitude, and that would be the end of it—but it didn't work out that way. One day became seven, then a week became a month, and before long Savva and I had taken up with Abdul's group as they planned an attack against the British.

I sometimes wondered if our time together had been peaceful

because we couldn't speak to each other without an interpreter. We
got by with looks and gestures and long hours in each other's arms,
and Abdul's seemingly inexhaustible passion. But I knew the day was
coming—soon—that he would have to sire children: it was expected
of him as well as a necessity to sustain his way of life, much as it had
been in St. Andrew in my day. We could not stay a couple. I'd have
to move on or stand by as he took another wife. Besides Jonathan,
Abdul was the only man to whom I would've happily given a child if
I could have. It had been made clear long ago that this wasn't to be;
it was another of the things Adair had taken from me, and so I tried
not to think of it. It was only in rare moments like these that I felt
the weight of a regret that was impossible to appease.

Plus, in the long run, I was bound to disappoint Abdul, and the
disappointment would sting less if he had another wife—a wife who
would bear the burden of behaving in ways acceptable to the rest of
Abdul's tribe. My inevitable apartness from him would be mitigated
by a wife who would age with her husband and ease him through all
the stages of his life, who would give him children and make his life
complete. Besides, once we returned to his tribe he would undoubtedly be expected to take a proper bride, one of his own people, a respectable virgin who had never appeared in public without a chador.
His reputation among his people might be forever tarnished by his
association with a scandalously independent, foreign woman. I had
no desire to see Abdul shortchanged because he'd had the misfortune
to fall in love with me.

I intended to encourage Abdul to choose a bride when we visited
his village, but that day never came. Abdul was killed in a clash not
far from Jalalabad, a ferocious battle won by the British, who then
went in pursuit of the fleeing Afghans. Thank God, Savva had stayed
with me. He bundled me up and led me away as I grieved. Kabul
was close and home to a contingent of expatriates among whom we
could hide. I spent months consumed by the loss of Abdul, sure that
I would never find another man as gentlemanly or as brave. As soon

as I could function again, Savva spirited us west to Turkey, then on to Greece. Even with the distraction of pretty island boys at Minos, we rested only a brief while, until Savva had gambled and smoked his way through much of our money, could stand the quiet no more, and demanded another adventure.

CASABLANCA, PRESENT DAY

I woke up from the dream disoriented. I hadn't thought about Abdul in a long while, and it struck me for the first time—as I pictured his face, his way of moving, his strong presence—just how much he reminded me not of Jonathan but of Adair. Abdul had been more generous than most men would be in trying to fulfill my wishes. He had been unapologetic whenever he exhibited his fundamental nature—slicing the throat of an opponent in battle as unflinchingly as another man might slaughter a sheep, for instance. We had been unalike in many ways, Abdul and I, but I had been unaccountably drawn to him.

The more I thought about Abdul, the more I started to see that he hadn't been an anomaly. When I counted up the men for whom I'd felt the most passion, I realized, with horror, that these men all had more in common with Adair than with Jonathan. All had been direct and unapologetic about their natures. Most preferred a bit of roughness in bed.

But the most frightening realization was that all of them had loved me even though it was not in their best interests to do so, even when they knew they would suffer—a loss of prestige; the forfeiture of wealth, a title, or independence; separation from a respectable wife—each had made the sacrifice in order to be with me. Unlike Jonathan, not one of them had shown the least ambivalence about our relationship. Even Adair, I now saw.

I had loved Jonathan before I knew what it meant to give myself to someone. The joy I had felt in the beginning was the sweetest I would ever know, but it had soured over time. For much of my life, when I thought of Jonathan, I felt sadness and bitterness. I still hurt when I thought of his trespasses against me. I know it's possible for love and hurt to coexist—anyone who has been married knows that—but when does the hurt, the disappointment, become too much? What had I carried with me all this time? Had I been in love with a ghost, a man who had ceased to be a long time ago?

Whereas, when I thought of Adair, I knew I should be terrified of him, I knew he was capable of doing horrible things, but I also couldn't help being overtaken with excitement, too. It had been like being courted by a demon, heady and intoxicating. My stomach fluttered at the memory of it. I had been loved by a man who would do anything for me: lie, cheat, steal. Murder. How many women could say that? As frightening as it had been, it also had been a singular love.

Exactly the way I had felt about Jonathan, once upon a time.

I sat upright, holding a pillow to my stomach as though it had some magical power to keep down the bile rising in my throat. The belief I'd held most sacred in life, the star by which I'd charted my course, had been an illusion. Even if I'd had a perfect love with Abdul and the others, each had come about because, subconsciously, I'd sought to re-create what I once had with Adair. The truth of this realization fell into place like tumblers aligning in a lock. It had been Adair all this time, not Jonathan. Adair, the monster, was the one I had loved all along.

This couldn't be. For a moment the inside of my head spun like a top, or perhaps it was my world flipping topsy-turvy and crashing around me. I'd always prided myself on following my heart, but I could not—would not—accept this. It must be mad lust or some kind of sick attraction dressed up to look like love. It must be trickery, one of his spells to make me think I loved him. It must be insanity brought on by Jonathan's death. I could not be in love with a monster, I vowed. I would not let myself be in love with the devil.

PART TWO

TWELVE

For Luke, the best medicine in the world was seeing the screen door to Tricia's house open with a bang and his daughters fly out, running straight at him as he stepped out of his rental car. He scooped them up in a bear hug, swinging them around the way he did when they were very young, like a chair-o-planes ride at the amusement park, while his former wife watched from the front porch. He felt fine for as long as he held them, but as soon as he set them down and they ran off, excited as puppies, he was filled with sadness once again. He looked up to find Tricia's eyes studying him with concern, and she returned his heartbroken smile.

She embraced him warmly on the top step. "How was your flight?"

"Fine, no problems."

"Well, come on in and make yourself at home." She ushered him into the foyer, where Richard was waiting, in his flannel and denim, to greet him. They'd met before, but Luke had forgotten that the man was built like a bear, right down to the full beard. Richard gave Luke a respectful nod as he entered the house.

Luke shook his hand. "Hey, thanks for letting me come by like this, with no warning. . . ."

Richard shrugged. "It's all the girls have been able to talk about. We're real glad you can spend some time with us." Luke had wanted to dislike Richard when they first met, for luring his wife back to her hometown when they were still married. But it wasn't possible: Richard was so easygoing, so down-to-earth. Luke could admit now that it hadn't been Richard's fault that Tricia had left: the marriage had been over for a while. At least she'd found herself a good guy.

Luke stood in the kitchen with a mug of fresh coffee in his hand and watched his daughters through the patio door as they helped Richard put out tables and chairs for Winona's birthday party later in the day. Tricia stood at the island in the kitchen decorating the birthday cake—pink lemonade with vanilla frosting—in concentrated silence, each letter squeezed out with the practiced hand of a calligrapher. The familiarity of the moment—minus Richard, of course—reminded Luke of birthdays they'd celebrated when they were living in his parents' farmhouse, leaving him feeling momentarily disoriented.

He'd told Tricia the truth when he called from the airport in London: that Lanny had left him and he needed a place to stay and collect his thoughts. Despite their differences and the fact that their marriage had fallen apart, Luke could always count on Tricia's dependability. With no questions asked, she told him to get on a plane and that the sofa bed in the basement would be made up and waiting for him.

After a full day of flying and driving, Luke still hadn't made sense of what had happened since the night Lanny walked into his ER. Then again, he'd actively tried to block her out of his mind while traveling, for fear of having a meltdown alone and in public. He'd shut off his cell phone and stuffed it into his suitcase to avoid the temptation of checking for missed calls that never came.

"More coffee?" Tricia asked, rousing him out of his reverie.

"What? No, thanks." He'd always been a heavy coffee drinker, needing it to get him through his shifts at the hospital, but he didn't think it would help today to be wired on caffeine.

"You going to be okay?" she asked.

"Me? Yeah. Sure. It was a shock, her leaving like that."

"She didn't give any hint? No indication that this was coming?" There was an edge to Tricia's questions. She hadn't liked Lanny to begin with, and now there'd be no way to redeem her in Tricia's eyes. Talking with his ex-wife was going to be trickier than Luke thought: he couldn't tell Tricia the truth about Lanny, and without knowing what made her unique, there was no way Tricia would understand why he was so depressed by her departure.

"No. It was out of the blue," he answered.

"She was too young for you, Luke. Too immature," Tricia said, briskly but not unkindly. "What were you going to get out of it in the long run? It's for the best that it didn't drag on too long. It'll be that much easier to put behind you." She moved the cake stand to the credenza in the dining room and then stepped behind him to rub his back. "I'm sorry that you got hurt, Luke, really I am. But she wasn't right for you."

"You didn't know her, Tricia. I didn't go away with her because I'm having a midlife crisis. It wasn't about sex. I want you to know that."

"Okay, I believe you. But what kind of future was there for you with her? She didn't sound stable, getting into all that trouble. . . ."

She didn't come out and say, *What were you thinking?* But after seven years of marriage, he could read her mind. And after being peppered with questions from Tricia over the past three months, he knew what she thought about Lanny. Tricia believed Lanny had tempted him with her glamorous life abroad, lured him there with promises of never having to worry about money again, making Luke abandon his steady job at the hospital. Luke could tell that Tricia was holding back, and he appreciated her restraint. He knew she wanted to shake him and ask: *How could you leave your daughters behind? How could you choose that woman over your own kids?* Maybe pleading temporary insanity *would* be his best defense.

"No, I guess she wasn't all that stable," he agreed, to make Tricia think he hadn't entirely lost his mind.

Tricia stood beside him and stared out the back door, too. "Not that I'm rushing you, but . . . have you thought about what you're going to do next?" Luke shook his head. "Joe Duchesne still calls here looking for you," she continued, keeping her voice even. "I told him I didn't know where you were, of course, but he wanted me to tell you, the next time we spoke, that you have to turn yourself in. He just wants to ask you some questions."

Luke snorted softly. "I don't see any reason to go back to St. Andrew. I'm certain the hospital has suspended my privileges. They'd have to, under the circumstances. There's nothing for me there now."

"That can be fixed, once you talk to them and explain what happened. Everyone will understand." That seemed unlikely, but Tricia pressed on. "The hospital, your practice, the farm—that's your life, even if you don't stay in St. Andrew. You have to deal with the police and the questions, even though it's not going to be pleasant. It's not like you can just walk away from that and start over as a different person, Luke."

If Lanny had stayed with me, I could have, Luke thought. *I could leave this shattered life behind. But for the girls . . .* He needed to be a father to his girls.

"I'm sorry. . . . It's too soon for me to be bringing this up." Tricia patted his shoulder and stepped over to the sink, running water over the mixing bowl and measuring cups. "You stay here for as long as you need to. Spend time with the girls. Before you know it, everything will fall into place. You'll know what you need to do, and the past few months will seem like a distant memory. It'll seem like something that happened to someone else, not to you. You'll forget all about her."

Tricia's presence dissolved into the background as she washed dishes, lost in the ordinary sounds of domesticity, the clink of glass and metal and sloshing water. Luke knew that he would never forget Lanny. She may have tossed him out of her life and he was hurt, but he couldn't harden his heart to her. He worried about her, and wondered if there was a reason he hadn't heard from her. He realized he would never stop worrying about her; he would always wonder where she was and what she was doing, if she was happy, if she was safe. She would haunt him the rest of his life.

THIRTEEN

BOSTON

Patience. Adair was tired of Jude telling him to be patient, tired of his never-ending stream of excuses for not learning Lanore's whereabouts and of his irritating habit of telling Adair to relax. How could he possibly relax until he found the woman who'd taken two hundred years from him? The only person—man or woman—who'd gotten the better of him? Too, he was frustrated by his helplessness in navigating this strange, fast-paced world in which he suddenly found himself. And this lack of control put him ill at ease.

Adair had been born impatient; he knew this from his earliest days, when he had thrown toys at servants and kicked the household hounds to get them out of his way. It wasn't until he was in his teenage years that he learned from his father, a duke and liege of a small kingdom, the value of hiding one's feelings. It was a rare ruler who wasn't spied on, constantly under the gaze of his courtiers, servants, and tenant farmers. Through his father, Adair learned that the most effective rulers were those with the most self-control, and through observation he came to understand the value of keeping his temper in check.

In the brief time Adair had been free, he noticed that the pace of living in this new age made it harder to be patient. He figured it had to do with the immediacy that technology enabled. Life had been easier in the old days, when information traveled slowly: news came by courier on horseback or wrapped in gossip passed along by merchants or by pilgrims taking a night's refuge under a kind stranger's roof. The hardest adjustment to modern times was not being able to think before he needed to act; new information came at him endlessly, making each decision tantamount to gambling. These intangibles—news, feelings, lies, opinion—were typed up on keyboards by millions of hands and rocketed around at such numbers that he could literally feel their urgency thrum in the air. Energy pushed and pulled violently around him, prickling at his skin, needling him. *There is more than you could ever hope to know hidden in the ether,* it seemed to be telling him.

Adair rubbed his eyes in exhaustion and frustration. He was restless: living in Jude's glass house was like being kept in a box, only slightly better than being trapped behind the wall. He needed to be on the move to feel as though he was making progress or the rage that ticked under his skin would find a way to erupt.

He burst out of the house without telling anyone, joining the trickle of people on the sidewalk. His thoughts turned inward as he walked, not looking into the faces of the people who passed him for fear he would misinterpret the slightest gesture—a raised eyebrow, a grin on an idiot's face—and strike out in anger, unable to check his misdirected rage in time.

He started on the trail he'd taken the day he was freed from his prison, eventually walking the many blocks through the city to the place where his mansion had once stood. The site was roped off with white-and-red tape and sawhorses, with signs declaring it a construction site. The mansion was gone, and in its place was a bare lot, every stick and stone cleared away. A large metal excavator stood idle beside the beginnings of a pit that loomed like an open grave. Adair stood behind the fluttering tape with his hands thrust in his pockets, the wind carrying his stray curls before his eyes as though to spare him the sight of his former prison. But it was a prison no more. Funny to think that this once damnable place, the scene of his persecution, was now . . . nothing. There was nothing at which to hurl his anger: no house, no cleft in the earth, not even a sufficiently deep hole into which he could pour his rage. It had been stripped of all significance.

Just then he noticed from the corner of his eye a woman at the other end of the lot, also staring at the site where the house once stood. He couldn't see her very well at that distance, but he sensed something familiar about her. She wore a green wool coat with a hood that obscured her face as completely as a monk's cowl, but she appeared to be slender, and blond corkscrew curls poked like wild ferns from around the edge of her hood.

From a distance she looked like Lanore, though he knew that was impossible: he would have felt her presence, or so he assumed. There might be a chance she had found a way to dampen her presence, to blind him to her. She had succeeded in putting up that damnable wall and hiding his presence from his followers for centuries, hadn't she? She could be the woman in green—or it could be that he was just desperate to see her again.

And if it was Lanore . . . Adair could just imagine the sinking feeling in her chest as she looked on the desolate lot and realized he'd been released like a malevolent djinn from his lamp and that no protection stood between them anymore—none at all. Her throat would tighten and she would have difficulty swallowing as the seriousness of her situation became fully apparent. And then, as though the woman in green had read Adair's thoughts, she turned and hurried away, her footfalls clattering noisily up the empty street as though she were trying to outpace the judgment that awaited her.

He kept a good distance between them as he followed. The streets were deserted at this hour on a Sunday: children were indoors for early dinners, lights had been snapped on, and blinds were drawn against the dusk. The woman turned down a street Adair remembered from the day he was freed because the houses were all marked for demolition. In the middle of the block stood the warehouse he'd ducked into that day. Thinking ahead, he saw that if she continued straight, she'd come out in a populated area where the houses were occupied and the streets were busy with traffic; but if she turned left, she'd go right by the empty warehouse. He would leave it in fate's hands. Fate would decide whether to deliver Lanore to him that day.

Adair cut through the building at a jog and with a little searching found a door that opened onto the deserted side street. He crouched behind a row of corroded metal barrels, wondering how long he should wait to see if she would pass by, when he heard footsteps on the gritty pavement. Adair waited until the woman had just passed the stand of barrels—the flash of the green overcoat unmistakable—before he stepped out and seized her, carefully clapping one hand over her mouth.

He pushed her ahead of him into the building. His gaze went instinctively to a dark corner under a flight of metal stairs on the other side of the warehouse. At first she didn't react, as though in shock, but halfway across the open floor she started to struggle in his arms, to dig in her heels. She was a fraction of his weight, however, and her resistance amounted to nothing against his fury.

Of course, he knew this woman was not Lanore. He knew by her scent, the way she breathed, the way she moved. She was young and pretty in a way not unlike Lanore, but the resemblance ended there. No matter. This woman would have to do: there was no stopping the hatred rising inside him. Adair's anger over his betrayal and his broken heart came thundering down like a landslide. He threw his victim on her back as she cried out in terror and stammered unintelligibly, the sound of her voice blanked out by his rage.

There were words he wanted to say to her—*Treacherous whore, betrayer*—but they wouldn't come out of his throat, caught as though snagged on thorns. *Heartless witch. You left me in darkness. Two hundred years of solitude, terrified that it was never going to end. I loved you as I loved no one else, I trusted you, and you buried me alive to be with* him.

He struck the figure beneath him with his fists until the hands held up to protect her face fell away and the face itself was a bloody open wound. By then he'd torn the green coat open, reached down to free himself, and pushed into her, his bloodied hands pinning her limp form to the floor to withstand his thrusts.

He collapsed onto her when he came, climaxing so fiercely that he saw stars of white flare before his eyes. He was still enraged but embarrassed that he had been unable to keep himself from destroying this woman. She was not dead yet but certainly beyond saving, and so with the last of his anger he reached for a loose brick nearby. The feel of the brick, its dusty bloom and mildewed smell, brought the chalky taste of his basement prison to his mouth and angered him enough to bring the brick down against her skull twice, three times, until the bone cracked like a walnut shell and she went completely still.

Adair sat back on his heels, breathing hard. As he looked down on the woman, her identity now obliterated, his stomach lurched. The remains alone could fool him into believing he was looking down on Lanore: *his* Lanore could be lying inert before him, destroyed by his hand.

In that awful moment, he realized that he *didn't* want this to happen. He did not want Lanore to die and was frightened to realize he *was* capable of killing her, that he could be completely engulfed with rage, swept away, to emerge on the other side with blood on his hands. The thought that he could lose her forever clawed at his heart, creating a darkness into which he could pour himself and never, ever touch bottom.

How could he have done such a thing to an innocent woman? There was no better proof that he truly was a monster. Even to himself he seemed a figure created out of pure hate, a vortex of fury that rose from some hellish unknown place. He disliked being out of control: it smacked of weakness and failure, two things he looked down on in others and wouldn't tolerate in himself.

Adair stood and examined his clothing for bloodstains and luckily found only small ones, unnoticeable under casual inspection. His bloody hands could be hidden in his pockets. He glanced back at the body one last time; it wasn't in the open but lay behind a stack of pallets, only her feet visible. She wouldn't be found immediately. He staggered outside and began the walk back to Jude's house, the cold air welcome on his overheated face. It would take the murderous flush from his cheeks and wash away the smell of death that clung to him.

Adair's stomach twisted as he hurried along, his thoughts a mess, upended in fifteen violent minutes. Lanore was his weakness, his Achilles' heel. He understood that he would need to find a way to control his emotions, and after all that he'd been through, that would not be easy. It seemed his nature was one of violence and rage, and he wondered if he *could* change. He would *have* to be disciplined; he now understood that he wouldn't be able to bear it if he killed her.

Adair loved Lanore, he hated her, but he was unable to take revenge against her and more compelled to find her than ever. His love for her was sublime, and it was also a bitter curse, running through his veins like an infection. He needed no more proof to see that he was damned, irredeemable and damned, and there was nothing he could do about it.

FOURTEEN

A dair had a vivid picture in his mind of Lanore's hometown: she'd described it to him as an isolated village separated from the rest of the world by a vast, untamable forest and a wide river. At the time it was 1816 and America was young, with only a handful of settlers spread over as much land as the rest of the known world—or so it seemed—and Adair dismissed her account as that of a girl who'd seen little and knew nothing.

But after traveling to St. Andrew, Adair had to admit that it was difficult to get to, even by modern standards. He had his first taste of the airship that Jude had told him about, only this one was a tiny commuter plane that rattled and shimmied throughout the flight, seemingly ready to break apart at any moment. The rest of the trip from Presque Isle to St. Andrew had to be made by automobile, following a long, lonely route that took him through endless farms and empty fields. He passed through forests that so reminded him of Saxony and Bavaria, he half expected a band of brigands to come bursting out of the wood on horseback.

Adair was actually looking forward to seeing the town of St. Andrew. He wanted to go to the place where Lanny had grown up and see the town that had shaped the woman he had loved. She brought out a youthful, almost lovesick curiosity in him, and though Adair would never admit it, he was eager to know every tiny detail about her, and that included visiting the places from her stories, if they still existed—if they had not been razed and rebuilt entirely differently, like the cities from his past.

As Adair got closer to town, he began to sense that he probably wouldn't find many answers on this trip. The sensation in his head was weak, so it was unlikely that Lanore was nearby. Still, the keening had been inactive for so long that he felt he could no longer interpret what it tried to tell him, and he was buoyed by the slim chance that Jonathan could be here. It could be a sign from the forces of the universe that he'd suffered enough, that they would deliver one of his tormentors to him, and he wanted to believe that the cosmos was on his side.

Jude had not been as optimistic about what he might find. "From what Maurice gave you and what you found out from that aid agency, it's a safe bet that Jonathan went to Maine with Lanny," the Dutchman had reasoned. "But there's nothing to indicate that they're *still* there. Let's have Maurice look for new financial activity on this man Schneider before you go up there."

Adair waited while Maurice checked Schneider's credit card activity and bank accounts, only to find that they had gone abruptly dormant a few months prior. And St. Andrew proved as logical a starting point as any other, given the hacker's trail of data. The thought that Lanore might be close was irresistible.

"I must at least satisfy my curiosity that she is not there. I must *do* something," Adair told Jude. "Waiting in this house is driving me mad."

But Jude had other concerns, too. "Do you feel you're ready to go out on your own?" he asked after a minute's hesitation. "There was a

story on the news that a girl was killed over by the old mansion. . . .
The police said it was especially brutal—'excessive' was the word they
used, like something a lunatic might've done. . . . It was you, wasn't
it?" Jude's hesitant tone surprised Adair—no one likes to be taken
for a madman—and made him pause on his way to the waiting taxi.
"They showed the dead girl's picture on television. She looked a lot
like Lanore, I'll give you that," Jude continued, his eyes carefully
downcast, "but you can't go killing everyone you please. What if
you get up to St. Andrew and Lanore isn't there? What will you do
then?"

Adair couldn't admit to Jude that the bloodletting had changed
him. In order to keep his sanity while he was behind the wall, he had
had no choice but to suppress his rage, winding it tighter and tighter
until it was like a weapon, coiled and ready to go off when he finally
met up with her. But it was as though he'd wound it too tightly and
something inside him had cracked when he'd killed that girl. He'd
unleashed his rage in a single act of violence against an innocent
woman unlucky enough to cross his path. And for what? His crime
merely filled him with deep remorse and shame. He vowed never to
allow himself to fly into such a blind fury again. A small piece of
him worried irrationally that somehow Lanore had been hurt by the
release of his rage, that his evil intention had touched her. Superstitious, yes, but now he was desperate to find her, or evidence of her, to
be sure that this wasn't the case.

And, too, he sought to make a pilgrimage of sorts. He couldn't
shake the feeling that all his troubles could've been avoided if,
two hundred years ago, he hadn't sent Lanore on her own back to
St. Andrew to fetch Jonathan. If he'd gone with her, he would've
claimed Jonathan's body for his own and never given Lanore the
chance to plot against him. All the misery of the past two centuries
would've been avoided if not for this one instance of shortsighted-
ness on his part. He would force himself to make the trip now, in

contrition, and with luck, fate would accept his offering and turn back the hand of time to deliver Lanore to him.

As he drove into St. Andrew, Adair was amused to see that the town was not so different from those he'd known in medieval times. Rows of tradesmen's shops lined the main street. Laggards shuffled up and down the sidewalks for something to do while old men sat sunning themselves on park benches. A tavern and a church, the two anchors of every town, stood across from each other in the square. Adair found lodgings at a public house that went by the name "Bed and Breakfast," its accommodations more fussy and claustrophobic than he would've preferred, but it was in the center of town and seemed a good location from which to gather information.

He carried his suitcase to his room and locked the door before pulling out his two books of spells. Running his hand over the time-worn covers, he slipped them under the mattress, securely locking the door behind him again when he left. The woman at the front desk directed him to the only bar in the downtown area, called the Blue Moon—which could not be missed, in any case, for the glowing blue crescent in the window— and Adair settled into a midday conversation with the barkeep and a handful of patrons.

Two of them recognized the name Rolf Schneider as the man who'd passed through town with a girl, seemingly just another couple of tourists traipsing through St. Andrew. But everyone knew the girl's story: that she'd murdered her companion and left his body in the woods, and then managed to escape from the county hospital, taking one of the doctors with her. Adair took in every detail, including the names of the doctor's former wife and children, and the town where they now lived.

Had anyone seen the girl? Adair asked. Could anyone describe her? The patrons shook their heads, advising Adair that the only people to see her were the police and the night nurse at the hospital. Adair bought a round of drinks and sipped a watery beer while he mulled over the curious series of events that he could not have guessed on his own, not even if an oracle had whispered clues in his ear. Jonathan was dead, and that meant Lanore had killed him, for it couldn't have happened any other way. Adair couldn't imagine what would've persuaded Lanore to let Jonathan go after hundreds of years together. She couldn't have tired of him, could she? He burned with curiosity to know what had happened between the two.

Having gathered all the information he could, Adair bid the patrons good night, slapped money on the counter, and went back to the inn. He retrieved the books of spells from their hiding place and began skimming through the pages. Although Lanny's tracks ran cold at Jonathan's grave, Adair was undeterred. It would take very strong magic, but Adair had come to find Lanore, and that meant he had no choice but to reanimate Jonathan and retrieve the clues from a dead man's memory. The task was daunting: if rumors about the resurrection spell could be trusted, it was an act that required the highest degree of skill and power. An act that was considered by many to be dangerous and blasphemous, and one that for a number of reasons—chief among them being a sense of deep foreboding—Adair had never attempted. Even if the spell succeeded, Adair had no idea what condition Jonathan would be in, if his mind would be wiped clean, if he would be of any use at all. . . .

Still, Adair wanted nothing in this world more than to find Lanore, and to do so, it appeared he had to ignore his unease and undertake the darkest of the dark arts, the most profane of its acts. He would bring a soul back from the land of the dead, and the consequences of this—for surely there would be consequences—would be his to bear. He was willing to defy the powers that governed the universe to possess Lanore once again, and having made his decision, he began to marshal the strength he'd need to make this happen.

FIFTEEN

Dusk had settled over the Great North Woods by the time Adair found the police station. The building sat by itself on a deserted logging road, set far from town, which was quiet anyway except for the high tourism season, and closer to the logging camps where most of the trouble happened the rest of the year. A black-and-white SUV sat parked in front, speckled with dried road salt, although it was approaching summer.

It was empty inside the station, with no signs that anyone was working. The entryway was cramped with filing cabinets and haphazardly stacked boxes, and as warm as a closed attic. "Hello?" Adair called out. "Is anyone on duty?" His voice sounded lonely against the background whir of a fan.

"In here," a man called back, and Adair followed the voice down the hall to an open door. A dull brass plaque on the wall read "Sheriff Joseph Duchesne." The man behind the desk looked nothing like a sheriff, not even in a backwater town such as this. He had neither the physique nor the bearing for the job, and was an awkward specimen, all elbows and knees, with a prominent Adam's apple begging to be struck. Further, he had a face that solicited neither trust nor respect, the face of an incompetent cheat, and the sheriff betrayed a hint of fear when he saw Adair.

"You're the sheriff," Adair said doubtfully.

"That's why I'm sitting behind this desk," the man replied impatiently. "Can I help you?" He eyed Adair suspiciously; it was plain that the sheriff was wary of out-of-towners.

"I heard that you saw the woman who came through here some months ago."

"We get a lot of people come through here," the sheriff replied coolly, but it was clear that he knew whom Adair was talking about.

"I'm referring to the girl who allegedly killed someone: a young woman, blond hair, very slight. Beautiful," he added with a hint of melancholy.

"Yeah. That's her." The sheriff sat up taller, eyes narrowing. "What do you know about her?"

Adair ignored him. "And the man she killed? Did you find the body?"

"Sure, we found him, but—"

"And what did he look like?"

The sheriff pushed away from the desk. "Now, hold on a minute. This woman you're asking about is involved in a serious crime, murder in the first degree. The case is still open, and it seems you might know something about it. I'm going to have to call in one of my officers as we need to ask you a few questions, Mr. . . . ?" Duchesne hung on the word, waiting for Adair to give him his name as he picked up the receiver to dial. Adair stepped over and pressed the button, disconnecting the phone.

"I asked you what he looked like—the dead man." Adair took a deep breath to slow his emotions, and tried not to imagine breaking this annoying little man apart with his bare hands. He'd crack like a crab claw, there was so little flesh on his bones. "Would you say he was a good-looking man?"

The sheriff's face reddened. "What kind of question is that? What are you . . . some kind of homo?" He rose unsurely, like a man unfamiliar with danger, his hand hovering indecisively over his holster. Adair moved in and slammed him against the wall, pinning him there.

"What does it matter to you if I swive men or women or livestock? You will answer my questions or I will snap your miserable neck. Do you understand?"

The sheriff sputtered and choked in Adair's grasp, their eyes locked as he struggled for air. As far as Adair was concerned, the sheriff was like a chicken whose body still twitched even though its head had been severed: he was already a dead man, he just didn't know it yet. Adair tightened his grip and slammed him into the wall a second time. "Where's the body now?"

"The body?"

A third slam, and the wall cracked beneath him. "The dead man. What was done with his body?"

"I'd have to look at the records right over there." Sheriff Duchesne lifted his chin in the direction of a filing cabinet. Adair dropped him to his feet and gave him a shove. The sheriff didn't try for the door, perhaps because he was already at the limit of his courage. He found the file in the second drawer, his hands shaking as he shifted through the papers inside.

"Usually we cremate the unclaimed bodies, but the paperwork says the crematorium wasn't working and they sent him back. According to the records, we buried the body."

"Here? In town?"

The sheriff nodded.

Adair slid the sheriff's gun out of his holster and shoved him toward the door. "Take me there."

Adair found a shovel in the back room, tucked behind a giant bag of road salt and two pairs of galoshes, and threw it in the backseat of his rental car. He put the sheriff at the wheel with a warning about what to expect if he tried to escape; the sheriff, now as meek as the docent at the museum, obeyed. They drove to an empty field on the edge of a shaggy wood, and Duchesne led Adair on foot to the grave site. Darkness had fallen, but the night was still and cool. A few blackflies buzzed about their heads. A metal marker sunk in the ground read "B17."

Adair handed the shovel to the sheriff. "Dig."

It took a long time to reach the coffin, and Adair spent this time pacing along the rim of the plot, mentally stepping through the spell he'd learned eons ago from old Henrik, the one copied on a piece of parchment and stuffed in his ancient book. He recalled that session with Henrik, holding his breath as the chick fluttered back to life, then sat inert, its butter-colored down trembling with every tentative breath. How he'd wanted to put his hands over it and crush it, send it back from where it came out of *mercy*. . . . But he'd let that feeling pass, because even at fourteen, he had been a man of science and he knew he had to resist feeling pity or fear.

He feared that he'd have the same outcome now, but he couldn't let fear stop him from trying. In any case, the situation wasn't the same: Old Henrik had been a dabbler, weak. Adair was confident that he was massively more powerful than his tutor had ever been. But if the result was unsatisfactory—if the creature that came back was a monster—Adair promised himself that he would smother Jonathan with his own two hands, once he'd collected the necessary observations.

Uncertainty battled with determination, however, twisting his stomach. He wanted Jonathan's body for his own—one look at the photograph from the refugee camp confirmed that—but the thought of taking over a body that had been dead for a while was unsettling, to say the least. He'd seen many a decomposed body and knew well the strange emptiness of a lifeless form, but a dead man left to rot on the battlefield was quite different from one that had been moldering in the ground for months. There was also the question of what to do with Jonathan if they switched bodies; not even Adair would be able to release his soul through death. Adair felt a pang of compassion for Jonathan (they had been friends once, after all) but pushed it away: it was one more thing that could not be helped, and it wouldn't be the first time he'd condemned a man to purgatory to further his own desires.

The shovel made a hollow sound as it struck the top of the plywood coffin. When the sheriff pried off the lid, they both retched at the smell of cadaverine, the noxious gas produced inside Jonathan's fermenting, unpreserved body. Adair then had Duchesne heave the body bag to the surface before dispatching him with a blow to the back of his head with the shovel.

A black vinyl body bag in a plywood box, sunk into an unmarked grave. What a sad ending for the town's favorite son, Adair mused. *How ignobly they have treated him.* Adair took a deep breath before unzipping the bag.

The contents sloshed beneath him, so Adair knew to expect some advanced decomposition. The flesh was no longer solid but a heavy black custard held together by Jonathan's clothing. The face that had once been the personification of beauty was now only slime clinging to a skull, scattered eyelashes embedded in the muck, and the teeth beginning to show through. The outcome would've been much better if they'd treated the body in the usual way, but the town wasn't about to waste money preserving an unidentified corpse.

Adair collected his wits and uttered the proper words over the body to reanimate Jonathan's decomposed form. Did the actual words matter, or did it depend on the will of the man who spoke them? He had to believe it was the latter, for the words had been known to practitioners of dark arts for hundreds of years, but he'd heard few claims of success. He could believe only the strongest Adepts would be able to raise the dead, and naturally he put himself in this class. There was the question of whether the most accomplished—and hence wisest—Adepts would attempt the spell, given the taboo against piercing the veil between the two worlds, but this was the sort of self-restraint that Adair rejected. True discoveries were made by the bold. If only God could know both worlds, the living and the dead, Adair would dare to steal a bit of God's might.

Within seconds, a familiar and welcome power came over him—gently at first, then surging along every nerve and muscle in his body, crackling through his bones and squeezing the breath from his lungs. This surge of energy connected him to Jonathan's body, and for a moment he was connected to what had to be a residue of Jonathan's consciousness at the last moments of his life: remorse, sadness, and bitterness as he waited to be released. Uncomfortable thoughts came to him, too: the dark abyss of his imprisonment lurked at the edges of his perception. It hovered beyond the glorious bright power that gripped Adair, emanating menace and loneliness. It made sense that this huge, dark presence might be associated somehow with the glorious power he sought to tap: they were both forces of the universe, after all. But the dark presence worried him. It felt threatening in some way.

The recomposition process was painfully slow, to his great irritation, and Adair was sure that the darkness was keeping him from a rare sight. Even by moonlight, he could tell that the gelatinous mass was solidifying into a dusty white creature. Then hair began to sprout and features to emerge, but the body remained as white as alabaster with lavender pooled around its eyes and mouth, as with the exhausted or anemic. When the eyelids fluttered upward, the right one sagged, and then the right corner of the mouth failed, as though Jonathan were a stroke victim. Thank God, the eyes were not dull and lifeless, but overall something was missing. Adair could not quite put his finger on the problem, but something was very wrong.

"Ah!" At length Jonathan spoke, and when he did, a last puff of cadaverine escaped into the air and hovered over his head like a wisp of smoke. "Hah! What is this? Where am I?"

"Jonathan," Adair said. He was reluctant to touch him, afraid to disrupt the regeneration process before the body had set.

"Yes, I am Jonathan, though I thought I was Jonathan no more." He spoke like a mystic in a trance, buffered from being fully present.

"Do you know who I am?"

Jonathan's eyes fluttered over Adair's face once, and despite the clumsiness of his half-formed face, Jonathan winced in recognition. "Yes, I remember you, Adair."

"And where did you come from, Jonathan? Where were you a moment ago?" It was the question that had burned in Adair's mind ever since Henrik's baby bird had come back to life.

"I was . . . I was in another place . . . not like this one. Dark and cold, and as aimless as ocean currents."

"Not like here? Then where were you?" Adair asked, anxious

"Where am I now?"

"Home. You are in St. Andrew. Do you remember how you ended up in this grave?"

On hearing the name of the town, the corpse's face looked pinched, and a shiver of distaste ran across it. "Yes, I remember."

Adair tried again, his temper growing sharp. "Were you dreaming before I woke you? Was it like a dream?"

"It was not . . . like here."

"And were you alone, Jonathan? Was there anyone with you, someone you knew, perhaps? A loved one?"

The cadaver frowned again. "No one I knew, no."

"And what"—Adair paused, humility and timidity returning for this one question—"of God? Have you met a deity? A higher power? And what of the devil? Have you seen the dark master?"

"I have seen no one," Jonathan said, "except the queen of the underworld."

Adair sat back on his heels. The answer was unexpected. The queen of the underworld? He had no idea what Jonathan meant by that. Apparently, there existed a next life, judging from the fact that

Jonathan's dead soul had come back from somewhere, and in this next life there existed something that could be interpreted as the queen of the underworld. Adair felt a surge of panic. He thought of his books: he needed the old stories and reference material to puzzle out this mystery.

When Adair turned to Jonathan to ask another question, however, he saw that he'd fallen unconscious. He jostled Jonathan's shoulder and pulled a lower eyelid down to look on a filmy brown eye in which he saw a tiny ticking pulse, a repeating flicker of animation. Satisfied that Jonathan had not been pulled back into the void, Adair bundled him up, stinking clothing and all, tucked him into the rental car, and drove away, leaving the heaps of dirt and the body of Joe Duchesne beside the open grave.

SIXTEEN

Adair drove straight out of town with Jonathan lying across the backseat, a coat thrown over his body to keep him from being seen. He needn't have bothered: not one vehicle crossed his path the whole drive south through the last hours of night, through lonesome logging territory and past potato farms. It wasn't until he was halfway to Boston that he realized he'd left his belongings at the bed-and-breakfast. No matter: he obsessively kept his two books with him at all times, and they were all he needed and the only things he couldn't afford to lose.

Adair sped back to Jude's house, driving only slightly above the speed limit to avoid attracting the police. The last thing he needed was for a local lawman to approach his window and detect the smell of rotting flesh. Back in St. Andrew, the clues chained together so easily that even a child would be able to follow them: the sheriff was dead, a grave had been pilfered, and the stranger who had been asking questions about the missing body had fled town under cover of night. He'd used a false identity for all travel arrangements and there was little chance of being discovered, but there was the risk that he might have left some clue behind. Adair would leave it to

Jude to clean up any problems that might arise. He was like a clerk, unimaginative, made to handle minutiae.

Driving in darkness down empty roads, Adair thought back to the potter's field and the unease he'd felt at Jonathan's grave site. Standing there, looking down into the deep, earthy hole, he experienced the same sensation he had felt during his own entombment, when the walls and floor of his tiny cell would fade away and leave him feeling as though he was floating in sheer openness. Worse still, there had been times when he hadn't been able to feel the boundaries of his body, when a steady but immutable force had pulled on his consciousness until it thinned and fanned out and dissipated into the void. At those times it had been as though his physical self ceased to be and he became nothing more than a speck in an endless ocean of nothingness. It was the identical sensation he'd felt standing beside Jonathan's open grave.

And then, there was this disquieting mention of a queen of the underworld.

As Adair struggled with the concept of an actual deity, a queen who ruled over the afterlife, he felt the black abyss tug at him again, as surely as he could feel his heart beat faster. Perhaps the sentient creature waiting in the world beyond was linked in some way to the abyss. Perhaps she could not only cope in the vast void but commanded it, too. The prospect of a being with so much power frightened him, for he knew his limitations: he wasn't a supernatural creature but a man. An extraordinary man but not a god.

ROMANIA AND ENVIRONS, 1300S

The primary reason the physic had chosen to take the elixir of eternal life was to continue his study of the forces of the universe, the seen and the unseen. Now he had the rest of time to track down the wisdom of practitioners of magic who had come before him, and to surpass their knowledge with his own groundbreaking discoveries.

After consuming the elixir, however, the physic found there was another benefit, one that he hadn't expected: he began to experience life more vividly. He was stronger than he'd ever been and could run so fast that it seemed like flying. His senses were heightened: colors were brighter, smells sharper. It was as though he'd been sickly his entire life and suddenly had been given perfect health.

Still, his body had shortcomings for which there was no compensation. It was the body of an old man and, as such, was subject to all the prejudices held against the elderly. People assumed he was slow and feeble, and either tried to brush him out of their way, or were overly solicitous, tripping over themselves to help him, even when no assistance was requested. As much as either reaction annoyed him, he kept his condition to himself, though he would have liked to slap aside the Samaritans' offers of help or pummel the thieves who assumed he was senile and tried to pick his pockets. Adair checked his temper, realizing it was best not to disabuse these fools of their assumptions and show them that he was as vigorous and alert as any of them, because that would only bring suspicion down on him. He couldn't risk being reported to the inquisitors. He had no explanation to give them for his rejuvenation, and so had no alternative but to play the graybeard.

If he was delighted with his renewed strength and sharpened senses, one aspect of his rebirth was an unwelcome surprise to him, and that was restoration of the sexual longing of his youth. The physic found he had the insatiable desire he'd possessed at sixteen—no, it was worse this time around, far more intense and unwilling to be ignored. Also, unlike his teenaged self, this time he *knew* exactly what he was missing. He'd never married but had satisfied himself throughout his life with whores and willing servants—maybe a little less frequently than if he'd taken a wife, but that was the sacrifice he made for his calling. Science and alchemy were all that he cared for, and left him with little interest in the company of anyone who didn't share this passion. Now, to his frustration, he couldn't put the thought of sex out of his mind. It was as though desire had infiltrated his system through his bloodstream and ate at him from the inside out.

But what good was this ravenous sexual appetite to a man so old and ugly that no woman would willingly accommodate him? He had grown so repulsive that even prostitutes turned up their noses at him. Because his hearing was sharper than ever, he could hear them whispering at his approach: *Here comes that dirty old man again! He can't get enough—and at his age! It's a disgrace.* If only he could be a young man again, the story would be very different. The whores would fight for the chance to bed with a man of such virility. As it was, he was no more than a freak with an unnatural sexual appetite.

He vowed to go to the street women less frequently, but that meant he had to find other outlets for his desire. In desperation, he turned to an urchin who was selling himself in the alley, a boy of twelve or thirteen. The physic expected to be disgusted by the sight and feel of the boy's body, even though he had the boy face the wall so he could take his pleasure from behind, but this wasn't the case. The revelation that he could experience pleasure with someone of his own sex shook him so badly that he sat in the dark with a bottle of strong wine, trying to eradicate all memory of what he'd done.

As he brooded, questioning his manhood, he began to see that there were desires inside of him that he'd never let surface, secret thoughts that he'd smothered. And yet, he wondered, if he'd denied himself *this* pleasure for fear of damnation, what else had he missed? He had nothing to lose now. Why not give his dark desires free rein? Surely his transformation had put him in a realm where the laws of man didn't apply. Not to him.

That was the moment that the physic parted ways with his fellow men: he no longer considered himself bound by the conventions that had restrained him his entire life. To have these extraordinary abilities and yet behave like any other person—seeking permission for his acts, self-censoring the voices in his head, restraining his hand—was a waste of his gift. No, he was immortal now, and he intended to do as he pleased, to see what heights he could attain. There must be a reason he was singled out for these incredible powers, he reasoned; it would be wrong and a waste of this gift to hold back in any way.

It wasn't until 1349, when he was back in his homeland in the employ of a Romanian count, that the physic learned of a possible solution to his imprisonment in his old man's body. The position as physician to Count cel Batrin was as much a contrivance as his other appointments; the real reason he went to work for the count was that he'd heard a monk with otherworldly powers had once lived in that area. The number of fabled alchemists was few, and their world small. Once a man attained a certain level of prowess and was considered a master of the practice, or what would one day be known as an Adept, his name quickly spread among practitioners. His feats would be compared to those of other Adepts. From wandering apprentices and devotees of magic, the physic heard of other practitioners and tales of their wondrous deeds. He heard of lineages, of Adepts passing their special capability on to their students—disciples who could be traced back through generations of training.

Lines were often cut short through the intervention of the church—important work lost when a master and his disciples were found and executed for heresy. Inquisitors used their victims' collections of notes and receipts to build the pyres at which these men were roasted. *So much knowledge lost*, the physic fretted. *What a waste*. It was his duty to preserve this knowledge.

And this was how he ended up in cel Batrin's employ, trying to find out as much as he could about a monk who'd practiced alchemy several generations earlier. The old man guessed that there might still be followers of this man living in the area, disciples with copies of their master's recipes. The monk's name had been Nicodemus, and the physic had heard it rumored that the man in question was able to send a soul into another body.

As enticing as the prospect was, the physic was skeptical. He'd tried many times to create a potion for this purpose based on his knowledge of the properties of elements—tried to find the weight of a soul by taking careful readings of bodies before and after death, for instance—but nothing came of his attempts. How had the monk managed to remove the soul in the first place? What happened to the body receiving the new soul? Did the two souls coexist in some way, or did the new soul supplant the old one, and if so, what happened to the body's original soul? He wrote his questions on scraps of parchment, formulating the inquiry in his mind with scientific precision, but never figuring out the answer.

The physic went out evenings to investigate the whereabouts of this Nicodemus's legacy, as such things were best done under cover of darkness. He found the oldest among the villagers and questioned them thoroughly, raking through their memories for the smallest of clues. He went to the places where the reputed master alchemist might've lived or worked, excavating caves for rare minerals, picking through moss and mushrooms on the forest floor. He searched the monastery's vaults; he rummaged through cottages while the occupants slept. He was like a nighttime phantom looking for secrets to spirit away.

In the meantime, he'd acquired a Roma boy, Adair, to be his servant. The boy was chosen especially for his comeliness. The physic had no intention of stealing the peasant's body when they first met, as the boy was too young and underdeveloped. It wasn't until the boy was older and had blossomed into his fullness that the physic realized the potential. But by then, he had already disfigured the boy with scars from a ferocious beating—deserved, as he was caught running away with stolen recipes—but nothing could be done for that now. The physic had been swiving the boy regularly, but that would end, too, as the thought of raping a body he would one day inhabit repulsed him. The factor that settled the matter, for the physic, was that the boy had a tremendous manhood: not so long as to be a drawback—the physic imagined there were times when a man's yardarm could be *too* long—but thick, like a personal battering ram. The thought of being the owner of this weapon and getting to wield it made the physic giddy.

Meanwhile, he'd begun to uncover clues in his investigations about the monk's work, and the physic felt he was close to finding someone who could tell him more. So he decided to give the peasant boy eternal life to ready his body to receive the physic's soul once the spell was found. In the meantime, this would safeguard the body against accident. The more the physic thought on it, the more sense it made: he found the boy's body suitable, the face pleasing. Others seemed to think the boy handsome, too. If the worst should happen, the physic might have to wait months or years before finding another acceptable body.

Besides, he'd begun to sense mutiny in the boy's heart. The physic had recently taken him on a pilgrimage he made every decade, to go over accounts with the manager of his estate. He had taken the boy and noticed that the trip had changed him. Perhaps it was a reaction to seeing the vastness of the physic's wealth, but it seemed to have been too much for a peasant who'd been poor his entire life, and had put ideas into his head. In any case, since their return, the boy was as skittish as a cat around him.

The physic picked an evening soon after for the peasant's transformation. He drugged the housekeeper's drink so she would remain asleep should things grow ugly or loud. That night, the physic lured the boy down to his chamber in the cellar by baiting him with the promise of teaching him to read. While skeptical, the boy was tempted enough to follow him, and as soon as he bent over the pages to begin his lesson, the physic grabbed him and forced him to swallow the elixir that he kept in a vial on a leather cord around his neck.

The spell required time to take effect, for the body to die and allow the soul to return once it was stripped of the troublesome requirements of mortality, or so it had been the physic's observation. By morning, the servant's transformation was complete and he woke with the power of the rejuvenation coursing through his virile body. How the physic envied that youthful body, recalling how he had felt taking the elixir at the age of eighty-seven. He could only imagine what it would do to a man in his early twenties.

As it turned out, the physic discovered the old monk Nicodemus's work through the simplest route. By then, he'd gained Count cel Batrin's trust and could be freer in his inquiries. The castle and its occupants were mad for the magical arts. Not that anyone openly professed belief, for the church zealously hunted down those who worshipped Satan, and anyone foolish enough to admit such leanings could expect to be tortured and killed as an example to the rest of the kingdom.

No, the count's interest in magic seemed to be for his entertainment as well as his court's, and so the physic obliged them with harmless demonstrations of legerdemain just short of the heretical: flash powder and prognostication, potions to induce hallucinations, states in which the men were susceptible to the suggestion that they were flying or invisible. Of course, the physic had in his possession spells and potions that could make one temporarily invisible and the like, but he didn't dare let anyone know. However, these simple antics endeared him to the count and earned his trust, enabling the physic to travel more freely inside the castle.

It was while exercising this freedom that he learned there was an old man who had made himself the keeper of the kingdom's history. By day he kept the treasury in order; he knew where every piece of silver plate and jewelry was stored and how many gold pieces were packed away in special trunks, and he wore the keys to the vaults on a belt around his waist like a chatelain. But in his spare moments—at night in his chamber, with quill in hand—he kept track of all the stories told about and within the kingdom.

So one night the physic paid a surprise visit to the treasurer, bringing a goatskin of strong wine. The treasurer so enjoyed having an audience to hear the stories that he'd meticulously collected over the years that the physic didn't even need the wine to loosen his lips. Nonetheless, the bright-eyed old man sipped the wine gratefully and told the physic everything he'd heard.

Apparently, there had once flourished within this kingdom a secret sect of monks who, it was said, had a deep and abiding interest in the dark arts. True, it was a perverse interest for a brotherhood of monks, but then, everyone knew that not all monks joined the church because they wished to devote their lives to God. Some just needed a profession, and becoming a monk was better than soldiering, as it was less strenuous and not at all deadly. Others took it up because food and shelter were provided and they often learned some useful skill; still others were either too lazy or physically unfit to manage any sort of manual labor, but content to do a job that required only a modicum of obedience in return. As in every walk of life, there were some drawn to a profession diametrically opposed to their innate character: just as there were lawmakers and sheriffs who stole and cheated, there were priests and nuns who flirted with the devil.

To all outward appearances, everything at the abbey appeared normal, with no indication of anything amiss. The order was known for beekeeping and kept the village and the castle supplied with honey and beeswax; their bees pollinated the farmers' fields, and the monks' interaction with the villagers was always cordial. Then one night all the monks disappeared save two. One had been there longer than anyone could remember; an outspoken, headstrong old man so ancient that he'd shrunk to half his former height and could barely walk, so he was carried on the back of a much younger monk most of the time. The second was a recent addition to the brotherhood, an acolyte. But the acolyte wasn't found within the abbey's walls: he was found in the woods, his tunic torn and stuck with thorns from hiding in the brush to escape the monks' search party, or so he claimed.

The young man was covered with bruises, and restraints had left welts on his wrists. He said, to the amazement of everyone, that the

brotherhood was dedicated to the study of the black arts and had discovered a way to live forever. They'd accomplished this by learning to
send their souls into the bodies of others, trading their aging bodies
for those of the incoming acolytes. Then they'd dispose of the elderly
bodies with the acolytes' souls trapped inside.

The ancient monk, it seemed, had refused to follow the others,
preferring to stay in his own body (though he did manage to prolong
its usefulness, as he confessed to being 125 years old at the time of
his capture). When the monks discovered that the acolyte had escaped and couldn't be found, they fled the abbey in anticipation of
their inevitable discovery.

"And the name of the monk who had developed this spell—was
his name Nicodemus?" the physic asked, breathless.

"I believe that is the name he was known by," the historian said,
nodding in agreement before continuing his story. Only the ancient
monk had any knowledge of Nicodemus's spells and powers, but
he refused to divulge any information on the grounds that no good
could possibly come of continued interest in the subject, particularly
if passed into the wrong hands, and vowed to take the knowledge to
his grave.

"So that's all there is to the tale," the treasurer said to the physic,
draining the last of the wine, oblivious to the physic's crestfallen
look. "That is probably why this village still has such an interest in
the dark arts," he added, "for we have had in our time such a tanta-
lizingly close brush with it."

"I take it the old monk had no relatives survive him," said the
physic, already resigned to having reached another dead end.

"Actually, his granddaughter still lives in the castle," the treasurer
said offhandedly.

"A monk with a granddaughter?" the physic asked, eyebrows
raised.

"Well, we've already established that he wasn't a very devout
monk, haven't we?" the treasurer answered. "The man condoned

murder and worshipped the devil—or so one presumes; having taken a mistress seems the least of his trespasses. He had a mistress who survived him, and the mistress bore a child, and so on. The girl has the gift of prophecy, they say, as well as a touch of madness. She lives in the very lowest part of the castle, near the dungeons."

The physic thanked the treasurer for his time, then quickly made his way to the level underground, past the cold storerooms and the buttery. As he got closer to the dungeons, he went from chamber to chamber with his lantern until he found her. His shadow had barely crossed the cell's threshold when the woman sat bolt upright as though he'd called out to her by name. "I can feel your intentions from here. You're here for my grandfather's secrets," she said. "Come no closer. I'll give you what you're looking for, as you mean to take it anyway, and I feel murder in your heart."

The woman was no older than thirty, he figured, and looked as though she'd been raised in the wild. She wore rags and was barefoot, and her ginger hair was matted like the nest of a feral beast.

"Why do you live in the cellar?" the physic asked, holding a cloth to his nose against the stench from the prisoners' cells down the hall.

"I'm safer here, away from the likes of them," she said, tossing her head in the direction of the upper floors. "I'm mad, or so they prefer to say. In a town obsessed with magical arts, it was preordained that I would be an outcast. They believe I am afflicted by the same evil spirit that was rumored to have possessed my grandfather."

She seemed so lucid that the physic thought she might be pretending to be touched to keep the townsfolk at bay. He sensed that a power swept through the room and through her, too, though she seemed to be unable to harness it—to her obvious misfortune. He understood that it would do well to see her as a cautionary example: if you couldn't control the forces that touched you, *they* would control *you*.

"So you know why I'm here," he said, pacing outside her door.

"You want my grandfather's book," the woman said, drawing

a bound volume from its hiding place in the wall and tentatively wiping a finger across the mildewed wooden cover. "I've kept it hidden, as my mother instructed me, all my life. It contains potent magic that neither she nor I have the power inside us to command. But you do." She slid the book across the floor and it came to rest neatly at his feet, as though it had been waiting for him. "A piece of my grandfather's advice for you: better to be a sinner than a hypocrite, especially when you've no reason to obey the foolish demands of the mob. Don't forget." With that, she pressed back into the shadows.

He thought momentarily about taking her with him. The woman obviously had a born connection to the unseen world and there had to be a utility for that. On the other hand, she wasn't in control of her gifts, and he wasn't eager to find out whether he was powerful enough to handle them himself. In any case, his curiosity fell away once he felt the power in those pages as his hand touched the book. He smiled at her with the hungry gratitude of a wolf, tucked the folio under his arm, and left the dungeon for the privacy of his keep, eager to explore this latest acquisition.

SEVENTEEN

MAINE

When the sky was half lit by dawn, Adair pulled the vehicle to the side of the road. With light enough now to see, he leaned over the seat and drew the coat away from Jonathan's face, hoping to find that a major transformation had transpired in the past few hours.

Jonathan's skin was at least a few shades closer to a normal hue, and the stink had mostly dissipated; having the windows down during the drive had done much good in that respect. However, Jonathan did not appear healthy. His appearance reminded Adair in no small measure of victims of the Black Death, his pleasing face distorted by swelling, and purplish blooms peeking from the open collar of his shirt.

Adair didn't realize until then just how badly he'd wanted this gambit to work, and work perfectly. Raising the dead was hard enough; restoring a body to its original state, when its original state had been absolute perfection, was probably impossible. While there was a chance Jonathan would improve, Adair decided to prepare mentally for failure and resolved to view this as an experiment, a chance to observe in the hope of doing better the next time he tried to raise the dead, should he ever attempt this spell again. In his heart, however, he felt the ache of disappointment.

Adair was staring at Jonathan, wondering if he'd ever regain consciousness, when his eyes popped open.

"Have you been awake long?" Adair tried to hide his surprise and delight to see Jonathan's corpse shudder to life.

"I don't know. Am I conscious now? This is not a dream?" The voice was Jonathan's, but it sounded as though it came from far away.

"Can you move?"

Jonathan floundered, finally using the back of the seat to push himself upright. It pained Adair to see him so crippled, to see that once flawless physical specimen now ruined. His stomach clenched, for he wasn't totally without pity.

"It's like putting on a suit of clothes you haven't worn in a while. I never thought I'd feel like this again—made of flesh and bone," Jonathan remarked. And correspondingly he moved in a strange, disjointed fashion, as though his skeleton had been put back together differently and he had yet to figure out how this new system worked. As he sorted himself out, he continued to grumble at Adair. "Why did you bring me back? It's an obscene thing to do to a man who has made his peace with this world."

Adair couldn't argue with him on that point as he, too, felt he might have crossed a line, though he would not admit this to Jonathan. "I have need of you: I have unfinished business with you and Lanore. But first, I want to know how you ended up in the grave. It must've been by Lanore's own hand, for it could not have happened any other way, and yet, I wouldn't have imagined she'd *ever* let you go. Did you drive her to kill you? You must've done something very horrible indeed to make her wish to be rid of you."

A flash of anger cleared the fog from Jonathan's eyes. "Don't be ridiculous. She didn't end my life out of anger. She did it because I *asked* her to. I was tired of living. I'm sure even you've felt this way at some point. I thought I was hurt beyond caring"—he shook his head ruefully at his folly—"and wanted to escape as quickly as possible. I went to Lanny and begged her to help me. She fought me like the devil, but in the end she gave in. Is that what you wanted to hear?"

Despite the regret in Jonathan's voice, Adair was struck by the selfishness of his act, to ask someone who loved him dearly to end his life. What had compelled her to agree? Was it because of her boundless love for him, or her guilt for having made him immortal against his will? In either case, it was an untenable position to be put in, and still she had not denied him.

"Not so fast. I want you to tell me *everything*. You asked her to end your life, but why did you wish to leave her? Had you tired of her after two centuries of companionship?"

"Tired of her? No, you've got it wrong. We were together for only a few years, right after we'd escaped from you. . . . I saw from the start that it was no good between us and could never be. She wanted more from me than I could give her. My presence only made her miserable, so I thought it would be best for her if I left. We've been apart ever since. I only sought her out again because I needed her to release me. And, to my shame, I bullied her into letting me go."

So they had *not* been together, happily enjoying each other's company, laughing at the cruel trick they'd perpetrated against him, as Adair had feared. And while he was pleased to find out that Lanny had not been in Jonathan's bed all this time, it also pained him—irrationally, contradictorily—to learn that Jonathan had deserted her. The agony she must've felt at losing him. She must've been inconsolable, living with the pain of his rejection all these years. How she must've doubted herself every day, doubted that anyone would love her. For he'd known these doubts, in his own way, after she'd betrayed him. He'd sat in darkness and wondered for the first time if he was so monstrous as to be unlovable. The evidence seemed undeniable.

Instead of being pleased to hear of her suffering, Adair was surprised to find he was *angry* with Jonathan for hurting the woman he loved. How dare this self-absorbed popinjay, this undeserving jackass, treat her this way? It was the height of ingratitude: Jonathan could search the world and never find someone who would love him as truly and completely as Lanny had. How arrogant of him to think so little of her devotion! Adair, his skull ready to explode with rage, fought the urge to lunge at the man he'd just resurrected and break his neck.

It made no sense, and yet it was undeniable: Adair loved Lanny so much that he couldn't bear to think of her hurt, no matter the reason. When he'd calmed down enough to speak, he fixed Jonathan with a stare and said, "How did she ever fall in love with you? I shall *never* understand it. . . . Of all the men she could've had, why did she pick someone as selfish and unfeeling as *you*?"

But Jonathan was not insulted. "Do you expect me to disagree?" he asked grimly. "I'd known since we were children that she was wrong to love me. But at the same time I never asked for it, either. She gave her love to me, Adair; she laid it at my feet and hoped that I'd reciprocate. And I'll tell you this: it wasn't easy, knowing I didn't love her the same way."

"And yet, you managed to take her to your bed—"

"It was what she wanted, but I felt guilty every time we were together! Eventually it got to the point where I couldn't live with the guilt any longer, and I left her." Jonathan's voice, which had been thin and ethereal, thickened with regret.

To his great surprise, pity surged through Adair. Pity for his rival, a man who'd tossed Lanny's love away, and *still* didn't seem to realize what he'd given up, or the folly of his arrogance. Was it possible that the defect was in Jonathan? Adair wondered. Did the man have no need to be close to another living soul? Too, he felt pity for Lanore, who—Adair realized with a sinking heart—would never stop loving Jonathan, even in death. And he felt pity for himself, for he'd never felt more alone.

"It might please you to know why I went to Lanny," Jonathan said, hesitating for another second before giving in with a sigh. "You might say I got my comeuppance. You see, I fell in love with a woman, only to lose her. As you know, three years, five years, it's like the blink of an eye to us. I'd only just begun to know what love was and then she was gone, killed in a car accident. I went crazy with grief and somehow got it in my head that we would be reunited in the hereafter. I was in so much pain. . . . I wanted to believe there was a way to fix things, to get what I wanted."

"And were you reunited with this woman?"

Jonathan turned away. "It didn't work out that way."

Good, Adair thought. There was justice in the universe after all; no soul deserved happiness less. "And what did you find in the afterlife?"

Jonathan only shook his head. "I can't seem to remember anything concrete about the beyond. It's strange: when I try to remember, any thoughts that come to me break up right away, like mist. It's as though memories can't cross over to this side. They might return to me with time. . . . But all those questions about the afterlife: that's not the real reason you brought me back, is it? You want to go after Lanny; you're looking for revenge. I won't help you."

Adair fought to remain nonplussed, not to vent his frustration through violence right away. "What a gallant corpse you make, for being such a cad in life. Your scruples don't extend to *me*, though, do they? She had your help to trap me, if I'm not mistaken. You must've helped brick up that wall. I'm entitled to seek vengeance from *you* as much as from *her*."

Jonathan did not wither at this accusation. "Lanny had her reasons for stopping you. She was trying to protect me, for one. She told me that you had tricked everyone into thinking you were the peasant boy, this victim, when you weren't. She knew you were the horrible monster of your own story."

"I know she had discovered my secret. She told me, right before she tricked me. She is a clever one. Too clever a girl for you, Jonathan. Perhaps too clever for me," Adair acknowledged.

"She said you planned to swap our souls, that you wanted to take my body, and that's why she had to stop you. The ironic thing is I would've happily given you this body, Adair," Jonathan said, almost laughing, leaving no doubt as to his sincerity. "You have no idea how sick I'd become of all the attention, the fawning. Being touched, stared at, chased. When you are attractive, people think you're a public commodity, like a piece of art or a statue. I was always on display. If you'd asked, I'd have switched places with you in an instant."

For once, Adair was at a complete loss for words.

"That's why you brought me back from the dead, isn't it? You thought you'd use my body to trick Lanny into coming back to you." Jonathan's smile was lopsided and macabre, like that of a rotting jack-o'-lantern. "I imagine you might be thinking twice about that plan now. Are you disappointed with the way I've turned out? Take this body if you want it. It can't be very appealing, but you're welcome to it. Take it and set my soul free."

In the course of a few moments it seemed that Jonathan had gained the upper hand. How had this happened? How had a man just brought back from the dead been able to set him back on his heels? It was very unsettling. "So much for your noble intentions," Adair said defensively. "You're ready to let Lanore fend for herself once you've got an easy way out. Is it because you are anxious to return to the arms of the queen of the underworld? Is this another case of a woman being fascinated with the magnificent Jonathan St. Andrew? Doesn't it ever get old?"

"I have no choice in the matter. And if she was 'fascinated' with me, as you say, it was due in no small part to you."

"Me?"

Jonathan touched his arm. "The tattoo—that's how I came to her attention. She knew the design. It meant something to her."

Adair thought of the original tattoo, the one on his back, which he'd had reproduced crudely on Jonathan's arm. He needed mirrors to view it, and it had grown indistinct as the ink bled into his skin with time. He'd wanted to assume the design was meaningless, nothing more than a Roma scribble the peasant boy had etched into his skin for amusement, but he saw now that he'd been whistling in the dark: it had greater meaning, which he'd intuited all along. It was that intuition that had driven him to have Jonathan marked in the first place, many years ago.

"So it was not your handsome face that drew the attention of this woman but the tattoo. . . . And, pray, what did she say? What did it mean to her?"

Jonathan shifted his misshapen face away from Adair. "As I said, as long as you threaten Lanny, I have nothing to tell you. You'll get nothing more from me."

"As luck would have it, I don't require your cooperation, Jonathan, not really. All I need is your *presence.*" Adair turned back to face the steering wheel but couldn't keep his eyes from the rearview mirror and the unsettling sight therein. "For now, all I need you to do is finish setting into flesh, you emperor of worms, and we'll see if we can't put you to further use."

Adair wondered if Jonathan's body would ever return to its original state. Even if it did, he wasn't sure he wished to move his soul into it, take it up as a hermit crab appropriates a new shell. The mechanics of taking on the body—there he had no concerns. He knew that he could execute that spell properly, for he'd done it once already—only once, but it was burned into his memory forever, for it had been a singular experience. The thrill of wielding such otherworldly power was not one he was likely to forget.

HUNGARIAN TERRITORY, 1358

With the old heretical monk's book secured, the physic took it back to his keep and set about finding the spell he desired. First, he had to puzzle over the writing, which was in the archaic Romanian of the old monk's time. Once he could make sense of the words, he was distracted by the range of the collection, for this told him how capable the sect had been at magic. He chuckled over a couple of the spells in which the approach was wrong or the execution inelegant, and anyone with common sense should've been able to think of a better way to accomplish the task. And he wondered about the usefulness of other spells. A few seemed pointless, more trouble than they were worth.

The physic had come to the conclusion that, far from being Adepts, the sect was nothing but a bunch of bumbling amateurs . . . until he came to the spell in question, the spell that would free him from his body. He read through the words twice, surprised by the spell's elegance and simplicity. It was truly clever, and undoubtedly the best work the monks had ever done.

Now that he had the means to effect the exchange with the peasant boy, the physic began to make plans. It would take place in his chambers and away from Marguerite, he decided; he wanted no witnesses to the transformation, wanted no one to even guess that he had taken over the peasant boy's form. Transferring his fortune to Adair's name would be easy because of the rule of the seal: as long as he carried the family seal back with him to the estate, he wouldn't be challenged for ownership.

Convincing the boy to come down to the chamber proved tricky, however. Now that his body was impervious to harm, he'd gotten cocky: the physic saw that he'd miscalculated when he'd decided to grant him immortality. He'd bestowed the gift too soon. He'd hoped that being the recipient of such a gift would make the boy loyal to him in gratitude, but instead, he acted above his station. The boy was testing him, forming plans in his head, and the time had come—none too soon—to put a stop to that.

The physic waited at the foot of the stairs with a rope in hand. "Adair, come to me," he called as he might call a dog. "I need your assistance."

The response was curt and impudent. "Why should I, old man?"

But the physic was prepared. "I have something I must share with you. I want to show you where I keep the seal to my kingdom. If something should happen to me, I want you to have it." The boy knew the rule of the seal from his time at the estate. The boy's greed could be counted on: it had already proven to be his weakness. The peasant wasn't clever: he might see one step ahead but not two or three, and when treasure or property was dangled before his eyes, all intelligence went out of his pretty head and he'd snap at it, like a chop on a string held out of reach.

At the sound of the boy trotting down the steps, the physic readied the rope, and as soon as he came around a corner, the physic caught his wrist and reeled him in. The boy didn't make it easy; he struggled as the physic completed the steps, anointing them both with the required oils while uttering the necessary words. He dug his hands into the peasant boy's shoulders and held on for all he was worth, unsure of what would happen next.

It was the single most extraordinary sensation he would ever experience. He felt as though he'd fallen into a million grains of dust, and a breeze cut through his essence and lifted him, carrying him on the air. At the same time, he felt—more than that, he *knew*—that the boy was experiencing the same thing, but through a prism of terror, because it was unexpected. They passed through each other—dust motes on the wind, fanning, spreading, thinning—and the physic became a part of the boy's consciousness, and the boy part of his. In that instant he learned all of the boy's life: his miserable father, the camaraderie of his brothers, his shame at being raped, and his terror of the physic's furies. To the physic's embarrassment, he knew the boy was being given every crumb and tidbit of his life, too, experiencing every failure and every slight. He knew everything the physic knew, down to each spell and recipe. He could be as powerful as the physic without the intelligence or temperament to control such power. As far as the physic was concerned, that sealed the boy's fate; even with the boy trapped in an old man's body, there was no way he could be allowed to live.

The transference passed and the physic, keeping his wits, overpowered his adversary at once, manacling him to the wall. How strange to wrestle his former self to the ground, to fit the handcuffs to his ancient, bony wrists. Bewilderment stared back at him from that familiar face—and what an ugly face it was! He saw how his former self truly looked now as it cringed before him. His former face was a thick map of wrinkles. His eyes had narrowed to slits. Age spots dotted the waxy surface of his skin, and white hairs sprouted from the least appropriate places. His nails had become as yellow as the claws of an old dog. But the expression on his face had changed, and this was for certain: it was the peasant boy's eyes staring back at him in disbelief.

"What has happened?" his former self whispered.

"You are now in my place, and I in yours." It delighted him to hear that he spoke with the boy's voice. Everything about the boy's body pleased him. As good as he'd felt when he first experienced the immortality spell in St. Petersburg, he felt a hundred times better now. Naturally, this was due to the fact that the boy was younger and spry, but having been a field hand, he was more robust, too. He felt strong as a titan, as though he could knock down the stone walls of the keep with the push of a hand. He was sure that he could run for hours and never tire, that he'd never need sleep again. The tug of sex was stronger, too, and he saw how frustrated the boy must've been, forced to satisfy an old man's needs and make do with an ugly servant girl when he wanted to swive every woman in the village.

His former self lifted his chained hands, imploring. "What do you plan to do with me?"

"For now, I plan to keep you here. Go ahead and scream all you want. You know Marguerite won't hear you." He double-checked the locks on the manacles before climbing out of the cellar, and standing on the upper floor as his eyes adjusted to the darkness, his gaze fell upon Marguerite's sleeping form. His lust was such that it needed immediate appeasement, and the housekeeper would do.

In the morning, he told her that the old physic had decided to leave the count's service and that she should leave, too. But she saw that the shelves and desktop still held the physic's books and supplies and seemed not to believe him, so he pressed a small purse of gold in her hand and threw her out, ordering her to return to the village. Once she was gone, he brought his captive up from the cellar with his hands still bound, though it seemed an unnecessary precaution, for the man's expression was vacant and he probably was near madness. The physic saddled the horses and then went back for his prisoner.

By chance, his eye fell on the books of alchemical secrets that stood on the table, his Venetian manuscript and the old monks' book of spells, and he decided quite suddenly to take them with him. Of all the things in the keep, the books were the only ones that were irreplaceable, and even though he intended to return, he could easily imagine the risks in leaving them behind. There was a chance that Marguerite might come back, perhaps even bringing the count's men with her. So he wrapped the books in a cloth and tied the package across his back, then dragged his captive outside behind him.

They rode for over an hour to the west, then followed trails up the foothills of the great mountain range. He knew the mountains were like honeycombs seeded with caverns and chambers, so many that no one person knew of them all. He'd heard that Gypsies or brigands sometimes used the caves to hide from pursuit, knowing they would be safe there, as the villagers believed ghosts and demons took up residence in their deep recesses and wouldn't go near them if they could help it. He'd once run across a cavern that was very deep, like a tunnel falling straight down. He'd thrown a rock into it, and never heard the rock hit bottom. This cave was their destination.

He brought his captive to the edge of the drop. "Take a good look; this is to be your new home, and I think it will be your home for a very long time. For you see, the body you inhabit is immortal, just like the one you've given me, so even though you'll be at the bottom of this pit, bones broken from the fall, you won't die. Your bones will knit and heal. And even though you'll not have food or drink, you'll neither starve nor perish of thirst. No, you'll live on in this hole in the earth for eternity if no one finds you and pulls you out, and I very much doubt that will happen. So take your last glimpse of sunlight, and say good-bye to all that you know." Before his prisoner could utter a word, to either beg for mercy or damn him to hell, Adair pushed him over the edge and watched his former self crumple and fall from view. The boy cried very little, the weak old voice dying away quickly, and just as before, there was no report of an impact at the bottom of his fall or anything that could be seen in the darkness. Satisfied, the physic climbed on his horse, set the other one free, and rode back to the keep.

To think back on it now, Adair was struck by the irony that Lanore had chosen to bottle him up in nearly the same way that he'd imprisoned the peasant boy. It had to be a coincidence, he thought, for he'd told no one his true story, not one person in his hundreds of years of existence. It sent a shiver through him to recall his time in that dark, narrow space, and how he'd nearly gone mad. . . . But to think of the peasant boy enduring this torture for three times as long! He had to have lost his mind, for sure. Or, if God had taken pity on him, he might be in a state of suspension, slumbering like a bear in winter, but in his case slumbering without interruption. Sleeping for eternity.

On returning from his journey to the cave, Adair had learned how little the villagers cared for his former self, for the keep had been ransacked and burned as completely as a stone building can be.

Marguerite must've communicated to the villagers that the hated old physic was gone, and so they came to take their fury out on his possessions. They despised and feared him so much that they hadn't stolen anything from the keep but let it all burn. The physic stepped through the smoldering heaps of still-hot ash, overturned furniture now broken into bits, all his supplies either burned or tossed and trampled. He went into the cellar to find that his bed had been made into a pyre. There was nothing to be done but unearth the seal and the last of his money from its hiding place behind a stone in the wall before bidding adieu to his life as a physic and venturing out in search of his new life as Adair.

EIGHTEEN

BARCELONA

Before I left Casablanca, Savva gave me a gift: a list of Adair's other companions. "There may be others I don't know about, ones that came long before me, but not many, I'd wager." He furrowed his brow as he looked over the names a second time. He'd put them in a rough chronological order. A few were known to me—Alejandro, Tilde, Dona, for instance, and Jude—but most were not.

"So many," I murmured, glancing down the list. Though I'd learned from Dona that there were more like us in the world, it had never occurred to me to seek out any of them—except for Savva, of course. I thought they would all be mean and deceitful like Tilde and Dona; even Savva could be trying at times. My world had shrunk over the years—when you need to keep the facts of your life a secret, it's easier to withdraw from society than to keep track of the lies you must tell—but I was never tempted to seek their company.

Of the dozen people on the list, Savva knew the whereabouts of only three. He pointed to the name Cristobal Ramirez, an alias that was immediately followed by Alejandro Pinheiro in parentheses. "I would talk to him first: he's probably in touch with a few of the others. You could track down all of them that way, and now that Adair is free, there might be some benefit to doing so."

It seemed that Alejandro, the deferential, watchful man I had known in Adair's household, was now Cristobal Ramirez, a photographer with an address on the Ciutat Vella, which a guidebook said was in a fashionable part of the city. It wasn't surprising that Alejandro had taken up photography: he'd always been observant, and the occupation sounded like a good fit for him. There was a degree of exploitation involved, a willingness to stare hard and not look away, to *use* what you see through the lens. Among Adair's minions, Alejandro's job had always been informant, the one who quietly took in everything and reported it back to Adair, and the recollection of his hidden cold-bloodedness sent a chill down my spine.

He had been one of the sadder members of our group. He'd been born into a wealthy Jewish household in Toledo, Spain, at an unfortunate time, at the height of the Inquisition. Imprisoned and tortured, he implicated his sister for witchcraft to secure his own release, and was paying for that act of betrayal for eternity. He hated himself. He renounced his religion, even pretending for a time to be a defrocked priest and a Papist sympathizer. His battered psyche didn't stand a chance against his tormentors—not the inquisitors, not Adair.

The address for Alejandro's studio led to a row of low buildings along a well-kept street, with stores and a chic bar on the ground level designed to appeal to fetishists and sex fiends. The door I was looking for was next to the bar and labeled "Cristobal Ramirez Photography." Behind the door were stairs leading to another door at the top, which opened into a small waiting area with high white walls and a white counter without a receptionist behind the desk. The room functioned as a gallery and displayed nothing but oversize photographs of men: some full-body portraits, some close-ups. The subjects were young, old, handsome, quirky; each image captured some secret truth about the individual, revealing almost to the point of being exploitive.

These photographs were so strong that it was nearly impossible to look away, and as I stepped from one image to the next, I marveled at Alejandro's mastery of the ability to look unerringly into people's souls, a skill that had no doubt taken lifetimes to attain. Just then a door opened behind me, hushed, followed by the soft padding of feet. "Can I help you?" asked a familiar voice.

I turned, smiling despite my anxiety about seeing him again. "Alejandro!"

He had changed so much that I wouldn't have recognized him on the street. The locks that I remembered as glorious and glossy black were gone and his head was shaved bald, leaving a blue-black cast to the scalp where his hair was beginning to reassert itself. He wore tiny round spectacles with yellow lenses over his beautiful deep-brown eyes, an odd affectation. The priestly black cassock was gone, of course, replaced by twenty-first-century equivalents: a black cashmere sweater and loose gray pants. A loop of prayer beads circled one wrist.

"Good God! It really *is* you—Lanny!" I took my cues from him then: he held open his arms so we hugged—but not too warmly— and he placed an air kiss on each of my cheeks. "I was just think-ing of you the other day and then, out of the blue, I hear from Savva, telling me you want to pay me a visit. A remarkable coinci-dence, wouldn't you say? It is as though fate were trying to tell me something."

He led the way into his studio. We sat at the far end from where he did his shoots, the back wall festooned with long, seam-less backdrops hoisted on heavy rolls overhead. Otherwise the space was empty. I took a seat at a café table tucked against a wall while Alejandro fiddled with an espresso machine.

"I should've tried to contact you earlier. I'm sorry it's been so long." Why hadn't I sought him out? I wondered. He hadn't been *so* terrible to me in Boston, had he? In that den of wolves, he had been the only one to treat me kindly, aside from Uzra. He'd taken care of me when I'd fallen afoul of Adair. True, he'd had a part in bringing me to Adair in the first place and sometimes wheedled and cajoled me into doing Adair's bidding, but I wanted to believe that had been beyond his control, that all those things had been done under duress. In his heart, I knew the Spaniard was gentle and kind. And I wanted to trust him. I needed him.

"How have you been?" I asked. "You seem to be doing well."

"Do I?" He peered at me playfully over the top of his eyeglasses. "The photography, you mean? We must have our hobbies to keep us occupied, don't you find? And what about you? What do you do to keep busy these days?"

"Not much of anything, if I'm being honest," I reported drily.

Alejandro continued. "I already know that you are no longer with Jonathan. Savva told me some time ago, and I must say it came as a complete surprise. It didn't seem as though you two could live apart from one another." A lie told out of kindness. "So tell me that you and Jonathan are together again. That would make me happy."

I tried not to flinch, though the question hurt terribly. "Jonathan is gone. He wanted to be released, so I . . . helped him."

Alejandro regarded me with cool curiosity, seeing a side to me that he hadn't known existed. "I never would have thought you capable of such an act. Even Adair would consider it very carefully before taking the life of one of his companions, you know."

"In my case, it was completely out of compassion."

"But to kill a man you loved! It is a very difficult kind of compassion, no? How many people could do such a thing to their lovers? One in a hundred thousand, a million?" The way he said this, there was no question that he thought there was something wrong with me. Again Alejandro regarded me stiffly. "What a terrible thing to have on your conscience. I'm sorry, my dear, for your loss."

My skin crawled uncomfortably; I had to change the subject. "Tell me about the others—are you in contact with any of them? Do you talk to Dona or Tilde?"

"Yes, I've been in touch with them, but . . . why do you ask? Do you really care to hear how they are? You didn't seem to like either of them before."

"It's hard to like someone who doesn't like you," I replied.

"That's true." He lifted one shoulder in a half shrug. "Yes, I know where they both are. We became close after you left. We had no choice: we had to pull together. That useless lawyer told us that Adair's money had been transferred to Jonathan, but you all had disappeared, you, Jonathan, Adair. None of you came back. We were left penniless. Shall I tell you what we went through—selling possessions, depending on the mercy of those heartless Bostonians—when it became clear that Adair wasn't going to return?"

There was a tremor of fear and anger in his voice for everything that had happened back then, even now, two hundred years later. "It sounds as though you had a terrible time of it."

"Tilde and Dona, they suffered, too. We'd served Adair for ages and ages, and by that point we were used to having a master. It took a while for us to realize we were free, and to grow strong enough to go our separate ways." He gave me a coquettish look. "So there is my story. Now it is your turn, Lanore. Are you going to tell me what happened to you, why you disappeared? Even Savva did not know how you happened to be free of Adair. He said you never told him that part of your story."

Confessing to Alejandro was harder than I thought it would be. There was an edge to him, a slight bitterness. He knew I had something to do with Adair's disappearance.

He fussed with his espresso and then continued, as though he didn't expect me to have a response. "I have so many questions, you see, about what happened to you during that terrible time. You know what I find interesting? Since the day you left the household, I had not felt Adair's presence. It stopped at the same time he disappeared, when—you said—he went to Philadelphia and you and Jonathan were going to join him. Do you remember?" He forced a smile. "I cannot say to lose Adair's presence was a bad thing. It was like being normal again, not like being a schizophrenic with a voice in my head all the time. You know what I mean: the *relief*? Of course you do." He paused and took a sip of espresso, letting me see slivers of his eyes over the rims of his glasses. "And then, a few weeks ago the presence came back. I had so completely forgotten what it felt like that I thought it was a migraine." His right hand gestured to his temple. "That's when I thought of you. I hadn't had this feeling since the last time I had seen *you*. You feel it, too, yes?"

"Yes, I do." Suddenly it occurred to me that Alejandro might know more than I thought. After all, I didn't *know* why I could feel Adair's presence again. I didn't know what actually happened back in Boston. I was only guessing that it meant someone had freed Adair; if indeed someone had, I didn't know who it was. Maybe searching out Alejandro wasn't a good idea.

"So, do you not think it is an amazing coincidence that Adair is missing for two centuries, no one has heard from him, and then he is back, and suddenly you show up at my door." It was not said as a question.

"No, it's not a coincidence," I admitted.

"It was you, wasn't it? You did something to Adair, two hundred years ago. You *stopped* him. You didn't kill him?"

I lowered my gaze. "We both know that's not possible."

He drew in a breath. "I searched for him, you know. I couldn't believe he would leave us like that, me and Tilde and Dona." Pain seeped into his voice, and liquid sparkled in Alej's eyes, behind his glasses.

"Adair was *so* taken with you and Jonathan. He made no secret of it. This happened every time he made a new companion. The new one becomes the apple of his eye. You bask in his attention, thinking it will never end. Then, one day, he brings home a new pet, and you feel it is just a little bit colder in his presence; he does not have time for you as he once did. But he had never deserted us *completely* for a new favorite, not in all the time we'd been together, so naturally I was devastated when there was no word from him—nothing. I hadn't been without him in many lifetimes. I didn't care if he had run off with the two of you. I was frightened. You can't imagine how frightened I was."

"Yes, I can," I replied. During the years Jonathan and I had been apart, what kept me from complete despair was the knowledge that he was still out in the world. I'd carried that knowledge close to my heart, and it had been a comfort in my loneliest times. Since his death, that space had been empty and was still raw.

Alej didn't care for my intrusion upon his recollections, and he studied my face ruthlessly, reading my sorrows as though they were tea leaves. "Oh, that's right, you have lost Jonathan, haven't you? So you know what that pain feels like." His smirk was enigmatic, half triumph, half hurt. "All right, I will admit that you, too, have suffered, and my heart goes out to all who suffer," he said. "But you are the reason Adair disappeared, and for that, I don't know if I can completely forgive you. I am only being honest with you," he added, unable to help himself. Savva was right about that: Alejandro couldn't bear to be at odds with anyone.

"I'm sorry if I caused you pain," I said. "If it helps, there were many times I was tempted to undo what I'd done. But we both know, Alej, the world is better off without Adair. He's a dangerous, unpredictable man. Remember how cruel he was to us! I didn't think anyone would miss him. I thought we *all* wanted to get away from him, and that he was keeping you and the others against your will, as he had with Uzra."

"Well, of course, there were always moments when I didn't want to do as he demanded, or when I wanted to be free of him, if only for a short spell. Life with him was tumultuous, you know that, but you are remembering only the bad times. Think of all the pleasant times we spent in each other's company, the balls and parties. The evenings together at the table in the cook's kitchen, like a family. He dressed you in the finest silks, gave you jewels to put in your hair, treated you better than anyone had. He had his good qualities, too, whether you choose to remember them or not. He saved each of us when he could've let us die. There were times when I feared him, yes, but I didn't wish to see him hurt. I loved him in my own way."

"That wasn't love, Alejandro. What you felt was gratitude."

"Different words for a feeling in my heart. I felt a *type* of love for him. We all did. Even you, Lanore. Remember, there was a time when you loved him."

My face grew hot as I recalled my earlier epiphany; yes, I couldn't deny that I loved him on a primal level. He was able to ignite my desire like a flame to tinder, with just as much potential for annihilation. But I questioned whether that was love; whatever it was, it was self-destructive, and I couldn't put myself in its path again. "Maybe so. . . . But remember, I was young when that happened. No one had ever shown me that kind of attention. As you say, no one had given me as much as a tin clip for my hair, let alone jewels. I was swept up by it. I got confused and was carried away."

He smirked as though he didn't believe me. "And now Adair has returned and is looking for you because of what you did to him, and you ask for my help."

"Yes, that's so, I'm afraid. He's going to want to take his revenge on me, Alejandro, and you know what that means."

His soulful dark eyes swept over my face with real pity. Yes, he knew what that meant. "I am sorry for you, Lanore, but I don't know how I could help you. I cannot stop him."

I leaned across the table toward Alejandro, my hands reaching for him. "Savva said you might know of someone who can help me—

someone who might know something about Adair's powers. You've been around so much longer than me, from when this kind of magic was part of everyone's life. Nowadays, people don't believe that magic exists, but I have to think that there are still people who study it, and they've just gone underground. Savva says you know these people. You can put me in touch with them."

He swirled the last of the coffee in the tiny cup, frowning at the dregs as though they displeased him. "And what would you ask of them? Do you want someone to tell you how to end Adair's life? Because I wouldn't have a part in that. . . ."

"No, I'm not looking for anything like that." And then I said something that startled me, something that I didn't even know I was thinking. "I want someone to change *me*, to make me mortal again."

"And why would you do that?" he asked, but we both knew the answer: so I'd be able to die and be spared endless suffering at Adair's hands. To escape the same horrific fate as Uzra, being punished for eternity. It seemed more like putting right the natural order of things, tipping the world back on its axis. And maybe, subconsciously, that was why I had left Luke: because I was looking for a way to end my life, and surely Luke would try to stop me from doing that.

My words seemed to have opened a door in Alejandro's heart. He studied me for a long time, and I could feel his eyes on me, reading my face for clues, trying to determine my sincerity. "I cannot give you an answer, just like that. I need to think about it," he said at last. "Stay in the city for a few days. I'll be in touch."

NINETEEN

BOSTON

Adair drove straight through to Boston, stopping only to refuel the car. He thought he would use the time to question Jonathan, but the reanimated corpse had slipped back into sleep. With a touch of his flesh—just above tepid, with the unmistakable resilience of living tissue—Adair knew Jonathan hadn't expired, but he couldn't be roused. They arrived at Jude's town house at dusk, Jonathan waking with the waning of the day, and Adair escorted him quickly to the entrance, banging on the door furiously.

"Coming, coming. . . ." Jude stood on the threshold, spectacles pushed on top of his head. "Where the hell have you been? I've been—" The Dutchman stopped in mid-sentence as he looked at the man beside Adair. "You found him?" He looked incredulously at Adair, who nodded as he kicked the mud off of his shoes. "So this is Jonathan, the fabled prince of the snowy north. . . . You don't know how long I've waited to meet you." Jude extended his hand to his disheveled guest but seemed to think better of it as soon as he touched Jonathan's reanimated skin. "But you don't look at all as I'd imagined. . . ."

"That's because until this evening, he has been dead for three months." Adair brushed by, leading Jonathan by the elbow into the house. Jude looked up and down the street before closing the door, then followed Adair.

"Look, you should've called me before you showed up here. What if the housekeeper had answered the door? What would she think about your friend? And that car outside: is that the rental from Maine? You weren't supposed to drive it all the way back, you were supposed to catch a plane. . . ."

Jude's voice was like the drone of a mosquito, an unintelligible buzz drilling into Adair's skull, disrupting his thoughts. It seemed plain that Jude had been ruined by two hundred years of freedom. What's more, Adair realized that every one of his minions might be worthless to him now, as ungrateful and demanding as the Dutchman. As much as he needed Jude, Adair would have no choice but to get rid of him if he continued to act above his station. At least there was Pendleton. Thank God he'd taken Jude's advice on that, Adair thought. Pendleton was coming along and, having just gone through the transformation, was still properly afraid of Adair and his powers. Perhaps he would be able to take Jude's place before long.

He turned on the Dutchman. "You are not here to tell me what to do and how to behave. You are my servant, here to service my needs—without comment. You must show due respect." Adair turned his back to Jude as he added, "And take care of the car. I don't care *how* you take care of it, just see that it's done."

"I'm only trying to help you, so next time you'll call less attention to—"

Adair lunged and grabbed Jude by the throat, then dashed his head against the fireplace's stone mantel. He'd acted with animal instinct before he even realized what he was doing. The soft slate cracked under the blow, but not before splitting the skin open over

Jude's right temple and sending fat drops of crimson blood to the blond hardwood. Jude's eyeglasses fell from the tangle of his hair to the floor in a clatter. Adair pinched Jude's windpipe shut for a few long seconds before releasing him, and Jude fell against the wall, clutching his throat and gasping for air.

"I am sick of your condescension, Jude. Being free all these years has allowed you to grow insolent. When the day comes that I no longer need you, you should hope that I think of you with gratitude for your loyal service, and not with disdain for your insubordination."

Pendleton stepped forward, troubled. "Adair, is this necessary—"

Adair cast a threatening look at him. "You and Jude may have been friends once, and you may feel a certain loyalty to him, but make no mistake: do not try to come between us, especially when it comes to matters of discipline. It is not your place and I won't permit it." With that, he bent down and seized Jude by his collar, pulling him close to look him dead in the eye. "Let this be the last time I have to warn you. Do not try to tell me what I can and cannot do. Your petty rules don't apply to me"—the very thought made his skull buzz with a long-forgotten truth—"and you'd do well not to forget this."

Jude said nothing but nursed his wounds like a beaten dog. The flow of blood from the cut on his head slowed, and then stopped. Adair turned to Jonathan, who until now had remained out of the fray, his eyes glassy and faraway. "You and I will talk soon. I want to know more about this queen of the underworld. In the meantime, finish knitting that muck into flesh and bones, for God's sake. See if you can restore my perfect vessel." Adair pointed at Jude. "Put him in a room upstairs, and make sure he can't escape."

Adair waited several hours before visiting Jonathan, secretly glad for the time away from him. Not that he would say his spell had failed—the fact that he'd managed to pluck the right spirit from the underworld and drop it into the right body made it a success, as far as he was concerned—but it hadn't turned out as he'd hoped. He would be glad to give the spell a few hours: maybe all that ruined body needed was more time to heal, though he suspected that this wasn't so. The magic that had been Jonathan's beauty seemed lost forever. A shame, but change was the nature of the cosmos, he was coming to see; nothing was impervious to change, not even him.

Tired of worrying about Jonathan, Adair decided to look in on Pendleton. He knew he shouldn't have left Pendleton so soon after the transformation: it was never a good idea to let them have too much time to think about what had happened. Too, Adair wanted to be brought up to date on the transfer of funds from his offshore accounts to his new trust in Switzerland, not to mention Pendleton's progress in tracking down Lanore. He also wanted to gauge how perturbed Pendleton had been by the scene with Jude. It might do well to have a word with him and settle any qualms. Breaking in a new companion was like training an unfamiliar dog. If treated too harshly in the beginning, Pendleton might become completely fearful; too little attention and he might become too independent and chafe when given direction, then grow furtive, as sneaky and untrustworthy as the Dutchman.

But as Adair stood outside Pendleton's room, he heard his latest minion talking on the telephone and, judging by the softness of his tone, he was speaking to a friend. The possibility was disturbing, as Adair had made it clear to Pendleton that he should not be in contact with anyone he had known.

He took the phone from Pendleton as soon as he stepped into the room. "Whom were you speaking with? You know you're not to talk to anyone from your past. That life is over."

"It wasn't anyone who knew me, I swear. And I didn't give my name—" Pendleton broke off his feverish apology. "Look, I know you say it can't be done, but I'm asking you to reconsider and let me return to my old life. My professional reputation—it's the culmination of a lifetime of work. I'm at the top of my game, a leader in the industry. I can't just walk away from all of this. Give me another year to enjoy it; then I'll go with you willingly," Pendleton pleaded.

Adair had heard others make a similar request and knew only too well that it was impossible. He shook his head. "It doesn't work that way. Your health has been restored; you are no longer at death's door. There would be questions if you were seen now, in your current condition—questions you would not be able to answer. As far as the rest of the world is concerned, Pendleton Kingsley is dead. Your family and colleagues have accepted it, given your illness. No one will come looking for you. We've given you a new identity. It's time for you to start over."

"I don't want to be someone else. Don't you get it? I'll never be this successful again. Let me remain as Pendleton Kingsley. I'll be more useful to you this way. My name carries a lot of weight."

"Yes, but we would not be able to explain Pendleton Kingsley's miraculous recovery. You must face the fact that you are no longer the man you were and you can never be him again. I know that is hard to accept, and it will take a long time to put it all behind you, but there is no alternative. Besides, look at what you've been given. You now know the greatest secret of human existence, that there is much more to life than we had been taught to believe. I would think that someone with your intellectual curiosity would be eager to explore this new world and would happily leave his old one behind."

Adair had said these words at some point to all his new companions, but for the first time the promise in them fell flat. He knew what he said was true—the best part of the transformation was at the beginning, when everything was new—but he also knew that the excitement would run dry soon enough. He was not unsympathetic to Pendleton's situation: it was hard to let go of your past, hard to put your successes behind you. Hardest of all was to walk away from the people who had cared for you. He remembered feeling sadness and regret, though he knew there were damn few who had loved him.

Adair's mother had felt some tenderness for him, he was pretty sure, as had old Henrik. And Lanore.

Adair stood abruptly. He didn't wish to crush Pendleton's spirit if he didn't have to, but he'd grown weary of this conversation and he knew he had a larger problem to deal with. "If you cannot accept what I have told you, the only alternative is for me to end your life, the very thing you sought to avoid by making this deal. Those are your only two choices." More kindly, he continued, "Don't forget that you still have the skills that earned you this reputation in the first place. Those can't be taken away from you. And I need those skills, Pendleton."

His encouragement fell on deaf ears. "You chose me because of what I can do for you, didn't you? You're never going to let me go."

"Eventually, I will. When I no longer need you and you've proven you can take care of yourself. For now, however, I'd prefer you to stay." Better to encourage him and to make his participation seem like an option; Adair couldn't imagine fighting for one more person's loyalty, not at the moment. "And what of your efforts to find Lanore? Have you had any luck?"

Pendleton shook his head. "I need something more to go on . . . a name, a location. . . . If you could get anything from"—he blanched at the thought of the creature he'd seen, the one in the room next door—"that *man*, it would be a big help."

"I'll try. One more thing: the money you owe me. How is that coming along? There have been no problems with the transfer, I trust."

"No, it's proceeding." There was another hesitation, a tentative look. "I'm grateful for what you did for me, don't get me wrong . . . but . . . do you really need to take so much? If it's left for my estate, it will do so much good. I made provisions in my will for my estate to go to charity." He winced reflexively, expecting an outburst from Adair.

But there was none. "So these institutions can name a building after you, ensure that your memory lives on? I have no interest in appeasing your vanity. I gave you a miracle," Adair pointed out calmly. "A miracle you could get from no one else. I named my price; you accepted."

"I know I did. . . . What I meant to say is . . . it took me a lifetime to earn that amount of money, and you wouldn't believe how hard I had to work. . . ."

"Really? Do you think I have never worked in my life?" His calm was broken by a thin crack of anger.

"That's not what I meant. . . . I'm not criticizing. . . . It's just that you don't seem to need that kind of money. You're not running a corporation, so I don't get it. What's the purpose of taking all my money away from me?"

The expression of suffering on Pendleton's face almost prompted a smile from Adair. In some ways, it felt as though Pendleton were a child; had no one taught him these things when he was a boy? "Why, to teach you humility, of course. What is money, when it can be so easily lost? A reputation, ruined in an instant, made worthless? Knowledge and experience, the stuff you keep in your head, is your true fortune. Knowledge is the only thing that can't be taken away from you. Reflect on that, Pendleton," he said as he took his leave.

And now, with nothing else to keep him from dealing with Jonathan, Adair stood outside the door to gather his strength for what would certainly be a difficult confrontation. Jonathan was unlikely to agree to betray Lanny, and Adair wasn't sure what leverage he had over him.

He found Jonathan sitting on the edge of the bed. It was difficult to tell, given the dimness, but he appeared to be continuing his metamorphosis, the primordial goo setting into strands of muscle fibers, the fibers knitting together into flesh. His muscular shape was returning, the swelling under his jaw had gone away, the bruises had faded. Adair reminded himself not to let his impatience for progress keep him from marveling at the miracle of Jonathan's transformation. Men disintegrated into dust every day, but how many times in history had one reversed the process?

Adair dropped some clothing on the bed next to Jonathan. The things he had on were disgusting, stiff with dried fluids and smelling of the grave. "Something for you to change into. . . . It won't fit very well, but it will have to do for now. You need a bath, too; that might bring you a way toward feeling human again," Adair remarked as he dragged a chair closer to the bed. "How are you?"

"Little different from the last time you saw me. In my mind, I know I'm Jonathan. Everything is the same. And then I look in the mirror, and I know that isn't true. I was dead, for God's sake. You should've left me alone," he said bitingly.

"So hostile, Jonathan. *I* should be the angry one, don't you think? At least you were dead when they buried you: *you* buried *me* alive." His anger began to rise like mercury in a thermometer, but he tamped it down before proceeding. "Look—we were friends for a while, weren't we, Jonathan? When you lived in my house, I treated you well. It pains me to think I might have to hurt you now. Just tell me where to find her and what name she goes by. That's all I need from you."

"Or what? You'll torture me? Kill me? By all means, go ahead," Jonathan said. "You've no idea how little those threats mean to me."

"You should not take me so lightly. I could break you easily, Jonathan. I sense that you've never really been hurt. Pain can make a man do things that he never thought he'd do."

Jonathan stared at Adair coldly. "I never did understand you, Adair. That's the only way you know how to get what you want, to threaten and hurt. You are strangely inhuman."

"Inhuman? That only goes to show how little you know your fellow man. I am not unlike many of our brothers." Adair pulled his chair uncomfortably close. "We are a brutal lot, we humans, always fighting and clawing for what we want. But you wouldn't know about that, would you? Raised as a little prince, always coddled, especially by the fairer sex. You were not exposed to violence much, I think, whereas the period in which I was raised would be considered very violent by your standards. You could be punished for anything: for displeasing your master, for thinking the wrong thoughts. For taking a crust of bread that didn't belong to you, you might have a hand or foot cut off, or a brand seared into the side of your face, so everyone would know you were a thief. You could even be killed over such a trifle. There was no law, no appeal. And the church was the worst offender: they perfected the practice of torture, you know, trained their own cadre of torturers to assist the inquisitors. I lived through such times, through the epoch age of cruelty. So you may think me inhuman, but I am only applying what I know.

"Did you know that I had invented the perfect device for punishment? I called it the Reformer." Adair brought his face to Jonathan's, their cheeks brushing so he could speak softly and deliberately into his ear. "It was a harness for keeping the body, head, and limbs in the perfect position for the application of certain *sexual* torments. Like a bridle and saddle, it was used for breaking a beast. Only in this case, the beast was a man, not a horse. It was a most effective device for breaking rebellious spirits." He leaned back in his chair and fixed his eyes on Jonathan. "Lanore was put in the Reformer once, did she tell you?"

"No. She never mentioned it."

"I'm not surprised. It's not something you want others to know about you: that men performed every sexual act imaginable with you while you were bound and helpless. But she did endure it, right before I sent her to St. Andrew to bring you to join me in Boston." He felt a sharp pang of regret at revealing this to Jonathan, for shaming Lanore this way. It was a most regrettable incident, and he would take back every hurtful thing he had done to her if he could. But he felt he had to tell Jonathan to impress upon him the seriousness of his predicament and induce him to cooperate.

"Had I known that, I would've come to Boston expressly to hunt you down and torn you apart with my own hands."

Adair let Jonathan's threat hang in the air. He pushed the chair back as he got to his feet. "As I said, I don't want to hurt you, Jonathan. I don't like threatening you, but I want you to understand that there are ways I can hurt you. For instance, I could wait until Lanore's return to humiliate you, if you follow my meaning. To do to you what I have done to her. She should witness what happens to you as part of *her* punishment. After all, she is responsible for it."

Jonathan would not be rattled. "I don't see how you could hold her responsible for *your* actions. It's clearly your choice if you decide to torture me."

"Don't pretend that you don't hold her responsible for what's happened to you. *You* should be cursing her, too, for you have been her puppet the same as I."

"I've hardly been a puppet of Lanny's, unless you think her a very poor puppeteer," Jonathan said. "All she's ever wanted is for me to love her, and as much as she's tried, it's the one thing I've been unable to do."

It was maddening talking to this man. Adair could understand Lanore's frustration in trying to get him to surrender to her. He was as elusive as a snake; it didn't matter how many times you struck, he would always weave between the tines of your pitchfork. Nor had Jonathan risen to the bait. No, Lanny had not been able to make Jonathan her puppet, any more than he had been able to get Lanore to return his affection. *We are all humbled by love*, he thought.

This talk with Jonathan wasn't going at all as he'd hoped. It should've gone easily enough; most people he'd threatened in the past had always done as he asked, eager to avoid pain. Frustrated, Adair felt his anger flare up and threaten to engulf him entirely, and he had to hold fast against the urge to snap Jonathan's neck. "I see what you are up to, Jonathan, with your damned passivity, and it won't work. You make yourself like water, slipping through a man's fingers, impossible to pin down. But you will not goad me into killing you."

Jonathan only gave him an enigmatic smile. "Face facts, Adair: there's nothing you can do to persuade me to help you. You have no power over me, none at all. But there *is* a woman with extraordinary powers—powers much stronger and more absolute than yours—and I must think that once she's gotten over her surprise at my disappearance, she will come looking for me. Have you thought about that?"

TWENTY

BARCELONA

I wandered the city while I waited to hear from Alejandro. My audience with him had not exactly been warm, and his silence left me with the suspicion that he might be buying time in order to act against me. I was too agitated to sit still, so instead of remaining in my suite, where I'd be at the mercy of my fears alone, I walked up and down the streets of Parc du Montjuïc and assessed my situation.

When I told Alejandro that I wanted to be made mortal again, I'd surprised myself. The realization that, like Savva, I might wish to end my life brought me up short. There had certainly been times in my long existence when I'd wished the spell could be lifted or, better still, had never been cast. Usually I'd felt this way when there was a person in my life whom I didn't wish to leave, a man I loved who was growing old and had started to wonder why I wasn't aging with him. That usually triggered an episode of impotent rage against my condition and I would be sad and upset, but eventually the will to live would come back and I would move on. This time, however, I was motivated by fear. I felt profound hopelessness over my situation, and fighting it was exhausting. It left me desperate for release—as desperate as Jonathan had been. I hadn't been able to refuse Jonathan his release; I hoped Alejandro would not be able to deny me, either.

I walked along the waterfront in an effort to still my mind. I found a bench overlooking the harbor and concentrated on chasing away the fearful thoughts. *Think of something else,* I told myself. The strong Catalan sun reminded me of Pisa, the first place Jonathan and I settled after fleeing Boston. Our new life together started out grandly, but could anything withstand the complications that seemed to follow Jonathan wherever he went? I'd prayed that the unwelcome attention and temptations he'd known in Boston would ease—we were in the Old World, surely more sophisticated than the one we knew—and we'd become the couple I'd hoped we'd be. This is what I wanted and expected, the start of a long and happy life together, but it turned out to be the beginning of our end.

PISA, ITALY, 1822

It wasn't easy to convince Jonathan to flee to Europe after we'd imprisoned Adair. He came at me twenty times a day with arguments as to why we should return to our homes and families in St. Andrew. Even after we bought tickets for the European passage, the date of departure set, and our trunks packed, he brought it up again and again, whether we were at the theater for a night's distraction from our troubles or at the window of our hotel room, envying the moon its peace.

"Why not return, at least for a few years?" he'd ask each time. "If nothing else, it will give us the chance to make things right with our families, to see that they'll be able to get by without us. For their sakes, Lanny, not ours. Please."

And so I had to be the hard-hearted one, the one to insist that we could not go back to St. Andrew after we'd left under such damning circumstances. Jonathan and I had disappeared from town the same night, so people likely assumed we'd run off together, though the truth was that I'd used Adair's potion to bring Jonathan back to life after he'd been shot and then whisked him off to Boston as Adair had ordered. Jonathan undoubtedly still felt guilty about leaving his wife, Evangeline, and his daughter, but Evangeline's heart was already broken and our reputations already blackened: returning would only bring the whole mess to the surface again, giving rise to questions we could only answer with lies.

Besides, I knew it would be hard to leave home again once we'd returned, for I'd done it myself. Being with your loving family is no small comfort when you believe you are a monster, and it is terribly hard to leave your home, a place where you belong, to face the unknown. It would be impossible to get Jonathan to leave St. Andrew a second time, even if we were on the verge of being tried as witches.

In the end, Jonathan's arguments didn't matter; they were all trumped by the fear that Adair might follow us to St. Andrew. Jonathan asked me every day if I felt a glimmer of Adair's presence in my mind, but it had decisively disappeared when we'd cast him behind layers of rock and brick.

Our ship landed at Genoa, but we'd decided to press on and ended up in Pisa. Since we knew nothing of the town, we took a room at the first inn we saw, a rustic place that was below our station but convenient enough. The proprietor gave us his best room—best, despite grimy walls and coarse blankets, and feathers working out of the mattress—and bid us good night.

The next day we went into town in search of an English-speaking banker or barrister who could handle the transfer of funds from one of Jonathan's accounts and help get our affairs in order. We returned to the little inn to find an invitation from an English lord to have dinner with him later in the week. We didn't recognize his name, and the only people we knew in Europe had been the other passengers we'd met on the ship. We debated whether to accept the invitation, distrustful of anyone who would invite complete strangers to dinner the minute they set foot in town, and put it aside for the day.

In the morning we found a barrister who spoke English, though he had as difficult a time with our American accents as we had with his Italian one, and at the conclusion of our dealing I thought of the invitation and asked if he knew the host. The barrister wrinkled his nose and called the English lord "a bad man," and gave the impression that we might be thought disreputable if we dined with him. We didn't know what to make of the lawyer's reaction, but by now were desperate for the company of people with whom we could converse. We decided to accept the invitation; at least we'd learn about the town and its inhabitants and then judge for ourselves what company we chose to keep.

On the appointed evening we went to the address on the invitation. From the outside, the house seemed beyond reproach: it was a small palace, beautifully kept, with rosebushes forming a frothy pink border down one flank. As a footman led us to an unlit parlor, I noticed that the house was not as well kept inside as it was outside, as though the occupants didn't care—or had little need—to impress visitors. Books were piled high on tables and even on the floor in wobbling towers. Flowers stood neglected in their vases, dropping petals. A pair of small pug-faced dogs circled excitedly at our heels, and from the cool, darkened parlor a woman's voice called out in heavily accented English to pay the dogs no mind.

She stepped out of the shadows to greet us. The mistress of the house was even younger than I and small, white, and delicate like a camellia. While it was clear that she was a member of the upper class, she gave an impression of sullen indifference, as though her life was forever spoiled and nothing could make it right ever again. "I am the countess Guccioli. Welcome to our home. Please, won't you have a seat?" After her initial wide-eyed surprise at Jonathan's unexpected handsomeness, she did an admirable job of disguising her interest. "Lord Byron will join us in a moment," she said as she fanned herself against the heat. We rustled in our chairs, impressed by our hosts' royal titles and still curious as to why they thought to summon us here.

"How fortunate that you are able to join us this evening," she said. With her strong accent, I couldn't tell if she was being sincere or sarcastic. It was plain that we were of no interest to her: if anything, she seemed mildly annoyed that we'd accepted the invitation from the lord of the manor, as though we were imposing.

In the awkward silence that followed, we all watched as the footman returned with a tray, glasses and pale golden liquid sparkling inside a tall decanter, and the countess was about to force herself to come up with a remark to entertain us when a man rushed into the room.

"Ah, you made it, I see," he observed, stopping for a moment to kiss the countess on her cheek, and I got the impression that there'd be hell to pay if he hadn't. After he introduced himself, he instructed us not to worry about using his title and that we were to call him by his given name, George, or Byron if we preferred.

I was immediately enchanted by Lord Byron. Neither painting nor words could ever truly capture his magnetism. While he might not have been classically handsome—and it was hard to judge any man fairly with Jonathan standing beside him—there was a sensuous interplay between his features that was impossible to ignore. His eyes burned with dangerous intellect, but what was truly mesmerizing was the dissonance between his cool, aristocratic gaze and his almost savage, lush mouth. Even his nose, with a slight patrician's bump, made him more exotic than the average pasty Englishman. I detected a slight limp, but Byron made no acknowledgment of this, and it was only later that we learned he had a clubfoot.

"So good of you to come, despite the mysterious circumstances," Byron said, flashing a twinkling, sly grin first at the countess—who returned it with a grimace—and then at us. "You don't know who we are, we don't know you. . . . Four strangers in a town that's mother to none of us. . . . It's bound to make for an interesting evening, don't you agree?" he asked, reclining on a divan in a striped banyan, which he wore over his shirtsleeves, his fingers stained with ink. "Did you know you're the first Americans to come to Pisa since my arrival? As the city is obviously of little interest to your countrymen, might I ask what has brought you here?"

Jonathan and I exchanged cautious looks: we hadn't yet agreed on a story for Pisa. I assumed we would continue the fiction we'd constructed for the voyage over.

"Is it your honeymoon?" the countess asked.

"Yes," I said at the same moment Jonathan said "No."

"Let me guess," Byron said, warming to the subject. "Are you wayward lovers on the run? If that is the case, you may rest easy for you are in like company, as Teresa and I are living in disgrace here. I am properly divorced, at least, but Teresa has run away from her husband, poor fellow." The countess's doll-like face took on an expression of horror both at his ready disclosure of their delicate situation and his expression of sympathy for her husband. He hurried to explain. "Oh, everyone in town knows of our circumstances, mine and Teresa's. Better you hear it from us. As for the count . . . he is not a bad chap, but not exciting enough to keep the countess's interest, I'm afraid. That's what he gets for marrying a much younger woman." He tipped the glass in his lover's direction before taking a healthy swallow.

"George," she replied archly. "You mustn't tease me like that in front of our guests. They are not acquainted with your wit or your poetic temperament. They do not know how you joke." I got the impression that, far from being the type to disguise his meaning with humor, Byron was unusually forthright, as though it wasn't in his nature to keep from making his opinions known, no matter the topic.

"Of course, my dear," Byron said, rushing to placate her. "Surely, our guests know that I am teasing. All they have to do is take one look at you to know that it would be impossible for any man not to fall truly, deeply in love with you." I squirmed; I did not want to provide an evening's diversion for the couple and wished to hear neither their squabbling nor their fawning.

"So, did you say . . . how you two . . . ?" Byron prompted, pointing first at me and then at Jonathan.

"Yes, yes, you've found us out," I rushed to answer, lest Jonathan contradict me again. By confessing that we were also disgraced and living outside polite society, we endeared ourselves to the poet, and even the countess warmed a bit. Over dinner, Byron elaborated on his tale, explaining that he'd been exiled from his homeland, although he didn't fully explain why. He only hinted of his accomplishments as a poet, perhaps expecting us to already be familiar with his work, and was visibly disappointed when Jonathan confessed that he'd never found much enjoyment in reading.

We stayed at the villa late into the evening, listening to Byron's tales of his tumultuous life, his adventures with other young English poets, and the stories got bawdier as the evening wore on. How Jonathan and I would've liked to tell Byron a story of our own adventures, but we held our tongues and played the role of dull rustics from America.

As we left, agreeing to rejoin our hosts the following evening, I noticed the expression on Byron's face as he looked at Jonathan. It was a look I would see directed at Jonathan from certain men many times in the years to follow (and, if I was truthful, it was a look I'd seen from select men in the village of St. Andrew): a combination of admiration and longing, with a touch of hostility, too, as though they were jealous of what they saw in Jonathan. I wouldn't fully understand until later that Jonathan's intense beauty stirred up longings and fears in some people, who then projected their expectations or resentments onto him. It was a burden he was doomed to carry his entire life.

There, in Byron's curious gaze, I saw that look again: the one that said the British lord wished to know Jonathan in a more intimate way. Because Jonathan never showed any inclination toward men, I worried that one of his admirers might someday seek to destroy what he could not possess. Once I learned more about the infamous Byron—which I did in short order from the gossip-loving residents of the town—I would understand that it was the look of an old desire rekindled, and that Byron was all the things alleged of him.

When I brought up my suspicions to Jonathan that evening, his response was that these were fancies: Byron was a poet and therefore an intense man, but I should not imagine that he harbored some proprietary interest in us. His response made me wonder if he didn't welcome this attention. It might've been simply that he was happy to have someone for companionship besides me, or he might've been impressed by Byron's title and privilege, and I pushed the darker thoughts from my mind.

We went back the next evening, and more evenings than not for the next two weeks, until even Teresa's chill began to thaw. The couple held small dinner parties to introduce us to important towns-people, at least those whose reputations could withstand association with the notorious Byron. I must admit, however, that the best evenings were spent alone with the pair, as the sole recipients of Byron's wit.

I felt that we four were destined for an unorthodox intimacy, our fate driven by Byron (for he seemed compelled to take every aspect of his life to the extreme) as the rest of us simply followed his lead. It started the evening of a terrible summer storm that broke out just as Jonathan and I were leaving their home. Within minutes, the down-pour turned roads into rivers and wind lashed the trees until they sounded like a shaman's rattle, attempting to drive out evil spirits. Being considerate hosts, Byron and the countess insisted we stay the night and somehow—the amount of wine probably was to blame—all four of us ended up in Teresa's chambers, where we lounged on the bed and listened as Byron told more stories and recited verse from memory.

I woke in Jonathan's arms as though he'd guarded my virtue all night, while Byron and his mistress were asleep on the pillows. Obviously, the courtship phase of our friendship was over, and Byron invited us to leave the tumbledown inn and stay at the villa for as long as we wished. We moved that very day.

By the end of summer, Pisan society seemed to have forgiven the four of us—two pairs of illicit lovers living in one household—or perhaps we were too delicious an object of speculation to ignore, and we were again invited to parties and the like. These events reminded me all over again what it was like to be in public with Jonathan, for at each event he was relentlessly hounded by gorgeous, dark-eyed Italian women. They flirted with him behind fans, boldly engaged him in conversation when he stopped at the punch bowl, and dragged him onto dance floors. Even the shiest trailed in his wake like baby chicks, and I wasn't the only one to notice.

We were at one such party when Teresa meandered beside me to watch Jonathan's blessing and curse play itself out once again. "My dear, my heart goes out to you," she murmured to me behind her fan. "The brazenness of those women. . . . It is not as though we are in Venice or Rome, where women can behave quite appallingly, as bad as any man." She exhaled in resignation; there was something that she felt compelled to share with me. "You see, I have been subject to the very same disrespectfulness. It is hard living with George, you understand. He naturally commands great interest wherever he goes. But there are always women who seek him out, women without the slightest interest in his poetry. Poor, confused things, drawn to his brilliance like moths to a flame, though they don't understand why.

"With Jonathan, their interest is not so mysterious." She gave me the smile with which I had become familiar, which I now saw was a smile of pain. "Women see a beautiful man. They have their husbands and their families, but still, they wish to know what it would be like to spend one night with him. One night is all they want, a memory to keep them warm when they are old and ugly and their old, ugly husbands are still chasing young girls," she said.

Her words made me wonder if that's why she was with Byron, so that she could one day find comfort in her memories of when she had been loved by a legendary poet. "We are destined to share the same sorrow, Lanore," she continued. "We are not to blame; we don't choose with whom we'll fall in love. And these men, they know what they are doing. . . . I didn't ask to fall in love with George. He wooed me even though I was married. He saw I was unhappy, yes, but also . . . it is his way. He must have someone close who adores him, someone to witness his every triumph and comfort him at every slight. Without this, he cannot be happy." It wasn't until Teresa lowered her fan that I saw she was crying.

Teresa's sorrows struck so close to my own that I was seized with anger on her behalf, and frustration for myself. How did we come to find ourselves in this same impossible situation? Mine seemed worse, for Jonathan and I were bound to each other for more than just love or companionship, as we had no idea what to expect from the infinite future that stretched before us, and feared the terrible reckoning that was sure to come with Adair.

Weakened, I was ready to quit the party and hide in the safe solitude of my bedchamber, but of course I could not. I had to wait until the others were ready to return home, trying not to follow Jonathan's activity from afar, for it would only cause me further hurt. At one point Byron found me by myself, turned away from the gay crowd, and ushered me onto the dance floor. "You look so sad, my dear. You mustn't let Teresa dampen your spirits; I saw you speaking with her earlier. She is rather good at making others feel whatever unhappiness has seized her at the moment. I do hope you haven't let her get under your skin."

Before I could reply, however, we passed Jonathan, standing beyond the dance floor, trapped by a gaggle of women clustered around him. Lord Byron followed my gaze. "Ahh . . . I see. How tiresome this must be for you, Lanore." Byron's voice was low and knowing. "You mustn't hold it against him. It's not as though he can do anything about it, save wearing a mask in public," he said gently.

"I know." I had told myself this countless times, for all the good it did.

"He doesn't mean to hurt you."

"I don't think he knows of my pain at all. I don't think he even sees me here, hurting. My feelings mean nothing to him."

"Oh, surely not. But you must understand that men look at love differently."

Later, when we returned to the villa, Byron would write these words on the back of my fan, the one that would one day hold court in the Victoria and Albert Museum: *Man's love is of man's life a thing apart, 'tis woman's whole existence.* "A reminder for a day to come, when I am not standing beside you," he teased me. I should have seen—as Byron saw; as Teresa understood—that to be with Jonathan, I had to accept that he would never be mine, not entirely. As much as I wished for it, we would never be each other's complete world, a union of two, protecting and sustaining each other. I wanted to believe it could work between us, that there was a way to change him, as though changing *him* was all it would take.

"It might be time to take our leave," I told Jonathan that night before bed. As convenient as it would have been to stay in Pisa, Lord Byron attracted much interest, and sooner or later Adair would hear that the rogue English lord was housing a spectacularly handsome new friend.

"Whatever you wish," he replied, like a husband who long ago stopped listening to his wife. By his response, I knew Jonathan didn't wish to leave, and he wouldn't actively argue with me over the matter: he simply would take no action whatsoever, and in this way we stayed on and on with Byron and Teresa. Most of the time it was easy to be in their company, each day as intoxicating and sweet as wine laced with honey. Byron regaled us with stories of his travels through Mediterranean countries (and I squirreled away all the details, in case Jonathan and I needed to hide there someday). He told us of a stormy summer spent near Lake Geneva with the poet Percy Bysshe Shelley and his wife, Mary, boating during the day with Shelley, evenings spent outdoing each other with improvised tales and poems. Jonathan warned Byron that he'd get no poems from us, for we were not of that mind, and Byron said it didn't matter, but I wonder now if he wasn't looking to re-create some aspect of that idyllic summer by taking us in.

Byron's mood was as changeable as a winter sky, and it was not uncommon for him to suddenly bolt from our company, upset by a perceived slight. Jonathan was rarely to blame, for he tended to be easygoing around other men, and since Byron was our host, I sought no argument with him. His fights were usually with Teresa, and the pair could be counted on to break into a quarrel at some point in the day, twice if it was especially hot or unpleasant. I can't say it was entirely Teresa's fault, however, as Byron seemed to need discord and fireworks. He lived life so hard—eating and drinking to excess, then doing something sporting in an attempt to trim his waistline (as much as his clubfoot would allow), writing all morning and then tearing his pages into confetti—that it was inevitable that he'd explode in fits of ill-temper and exhaustion.

Often, after one of his outbursts, Byron wanted only Jonathan for company, and the two would disappear for an afternoon or evening. They might go for a ride under the hot Pisan sun, galloping at breakneck speed until both the riders and horses were bathed in sweat, or sup at an inn where Byron could entertain barmaids and patrons alike with stories from his tempestuous life or recite snippets of his poems aloud, dazzling all with his talent and remarkable memory.

It was this way that Jonathan learned of Byron's many stormy relationships with women, usually married women who fell madly in love with him and refused to let him go once he'd tired of fighting with them. He told Jonathan about the scandal that drove him from England, the rumored affair with his half sister, which he denied. No, he much preferred the steadier company of men, he professed, and that was the reason he usually traveled with a companion who shared his love of adventure and could provide a respite from his high-strung lovers. I understood immediately that this was what Byron wanted from Jonathan: he meant to make Jonathan his new companion, and take him along when he'd had his last fight with Teresa and decamped for his next adventure.

During these times when Jonathan and Byron were away and Teresa took to her chamber to nap through the brutal afternoon heat, I snuck into Byron's study to read the new pages of poetry he'd written in the morning. I did this both for pleasure and to look for clues to his possible intentions. I handled the pages gingerly, careful not to smudge ink or mislay them, not wanting Byron to know what I was doing. He was working on *Don Juan,* which was to become one of his masterworks, but aside from finding a passing familiarity between the story's hero and my Jonathan—though I think Byron, the egoist, styled the character after himself—there were no indications of the English lord's intentions.

So I badgered Jonathan, asking him to tell me what he and Byron spoke about during their times away. I suppose I was jealous in a small way, too, for I found the English lord to be fascinating company, so much more fun than Teresa. Finally, one night as we prepared for bed, he seemed ready to relent. He tried at first to brush my questions aside, as though I'd touched on something he meant to hide.

"You didn't tell him the truth about us?" I asked, my alarm growing.

He gave me a dirty look as he pulled his shirt over his head, baring his chest. "What can I say, Lanny? I may have spoken a word here or there about our troubles—nothing of Adair and his bags of tricks; I wouldn't know what to say without making us seem mad.

No, I've only told him a few stories about my childhood, of my family and growing up in St. Andrew. That is all."

"And what did you tell him about St. Andrew?" It was such a quaint town, I could hardly believe it would be of much interest to the worldly Byron, but these were threads he'd given Byron, threads that led back to our true identities.

"We talk about . . . oh, the sorts of things that interest men and . . . he admitted that he was curious about my first sexual encounter." He shook his head at recalling the conversation. "I was near drunk and perhaps I wanted to impress a man as worldly as Byron, for against my better judgment, I told him—" And then he stopped.

"Told him what, for God's sake? It can't be as serious as that. . . ."

He gave me an aggrieved look; how he hated to be prodded. "It was Joanna Kilpatrick, a friend of my mother and frequent visitor to our house, who was my first lover. Oh, Lanny, do not look at me that way. Do not hold me in such contempt before you have heard the rest of the story, for you will have reason enough to despise me then."

I was shocked into silence. I'd always believed Jonathan had spent his virginity on a similarly inexperienced girl his own age, but this wasn't the case, Jonathan explained as he took my hand. He was very young when it happened, thick into puberty, not yet accustomed to the tricks his body played on him. He'd been sent to carry a few things over to the Kilpatricks' house and the lady had seduced him, even as her husband worked in the fields outside their house. Mrs. Kilpatrick had walked right up to him and put a hand on his cock, which had unsettled him.

"She had decided in advance how she would put me in her service, and was determined to secure what she desired," he said, blushing. He ended up on his back on the floor as Mrs. Kilpatrick straddled him, her bodice undone and her skirts gathered around her hips as she rode him. Jonathan had barely buttoned and arranged his clothing and was headed out the door when he ran into Mr. Kilpatrick returning from the fields. Seeing the flushed cheeks of his wife and the boy, and not being a total fool, Mr. Kilpatrick accused his wife of mischief, which she denied. Without proof, the husband reluctantly retreated from his accusations and Jonathan was allowed to make his escape.

I stared at Jonathan, unable to find words. What an unromantic indoctrination into the mysteries of love, to be simply petted to arousal and used like a hook on the wall for Joanna Kilpatrick to scratch her back. I recalled the Kilpatrick woman; she had possessed a strong character and had bullied her way to a position of respectability in the village. It took a determined soul to argue against Mrs. Kilpatrick when her mind was made up. That didn't give her the right, nonetheless, to seduce a young boy, and surely the fiery-haired housewife had taken advantage of other young men as well. My stomach became quite unwell the longer I thought about his confession; Kilpatrick had her pick of the axmen, all living without their wives or sweethearts and grateful for female attention. Why had she turned to Jonathan?

"It was a long time ago. You shouldn't let it trouble you now, not after all we've been through together," Jonathan said to me, and that was true enough: we were hardly a pair of innocent newlyweds, and after all the men and women we each had taken to bed in Adair's house, what was one more? However, the more I thought about it, or tried *not* to think about it, the more it hurt, until tears started rolling down my cheeks.

"Ah, Lanny, don't cry over Joanna Kilpatrick," Jonathan said, lifting me up and setting me on the bed to face him. He took the edge of the sheet to daub my tears. "I'd hoped you would never hear about it."

"I thought you told me everything," I said, reproaching him between sobs. "I thought I was your confidante."

He took a deep breath. "You were, I assure you. But a young man cannot tell everything that he experiences, especially at that age, to a young lady for whom he has feelings. I was trying to shield you."

I should have let our conversation end there—I should have let it lie—but I was still blind to Jonathan's true nature, so I asked a question better left unsaid. "Is there anything else you haven't told me? I want no more surprises. I want honesty between us, Jonathan. Don't ever lie to me, even if you think to spare my feelings."

He took a deep breath and eyed me warily, but took me at my word and proceeded to tell me a tale I wished I'd never heard. For it turned out there was a side to the town of St. Andrew that I never knew: men and women who took their pleasures on the sly, a waltz of secret lovers who danced right under the noses of the rest of us. They did not organize their activities—there were no orgies held like Black Masses in the thick north woods—but rather, they were individuals of a common taste who sought to lighten the burden of their hard lives with illicit sexual consort.

Jonathan was indoctrinated into this group early in his life and admitted to dancing with many partners by the time he was seventeen. He proceeded to name every one of them, for that was what I wanted; hadn't I begged for there to be no secrets between us? Thank goodness none in my family had been drawn into this sect, though it made me wonder if Nevin had an inkling of the darkness Jonathan was involved in, since he'd warned against him so vigorously. Among Jonathan's most shocking admissions: he'd had his own mother-in-law, Katherine McDougal, though it had happened years before his arranged marriage to Evangeline. And he once let Titus Abercrombie, the town tutor, touch his cock in the woods behind the schoolhouse, though he allowed the old man no other liberties. "He wanted it so badly," Jonathan explained, now full of regret, "and I was drunk on the power I held over him."

He moved closer to me and took my hand. "Lanny, you must believe me: I fell under Joanna's influence—quite literally, for it is difficult for a young man to refuse a woman when she has his privates in her hand—and after that I felt, well, do not laugh at me, but I felt shamed, *dirtied* by what I had done. And the veil was lifted from my eyes; it wouldn't be an understatement to say that I was consumed with a desire for pleasure and I realized there was no shortage of women who would accommodate me."

I managed to find my tongue. "So you had no reason to give yourself to me, an unworldly girl—"

"That is not what I meant, Lanny! Do not twist my words," he snapped, though his anger subsided quickly. "I didn't turn to you because my desires seemed so sordid, so base. It seemed fitting that I should satisfy myself with women who had no expectations of me."

"That is why you took up with Sophia." I understood then why Jonathan had started an affair with Sophia, a new bride to an oafish, insufferable husband.

"I didn't expect to come to care for her, to be frank." Sadness passed over his face. "That was the start of our troubles, Lanny, yours and mine. Because if I hadn't chosen that moment of weakness, after Sophia's death, I never would've gotten you pregnant—"

"And my father never would've sent me away to Boston." And . . . neither of us needed to go on. We sat lost in somber thoughts at the recollection of the demon we were sure was on our trail.

Our time with Byron and the countess ended a week later. As for my premonition that Byron had designs on us, there was one night when we four ended up in bed together, drunk and behind a barred door, safe from inadvertent discovery by a servant. Surprisingly, the evening passed tamely, for Teresa would not let Jonathan have her, and Byron seemed content to observe Jonathan swive me with great gusto. Perhaps all the poet wanted was to see Jonathan in his natural glory, for Byron scarcely looked away as we coupled.

Days later, Byron told us he was decamping for Genoa; he had tired of living in a fishbowl, he claimed, with all eyes in the village upon him. He smiled at us like a fox, hope gleaming in his eyes. "You're welcome to come with us. I've been invited to borrow a friend's villa. There's room for all." To my great relief, Jonathan declined the invitation, and by week's end we were on our way to the next unknown destination. But in the course of that summer, the damage had been done. Watching Byron and Teresa made only too clear what future unhappiness awaited me—while not blameless, Jonathan would always be trapped by his beauty the way Byron had been trapped by his notoriety—and we struck off on our own again, our fragile relationship well on its way to crumbling past the point of salvation.

TWENTY-ONE

BOSTON

After his last encounter with Jonathan, Adair avoided him for an entire day. He kept to his room, where he scoured his books for a mention of this queen, and to the parlor, where—unable to shake his unease—he scowled down on passersby from the huge front window. He resisted the urge to see how Jonathan was coming along. He still smarted from Jonathan's last remark, that this mysterious and powerful deity was sure to be surprised by his disappearance and would come looking for him.

Adair knew that he'd acted hastily in bringing Jonathan back from the dead. He wanted to believe that, under other circumstances—if he'd merely been conducting an experiment, for instance, or testing a new spell—he'd have been more patient. He'd have researched the spell's provenance and brushed up on each ingredient's properties; in short, he would have prepared thoroughly and known exactly what he was getting into. But he'd rushed to use magic, like a novice who doesn't know the danger and blunders foolishly into the unknown, and now he would suffer for it.

Jonathan's enigmatic reference to a woman with extraordinary powers had rattled Adair. She wouldn't be a flesh-and-blood woman, of course, but then he was hard-pressed to envision what she *would* be. Most likely an entity of some kind, a demon or djinn, if there were such things—though he'd never encountered one in his dealings. If she was, indeed, the force that kept the worlds of the dead and living from ever meeting, she would be another type of being altogether. She would be among the most powerful forces in nature, an entity that might be thought of as a deity.

Only now did he realize his folly: he'd made a grave error by provoking such a force without protecting himself first. It was like calling a tsunami forth without making sure you were a safe distance from the shore. Practitioners of the dark arts wrapped themselves in spells or stood in elaborate circles of charms to be safe from the spirits they unleashed, but he hadn't thought any precautions would be necessary—not to wrest one soul back from the afterlife. But that soul was Jonathan, and nothing about Jonathan could ever be ordinary, apparently. Adair blamed himself for not looking beyond the obvious, not imagining that extraordinary measures might be required.

If this queen of the underworld came looking for Jonathan, as Jonathan seemed to feel she would, Adair could see no choice but to let her take him. A damnable outcome, after all this trouble, and he struggled to come up with a way to keep this from happening. He was, after all, the ultimate lure for Lanore. She wouldn't let hell itself stop her from coming to him if she knew he was alive. It pleased Adair to imagine her shock at learning Jonathan was in his custody. She would be desperate enough to do whatever he asked. But as with everything worthwhile, this, too, came at a price: Adair would have to witness her absolute *elation* at seeing Jonathan again, and be crushed to know that she'd never feel that way for him.

As for taking possession of Jonathan's perfect form, he was ready to admit that the body was beyond redemption and would never be fit to occupy. Better to release it and send the gigolo back to his mistress than to wait for *her* to come for him. Adair permitted himself no regrets. He was a scientist; it had been an experiment and it had failed. He would learn from this and move on, if that's what it came to.

Adair struggled with his doubts as he stood once again outside the room that held Jonathan. Objectively, he knew that bringing Jonathan back from the dead was one of his greatest feats, and yet it felt as though he had failed. And instead of being furious—for he hated failure above all things—Adair wished he could put everything aside and befriend Jonathan again, as though nothing had ever happened.

He knew he shouldn't let his guard down around Jonathan. He was a tricky fellow. After all, he'd helped Lanore banish him behind a stone wall, proof that he could be as merciless as she. However, just as Adair was finding it difficult to harden his heart against Lanore, he felt drawn to Jonathan, too, and found himself craving his companionship. He attributed his strange melancholy to exhaustion—and loneliness.

Another odd consequence, Adair noticed, was that although he desired Jonathan's company, it was difficult to be around him for long. Within minutes, he would feel an overwhelming urge to flee. It wasn't a matter of being nervous. It was more like panic, but he knew of no reason why he should have this reaction to Jonathan, and could only think it had to do with Jonathan's proximity to the next world.

Adair wanted no part of the afterlife. He was sure that hell awaited him after death. The judgment he was sure to face in the afterlife was the only thing he had left to fear. Despite being secure in his immortality and confident that he'd cast the spell correctly, Adair had always known there would be an end for him. That day might not come until the sun swallowed the earth, when time itself collapsed and the fabric of the universe finally unraveled, but he'd always felt in his bones that there would be this final reckoning. Nothing he'd done would be forgotten, and he'd be held accountable for all his sins and crimes.

When he knew he could avoid Jonathan no longer, Adair pushed the door open without knocking, to find Jonathan still sitting at the end of the bed, as immobile as a doll placed on a shelf. Again, Adair felt his nerves called to attention, tingling. His stomach twisted with a nameless anxiety, but he would not be deterred. "Come with me," Adair commanded.

Adair led Jonathan up a staircase that brought them to the rooftop garden. The space had been made into an outdoor room, complete with miniature trees and leafy green plants, furniture and lighting. Although a gardener kept the plantings trimmed and neat and the housekeeper kept everything spick-and-span, it had developed a forlorn air from disuse. After two centuries without a glimpse of the heavens, Adair ventured out whenever possible for a taste of nature, and found that the view from here was the best in the house. And sure enough, that night the sky was a luxurious expanse of purple with pinpoints of white, as beautiful as anything he'd ever seen. He sat and gratefully absorbed the night sky's quiet energy for a moment.

Under the starlight, Adair saw that Jonathan's transformation had continued and he almost looked like his former self again. His face had undergone a change, something Adair couldn't put his finger on, but whatever it was, it threw off the once-pleasing, classical proportions. His perfect face was perfect no more. It was more interesting, however. It made him seem like the kind of person a stranger wouldn't hesitate to approach, as opposed to the imposing beauty he had been before. He'd changed in other ways, subtle but undeniable. He had an ethereal quality that he didn't have before, almost as though he'd transcended his earthly body. He seemed lighter than air.

They sat in garden chairs and stared at the canopy of heaven for a while before Adair felt ready to present his case. "Lanore's trail has run cold. I can be patient no longer, Jonathan. I need you to tell me everything you know."

Jonathan hesitated for a moment. "I've been gone for months.

Anything I know is useless by now. She must feel your presence and knows that you're free. She'll be using a different name, and I doubt she'd go back home."

"It doesn't matter. Give me anything you have. The name you know, the address of her house. . . ." He thought of Pendleton and the hacker, and the miracles they'd been able to perform with only a tiny bit of information. He wanted to remain optimistic.

Jonathan shook his head. "I'm sorry. I can't help you."

Adair expected to feel rage bubble up inside him at Jonathan's refusal, yet it did not. There wasn't an inkling of the familiar white-hot anger, not in his head, not in his heart. Instead, he was flooded with despair, undone by his need for Lanore. Whether she meant to or not, she'd altered him and he was disturbed by this profound change. He was so weakened by the prospect that she was lost to him forever that he couldn't imagine going on without her. The depth of his devastation shocked him.

Only one choice remained, and that was to ask Jonathan for his help. If anyone knew the secrets to Lanore's heart, it would be him, and yet . . . Adair couldn't imagine asking. Adair was unaccustomed to *asking* for anything: he'd always taken what he desired, at any cost, whether it was the life of someone who possessed knowledge that he craved, or the maidenhead of a comely girl fate put in his path. How ironic that he was now reduced to confiding in Jonathan, his former rival, a man who had never truly loved Lanore and had taken her love for granted. It seemed that fate would not spare him this indignity; as a matter of fact, it seemed to Adair that fate was going to considerable lengths to humble him.

Adair sighed, his breath as heavy as water. "I need your help, Jonathan. I won't harm Lanore, I swear. I'm not looking for revenge. I only want to see her again. Lanore has changed me somehow. I can't think of her without going weak. I am helpless before her, if you can imagine. I admit that I spent decades behind that cursed wall, planning exactly what I would do to her when I found her. I wanted to break her neck; I wanted to hear her beg for my mercy. I thought about subjecting her to torments that now sicken me. To think that I ever contemplated doing such things to her! I *cannot* hurt her, Jonathan: I love her. Even the thought that someone might harm her alarms me. I only want to see her again, I give you my word."

He braced for laughter, for Jonathan to ridicule him, but Jonathan did neither of these things. He sat quietly and seemed to turn the thought over in his mind before he said, "People don't change, Adair. The world just changes around them. Why should I believe what you've told me?"

Adair drew back from him. "How can you say that people do not change? Look at you. The Jonathan I knew could love no one more than he loved himself, and yet eventually you fell in love and wed, and came to feel love as deeply and selflessly as Lanore. Can you not accept that I have changed as well? I would think my behavior would be proof enough. Do I seem like a man seeking revenge? Have I done anything to hurt you? I've admitted my weakness to you: what more evidence do you need?"

Jonathan let slip a half smile. "True, I wouldn't think such vulnerability possible of you or, if you're lying, that you'd be able to do so this convincingly. I almost believe that you're telling the truth."

Adair felt a wave of gratitude wash through him at Jonathan's words. He was being whipsawed by his emotions, moved so profoundly and intimately that he would not have thought another person could understand what he was going through. And yet Jonathan did, and believed him, and Adair took great comfort from this. He then realized how rarely he confided in *anyone* about anything. He'd not had a confidant for as long as he could remember.

Jonathan shifted his gaze to the starlit sky. "I think you are being honest with me. You *have* changed, Adair. And you're right that she's weakened you. . . . You're no longer the ogre that you were. But that's what love does. If it makes you strong in some ways, it makes you weak in others. What you gain, you lose elsewhere."

You lose elsewhere. The corners of Adair's mouth twitched; perhaps more than just his emotional state was being affected. After all, it was probably all connected, his mental and physical state and his extraordinary powers. He hadn't thought that his power might depend on the hardness of his heart or the iron of his will. He'd spent centuries building upon his knowledge of the physical world and cultivating a special kind of energy from the unseen one. But it was possible that he was now frittering it all away with the effort of finding Lanore. Perhaps he couldn't afford to be in love.

And yet, his need to see her was undeniable. He had to find her and look at her, touch her skin and stand in her presence one more time, even if it used up the last of his strength, even if it killed him. He couldn't believe that pursuing Lanore would be the death of him; to the contrary, he sensed that being with her would bring him back to the way he was before, whole and strong.

"Jonathan, all I know is that I *must* see her. No one knows Lanore's heart better than you. Now that you know I intend her no harm, tell me how to win her."

As little as Adair cared to be pitied, he was glad to see Jonathan's expression soften. "Well . . . first, you must accept that she may never love you, Adair. Too much may have transpired between the two of you for her to ever trust you. Without trust, there cannot be love."

"I will prove to her that she can trust me."

"That alone may take an eternity."

"I will wait," Adair insisted with palpable determination.

"You must also accept that there is nothing you can do to *make* Lanny love you. Love comes from within. A woman's love is an amazing and humbling thing. You've seen it in Lanny: her love is fierce. But *she* has to choose *you*, Adair."

"She will. I know you doubt this, but she loved me once, a little." Adair wasn't sure if he said this to reassure Jonathan or himself. "That time with Lanore . . . was the closest I have ever felt to being loved," he said. The recollection of that feeling made him momentarily happy, though at the same time he wished he might burst into flames and burn to ash to be spared this humiliation.

"Yes. That's the power of our Lanny: she can love the unlovable. I speak from experience," Jonathan said.

"So tell me: how do I get her to give me another chance?"

Jonathan smiled ruefully. "This will be the tricky part. You must show her that you're worthy of her. If you want her to love you, you must be the sort of man she could love. For Lanny, it's not like you'd have to become a saint. There is that temper of yours, though: you'd have to do something about that. But the one thing Lanny demands is fidelity. She must come first in your heart."

Adair frowned. "She's known me to have other lovers and has even been with them as well."

"You weren't asking her to love you then, were you? If you wish for her to make you the epicenter of her world, you must do the same."

Adair ticked over Jonathan's words, captured in his head. Fidelity, trust, sacrifice. "This change is no small thing," he said finally.

"No, but it will make you a better man."

"But how will I find her?"

"You have the answer. It's inside you," Jonathan said simply. "I think if you search your heart, you'll find it."

Adair's temper flared. "Don't speak in riddles. If you know what I must do, tell me plainly."

"I've told you all I know. And you feel the truth in it, don't you?" Jonathan continued. "You've always had the power to find her; it's been with you all this time. You've only had to wish for it."

"Wish for it?" As unlikely as this sounded, Adair felt a stirring in his heart that made him think it might be true.

"I've told you everything I know. And I am taking you at your word, Adair, that you will do her no harm. You would do well to remember that. Mark my words."

Adair placed a hand over the spot where his heart should be. "I promise you: I will do her no harm."

TWENTY-TWO

At least Jonathan's words gave Adair hope, though he wasn't sure how he was going to track Lanore down, let alone win her affections once he'd found her. She could be anywhere in the world. He wondered if his subconscious might be aware of her on some level and, if so, if there was a way to access it. The technique of projection came to mind, and he wondered if this altered state might lead him to the answer he sought. In all his years behind the wall, he'd tried to do it many times and failed. He had heard stories of Adepts who could project their consciousness out of their bodies, freeing them to roam far corners of the world, even other planes of existence, or so it was claimed. If he remembered correctly, practitioners often relied on external help—such as drinking a potion, or taking hallucinogens, or conjuring up visions in a soothsayer's bowl—to get any results. Adair had managed to attain deep meditation only during his imprisonment, but never the experience of completely freeing his consciousness. Yet Jonathan had said that the power to find Lanore was inside him, which made him think that he'd needed nothing more than his own mind to free himself all along.

To tap into his inner self, it was generally best to find a place of total stillness, like a monk retreating to a cave to pursue enlightenment. He could cheat on the darkness—it was impossible to block out all light given the surplus of windows in this house—but the walls needed to be able to dampen all sound and even block the movement of air, if possible. According to the stories he'd heard, waking in the middle of a projection was dangerous. Your consciousness could end up trapped in some netherland. The old practitioners would have a trusted attendant standing by who could be summoned by a predetermined signal—the ringing of a bell or a series of claps—in case the subject became disoriented coming out of his trancelike state. Although he had neither sealed chamber nor trustworthy attendant, Adair would not be deterred.

He decided to try right away, without hallucinogens or soothsayer's bowl. If he failed, he could consult his books and try again, but he was impatient, his curiosity piqued by Jonathan's words. He locked the door to his bedroom and lay still on his bed.

It was hard to quiet his mind after the talk with Jonathan. His thoughts wanted to race ahead. Adair concentrated on his breathing, clearing his mind, sinking further and further into pure thought. Deeper he went, until he left his body behind, until he felt he had no corporeal boundaries at all. He felt as though he had thinned and become dispersed like a cloud of gas or a spray of foam carried on the tides. He tried not to notice his surroundings in this abstract world, as it might distract him and break the trance. As it turned out, he needn't have worried, because he seemed suspended in a pale gray mist, and he gave over to being a shapeless creature, drifting contentedly.

A tug stopped his drifting and he fell like a leaf from a tree, settling gently to earth. He could tell he was in a different place by the feel of the air, its temperature and sensation on his skin. He opened his eyes, wondering where he'd ended up and if he'd found the right place.

He was in a city. That much was clear from his surroundings, a row of impressive three-story town houses that stood shoulder to shoulder, smothering the street in shadow. It was a quiet street, the kind of place where neighbors might watch what went on from behind their curtains. Whether this was a fabrication of his mind, the manifestation of a vivid dream, or a real city, like New York or London, he couldn't tell. He tried to ignore his uncertainty and remain present in the moment.

Another gentle tug guided Adair toward the building directly in front of him. Five stone steps led to a front door with a large glass windowpane encased in an ironwork frame of delicate arabesques behind which the occupant could see without being seen. He knew right away that it was Lanore's house. When Adair placed his hand on the doorknob, he was amazed to feel her presence in the metal. Touching the doorknob was like touching her hand.

Inside, he detected a scent that he associated with Lanore, her musk making a part of his brain fire excitedly, re-creating the feeling of being in her presence. She felt so real, so present, that he expected her to walk around a corner or to hear her voice carry down the staircase, and when neither happened, he felt his loneliness more profoundly than before. Coming here, where he could feel her presence again, proved to him that he had changed—he was now susceptible to loneliness and sadness. He didn't like this change; it hinted of weakness and impairment. *It's Lanny's fault; she's crippled me,* he thought. His anger flared once but died as quickly as it came. This new inhibition on his rage, at least where Lanore was concerned, still confounded him, like walking into a wall where there'd always been a door.

Love. It had corrupted him.

A quick intake of breath, like a snowflake pushed by the breeze, and he was in the front hall. It was hushed, like a funeral parlor. A large pedestal table stood on a priceless oriental rug, under a chandelier fit for a ballroom. On the table, there was a pile of unopened letters, the return address on all of them a lawyer in Boston. So many letters, and she had ignored them all. As Jude had explained when they'd puzzled through the miracle of Adair's release, the city most likely had sought to notify her of its intention to raze the mansion to make way for a highway. That notification was undoubtedly contained in these letters, which she'd studiously ignored. Adair wondered if, on some level, Lanore had suspected what they were about and might have wanted to see him freed, even if she could not bring herself to do so by her own hand. He felt a brief stirring of hope that his cause was not entirely lost.

The room he wanted to see first was Lanore's bedroom, saving the less intimate rooms of the house for later. He only had to wish it and he was there instantly, in a room dimmed by heavy curtains with walls painted the color of forest mushrooms. Her bed was an antique, Swedish, made up with silk sheets and its pillows still dented where her head had last rested. The sight of the bed saddened him, to be here in this place among her things, inhaling her smell. Adair stood with his gaze fixed on the indentation on the pillow made by her delicate head and felt the immensity of the task ahead of him. Proving his love as well as his worthiness to Lanore would take time—an abundance of time—the one thing they had in common.

On one nightstand was a collection of stray objects: an ancient Chinese teacup holding three loose pearls; a small book, slightly bigger than a woman's hand, *Madame Bovary*, a first edition from 1856; a handmade paper rose. On the other nightstand was evidence that another person—a man—shared the bed with her: a pair of drugstore reading glasses; a plastic dispenser of dental floss; a jar of liniment; a magazine with glossy pictures of men playing various field sports. Adair put a hand to that side of the bed, then staggered to sit as a surge of jealousy overcame him.

He went to one of the dressing rooms, the one that was obviously hers. Empty hangers and gaps along the clothes rod suggested that she had packed for a trip. He fingered wispy panels of fabric hanging from padded hangers, delicate pieces made of silk and lace, the touch of such feminine fabrics exciting him. He held one of her blouses to his nose: no trace of perfume, but there was her scent again. He rubbed his face in the garment, wishing he were a hound, able to track her down by smell alone. Her scent settled on his tongue and it was as though he could taste her, taste the tang of the skin of her inner thighs, the dewy undersides of her breasts. He felt the urge to wrap an item of Lanore's clothing around his member and stroke himself, but he released the blouse and willed the moment to pass.

Down the hall, Adair found storage rooms that had been half emptied of treasure, judging by a list left on a shelf cataloging the shipping dates of various items. He picked through the things that were left, examining each item as he came upon it: a pair of lush silver beaux arts serving utensils made to resemble looping lilies; a primitive-looking saber in a horsehide sheath; a crown fitted for a child's head. A stack of old photographs on a shelf. He didn't recognize the people in most of them, but then he stopped at one, a crumbling, faded image of a posed group from the turn of the last century, everyone heavily dressed as though for a skating party. He recognized her right away, even though she was nearly buried under a great fur hat and coat, a cocky expression on her upturned face, daring in her eyes. When had this picture been taken, and who were the other people? He had missed so much of her life, he realized with a pang of regret.

Downstairs, he found a desk in the corner of a room where it appeared Lanore tended to her correspondence. Adair pulled the drawers open one at a time and found nothing but stationery and postage stamps. Then, in the bottom drawer under an ancient dictionary, he found photographs of Jonathan. Jonathan in bed, his face half buried in a pillow, dark hair falling across a stubbled cheek; Jonathan driving an automobile and smiling lovingly at the photographer in the passenger seat; Jonathan, the picture of good health and with an expression of utter contentment on his face, taken days before Lanore would end his life.

Up until now he'd found no written documentation of her life, the bits of information that might lead him to her, but he finally discovered a small trove in a tiny cabinet tucked beneath the desk. It was locked, but he pried the door back with his hands, then pulled out files and began flicking through the papers. How strange to see the complexity of a person's life summarized in stacks of documents like this. Of course, for Adair, the record of his life was lost many times over, but he'd trained himself over the centuries to travel light. Unsentimental about most things, he preferred to remain a mystery.

He started by reading through her letters, reaching into opened envelopes, unfolding stationery and greedily skimming through the words contained therein, but was disappointed when it was mostly business correspondence. No invitations to parties or salons. No handwritten cards from friends, no gossip of the antics of guests at dinner the night before. A few bank statements, a letter from a government office seeking additional payments of some kind. A few notices for another woman, Annette Blanchard—perhaps her last pseudonym. . . . He noted the name to give to Pendleton.

Next, he fetched the fat stack of unopened letters in the hall. They were all from a lawyer in Boston, the earliest one sent to Lanny years ago. Adair read each letter in chronological order and came to understand the miracle of his release. It was as Jude had guessed: the state had sought to raze the mansion to make way for a highway project, and the entire neighborhood was to be destroyed. When she did not reply, the lawyer was unable to protect Lanore's interests. By doing nothing, she had ensured Adair's release.

At first he thought her a fool. How could the clever Lanore be so careless with such an important matter? *Unless* . . . he wondered if something else had been at play: her subconscious desire. He'd seen it before, after all: at a successful night at the gaming tables, a man might suddenly start making tactical choices that put him out of the game. Or during a siege, a noble made a decision that gave the opponent a means to sneak into the fortress. Perhaps seized by fatalism,

Lanny had allowed her house to be destroyed in order to force a reso-
lution. Perhaps she was exhausted by having a sword of Damocles
hanging over her and wished for it to be over.

He pulled another letter from its envelope: it was an invitation to
speak at a museum a year ago on the subject of ancient Chinese tea-
cups, of all things. Adair puzzled at the oddity of her choice area of
expertise; what in the world could've transpired to make Lanore an
expert on such an arcane topic? It implied that she'd been to China,
and not on a casual vacation. It was entirely possible that she'd lived a
lifetime there, and for a moment Adair was struck by the realization
that the woman he sought had been replaced by a woman with two
hundred years of experiences of which he knew nothing. Very likely,
Lanore had become a woman who had, in some small way, made
amends that might ameliorate the terrible things she'd done earlier in
her life, such as shutting him up in the wall.

As he shifted through the letters, Adair was suddenly struck that
there was no mention of men. One false name, Emily Bessender,
appeared everywhere, but there was no Mr. Bessender in the correspondence, nothing to explain the unnamed male presence in her
bedroom—or of any other man, for that matter. This struck Adair
as odd behavior for Lanore. He flipped letters over, looking for a
name scrawled on the backs, a name doodled absently in the corners.
Nothing.

He leaned back on the couch and stared at the stacks of correspondence on the coffee table, where he'd smoothed out folded papers
and tried to put them in some sort of order, unsuccessfully. They were
the letters of a woman who was foreign to him and were, frankly,
disappointing. Where were the passionate love letters? The unreadable scrawl of a man driven to madness by her beauty, her fickleness,
her games? Where were the pledges of undying love and promises of
long days of lovemaking, of time spent only in each other's company?
Had Lanore forsaken love once Jonathan had left her? It didn't seem
possible. Adair scrambled to find an explanation for her inscrutable

behavior and, finding none, pushed the stacks of paper to the floor in frustration.

He stood back and tried to recall what Jude was always saying to him: *Everything is done electronically.* Adair searched the house until he found a laptop in one of the storage rooms. It was clunkier than Jude's machines, and once the computer had come to life, Adair looked at the dates of the files and found that the records were several years old. There was information of value, drafts of letters and copies of documents, but not much that would help him now.

He went back to the bedroom and rifled through drawers for the man's belongings in hopes of finding identification or some clue as to his identity. All of his clothing and toiletries were new, as though he'd come from nowhere, as though he had no past and Lanore had created him from the elements like a golem.

Finally, Adair found what he was looking for: a few pieces of documentation kept in the drawer that held his socks. An official-looking letter with the seal of the French republic . . . a copy of a visa request. Adair squinted at the name on the paper: Lucas Findley. The back of his mind itched. He had heard it before in conjunction with Lanore. . . . Yes, when he was in the town of St. Andrew. The rustics in the restaurant had given him this name, too: the doctor who had helped Lanore escape. *Of course,* Adair thought, *of course she would keep him around*—and wondered why it hadn't occurred to him earlier, why he hadn't given this name to Pendleton. . . . Maybe he really had lost his focus after his imprisonment. There could be any number of possible explanations for where she was, what she was doing, and who she was with, but the name Lucas Findley seemed right to him.

He felt more nameless anxiety as he walked through the house wondering what he might've missed, pacing circles around the first floor and coming to a stop in a back hall, in front of a framed charcoal portrait of a man. A long second passed before he realized it was the drawing he'd commissioned of Jonathan. Lanore had taken it from the mansion. Even from the smudged image on the page,

Jonathan's outlandish beauty taunted Adair, his insufferably handsome face jolting him like a poke in the eye. The portrait had been
done shortly after Jonathan joined the household, his arrogance and
petulance captured to perfection by the artist. And yet, for all of
Jonathan's weaknesses, Lanore had chosen him—chosen to endure
his ill treatment of her over accepting Adair's love.

And now she was with this doctor, an ordinary man with nothing special to offer. It was too humiliating to bear. He took the picture down from the wall. Gripping the picture frame, he smashed it
against his knee. The frame broke into splinters, the glass into slivers
and shards. Adair pulled the drawing itself out of the frame and,
in one long stroke, tore it in half. His chest tightened, his temples
pounded. Her beautiful little nest, where she lived with this foolish
doctor, mocked him. Rage sparked inside of him, the inhibition that
held his anger against her in check lifted for an instant, and it took
nothing to make his wish real. *Burn it all,* he thought. *Burn the house
down. Leave her nothing to return to.* His last image as he drifted up
and away was of long orange flames licking the walls, greedily devouring everything in their wake.

TWENTY-THREE

BARCELONA

Two days later, an envelope, elegant and luxurious to the touch, awaited me at the front desk. There were no markings on the outside except my name in a neat, tiny script. I pulled out the folded sheet inside:

> *My dearest Lanore,*
> *You must forgive my lapse of manners in leaving you without diversion for the past few days. You must enjoy the hospitality of my house while you are in town. Please join me tonight for dinner. My car will pick you up at eight o'clock.*
>
> *Sincerely,*
> *C*

The *C* was a beautiful work of calligraphy, done by a practiced hand. I turned the envelope and the sheet of stationery over but there was no address, no phone number, nor any other way to contact him. My acceptance was a foregone conclusion.

There was no thought that I wouldn't attend, but as I dressed for the evening, I was apprehensive. There was the rather sinister manner in which the invitation had been extended—summoning me with a handwritten note carried by an unseen messenger—and I had to wonder if Alejandro had done this deliberately in homage to our mutual past, or because he took comfort from indulging in the old ways: paper correspondence delivered by a footman, sending a carriage for a lady.

Secondly, I was still ashamed from our initial reunion. It never occurred to me that the others—Alejandro, even Tilde and Dona— would be anything but overjoyed to be free of Adair. In the panic of fleeing with Jonathan and figuring out how to make my way in the world, I didn't think the others would be faced with this same dilemma. I felt I'd done them a great favor as the architect of their escape, never once thinking they were content living in Adair's company, and yet, here I felt like a criminal whose past had caught up to her.

Lastly, I couldn't shake the feeling that Alejandro had used the past few days not to try to decide whether to forgive me but to figure out a way to hand me over to Adair. It was clear from Alejandro's reaction that he'd never suspected me of being responsible for Adair's disappearance; he seemed too shocked when I made my confession to have faked his surprise. If Adair was free, he hadn't yet spoken to Alejandro. I reminded myself that Alejandro had been the kindest of the group, unable to overcome his sensitivity even though it had been a liability among Adair's companions. I trusted that Alej's tendency would hold out for a few more days and I could wait that long to see if he had anything for me.

A silver Mercedes appeared magically at the appointed time, like Cinderella's carriage, and carried me through the streets of Barcelona to an outlying neighborhood. It pulled through the gates of an old estate, and I was let out at the front of the house. Oddly, the solemn front doors were slightly ajar, so I stepped into the hall, which was as cool and dark as a crypt. Still, there was no one there to receive me and the house seemed unoccupied. Already uneasy, I was ready to retreat when I saw a figure at the end of the long hall coming toward me: Alejandro. His footsteps on the marble floor were the only sounds in the house; there appeared to be no servants, or perhaps they were otherwise occupied and discreet as mice. Alej could have been indulging his taste for the dramatic by staging an entrance, or perhaps it was another contrivance meant to put me on edge.

"Lanore! So good of you to accept my invitation. I've been on pins and needles, afraid you might disappoint me," he said, taking my arm and tucking it under his.

"I would've called to tell you I was coming, but I had no way to get in touch. No address, no telephone number," I teased, watching for his reaction, but he gave me nothing but his enigmatic smile. His appearance, too, revealed a shade more of his eccentricity. Gone was the sedate clothing he'd worn in his studio, the quiet clothing that let him fade into the background. Tonight he wore a mishmash of styles and periods: a jacket cut like a frock coat but made of tapestry, the fabric shiny from age; a satin shirt in the Cossack style; faded black jeans; and a crocheted pillbox cap, the kind I'd seen worn in northern African countries. All plucked from his wardrobe, no doubt, each a precious memory of another time.

"I didn't mean to be so secretive. It's just that I like my privacy, you see, and rarely give my address to anyone, and I suppose it's gotten to be a habit. I didn't mean to frighten you. It was just an oversight, I assure you," he said, patting my hand.

"And where are your servants? You don't live here alone, do you?" I peeked into rooms as we passed open doors, hoping to see someone putting out a tray of liqueurs or tidying up.

"Oh, yes, of course I have servants, but I've asked them to leave us alone tonight as much as possible so that we might feel free to talk about old times and our *secret*. It's a rare occasion that I get to be myself with anyone—I'm sure you feel the same way—so I thought to keep it as intimate as possible. There should be no other people on earth tonight, just us two." I smiled at him, but my heart was sinking bit by bit. Had he gone a bit mad, poor Alejandro? His outlandish dress, a mania for secrecy? Like Savva, it seemed that the world had exacted its toll from him.

Alejandro took me on a tour of the rooms, making an occasional remark about one object or another, but otherwise leaving me to take in what I saw on my own. I was struck by the similarity to my house in Paris in that it was stuffed with mementos of Alejandro's previous lives. It wasn't as ramshackle as my home had been, however; Alejandro had a more discerning eye and kept only beautiful pieces, and edited his collection so the overall effect was more harmonious than the unrestrained cacophony of my residence. However, unlike at my house, his collection seemed to lack sentimentality—no faded ticket stubs or theater programs to remind him of outings with long-dead friends, no moth-eaten sweater worn by a former lover—but that was Alejandro: polished exterior with his cards pressed close to the vest. The rooms seemed more like set pieces than a reflection of himself: what he wished his life had been, instead of what it was.

Seeing that he, too, had surrounded himself with possessions, substitutes for people and love that was gone from his life, made me sad for him. "So, what else do you do besides photography, Alej?" I asked at last, daring to break the hush. "Tell me, is there someone in your life?"

He pressed my arm firmly to his side as though I might try to escape. "Oh, my poor Lanore. Is that still your measure for happiness? Are you only happy when there is someone to share your bed or the breakfast table?"

I was surprised by his response: is that what he thought of me? "That might have been true in the past, but don't forget, Alejandro, I was practically a girl at the time. Twenty years old, and I'd led such a sheltered life, never expected to have to be on my own. Since then I've been on my own quite a lot; I suppose we all have. Everyone else comes and goes. Anyway, it's not the worst way to live—is it—to share your life with someone? I'm only saying that it would be a shame if you were alone, Alej, when you have so much to offer."

His expression remained guarded. "It is kind of you to be concerned for me, but you needn't worry. I'm not alone, except when I choose to be." He continued leading the tour, stopping at one room or another to show me his treasure, each piece worthy of the best museums in the world. We lingered for only a second outside his bedroom, long enough for me to take in the lush but forlorn still life of panels of burl wood and silk draperies, a clutch of bloodred poppies in a vase at the bedside. It was a beautifully composed room, but the bed, surrounded with pillar candles and bowls and incense burners, seemed more like an altar, a platform, or a stage than a place for rest. As a matter of fact, it reminded me in no small way of Adair's bedchamber.

Dinner was laid out in a large, formal dining room, the two settings placed together at one end. I had yet to see a servant, but someone had set out covered dishes still hot to the touch. Alejandro had put together an exotic menu: there was a bowl of tiny slivers of something pink, fried to a crisp, that turned out to be quail tongues; poached turtle eggs; and a salad bright with purple morning glories. I pointed to the latter and exclaimed, "But they're poisonous!" and he laughed and replied, "Not to us. You should try one; they're delicious. So many things that are poisonous turn out to be quite tasty. The liver of the blowfish is the best part, but it's also the deadliest."

"Where do you even find quail tongues?" I asked, using a small pair of silver tongs to disentangle a tongue from the rest.

"It was one of my favorite dishes when I was a child," he explained as he gently slid a softly poached turtle egg onto his plate. "I keep a covey of them in the aviary for just this purpose."

I tried one quail tongue and a morning glory to be polite, while Alejandro put a small portion of each dish on his plate and then darted from each like a hummingbird. I much preferred the bottle of sherry he set out. He was clearly playing a game with me: the theatricality of serving bizarre foods and hiding his servants. If it weren't for the sherry's numbing effect, I probably would have succumbed to nerves and fled from the house. I couldn't see the point to his game, other than to rattle me. Or perhaps his grip on reality had slipped and this was a reflection of what he had become. Adair's curse didn't seem to keep our minds from falling apart, just our vessels.

He waited until I'd eaten both items on my plate before he spoke. "You have been very patient with me tonight, Lanore, and I should not keep you waiting for my decision any longer. I will help you." I must've looked quite relieved by his answer, for he rushed to add, "You shouldn't get your hopes up, though. I am in touch with only a handful of the others, and few were interested in studying the dark arts. Most of us are afraid of it, and I'm sure that comes as no surprise to you. But there's one person who might be able to help." Alejandro took a small white card from his pocket and handed it to me. It had Tilde's name on it, with an address. "She's the one you want to see," he said quietly and firmly.

"I don't understand."

"A lot of time has passed, Lanore. Two hundred years can change anyone, and I would say that, of all of us, she has changed the most."

I stared at the white card pinched between my fingers. Of all the cold, selfish people Adair had collected, Tilde had been the most chilling. She'd committed the worst crime of any of us before Adair changed her: killing her husband and children so that she might marry a rich man who'd fallen in love with her. Time and again, whether luring men to squander their gold at Adair's gaming table or a poor girl to give her virginity to Adair in his bed, she had proved that her heart was the stoniest. I lived in terror of her second only to Adair, and here Alejandro was telling me she was the only one who could help me. Even he seemed vaguely apologetic for putting me in her hands. I looked into his eyes pleadingly and asked, "Don't you remember how she hated me? Why would she agree to help me now?"

Alej shook his head gently. "She didn't hate you any more than she hated anyone else, my dear, and certainly no more than she hated herself. Don't you understand? We all had to find a way to appease Adair in order to survive, and that was her way. Early in her life, she decided she must put her interests first; selfish, yes, though some might say pragmatic. She lived in a difficult time and a place more primitive and harsh than even the town you grew up in. There were events that had shaped Tilde by the time Adair found her, things that you don't know about," he chided me. "And don't forget, you have been selfish in your way, no less selfish than Tilde. I don't mean to be cruel, but you gave Jonathan to Adair, didn't you? And here you are, claiming to be a changed woman."

He still had that priestly, disarming way about him. And he knew of the shame I carried mostly in secret, of being the one to give Jonathan to Adair. Seeing me subdued, Alejandro continued, "She's sorry for everything she's done. She's not the same woman at all; she's taken on a kind of *spirituality*. She's been trying to find out who we are, and to do that, she's delved into the mysteries of the unseen world. She's consulted with scholars and practitioners from here to the ends of the earth. If anyone will be able to help you, it is Tilde."

As intimidating as this was, I wanted to believe him. I had to go along with it, anyway—I had no other choice. It seemed that part of this ordeal was to humble myself before my enemies, to ask for help from people I'd hoped to never deal with again. If my entire journey was about changing the type of person I was, about making amendments for the selfish things I'd done, it made sense that this, too, would be part of my punishment.

He took both of my hands. "Lanore, you know that I tried to protect you before. You can trust me now."

I studied Alejandro's card a second time, then slipped it into my purse. "Thank you, Alejandro."

When I started to push away from the table, he rose as well. "You are eager to start on the next step of your journey. I understand.

I'll have my driver take you back to your hotel. But I ask that you wait a minute longer; I thought of something I'd like to give you, something I picked up a long time ago that would suit you perfectly. Come with me."

We went to one of his carefully composed rooms, and he began to sift through a huge, antique Chinese herbalist's cabinet with dozens of tiny drawers, but he couldn't find what he was looking for. I excused myself to go to the bathroom and locked the door behind me, then stood clutching the sink, a bundle of nerves at the thought of seeing Tilde again. I feared her almost as much as I feared Adair. My throat was dry and my heart beat insistently in my chest. I exhaled slowly, trying to calm myself. *Give him five more minutes, then make your excuses and escape.*

As I passed Alejandro's room, however, I caught from the corner of my eye a glimpse of the past: dangling from a hanger on an armoire door, I thought I saw one of Adair's banyans, olive silk with stripes of gold, the same coloring as his eyes.

I crept into Alejandro's room quietly. All it took was fingering the silk and I knew it was Adair's old robe, now thin from an eternity of use. Seeing this empty vestige of him again made me recall Adair vividly. The movement of the hanger made the armoire door swing open and, as I tried to close it, something fell to the bottom of the cabinet. I crouched down to clear away whatever was blocking the door, and my hands closed around a strip of leather, greasy from use. I pulled out a maze of leather straps and buckles, a diabolical cage fashioned into a hollow human form. The last time I had seen it was in Adair's house in Boston, and here was the ugly contrivance again, sharp leather straps spattered with blood and stiff with human misery, unwilling to be ignored.

But the harness no longer held *my* shape, frozen for centuries: the shape was larger, straighter, too, and it didn't mimic a woman's curves. It hit me then: Alejandro had himself put into the harness, had himself strapped into a frieze of helplessness. . . . He'd actually enticed someone to strap him in and use it to reenact the punishments that Adair used to mete out. Alejandro had chosen to relive the humiliation, rapes, and beatings; he'd accepted them voluntarily, but why? When I thought about it, though, the answer seemed obvious.

"What are you doing?" Alejandro's voice called out behind me, chilly.

I held the harness out for him to see. "Alejandro, how in the world could you save this?" I could barely bring myself to ask.

The haughty expression on his face crumpled. "What else could I do? It was Adair's. I couldn't let some outsider find it. Think of the scandal; what would people have said about him?"

The truth, I thought. "But how can you do this to yourself, Alej?" I gestured at the shape captured in leather with a pained expression on my face. I could barely breathe. "You must stop hating yourself."

Those dark eyes stared back, full of shame, with a glimmer of relief at being discovered. "The only time I feel truly at peace," he said at last, "is when I am in the harness."

Perhaps I shouldn't have been surprised that he re-created the rituals of torture, punishment and absolution; he was a child of the Inquisition, after all. Or perhaps he only wanted a reminder of the most poignant and singular attention he ever got from Adair.

Alejandro and I were both Adair's casualties, shaped by our every interaction with him, his attention and his displeasure, the rewards he bestowed and the punishments he inflicted. I hoped that I had broken this cycle and was free from his influence, but apparently Alejandro was not. I wanted to help him cure himself, but didn't know how. "Oh, Alej," I said, dropping the harness to the floor. "I am so sorry for you."

I took his cold hand and warmed it with my own as we walked together in silence through the dark, empty halls. As Alejandro escorted me to the car, I waited until we were at the front doors to ask, "Will you go looking for Adair? I assume you want to be with him again."

The flush of embarrassment had faded from his face, but he still wouldn't look me in the eye. "I don't know. I am wise enough to know that the idea of something is often more alluring than its reality. I have mixed feelings. You understand."

I shivered. "No, I don't understand. I have no desire to see him—none at all."

"If I were in your situation, I would not want to see him, either. But I'm not afraid of Adair—not anymore." He looked at the dark horizon, avoiding my gaze. "I thought about him a lot over the years—as have you, I would think—and I believe I've come to understand him. I think he is not dangerous to everyone. He is a predator, yes, but in my experience, he preys only on a certain type of person. Think on it, Lanore. None of us were good people. We were not good to our families or neighbors. We did not honor God with the way we led our lives. God put predators on the earth for a reason, and this is why I am not afraid of Adair anymore. I believe God sent him into my life to help me atone for my sins."

He had a zealot's gleam in his eye, just as he always had. "Sorry, Alej, but I disagree with you. I don't think anything I did was terrible enough to deserve what I got from Adair, any more than I believe he has the right to punish us. After everything I've been through and everything I've seen, I don't believe in God anymore. I don't think there's been a reason behind anything that's happened to us, but of course we want there to be. We want life to make sense."

He let out a soft snort of derision. "If that is what you believe . . . if you have truly exiled God from your life, then you should go see Tilde. She can tell you things that may change your mind. She is your best hope, I think, to find peace in your soul."

I hugged Alejandro and gave him a weak smile as we said good-bye. He kissed both of my cheeks and looked in my eyes as he said *"Fuerza,"* then gave my shoulder a reassuring squeeze. I climbed into the sedan, and as we cut through the city like a ray gliding through deep ocean waters, I watched the city spool away and tried to throw off the profound melancholy that Alejandro had sown in my heart.

PART THREE

TWENTY-FOUR

Alejandro told me I'd find Tilde in Aspen, Colorado, on a skiing holiday with her stepchildren. I was surprised to hear she was in a relationship with someone who had children. I wouldn't have thought she had the patience and maybe it was a sign that she'd changed. She'd never seemed maternal, not in the least: witness the fact that she had poisoned her own children. That seemed like the kind of act from which a mother would never recover, something that would haunt her every day of her life, even if it had happened centuries ago.

The life she was now leading was just as unexpected. Alejandro emailed articles and photos from society magazines and international newspapers that featured Tilde in her various personas over the years: 1947, 1978, 2003. I was shocked to see that she let the press write about her and, more dangerously, take pictures of her. She was out in plain sight: photographed in a slinky dark-blue gown at a political fund-raiser in New York City, written up in a news article describing her work on the board of her stepsons' private school. Each time, she had a different name and was married to a different man.

Tilde was a chameleon, not only in identity, but in appearance, too. Even though she couldn't change her weight or height or the shape of her face, you'd have to look very closely at the photographs to realize it was the same woman. What gave her away—to me, anyway, who'd only lived with Tilde a few years—was her telltale stare. She had a way of looking past a person's expression, through any mask of deception you might wear, through blood and the bone and into the mind, and quite possibly into your soul as well. Not unlike Alejandro's ability with the camera, and it made me wonder if it had something to do with the way Adair chose his companions. Perhaps I had the gift, too.

These days she was going by the name Birgit von Haupt, widow of the president of a multinational energy corporation. In the photos, her streamlined, catlike form was clothed in an expensive, conservatively cut suit, her lavender eyes hidden behind very dark sunglasses. She was a cipher, at least to the camera's mechanical eye, and I could only hope that Alej had told me the truth and she was hiding a newfound compassion beneath her controlled exterior.

The articles said she was running her late husband's charitable foundation, which I took as a good sign, and her appearance was in keeping with what you'd expect from a woman in that position. Also, the fact that she was taking care of her husband's children seemed to indicate that she'd reformed—though she might have locked them up in a closet at night, for all I knew. It's funny: in that suit, standing in front of a limousine, she looked like Jackie Kennedy, too conventional to be a student of the dark arts. But, of course, appearances are deceiving.

Looking through these photographs of Tilde filled me with foreboding, however. It was one thing to reveal myself to Alejandro, but quite another to seek out Tilde. There was no real danger with Alejandro and I'd known it when I went to see him: he had always been a facilitator and a messenger, and unlikely to act on his own. Tilde, however, had been second only to Adair in cunning and sheer wickedness, and was perhaps even better than he was at deception. When strangers looked at her, they saw only what she wanted them to see, and she was so good at it that she could live in the public eye without being detected.

As I studied a photograph of Tilde, icy and aloof, I started to worry again that I might be walking into a trap, and put a stop to that thought abruptly. When would I learn to trust others again? After being free for centuries, probably neither Alejandro nor Tilde wanted to give up their freedom to serve Adair again. And for all my uncertainty, it didn't really matter, since I had no choice but to trust them. I could either use every resource I had in order to try to save myself, or be on the run forever. I was already growing weary of the pursuit, feeling worn down mentally and emotionally. I was starting to hear the sirens' call—weak and distant, but there—enticing me to surrender, to give in to the inevitable.

Alejandro assured me that I could find Tilde in Aspen for the next few weeks. He said she kept homes in multiple locations—a timber frame house overlooking a Norwegian fjord, a chalet in the Swiss Alps—each one cold and snowy like her place of origin, a northern kingdom whose name was now lost to time. As I made my travel arrangements, I noticed that the flight would take me through Green Bay, Wisconsin, the airport closest to Luke's family.

I hadn't forgotten about Luke: thoughts of him visited me in quiet moments, guilty thoughts for the cowardly way I'd left him and for cutting off all communication with him the way I did. I wanted to believe that as long as Luke had been exorcised from my life he was safe from Adair, but I was starting to see that this might not be so, especially since Luke refused to take the threat seriously. If Adair had learned of Luke and knew of his importance to me, he might go after him.

That I was passing through Green Bay seemed like fate—at least, that's how I *wanted* to view it. This was a chance to try to make Luke believe me. At the same time, I'd have the opportunity to see him again—and I wanted very much to see him again. As I typed in the change to my flight reservations, I knew by the unsettled feeling in the pit of my stomach that there was more to this detour than I wanted to admit. It was my chance to tell Luke—the last man who'd loved me and asked for nothing in return—that I was sorry.

There was a heavy chill in the air when I arrived in Green Bay in the late afternoon. I left immediately for Marquette, intending to go directly to the place where Luke's ex-wife, Tricia, lived with her daughters, a small farm on the far outskirts of town. As I drove, I tried to formulate what I would say to him, how I would explain that I'd come in order to close that chapter in both of our lives, and to impress on him that he and his family might be in grave danger.

The drive was long and took me through stretches of forest and farmland reminiscent of St. Andrew. The last few hours on the road took me closer to civilization, past state parks and small towns with names from the Native American tribes that lived there long ago. I drove by houses that looked as though they'd been made from giant Lincoln Logs, past weather-worn signs advertising snowmobile rentals and Sunday church potlucks. It seemed like a nice place to live and raise children; there was probably a need for doctors here, too. Luke could start over here, where there'd be fewer questions, and he wouldn't be known by the one bad decision that came to define his life.

The sky was dark by the time I found Tricia's home. The house was a modest split-level with a large barn and a two-car garage. A rental car was parked in front of the house, near an old but well-cared-for Camaro. The lawn between the house and outbuildings was patchy from years of children's play, and a swing hung off the branch of a giant old oak.

From where I'd parked, I could see into the house through a set of patio doors. The family seemed to be getting ready for dinner, a white tablecloth glowing under warm yellow lights. People passed by the tall glass doors, visible to me for only a moment. Two little girls, both with round faces and curly brown hair the same as Luke's, ran by, chasing each other, their high-pitched girlish shrieks audible outside the house. A woman about Luke's age, highlights in her dark-blond hair, set the table and occasionally looked up from her task to call out to someone I couldn't see. I assumed she was Tricia, her prettiness strained by fatigue.

Then Luke appeared, going up to his ex-wife to ask her something. I wasn't prepared for how he'd changed, his cheeks sunken and a few days' beard grown in. His clothing was disheveled, as though he'd slept in it. I'd done this to him. The abruptness of my leaving had overtaken him like a hurricane, sweeping him up and dropping him down in an unexpected place. You could tell Tricia was being patient with him— a nurse's forbearance in her manner—and I could understand why Luke had never said a bad word against her.

His daughters swooped by the door again, and his expression lost some of its melancholy as his eyes followed them. His lips moved; he must've said something fatherly, his mouth taking a slightly stern cast. I'd seen traces of that expression at times when he spoke to me, those times when my face had fooled him and he'd forgotten that I was so much older than him. In that scene on the other side of the glass, he looked as though he was meant to be there, in that dining room with that woman and those children, and I knew I'd made the right decision to leave.

Luke appeared to be adjusting to life without me. I was relieved, even as I was sad for myself, sad that I would never have a family like this to love and keep me from being lonely. I could not even have the comfort of one person in my life. That was part of Adair's curse, to be alone forever. I sat behind the wheel and started crying out of exhaustion, tired of the tussle of thoughts going on in my head, back and forth. Love, leave. Stay, go. I wanted this to be over.

As I took my hands away from my face, wiping away my tears, I saw that Luke appeared to be staring through the glass door in the direction of my car. Did he know it was me in this thick darkness? There was no doubt: I could tell by the twist of his mouth and the painful, hopeful look in his eyes that he saw through the glare and spotted me behind the wheel. So much for precautions.

I pulled out my cell phone and pressed his number on speed dial and watched as he reached in his pocket. He answered right away. "Don't tell your family I'm here" were the first words out of my mouth.

He hesitated. "Come inside and we can—"

"I'm not staying," I said flatly, my tone conveying that this was not to be a joyful reunion. "Can you meet me outside? Just for a minute?"

His brow ruffled. "Uh, sure." He turned away and slipped out of view as he walked away from his family. "Drive past the house and I'll walk down to meet you. That way they won't see where I'm going."

A few minutes later, Luke slipped into the passenger seat. Even by moonlight, I could see evidence of his devastation. He'd lost weight and his eyes were red-rimmed. He moved tentatively, blinking at me, as if asking for a sign of what to expect but bracing himself for disappointment. Luke had been through a lot in the past year—he'd lost his marriage and both his parents—and I could understand why he didn't want to be hurt one more time.

"So . . . what're you doing here?" he asked slowly.

"I wanted to see you," I said, then caught myself. "I want to tell you how sorry I am for leaving you that way. It's just that I didn't know what else to do at the time. . . ." I was making a mess of this apology and trailed off before I could do more damage.

"You still think you're doing the right thing?" he asked, his voice tense.

I nodded.

"So that's how you want it to be."

"That's the way it *is*, Luke. I—"

"No, listen to me. It's my turn now. I have a few things I've wanted to say to you, but you wouldn't answer my calls," he said, turning to face me. Outside the car the blackness of the evening closed around us like a curtain. It was just the two of us at the edge of the world. It was a time for honesty.

"Lanny . . . I thought I loved you. When you told me you needed me, I gave up *everything* for you. Have you forgotten that? My life is a wreck. My ex-wife thinks I've lost my mind, and maybe she's right. Right now she's not sure she can trust me with my own children. She thinks I might run off with them and disappear, like I did with you. And back in St. Andrew? I'm a wanted man. I lost my practice, my position at the hospital. . . . The only reason there hasn't been a board inquiry is because I've known all my patients since I was in elementary school and none of them have the heart to file a complaint."

Listening to his indictment was like getting hit in the stomach with a sledgehammer. These were all things I suspected or heard slip out in his telephone conversations with Tricia, but to hear him say it aloud, and with such bitterness in his voice, brought me up short. "I'll make it up to you."

"How are you going to do that?" he asked brusquely. "Lanny, I've been worried about you, not knowing why there was no word from you, if what you said came true and this psychopath had—" He broke off, unable to finish.

Memories of the pain Jonathan had caused me came flooding back. "I'm so sorry, Luke. I didn't mean—"

He held up a hand to stop me. "There's something else I need to tell you. You remember Joe Duchesne, the sheriff in St. Andrew? He's dead. Tricia's friends told her. He was killed by someone who dug up your friend Jonathan and stole his body."

His news sent an icy streak down my spine.

"So I guess you were right. Adair's on the hunt. I can't imagine anyone else would be robbing graves."

"He took Jonathan's body?" I choked back the urge to retch.

"Maybe he'll leave you alone, now that he's got Jonathan," Luke said, cautiously optimistic.

"No. He wants revenge."

Luke took my hands. "If that's the case, then I can't let you go off by yourself. You need someone to help you, Lanny. You can't face this alone."

I pulled away from him, causing him to flinch momentarily. "You can't come with me, Luke," I said. "Think of your daughters. If you're with me when Adair catches up to me, he'll kill you. Do you want your daughters growing up without their father?"

He fell silent.

"I can't be responsible for that, Luke. I want you to put all this behind you and get on with your life, doing whatever makes you happy. Life is short—for most people—you need to enjoy what's left of it. This has to be good-bye; it's the only way. Go back to your daughters—protect them. Take them someplace where you have no connections, where no one would think to look for you. Just go and hide until things have quieted down and you don't hear of any more strange incidents. Don't worry about me. And I hope you can forgive me."

He wasn't dissuaded. "Do you know what you're doing to me, Lanny, shutting me out like this? Knowing what you're up against . . . how can I let you go? What kind of man would I be—"

"You're a wonderful man, Luke. More than I deserve. But it's not your decision. Go back to your daughters and forget about me." I shouldn't have reached for his cheek, but I did—an indulgence, given that it was the last time we'd see each other. I fancied I felt all his love and despair in that one touch of his hot cheek. "I hope you can forgive me someday. You'll never know how sorry I am for dragging you into this mess."

Luke sat dazed and I worried for a second that he would refuse to get out of the car, or that he would figure out some way to tear my heart apart worse than he already had. But he wasn't that kind of person, thankfully, and after one more second's hesitation, he stormed out of the car, slamming the door behind him. My tears might've had something to do with his departure: Luke had a hard time remaining resolute whenever I cried, and I was crying already, sorry for all the hurt I'd inflicted on him.

Because he was right. I'd ruined his life, just as I knew I would the night I asked him to help me escape. I was rarely confronted by my duplicity. Oh, in the moment, I never believed I was hurting someone; I always tried to convince myself this time would be different, but the truth was I had been a hit-and-run artist my entire life, slipping away whenever a situation became too painful or too suffocating. I had Jonathan to thank for that. He'd taught me the art of living only for myself.

At least this time I could make amends. I could make sure Luke was taken care of. I wanted to know he was safe with his girls, safe and warm and dry when it was cold and wet and snowy. I needed to know that Luke would never want for anything, that he and his daughters wouldn't suffer any more than was unavoidable in this life. Because I knew from experience that a loved one's disappearance leaves scars.

To make this happen, I needed the help of my most trusted associate, Henri Renville, the Paris lawyer who managed my business affairs. He was famous for taking on clients in peculiar situations who demanded absolute loyalty; it was rumored he represented a few international criminals, an up-and-coming black market arms dealer, and the wayward son of a former African dictator. I figured I was among the less conspicuous of M. Renville's customers, although we'd been together many years and Henri had yet to ask any difficult questions of me. It would just be morning in Paris, too early to call most law firms, but not Henri: he had a policy of taking his clients' calls at any hour.

"Lanore! *Mon dieu,* where have you been?" His voice was thick with concern, almost paternal. "Why haven't you answered your phone or responded to the emails I've sent?"

"I'm sorry, Henri. I've been detained. What is it? Why have you been trying to reach me?"

"I hope you are seated, not driving a car or something like that, because I have bad news for you. Your house here, in Paris. It burned to the ground."

I suddenly felt flattened. The world turned a shade darker.

"Did you hear me? I've been in a terrible panic when I did not hear back from you. If the fire bureau hadn't assured me there were no human remains among the ashes, I might've suspected you had been in the building."

"I'm sorry, Henri, to have caused you worry. Do they know how it happened?"

"They have not finished their investigation yet. They have been asking the usual questions—very rude, really—wanting to know if you are heavily insured, insinuating that you might have set it your-self. I put them straight immediately, as you can imagine. 'You do not know Mademoiselle Bessender if you think she would be the sort of person to set fire to her own home!' I told them."

I could see how it might've seemed damning to Henri, though: I'd just sent away truckloads of irreplaceable antiques, none of which had been insured, because I hadn't wanted to explain to an insur-ance company how I'd come to own them. Then the house burns down. There were still some important records and sentimental items in it, though, correspondence with friends long dead, records of my previous identities. The only possession it would kill me to lose was the charcoal drawing of Jonathan, and so it was the first thing to leap to mind. I couldn't mourn my loss at that moment, however.

"You don't need anything from me right now, do you?" I asked.

"I think the police would like to speak with you as soon as possible. They've been very concerned, as you might imagine. Shall I have them call you?"

That was the last thing I needed to deal with just then. "No, not yet, Henri. I have something else I need you to take care of first. That's why I'm calling, as a matter of fact. I want to buy another house."

"Another one! If you don't mind me saying so, this might appear a wee bit suspicious to the police, seeing that your current home was recently destroyed. I don't suppose this new house is in Paris?"

"No, it's here in America. I want to pay off a mortgage for someone else, not to purchase a house for myself. I want to make a present of it."

"It is not a simple thing to do, Lanore. And it isn't smart, either, if you follow me. There are good reasons why you should keep your property in your name. Is this for your friend, the man who has been living with you? I do not need to tell you that relationships can change, sometimes precipitously. You should not be such a romantic." I had told Henri when we met that I was an orphan, and that led him to occasionally try to father me when he felt I needed friendly advice.

"Thank you, but there's no need to worry. I don't want any part of it, Henri. It's a simple little house. It belonged to Luke's parents, but they're dead now and Luke can't pay off the mortgage. I'd like him to own the property free and clear. I'll send the details in an email."

He sighed. "As you wish. But what about you, Lanore? What are your plans? Now that your house is destroyed, where will you live?"

"I'm fine. I'm traveling. I don't need a house right now."

"Whatever is going on, it seems to have left you rather sad—and it's never a good idea to conduct any financial transactions when one is emotional, you know. It's far better to look at these things with a clear head. Are you sure you don't want to think some more about what you are doing?"

"I appreciate your concern, but I've made up my mind."

"It's only that"—his tone was strained, which was quite unusual for Henri—"you've never done anything like this before. Never bought such a large gift for anyone. Especially not for a man."

"Is that what's bothering you?" Despite my worries, I laughed in relief. "Luke is hardly a gigolo."

"He did talk you into giving away all those beautiful things," he said, referring to the pieces we'd sent to museums. "They were worth a fortune. A *considerable* fortune."

"Yes, but in this case it was the right course to take. I do appreciate you're concerned enough to press the issue, but this is my decision. If you would execute my instructions, please, Henri, with your usual discretion." Meaning Luke would not be told who paid the mortgage. But he would guess.

"As you wish," he said, resigned.

Then I was compelled to add something. "I should say . . . you won't be hearing from me for a while. Nothing to worry about. It's just that I'll be going away."

"Away? But you're away now. How much farther away can one be? Will you at least tell me where you are going?"

"I can't say, Henri. I'll be in touch as soon as I can. Just don't worry."

"You say 'don't worry,' but how can I not? You've got me very concerned, Lanore, I must say. . . . Are you sure you're not in shock over the news of your house? I should have broken it more gently. . . ."

"No, Henri, I'm fine."

"No, you're not fine. It sounds like you're saying good-bye to me, in so many words. . . . Quite frankly, you sound so melancholy that one might think . . . I might worry that you are thinking of harming yourself." The words came out in an embarrassed jumble. How do you respond to a statement like that, from a man who has been taking care of you for decades? Especially when he's right. For soon I would cease to be, one way or the other; either Tilde would help me slip the bonds of my curse so I could end my life, or I'd spend the rest of my days in Adair's custody, a ghost, as Uzra had been.

"Don't worry about me, Henri. Tomorrow I'll be much better. I'm sure of it," I said to him, hoping I sounded convincing. "Good-bye."

I tossed the phone aside and held on to the steering wheel. Throughout the conversation, I'd held in my alarm at learning my house had been destroyed, for I knew it had to have been Adair's doing. I would've screamed out loud if I didn't think someone would hear me. In the span of a few minutes, my situation had become much worse. It was as though Adair was circling me like a wolf, just beyond the range of my vision. He'd killed the sheriff and taken Jonathan's body; he'd burned down my house. He was systematically destroying everything that was precious to me. It didn't seem I had a chance to escape. He was coming for me. I couldn't bear to think what torture he was capable of inflicting.

I closed my eyes and exhaled slowly, trying to calm down. I had a plan, I reminded myself. Find Tilde, pray that she is as forgiving as Alejandro says she is, convince her to help me. As I reached down to slip the transmission into gear, the passenger-side door opened.

"Luke, I—" I turned, my heart in my throat, thinking he had come back to try to get me to change my mind. Who else could it be, here in the middle of nowhere? But the man who'd climbed into the car wasn't Luke.

TWENTY-FIVE

There was something familiar about the man who slid into the front seat. I'd seen his features before—the impertinent grin, light leaping in his eyes like the flames of a bonfire—but his name eluded me. There was something odd about him. He seemed out of place, as though he belonged to another time. He waited patiently while I searched my memory.

"Jude," he finally said, tipping his head in a mock bow, a hand pressed to his chest.

Once I heard his name, of course I remembered him as the wild-eyed charismatic preacher I'd first met as a teenage girl. He had been Adair's emissary, scouring the New World for flawed individuals to turn into companions, and a new vessel to carry his soul. Sly and conniving, Jude had been perfect for the job. His appearance tonight could not have been a coincidence, and it didn't bode well.

"What are you doing here?" I asked, gripping the steering wheel tighter and trying to look past Jude's shoulder into the blackness. "Is Adair with you? Where is he?"

Jude unzipped his jacket, making himself comfortable as he settled into the seat. "Not in Michigan, I'll tell you that much. Now

I know why he sent *me* to watch the ex-wife's house: it's a wasteland around here."

I was relieved to hear that Adair hadn't bothered to come after Luke and had sent a lackey instead, but I still needed to know what he was thinking. "So he's looking for me. Where is he, Jude?"

"I don't know," Jude replied. "He doesn't tell me everything. You know how he is."

"I'm starting to recall, yes."

"You'll know soon enough: I'm bringing you to him now. And do us both a favor and don't think about giving me a hard time, because we both know I can easily overpower you, and I don't think you want to ride all the way to Green Bay in the trunk." He nodded at the dark road ahead. "Drive. Before long, you'll see a car on the side of the road. Pull up behind it. We're going to take my vehicle and leave yours here," he instructed.

A black sports car came into view beneath a stand of trees, as Jude had described. Jude took my elbow and led me to the second car, then pushed me into the passenger seat. He looked through my purse to make sure I had a passport and retrieved my suitcase from the trunk of my rental car.

Turning the key in the ignition, Jude swung the car onto the empty highway. Light flashed hypnotically overhead as we passed streetlamps, and just as I'd begun to think he meant to travel the entire way in silence, he spoke. "For the record, I don't have anything against you, Lanore. It's not like I was in any hurry to have Adair come back. I'd just as soon have lived the rest of my life without seeing him again. We all felt that way—Alejandro, Tilde, Dona. It was just that none of us were eager to attempt what you did. We knew what would happen to us if we'd failed."

"Lucky for you, then, that I succeeded." I held my gaze steady on him while he looked away, ashamed. I changed the subject. "How is he? Adair, I mean," I asked.

"How do you think he is? It's like having a hurricane blow

into your life and turn everything upside down," Jude said, hotly. "Or having a child suddenly left on my doorstep. I have to explain everything to him: phones, cars, televisions, computers. He knows *nothing*. It's a nightmare. And I forgot what it was like being around him. . . . He's a tyrant, a megalomaniacal despot. Once you've been free, you can't live like that again." His words spilled out in a torrent. He must've been desperate to complain to someone who could appreciate the impossibility of his situation.

"It's worse than you know, Jude. Why do you think I walled him up in the first place? He's not what you think he is, Jude. He's not the defenseless peasant boy he pretends to be in the stories of his youth. He's the physic, the monster in his own story."

By Jude's reaction, I could tell that I'd surprised him. "That's impossible," he said, but he sounded unconvinced, as though turning what I'd said over in his mind.

"He's more powerful than you know. You won't believe what he can do."

Jude kept his nervous gaze on the road. "Try me."

I drew in a deep breath and braced myself for his reaction: "He can put his consciousness into another body."

Jude was quiet. Putting the pieces together, maybe.

"He took over the peasant boy's body. And that's why he sent you and the others out scouting for someone like Jonathan: he was searching for a new body. That's why he had me bring Jonathan to him. He wanted a new vessel, one that was irresistible, whom people would want to befriend and trust. One that would give him everything he wanted."

There was still no objection from Jude, no questioning of my sanity. He stroked the corners of his mouth. "What makes you think this is what Adair was up to? What evidence do you have?"

"I saw a room at the old mansion that was just like the physic's workspace in Adair's story. He'd re-created it and tried to hide it away. It was chilling, Jude. It was filled with the ingredients from his story, the herbs and roots, all this ancient equipment," I told him. "I found his books, the two he talked about, the ones with all his spells. Then I made a terrible mistake. I took a few things to be verified, so I could be sure I was right about him. I think that's why he killed Uzra: he realized someone had been in the room and knew he'd been found out."

Jude seemed to be struggling with a thought as he drove, his hands restless on the steering wheel, his brow furrowed and his mouth pressed tight. "I'd known—all of us knew that he was interested in alchemy . . . magic . . . but it didn't seem like more than a casual interest. A lot of people in my day were; it wasn't that unusual. Then, a few weeks back, when Adair escaped, he came straight to my house. He was able to find me, just like that," he said, snapping his fingers. "The first thing he did was to look for his books of spells. I knew about the books—I'd seen them once or twice when I lived with him—but I didn't think much of it at the time. He never made a big deal over them. . . .

"Since he's returned, though, it's been intense. . . . He made another person immortal like us, he brought Jonathan back from the dead—"

"He brought Jonathan back from the dead?" I interrupted. His news left me feeling as though I'd taken a punch to the head. "I'd heard he'd gone after Jonathan's body, but you're saying Adair brought him back to life?"

Jude shivered. "He sure has, and it's the spookiest thing you ever saw. When he first showed up at the house, he looked only half-alive, like a wet, bloodless lump of meat. His corpse must've been in a terrible state, half-decomposed by the time Adair got to it, and looks like it's trying to rebuild itself—"

"Jude—no more details, please." My beautiful Jonathan reduced to a lump of raw flesh. That was what I'd done to him, taken away the magic that had kept him perfect and left him to rot and ruin like any other human. It hurt to hear Jonathan described like this. I didn't want to think of him in any way other than how I had known him. I'd been tormented these past three months, questioning whether I'd done the right thing by giving Jonathan his release, but I hadn't given a thought to what his body would go through.

"I'd say he's almost back to normal now," Jude continued, "but I didn't know him before, so it's hard for me to tell if he looks the same. As for his mental state, I'd say he's awfully *calm* for someone in his position."

My conscience had gotten the better of me now, and I hugged my upper arms to chase away the chill of my guilt. "Has he said anything about dying? What it was like to die? Did he mention if he was in pain at the end or if he wished he hadn't done it?"

"He hasn't blamed you, if that's what you're worried about." Jude rested one of his hands at the top of the steering wheel. "He claims he can't remember any of it clearly, but I think it's just an excuse to put Adair off, since he's so desperate to know about the afterlife. Adair's worried about what might be waiting for him on the other side."

My ears pricked up. "Is he?"

"Oh yeah, especially after Jonathan told him about meeting the 'queen of the underworld.'"

"'Queen of the underworld'?" I didn't like the sound of that, even if I didn't know what it meant.

"Out of the billions of souls in the afterlife, trust your boy Jonathan to come to the attention of the head girl."

"Did he say anything more about this queen?"

"Adair says he's her consort or something like that." Jude warmed to his tale. "It's not exactly clear what's going on, but it shook up Adair. He's afraid of this queen, there's no doubt. He says she's a powerful force, strong magic."

"I've never heard of a queen of the underworld," I mumbled to myself, thinking back to the conversations I'd had over the years, trying to find a way out of my condition. None of them—not the professors or the back-room magicians, self-professed alchemists or holy men—had mentioned a queen of the underworld. A tremor of awe and fear ran through me. As for Jonathan being her chosen companion, that didn't surprise me in the least. I'd never known a man or woman able to resist Jonathan, so why would a deity be immune to his appeal? "How is Jonathan? Adair hasn't hurt him, has he?"

"I wouldn't worry about Jonathan. He doesn't seem to be afraid of Adair; it's more the other way around. I'd say he's got Adair figured out. And you should know, Lanny: Adair has changed in some ways. Those two hundred years behind the wall changed him. It's hard to say how, exactly . . . knocked down a peg, maybe. He thinks before he acts."

I wasn't sure what to make of this news. If Adair was sparing Jude his vitriol, that meant he undoubtedly was saving it for me. As I thought over what Jude told me, he cleared his throat for my attention. "There's something else you should know. A few nights ago, he said he was able to go to your house in Paris. He didn't need to leave his room; he said he went there through 'projection.' He said that's how he knew you were with this doctor. That's why he sent me here."

The fire. Fear spiked in my heart as I realized that the fire that destroyed my home had been his doing, even though he hadn't actually been there. He didn't even need to strike a match. His mere intent could be dangerous. Why shouldn't it be? By his hand and intent—that was his curse.

And suddenly I was hit by the enormity of what I was up against. For whatever reason, the Fates had seen fit to allow Adair to bend reality to his will, to make the impossible possible, and there was no way that I would be able to defend myself against this. I could try to outrun him, but in all likelihood that would only make him angrier. He had Jonathan, he knew about Luke; he had at least two levers to try to control me, and probably more that I hadn't yet thought of. How had he been able to know which way I would turn, where I would run? How could he have been so many steps ahead of me?

I watched the landscape roll by outside my window, moonlight highlighting the horizon. My freedom was slipping away with every mile. I needed to get Jude on my side. "You know I'm not the only one at risk here. He may be after me now, but once he has me, it won't be over. He'll need you for the next thing, and the thing after that . . ."

He had no response for me, but I could tell he was listening.

"You know Adair's dangerous. He's shown that he can turn on any of us. And he lied to all of you the whole time you lived together, pretending to be something he wasn't. In truth, you don't really know him. None of us do. We don't know what he's capable of."

Jude snorted. "No kidding. I have been seriously freaked out since he came back."

"That's why I'm asking you to help me. We're in this together."

He was thinking about it, I could tell. He kept looking in the rearview mirror as though the answer were written there, or was afraid that something might come hurtling at us from the darkness, attuned to our treacherous talk.

"Has he talked about what he plans to do to me?" I asked, saying aloud the fear I'd tried to suppress, the fear I'd carried with me ever since I trapped Adair. "I expect he'll bury me alive, the same as I did to him."

I'd never been as afraid as I was at that moment. I was seized by a terrible chill, and my teeth started chattering, and my stomach tightened into a hard knot. There was nothing I could do to help myself. I wished I could fling myself out of the car to end my life, lose consciousness with a thud and a slap against asphalt, tumbling end over end like a discarded toy.

"Hey, calm down," Jude said, reaching for my arm. It was his attempt at sympathy, the way the butcher tries to soothe the lamb before cutting its throat.

"Who are you to tell me to calm down? You know what will happen to me, and yet you're taking me to Adair. Don't kid yourself that you're better than him!" I shouted at Jude.

"Hey, I could've—"

"You're doing his bidding. At least I tried to stand up to him."

"And look what it got you."

"It got you two hundred years of freedom," I spat back at him angrily.

He opened his mouth to speak, then seemed to think better of it. He hemmed and hawed, and his driving became more erratic as he thought. I tried not to hope that my tirade had gotten through to him, but finally he sighed and said, "I tried to warn you once, didn't I? In Boston, that time I checked in with Adair and there you were in his house, to my surprise. I tried to tell you that you were making a big mistake, but you threw me out."

"You don't want me to say that I should've listened to you, do you?"

He sighed. "Look, what would you do if I let you go? Can you go somewhere he won't find you? Do you have a plan?"

I was shocked, but didn't risk the moment by contemplating my luck. "I have an idea, yes."

He looked over his shoulder as though the devil might be in the backseat, a witness to his perfidy. "And it won't get back to Adair, even if he catches you?"

I shook my head. "I'd never tell him."

Jude slowed the car and made an abrupt turn, tires squealing in protest, and we were suddenly heading back the way we had come. I was speechless.

He shook his head ruefully, as though he regretted his actions already. "I haven't called Adair yet to tell him I'd spotted you, so he doesn't know I have you. As far as he knows, you never came out this way. I'll let you go, Lanny, because you're right: I don't need this on my conscience. Adair isn't the only one who's afraid of the afterlife." He stretched his neck as though the tension had become too much. "That advice I gave you all those years ago . . . I should've heeded it myself. But I was headstrong and thought I could handle anything. You, me, the others—we were stupid to accept his offer, even if it did come at the point of death," Jude said bitterly. "In my case it came as I was hanging from a rope in a warehouse in the Waterlooplein. . . . I should've known, after the things I'd done, to refuse an easy way out. Some things are worse than death. If I'd accepted that my life was over, at least with my death I'd have been able to make amends. So this is my second chance. I'll take it."

We drove the rest of the way to my car in silence, each lost in our own thoughts about the twisting path that had brought us here. Once we'd glided to a stop next to the abandoned rental car, Jude leaned over to open my door.

"Think of this as a small gesture of amends," he said. "Now go, and don't let him catch you."

I looked him in the face. "What are you going to do? Will you go back to him now?"

"I'll give it a few days, wait until I hear from him. He's got a new man to help him now, and you know how he always favors his most recent convert. Maybe he'll be done with me soon."

"Do you know what he's planning to do next?"

He shook his head. "No. He's stopped telling me things. I don't think he trusts me anymore."

I looked each way down the lonesome street. There were no cars on the road, not at this hour. I squeezed Jude's hand before stepping out. "Thanks."

"Don't forget: if the worst happens and he catches up to you, you were never here," Jude said, staring straight ahead. "Go."

As I sat behind the wheel and watched Jude drive away, I thought about how much worse things could've gone tonight. If Adair had come for Luke himself, everyone in that house would be dead. There would be corpses scattered throughout the house and across the lawn, Luke restrained and made to watch the carnage before being released from his grief by a blow to the back of his head. There would be more dead innocents, and it would make no difference to Adair, as long as I suffered.

I couldn't sit on the side of the road in a rental car, waiting for the police to question me come sunrise. I had to continue with my plan to see Tilde and throw myself on her mercy. If I felt any trepidation in placing my trust in her, I could take comfort from knowing that the others hadn't let me down. Alejandro had not closed his door to me; Jude found it in his conscience to let me go. Adair had been right when he said we were a family and that we had to be able to depend on one another, although I don't think he knew our solidarity would have this effect. There are unintended consequences to everything.

I turned the car south on the two-lane road, away from Luke for the last time, and resolved not to look back.

TWENTY-SIX

Luke slipped back into the house through the garage. The voices of his daughters drifted in from the living room, their high-pitched laughter folded in with good-natured growls from Richard and background noise from the television. They hadn't noticed his absence, but he expected his former wife had. Nothing escaped Tricia.

She looked up from the dishwasher. "Where were you?" she asked.

"Went out for a smoke," he lied.

Her shoulders sagged, a dirty dish in one hand. "You're smoking again? You know you shouldn't. I don't want the girls to catch you with a cigarette in your mouth." Tricia turned to look Luke in the eye. She read his expression in an instant—she always could—and said, "You're a terrible liar, Luke. What's really going on?"

Should he admit she caught him, or dig himself in deeper? He was tempted to try the latter, but his former wife had the instincts of a bloodhound. "I was talking to Lanny just now." He pulled his phone out of his pocket and gave it a wiggle; no sense letting her know the woman she despised had been parked fifty feet from the house. "Listen, Trish. I don't want to alarm you, but there's something I need to tell you. It probably won't come as a surprise, but Lanny is mixed up with some dangerous people. . . ."

Tricia crossed her arms over her chest, probably putting it together in her head: all that travel, the seemingly endless supply of money. Where did it come from?

"And now these people are looking for her. She called to warn me that her pursuers know about me, and because they're trying to get to her"—Tricia's expression hardened by the second—"the kids might be in danger."

"Dammit, Luke—"

"I need you to take them somewhere. On a trip, not to see your mom. Someplace no one would know to look for you."

"You have got to be fucking kidding me, Luke—"

"I'm serious, Tricia. I'm not saying this lightly, and I'm not delusional. These are really bad people. You've got to take the girls away. I'll pay whatever it costs, just take them someplace safe."

She shook her head, shifting her weight from one foot to the other. "What about school? I'm supposed to pull Jolene out of school for this? And work? I just got my shift schedule from the hospital for this month. What am I supposed—"

"Tell them it's an emergency. It doesn't matter. Just do it."

"This is great, Luke. How could you do this to us—to your daughters—by getting mixed up in something so dangerous? What am I supposed to tell them—or Richard? He's not going to leave. He's going to want to stay and work the farm."

"No, you've got to tell him to go with you. He'll be in danger. You're in danger. That's why I want you to take the kids somewhere." He faced up to her blazing eyes. "I'm sorry, Tricia. I didn't mean for you guys to get involved."

She made a noise that indicated she couldn't care less for his apology. "And how long do we stay away? Can you tell me that? Can't you just talk your girlfriend into giving these people whatever it is they want? Drug money, I assume."

"It's not drugs or money they're after."

"Whatever." She spoke crisply. "Whatever illegal thing it is she's involved in, can't you get her to take her lumps and do whatever it is she needs to do so that innocent people don't suffer?"

"It'll be okay. You just have to stay hidden for a few days."

"Oh—now it's just 'a few days'? What's going to happen in a few days?"

It was his turn to look away. "I'm going to go help her."

"Are you out of your mind?" Tricia shouted. The girls must have heard her because the volume on the television set rose appreciably; thank goodness Richard was paying attention. "Let your girlfriend take care of herself. She got herself into this mess, let her get herself out. You have other responsibilities to worry about, Luke. Jolene and Winona, have you forgotten about them?"

"Of course not."

"They're your first responsibility. Don't choose your girlfriend over them."

"I'm not. The reason I'm going is to make sure that the girls are safe—that *you're* safe." Luke's throat was constricted; his head ached. It was all too much for him. He was making promises, but he had no idea if he'd be able to keep them. "And I can't let Lanny face this on her own. What kind of man would I be if I did that? Not one the girls could respect."

"Don't try to be a hero," Tricia said, frustrated.

"I'm not looking to be a hero. I just want to be a decent human being," Luke said, almost wishing he could ignore this feeling inside him, the one driving him to go after Lanny. The urge for self-preservation was supposed to be stronger than the urge to sacrifice yourself for someone else. Maybe he was defective, he thought, raised by overly idealistic parents.

"And if something happens to you . . . if we never hear from you again, what do I tell the girls?" Tricia asked. Luke was surprised and gratified to see tears in her eyes.

"Tell them their father was an idiot."

Tricia laughed. "That's exactly what I'll do. Do you even know where she is, where to look for her?"

He checked his cell phone before stuffing it in his pocket. "Oh, I have an idea of how to find her."

TWENTY-SEVEN

T he driver I hired at the airport left me at the gate of an estate built on the side of a mountain. Clearly, Tilde guarded her privacy, being a public figure and wealthy beyond measure. According to the newspaper and magazine articles Alejandro had sent, her husband, the energy magnate, had died recently, leaving her with two stepsons. The husband had collected and raced vintage sports cars and suffered a fatal crash while taking a recent acquisition for a few test laps. Other than revealing that the widow had taken over her husband's charitable foundation, the latest batch of articles made no mention of her.

If I had to throw myself on the mercy of anyone on this planet, it was beyond ironic that this person would be Tilde. When we lived together under Adair's roof, I was terrified of her. She had been the most cold-blooded of all of Adair's chosen, the woman who, without any misgivings, procured unsuspecting girls and boys to serve as entertainment for Adair. Tilde had never seemed to care for anyone else, not even Adair: her own survival was all that mattered. Could a person like that change? I didn't want to be uncharitable; I wanted to believe everyone is capable of change, of acting selflessly, of becoming a better person. In my experience, the longer we lived, the more we understand and develop empathy for our fellow man, and are moved to change our selfish ways. I would hate to meet the person who was forever inured to the misery of others.

By the time I walked up the steep driveway to the house—the car itself was turned away at the gate and not allowed on the property—a handsome young man was waiting outside the front door for me. He was decoratively pretty, with the vapid expression of a fashion model, and seemed to have no curiosity about me. I wondered if he could be one of the stepsons. He listened as I told him that I was there to see Mrs. von Haupt, and he turned on his heel, expecting me to follow. He left me in a room that had a gorgeous view of a steep rocky slope and the majestic mountain range beyond. The grounds surrounding the house were covered in a thin, patchy crust of white in keeping with the earliness in the season, but the mountaintops were stark and brilliant, and thick with snow.

I knew I'd instantly recognize Tilde, as she'd made such an impression on me. No matter what she wore or how she styled her hair, I thought I'd always remember her sharp, eagle-eye stare and the way she carried herself, like a lioness. And those characteristics were still there in her photographs two hundred years later, but much softened. There were only traces of the implacable huntress she once was.

The woman who stepped into the room was tightly and elegantly edited, dressed head to toe in cream, the only contrast a pair of dark sunglasses over her eyes. Her yellow hair was cut in a gamine fashion, but she was too somber to be taken for a sprightly young woman. Her predatory air had been replaced by weariness.

She slid off her sunglasses as she walked toward me; her eyes were still lavender, giving her a coldness that could never be overcome. One last burst of nerves rippled through me. She smiled warily and reached a hand out to me. "Hello, Lanore."

We shook briefly, her firm hand like an icicle in mine. "Should I call you Birgit?" I asked.

She gestured to a pair of armchairs close to the fireplace. "When no one else is around, you can call me by my old name. I'd like that; I haven't heard it in a long while. Just please be careful if someone should join us. My stepsons are here with me; we're on a skiing holiday, one of my husband's family traditions, and I have a few friends with us as well. Needless to say, no one knows me as Tilde."

I picked up the differences in her manner immediately: she used the word "please," which I don't think I'd ever heard her use in Boston unless it was with heavy sarcasm. Her formerly shrill tone had been replaced by something calmer, soothing. And she kept her late husband's sons with her, hadn't relegated them to boarding school or left them with one of her husband's relatives. That, too, seemed unusual for the woman I had known.

"Thank you for agreeing to see me," I began, but she brushed my thanks aside.

"We must be ready to help each other," she said gently. "I'm sure you've found, as I have, that while we love our families and the special ones who come into our lives, our time with them is brief, and passes so quickly. We're comforted by their company while it lasts, but we have no one to help us put our lives in perspective. No one with whom to share the breadth of our life experiences, no one who can understand what we've been through. No one but each other."

She was so subdued and unlike the Tilde I'd known that I was starting to worry that something was amiss. Could a person change so drastically? In two hundred years, surely anything was possible. Her somberness, her listless gaze . . . And then I remembered that she was in mourning.

"I heard about your husband. I'm sorry for your loss," I hurried to say.

She bowed her head. "It was unexpected. Bruno was wonderful, one of those people you meet once in a lifetime. The newspapers only talk about his companies and his success with his businesses, but he was a considerate partner and a good father. I will miss him. I'm sure you've been in this position more than once yourself, losing the person who keeps you connected to life. I don't know about you, but I find it hard to enjoy life for myself anymore. It seems I'm only happy when the people I love are happy."

I nodded in agreement but inwardly was overwhelmed. I couldn't ask for more evidence that she'd changed than her last statement. She seemed devastated by the loss of her husband and, in contrast to the woman I had known, seemed to have become quite reflective and struggled to understand our bizarre existence. I was ready to trust her—and besides, I had no other choice at this point. I cleared my throat. "I assume Alejandro explained to you why I've come," I started hesitantly.

"He said Adair has returned after his long absence and that, for some reason, he was looking for you." She watched for my reaction while giving nothing away.

"And did he explain where Adair has been all this time and why he's looking for me now? Did he tell you that I'm responsible for Adair's disappearance?" It was harder to admit this to her than to Alejandro, maybe because I expected her to react badly, even violently. I suddenly felt very small and childlike sitting across from Tilde, waiting for an explosion of temper. In Adair's house, she'd been like a bullying older sister, relishing every opportunity to torment me.

But again, her reply was calm. "Alejandro told me something of that," she murmured.

"I'm so sorry if you were hurt by what I did, Tilde," I continued hurriedly to assure her. "Alejandro told me how difficult life was after Adair vanished, and I'm truly sorry for any hardship I may have caused you. I suppose it was selfish to do what I did, to take Adair away from all of you, but you must understand: Adair was going to take Jonathan away from me *permanently* and I couldn't let him do that. . . ."

She lifted her hand again to stop me from saying anything more. "You don't have to apologize to me. I'm *grateful* for what you did. I wanted to stop Adair—we all did—but I never saw a way. Or perhaps we were less courageous. . . ." She glanced away, ashamed. "Lanore, I wasn't always the woman you knew in Boston. After so many years with Adair, I became shaped by his nature. I did what was necessary to survive his temper, his moods. And that included hardening my heart against anyone else's plight. So, if anything, I should be apologizing to you for the terrible way I treated you."

It struck me that she had been Adair's victim, too, but while I had suffered for only a few years, she had spent centuries in his tyrannical grip. How could she *not* have changed under the pressure of his fierce will?

They all must've been twisted in this way—Alejandro, Dona, Jude, poor Savva—forced to become ruthless and calculating in order to survive. Fighting for just enough space to exist in the presence of a force as relentless as Adair. Perhaps Tilde wasn't the ogress Adair had made her out to be. It was he who'd told me her story, after all, not Tilde; he might've lied, as apparently he'd done about Uzra. He might've lied about everyone.

"Alejandro said you needed my help. It's yours, if I can be of service."

I cleared my throat nervously. "He hinted that you know about the magical arts, the source of Adair's power. I'm looking for someone who understands that sphere." My cheeks warmed as I fumbled for the right words.

She shifted in her chair. "Yes, I believe we should try to understand our condition. It makes sense, doesn't it? If you had cancer, you'd want to know all about the disease, its symptoms and effects, your options for treatment. Why should it be any different for us? That's why I've tried to study what some people might call 'magic,' to follow up on practitioners as I've heard of them.

"But if you're asking if I'm like Adair, if I acquired any power over the physical world, well, I'm sorry to disappoint you. I was with Adair a long time, nearly the longest of any of his companions, and during that time I saw him do things that are simply impossible. I've always known there was something unexplained—and possibly unexplainable—about him. I've sought to be able to understand what he is, where his power comes from, but I haven't come up with any answers, any more than anyone else. And as for *reproducing* it . . ." She trailed off, looking at me intently. "What is it, exactly, that you want?"

"I want to break the spell." I tried not to sound as ridiculous as I felt.

"Break the spell?" she asked. "Why on earth would you want to do that?"

We'd been free of Adair so long that she'd forgotten: *he* was the price for immortality. "Because Adair is coming for me."

Tilde flushed, bringing uncharacteristic warmth to those cheeks, perhaps out of embarrassment for having made me speak so plainly. "I see, and you're right. Now that he's free, that's something we'll all have to come to terms with. He'll come to each of us in turn, I have no doubt. . . . Still, to give up your life seems such a dramatic solution. Is that really what you want?" Tilde spoke passionately. "Think it through thoroughly, Lanore. Do you have any idea what might happen if your condition were, uh, alleviated? You might die immediately; we died as part of the transformation, after all. There's no guarantee that life would resume where it had left off, starting again at whatever age you were and progressing toward a normal mortal end. Your life might end immediately, right where you stood. Do you really wish to die? Have you no one to live for? No one to mourn your passing?"

The truth was I wasn't sure if I wanted to die. I was afraid of dying. Who knew what waited for me in the afterlife—God or this queen of the underworld—and what purpose could a hereafter serve if not to settle up the crimes one committed in this world? I didn't know if I'd accepted death, but I'd accepted that I had no other choice.

Tilde had raised good questions. I hadn't thought of the possibility that I might die right away. I thought I would keep my death as a possibility I could hold in abeyance, a poison pill to use when it was clear I couldn't escape from Adair. As for Tilde's second question, it would take brutal honesty to answer it. Have I no one to live for? It had always been Jonathan, just Jonathan. I thought it might be Luke. But now I'd given him up.

I twisted my hands in my lap. "No, there's no one. No one in my life, no one to come looking for me. It might as well be over."

Tilde looked at me uncertainly, then took in the purse at my feet, my abandoned jacket. I'd brought no suitcase, having forgotten it in the trunk of Jude's car. I was as I'd presented myself: a lonely soul, unattached and unprotected, blown on the wind and dropped at her doorstep. She couldn't doubt the truth of what I had told her. I was alone.

"All right . . . let me see what I can do. You're welcome to stay with us. I can understand how vulnerable you must feel, and you shouldn't be by yourself at a time like this. We have a spare room at the back of the house. Why don't you rest."

The same dark-haired young man who'd been at the front door escorted me now to a quiet cranny, a maid's room off the kitchen. On our way, we passed a great room with two young men—their hair was nearly as white as snow, and they looked so alike that they had to be brothers—sitting slouched on a leather couch in front of a television, playing some kind of video game. A few others rounded out the group: another handsome young man, a wide-eyed young woman about the same age as the brothers. They glanced at me wordlessly, with no introductions made: we could've been ghosts observing one another from our separate planes of existence.

I lay down on the single bed and listened to the voices from the great room, now mumbled and indecipherable, the murmur broken by the occasional flash of laughter. They might have been speaking a language I didn't understand, or it might have been the walls masking their words. The maid's quarters were cold and reminded me of a doctor's examination room, nondescript and spare. No computer, no television.

I must've fallen asleep on the maid's bed, because I woke to rapping at the door and had barely sat up when Tilde came into the room, a mug in her hand.

"I might have an answer to your problem. I don't want to get your hopes up, but I think this might work," she said, holding the mug out to me. "It's something I found in an old book of spells attributed to a group of thirteenth-century monks. The book's provenance has been confirmed, according to the scholars I've consulted—if that has any bearing on *anything*. I figured if you're looking for a remedy, we might as well start there as anywhere. This potion is supposed to lift all curses."

I looked into the mug of dark opaque liquid, a color between brown and green, like a frog. It smelled of bitter herbs and alcohol. "Do I drink it?"

"All of it. I've never made it before, let alone used it on anyone." She folded her arms across her chest, staring at the mug pensively. "It might not have any effect right away, and if it does . . . well, I admit, I'm a tiny bit curious to find out what will happen."

With Tilde watching, I drank down the entire contents of the mug. It tasted strongly of alcohol and something else I couldn't place, an unnatural bitterness covered by the taste of the herbs. Within minutes my muscles went slack all at once, as though I'd been hit on the back of the head. I fell on the bed, my mind functioning perfectly but unable to support myself upright. The physical change was so striking and so swift that I figured I had to be dying. *You wanted this*, I recalled. *Don't fight it*. It took all my forbearance not to panic and pump adrenaline into my veins in reaction to this weird sensation.

I opened my eyes to find Tilde leaning over me with a wicked grin, a grin I instantly remembered from our days together in Boston. She picked up the mug that had fallen from my hand. I was unable to move my mouth and ask Tilde what she had done to me.

"I figured it would be easier to knock you out than to hold you against your will. I wasn't sure if it would work on you—the date rape drug, Rohypnol—so I put enough in there to take down a horse. I'd let the boys take advantage of your sedation to have a little fun with you if I didn't think Adair would mind, but he probably wants that honor for himself—for starters, at least. God, I almost didn't think you would fall for it." She laughed that merciless, cheerless laugh that had rung through the halls of the mansion in Boston. "I thought it was all over when I said 'if anything, I should be apologizing to you.' . . . I thought, *Oh no, I've gone too far,* sure that I'd oversold it, but you didn't bat an eyelash. . . . You wanted to believe so *badly.* You haven't changed, have you? Still the gullible fool." Tilde dabbed at the corner of an eye, having laughed so hard, she was tearing.

"Okay, lie still now. Don't fight it. Just let the drug take you away. Adair should be here shortly. Have a little peace while you can. Time has caught up with you, Lanore. The reckoning you've been anticipating for centuries is just about upon you."

TWENTY-EIGHT

His wait was over. The time of deliverance was at hand. And still—the private jet had not been fast enough for Adair. He had twitched throughout the entire flight, barely able to tolerate the chatter of his companions. And now the car that picked him up at the airport—could it not go faster? He thought he might burst out of his own skin with impatience.

As they neared Tilde's house, Adair felt something fundamental shift inside him, as though a great force was bearing down on him and compressing his consciousness and energy into something as hard and dense as a diamond, for a purpose unknown. He couldn't help but think of the girl in the Wonderland story, a fantastical tale read to him by Pendleton, who admired it very much. Adair thought this was how the girl must have felt when she was shrunk by means of a magical potion so she could fit through the door to another realm. He felt he, too, was being changed, altered to fit the circumstances that lay ahead.

At the same time, he felt as though a storm front was descending on him. The keening in his brain was brighter and stronger—he could feel Lanore's presence building the closer he got—and his thinking was clearer than it had been since his entombment. Whatever had been interfering with his mind was suddenly swept away. He was being changed by an unseen force, made stronger, sharper, more intuitive, for reasons he couldn't guess. He had the distinct impression that he could see into the mind of every living thing while being able to keep each one separate and distinct, like having a conversation with everyone simultaneously. He was sure it was a trick or hallucination, a problem with his overwrought mind, but at the same time he couldn't ignore it. It was exhilarating.

Tilde stood waiting by the front of the house as his car pulled up. She trembled with visible excitement as he climbed the stairs, but fell back when he swept by her without a word of greeting, let alone a kiss or embrace. Crestfallen for an instant, she recovered to hug Jude and Alejandro each in turn, like siblings she had not seen in a long while. Pendleton hung back at the rear of the group, watching them as carefully as the newest child on the playground. The last to emerge from the car was a tall man in a long overcoat who peered up at the sun through dark glasses.

Adair stopped in the front hall, cocking his head like a bloodhound trying to pick up a scent in the air. "Where is she?" he asked Tilde over his shoulder.

"You needn't worry. She's here and can't get away. I wouldn't disappoint you."

Tilde wound around the others to step beside him. She lifted a hand to his chest, then—when he hadn't batted her hand aside—pressed her cheek against his for a long instant. "I've missed you."

As soon as Tilde's palm pressed against his breast, in that one touch, Adair was flooded with the knowledge of every day she'd lived since he'd been gone. It was similar to when he'd touched the doorknob during his projection to Lanore's house in Paris and felt her come alive to him, except now it was more intense (for being present in the flesh, he guessed). In that one instant, Adair knew everything there was to know about Tilde: what she'd been through for the past two hundred years and everything she was doing now.

He saw that she had spent the entire time living from husband to husband, killing one to live in solitary contentment off his fortune until it ran out, when she would find a new rich man and start all over again. She'd paid someone to tamper with the car of this last one once she'd tired of his egomaniacal ways. Since then she'd seduced both his sons for amusement and to fill some pitiful and implacable longing in her soul. *What a sad creature she has become*, Adair thought, *aimless and petty*.

"It's so good to see you," Tilde purred, and she pressed against him for a scant second, revealing her desire for him. Adair found it unnerving, like being licked by a tiger. He almost swerved for her cheek when he bent over to kiss her, when he realized that Tilde and the others would notice if he didn't kiss her on the mouth. It would not sit well with Tilde—nor would it do for him to betray his weakness for Lanore to a woman like Tilde, whose ruthlessness he had once depended on but now detested.

Adair cupped the back of her head and pulled her toward him, giving her the kind of kiss she would expect, the kind he used to give her, domineering and possessive. Reassured, Tilde sighed and relaxed.

She lifted her chin in the direction of the man standing beside Pendleton. "Who's that? I would almost swear—"

"It's Jonathan," Alejandro said.

"But what's happened to him? He doesn't look the same. I thought we would never—" she said, her voice rising in alarm. Jonathan regarded her with a bemused look as he pocketed his sunglasses.

Adair replied, "Don't worry, Tilde. What's happened to Jonathan will never happen to you—as long as you manage to avoid dying."

She swiveled back to look at Jonathan in horror.

"Yes, I'm back from the dead," he said drily. "All things considered, I think I look pretty good."

At that moment a shuffling sound came from the back of the

house, and the two brothers walked toward them with the quiet curiosity of a pair of housecats as they peered out from behind long platinum bangs. After one last uncertain stare for Jonathan, Tilde put her unease aside and extended an arm in their direction, waving them to her. "Let me introduce my stepsons. Josef, Mika, come here. . . . Boys, I want you to meet a very dear friend of mine. This is Adair." Her smirk was the same as it had always been, possessive and gloating. The smirk he'd seen many times before, whenever she would bring him prey—a frightened young woman, a young man helpless with lust—that she intended for him to share with her. Adair knew by her manner that Tilde meant for them to be lovers again, but he had no intention of letting that happen.

His ability to sense their thoughts and feelings continued, and he realized that he didn't even need to touch the stepsons for their stories to rush at him. A look was sufficient, part of this unexpected strengthening of his power, or perhaps it was the strength of their suffering. The older one was trying to appear worldly and sophisticated at nineteen, to be the kind of man (still a boy, really) who could fuck his father's wife and remain unaffected. His aura told Adair that he was unhappy and guilt-ridden, wishing he could be free of her yet under her control because of their secret.

But Mika, the younger one . . . Adair could tell that the boy was completely in love with her. His desperation seeped through his teenage ennui. He thought he'd concealed it, but the only thing on his mind was being with Tilde again, his desire betraying him as he shifted and fidgeted uncomfortably. He was, maybe, sixteen, and at this age a slave to lust. At the moment, he was nearly paralyzed by the desire to put his cock in her mouth. He wanted only to be lost between her legs and on her lips, and everything else in his life—indulgent as it was—came a distant second. No girl his own age could make him feel the way Tilde could, or so he believed. He'd do anything for her, and Adair knew that made him dangerous. It was stupid and incendiary to fuck both her stepsons, and Adair respected Tilde less for it.

The two boys stared back at him before Tilde dismissed them, hostility roiling beneath their calm expressions. For all Adair knew, they might have been good boys before crossing paths with Tilde, but now they would be forever warped by the shameful thing they'd done with her. They would always believe there was something fundamentally wrong with them, that they were bad inside, like rotted fruit. Tilde was a smart woman and he thought she knew better than to corrupt her own stepsons for sport. Nothing good could come of it. Adair wanted no part of this melodrama with Tilde and wished he had never found out about it. It only heightened his impatience to see Lanore and put everything else behind him.

Tilde, believing she knew what was on Adair's mind, touched his sleeve lightly. "You'll find her at the end of this hall, in the room behind the kitchen. I'll send the boys to the slopes, and I'll head into town with Jude and Alejandro to give you some privacy for your reunion."

"What about Jonathan?" Jude asked. "We can't take him with us."

"I'll stay in the car with him," Pendleton spoke, surprising everyone. He turned to Jonathan. "I'd like to ask him about his experiences. In the next world."

"All right, we'll bring him with us, but cover him up as much as possible. And have him keep his sunglasses on. I don't want him frightening my driver," Tilde instructed.

"Good," Adair said. "Maybe he'll be more forthcoming with you. And, Pendleton, if he does tell you anything, I want you to make a full report to me."

Tilde squeezed Adair's forearm. "The house is yours. Take all the time you want." Her eyes shone at the prospect of what was about to happen, as excited as a foxhound anticipating the kill. It was a good thing she couldn't see into his heart the way he could see into hers,

Adair realized, for she'd be disappointed by what she'd find. But he said nothing, watching her usher the others up the stairs to dress or retrieve coats, the sooner to get them out of the house and leave him to his prize.

"Don't forget your promise," Jonathan said in a low voice as he was led away. "You swore under heaven. Heaven will be watching."

"I remember," Adair replied, wondering if he'd be able to keep it, now that he was about to come face-to-face with Lanore.

TWENTY-NINE

I jolted awake. The keening in my head was now at a terrible pitch, and I knew at once that Adair had arrived. I looked down at my hands to see that Tilde had come in as I had lain unconscious and tied them together in front of me but had left my legs unbound; I shuddered at the realization that she'd no doubt left my legs unfettered for Adair's convenience. She was one of those women who had only contempt for their own gender, and took a perverse pleasure in a man's abuse of another woman.

His presence was strong enough to make it nearly impossible to think or listen. Even in the darkness of the tiny room, my vision went white from panic. I could make out other signs of his arrival: the slamming of the front door, followed by the murmur of several voices and then his voice, a distinct rumble to which my ear was still tuned. The thunder of his pitch reverberated down the hall and up the walls; it traveled through the pipes of the bed's metal frame. His voice passed through me in low waves, like sonar, each wave heralding his arrival. Each wave announcing he was coming for me.

The other voices fell away, or my frightened mind couldn't process them. His footsteps grew closer and louder, the sound carrying through the floorboards, my heart beating twice as fast as the foot-falls. I looked about desperately for a way out, but there was only a narrow casement window placed high in the wall, and I knew I'd never be able to free myself and get to the window in time. A far door opened onto a bathroom but it was small and plain as a shoe box, and offered nowhere to hide.

I had risen from the mattress on one elbow to scan for hiding places, when the door flew open. Adair filled the doorframe, so much bigger than I remembered, or perhaps fear made him seem larger than he really was. The other sounds of the house had dissolved, and all I could hear was blood sluicing in my ears and the beating of my heart, rapid as that of a hare that had been running for its life. My throat was dry as a long-rusted pipe, and I felt as though I was going to be sick.

He stepped into the room and closed the door. I could see his face better now, and it was both frightening and hard to read. He did not look at all as I had imagined he would when we came face-to-face again. He wasn't red with rage. He wasn't shouting or threatening me. He stood motionless in the doorway, seemingly unable to take his eyes off me, but I couldn't tell what he was thinking. I held the thinnest sliver of hope that he might let me beg for leniency or that I might find a way to deflect or lessen his anger the tiniest bit.

"Adair," I said once I'd found my voice. "Let me explain—"

In two quick strides he was across the room, his hand lifted and poised to strike me across the mouth—but he froze in place. I cringed, closing my eyes, but there was no strike. I opened my eyes to find he was staring at me. A sad, strangled gurgle sounded in the back of his throat.

"Please, Adair—"

"Don't. You are not to talk to me. Not yet," he said, choked with emotion. He reached for my face and I drew away reflexively, falling backward onto the bed. My pulling away angered him, and his expression changed swiftly and completely, like the striking of a match.

I tried to get up and he pushed me down, climbing on top of me with grim determination. He brushed his face up my neck and across both cheeks, drawing in my scent before taking my mouth with his. He wasn't kissing me so much as devouring me, and I could do nothing to escape him. His body over me, the smell of his skin and his hair, the taste of his breath—it was all so familiar, and so frightening. He leaned against me and held me in place like an animal as his hands searched lower, and then I felt my skirt being hiked over my hips, the blush of cold air on exposed skin, my panties being jerked down.

"Please don't do this," I started to say, but he was like a deadweight on top of me, and I could see that I wouldn't be able to dissuade him by begging for mercy. I was only to experience what was coming next. His hands steadied my hips and then he was in me, dry pain tearing as he pressed into me hard, over and over and over. He said nothing, didn't insult me, didn't curse, didn't even sigh, just ground his teeth with each thrust. I clenched my eyes shut and tried not to scream, and suppressed the urge to struggle, for struggling would only make it worse.

And then I heard the sound in the back of his throat. Not the grunt and groan of pleasure that I was used to hearing when we coupled. It sounded as though he might be smothering some kind of pain. He came quickly, slamming into me at the same time a strange cry escaped from his throat. It was a sound I'd never heard him make before, and it was unmistakably sad. I lay underneath him while he stroked my face and my hair, his breathing hot and tense in my ear.

At great length he climbed off me. I was wet with his ejaculate, my head pounding as though it might explode. With my eyes still closed, I listened to the metallic rasp of a zipper being worked. He didn't say one word to me, and I remained conscious long enough only to hear the door open and close behind me before falling into a dark, agonizing oblivion.

THIRTY

A dair stood in the hall just outside the room where Lanore lay aching in a tumble of damp sheets. He held a hand over his eyes, his fingers trembling. He was spent, his every muscle twitched. He wasn't sure how long he'd been in the room; all he remembered was the moment he spilled into her.

He hadn't wanted this, not for their reunion. He'd had every intention of talking to her, telling her of the change that had come over him since he'd been freed. He longed to tell her that he'd forgiven her and ask her to give him a chance . . . but when the moment finally came, he found it impossible to speak in her presence. He became tongue-tied as soon as he saw her, thick-tongued with lust. More than lust, he craved the closeness that came with being inside her. He wanted to melt into her, and wanted her to melt into him. But she hadn't shown the slightest sign that she would have him, and so he took her forcefully, unable to stop himself.

He'd taken her despite what he knew, for her life had rushed at him the moment he touched her, the same as Tilde's had come to him. He knew instantly of her years of loneliness waiting for Jonathan—and felt a pang of envy that she hadn't longed for *him* in that same way. Her feelings for him were a tangle of fear and revulsion for the things he had done to her and the others. He thought he felt a tiny glimmer of something like attraction, but it was small and weak, and he guessed it was nothing but a residual speck of the love she had felt for him in Boston, like visible light from a distant star that was already long dead.

Standing on the other side of the door, he wanted to beat his head against the wall with regret. For centuries he had thought about the moment when he would see Lanore again, at first choreographing elaborate scenes of revenge and, after his epiphany, wondering how he would make her understand that he had changed. Now the moment had come and gone, and it had been unlike any of the scenes he'd played over and over in his mind. It was too late, over before he realized what he'd done. He felt a jumble of contradictory emotions: nausea, triumph, remorse. He wanted to rush back into her room and apologize, and at the same time was disgusted that Lanore had reduced him to his present state of weakness.

All that *should* matter was that she was his again; it shouldn't matter how she felt about it. *He* was the one who'd been wronged, after all. There was no reason for him to feel as wretched as he did.

But he couldn't deny that it *did* matter to him. As soon as he laid eyes on her—at the exact same time revenge sang in his ears—he also wanted to hold her tight as his heart exploded with joy. This simpering, lovesick part of him wanted only to feast on the sight of her, to revel like a schoolboy in all the things he loved about her and had missed. He was delighted to find that the mere sight of her still moved him; her beautiful face still could make him weep. He put his hand to the door, hoping for a wild moment that it was not too late; he would tell her not to be afraid of him, he would beg her to give him another chance. She once felt something like love for him—he *knew* this was true, she couldn't deny it—and all he wanted was to make her love him again.

But his pride stopped him, and he took his hand from the door.

Adair went to the bathroom to wash his face. The water helped to calm him, and he stared into the mirror, remembering how she'd turned her face away from him and tried to resist his kisses. How she'd tensed against him and flinched when he withdrew his spent member from her. Jonathan had been right to doubt him: he couldn't make Lanore love him. He couldn't even stop himself from raping her, couldn't stop from being swamped by the swirl of his conflicting emotions. How would he ever be worthy of her love if those dark urges still lived inside of him? He had to fight to keep from smashing the mirror over and over until it was nothing but needles of glass.

He'd tried to get his emotions under control on the trip to Aspen from Boston. He'd hoped that, when he saw Lanore again, he'd find that his feelings had changed, that he wouldn't feel this giddiness and optimism or the desire to see his love reciprocated in her eyes. Things would be easier for him then: if it was not love, he could punish her to his satisfaction and then dispose of her.

But, maddeningly, the signs were that he still loved her. He wished there was some way to extract this love from wherever it resided inside him like a creeping vine, curled and wrapped around his organs and his bones, squeezing his heart and cutting off oxygen to his brain, insinuating itself into his very marrow. He'd rip out the strangling, cancerous growth if only he knew how. It was killing his vitality; the unstoppable force of his being was grinding against the immovable object of love, and he knew from costly experience that he would not win such a battle. He could not force someone to love him.

Adair showered to wash away all reminders of what he'd done to Lanore; he washed her juices off his groin and the smell of her fear from his memory as he drank a bottle of something strong. Still, nothing would alleviate the regret he felt for giving in to this flash of vengefulness and lust. Now, whiplashed by emotion, Adair wanted to inflict pain upon himself like a penitent. He thought about slitting his wrists to see if it would bring any relief, if bleeding off his self-hatred would harden him to her. He remembered how Dona used to cut his arms when he was drunk, thinking it ridiculous, a futile act. Now Adair understood why he did it, saw the allure of the act and the poignancy of its utter uselessness.

What a punishment God had sent to him. *God*—he hadn't thought of God in a long time, except in a disparaging way, and yet, as if he were a superstitious old woman on her deathbed, the name of God flew to his lips! The invocation of God at this bitterest, darkest time shocked him. It was maddening; what was this woman doing to him? She had turned him inside out, made him into something he was not, or was turning him back to something he had once been and tried to deny. He had been a young man when he decided to forsake love for science. Stupidly, he'd believed one had a choice in these matters. As it turned out, he was only human after all.

He wandered to the kitchen for something else to drink, opening cabinets until he found a bottle of wine, and stood in the middle of the room, uncertain what to do next. No matter where he was or what he did, Lanore's presence pulled him like a magnet; he was unable to be happy anywhere but at her side. With a groan, Adair resisted the urge to take two glasses up to her room, and instead drew out a chair and poured a solitary glass.

The others' return saved Adair from standing watch in the kitchen all night long. Tilde's stepsons and their friends were still skiing, but the others came back in high spirits, their voices echoing through the cavernous rooms. Adair figured they had fled, these otherwise blood-thirsty and heartless fiends, because they could easily see themselves in Lanny's position, suffering whatever horrors he was inflicting on her. But this, Adair knew, wasn't true: not one of them could invoke the emotions that she drew out of him. He'd never loved anyone the way he loved her.

Adair, sober despite having downed a second bottle of wine, joined his attendants. "I had been frantic," Alejandro was saying when Adair slipped into the room. "I had started feeling the presence again in my head, just like you, yes?" he asked as he looked expectantly from face to face. "I was wondering what it meant . . . when Lanore *shows up* at my studio. So I think to myself, *Could this be just a strange coincidence?* But no, I know it cannot be a coincidence at all. When she admitted that *she* was responsible for Adair's disappearance, I almost lost my composure right then and there—"

"I'd always suspected she had something to do with it," Tilde interrupted, nodding at the others. "Right from the start, there was something about her I didn't trust."

"—so I know I must do something," Alejandro continued, raising his voice to be heard over the others. "She cannot be allowed to get away with what she has done to Adair, but what am I to do?"

"Why didn't you just hold on to her yourself? Keep her until you found Adair," Pendleton asked to the Spaniard's surprise. He wasn't fooled by Alejandro's feyness, his pretense of delicacy; Adair appreciated that.

Alejandro feigned shock. "I couldn't think straight, for one thing, being taken unawares like that. But, my dear, me? Lay hands on someone? No, but I tell you what came to me: call Tilde. I was sure she would know what to do.

"So I fabricated a story to send Miss Lanore on her way, and then I called Tilde, and she told me to send a message to every one of the others we knew, to see if anyone had been contacted by Adair." He smiled, satisfied with himself. "And then I heard from Jude, and a day later I was in Boston, reunited with Adair, as though my desire to see him had made him materialize, like a dream. I was speechless with joy." He turned then and caught sight of Adair and his face lit up in rapture. "And I am still amazed to see him again with us like this. As though all this time was nothing but a nightmare, but it is over now. It is a miracle."

Adair grunted noncommittally, lacking the desire to engage with Alejandro's sycophancy. The truth was Adair had been as shocked to see Alejandro without having beckoned him. The Spaniard turned up on Jude's doorstep, assuming he'd resume his place in Adair's entourage. He brought a box of photographs with him and insisted on showing Adair picture after picture from his life: people he had known, places he had lived. The most embarrassing were of the house where he currently lived, which Alejandro had practically made into a shrine to his former master. He'd re-created Adair's bedroom down to its hookahs and bower of cushions. One of Adair's very own silk banyans hung by the bed forlornly. Worse yet, the Spaniard had brought with him the torture device, the web of restraints, and handed it over to Adair reverently, as though Adair could bear to use it now.

As the others gossiped and carried on around him, Adair regarded them critically. Had they always been so disagreeable and he'd not noticed before? Was Jude always so greedy, Alejandro so obsequious? Or, without a strong hand to guide them, had they let their worst attributes grow out of control? Adair hated self-indulgence, thinking it a curse of the lazy. He wasn't sure that he wanted to take up with any of them a second time; it would take too much work to reform them. Pendleton seemed the only one with promise, Adair thought; he might banish the rest of them, give his household a good purging, but spare Pendleton. A man needed at least one reliable servant.

And then there was Jonathan, sitting by himself, listening to the cackling magpies but making no comment. Adair thought Jonathan seemed subdued. Perhaps he was wondering what had transpired with Lanore, whether Adair had kept his promise. Or perhaps he could see that Adair had struggled with his emotions and lost.

At the mention of Lanore's name in the conversation around him, Adair felt a twinge near his heart as he recalled again what he'd done in the room down the hall. He'd had the chance to show her mercy and squandered it; she'd never trust him now. His former entourage chattered on around him, not suspecting that he was racked with shame, that he wanted to douse himself with gasoline and light a match, or hack himself into a thousand pieces. He would do anything to be free of his own miserable self, but there was no escaping his nature . . . or regret, either, as he knew too well.

The door opened and the skiers returned on a cloud of aimless talk and sarcastic laughter, their young faces red from exertion. Upon seeing the adults gathered around the fireplace, they quickly smothered all cheer and became sullen-faced teenagers again.

"Mika," Adair called over his shoulder to the youngest, his words slurred as his tongue thickened from the wine. "Come here, boy. I have an errand for you."

A dead silence fell over the room except for a sharp intake of breath from Tilde. The younger boy stepped forward reluctantly.

"I want you to go to the room behind the kitchen," Adair continued. "You'll find a woman in there. Bring her some towels and untie her hands so she can wash up."

The word "untie" cut through the air like a high, sharp bell, and the young ones glanced nervously at one another to see if they'd heard correctly. Shock melted into disbelief at what they'd heard, and one of them laughed, thinking it was a joke.

Jonathan started to rise. "Let me take care of it."

"Stay where you are," Adair growled without taking his eyes off the young orphan, who, despite being heir to millions, seemed as surly and insecure as a kitchen boy. "No. You'll do it, Mika. . . . You *want* to go see what I'm talking about, don't you? I can *feel* that you do. There's a good boy. Mind you don't listen to a word the woman says. She is a siren, and you know about sirens, don't you? They can drive men mad with their song."

"He's had too much to drink," Jude said apologetically to the boys. "He's kidding, obviously."

Tilde started for the hall. "Mika, stay where you are. I think it would be best if I handled this—"

"Sit down!" Adair boomed, shocking the room into stillness. "Did you not hear what I just said? It's Mika's job. I want him to prove himself to *me*," Adair said, his tone unmistakable in its warning.

Conflicting emotions battled inside; earlier, he had disapproved of Tilde corrupting the boy, but now, in his drunken state, Adair wanted to see how the boy would react when faced with someone weaker in peril, like coming across a rabbit in a snare. Does he let it go, or does he snap its neck? Or perhaps by sending the boy, an unknown quantity, to see his prisoner, he was tempting fate to upset his plans. As Adair sat with all those eyes staring at him, the room tense and uncomfortable, he realized that all he wanted was to make this spectacle stop. As though there was someone capable of stopping him.

The boy stared at him pointedly before walking off in the direction of the kitchen, and his friends wisely chose to disappear, heading for the staircase. Before anyone else could speak, the doorbell rang. Jude sprinted for it, seeming relieved for the opportunity to get away. Before long, however, they heard a man's raised voice demanding to see the owner of the house, a murmured response from Jude, and then the man's voice again, louder, and the name "Lanore" distinctly audible, as well as "police." Tilde started to rise but Adair raised his hand, bidding her to remain, and he lurched from his seat to follow Jude's path out of the room.

A tall, middle-aged man stood beyond the doorway, trying to get around Jude, who was barring the way. The man was harried and flushed, nervous but not about to leave without being persuaded more strongly. He pushed his eyeglasses farther up the bridge of his nose.

"I'm telling you, there's no one named 'Tilde' here," Jude was saying patiently as Adair stepped behind him.

"What's going on? Can I be of help?" He wanted to get a good look at this man he presumed to be Dr. Luke Findley.

"As I was explaining to your friend here, I've come looking for my girlfriend. Her name is Lanny. I know she's here. Her cell phone

GPS shows this address—" The man stopped speaking once he peered deeply into Adair's eyes, and discomfort descended over him visibly. "You're Adair, aren't you? The man she told me about. You're real. You really exist," he said with a touch of awe, his voice dry. Jude stepped backward, away from the door.

"Yes, I am. And you are . . . ?"

"Luke Findley. But you know that already, don't you?"

"It seems we both know a little about each other. Come in, Findley. Lanore is here, but you will forgive me if I don't send for her right now: she's not in a position to receive visitors." Much to Adair's amusement, this man obeyed like someone in a dream, walking slowly into the hall. From there, he took in the others, suddenly understanding that the stories were true. He peered more closely, curious and repulsed at the same time, but didn't comment.

Adair looked Luke up and down. "So you are Lanore's lover. To tell the truth, I am surprised. Do not take this the wrong way, but you are something of a disappointment. Not up to her usual standards. Lanore usually prefers her men . . . better looking."

"I heard you do, too," Luke countered automatically.

Adair was taken aback. The comeback was a surprise; perhaps he wasn't as harmless as he appeared if he had the courage to say something like this. Brave or not, however, Adair reacted as he would to any jibe and punched Luke in the face with a closed fist. Something cracked inside Luke's mouth, and blood dribbled from his bottom lip, which he had bitten through. He spit shards of a broken tooth into a palm.

"Take care you don't anger me further or you'll find out *exactly* how I like my men," Adair warned as he examined a scrape across his knuckles, a nick from the edge of one of Luke's teeth. "Do you think maybe her tastes have changed and she is looking for a father figure, old man?" he said while flexing his hand, the cut quickly vanishing as though it had never existed. "It never would have worked between the two of you. She wouldn't have been content for long. You'd have become nothing more than a lapdog for her, an amusement to keep her company. She hates being alone, you know. She'd welcome the devil into her bed so long as he promised to stay until morning." He watched the man flinch. "Yes, that's all you could ever be to her: a servant when you can be useful to her, a toy when you cannot. She can be ruthless, you know."

"I guess you'd know," Luke mumbled through bloodied lips. "She got rid of *you*, didn't she?"

One of the onlookers let out a hiss, another a groan, amused by the visitor's foolhardiness. This time Adair said nothing in response, just drove a punch hard into Luke's stomach. He leaned over Luke, who had fallen to the floor and was writhing helplessly. "You haven't a hope in the world against me. I advise you to try my patience no more."

He waved an arm at the pack of jackals at his back, suddenly tired of the audience. "Get out, all of you. Leave me alone with him." They shuffled out, casting sideways glances his way as he paced the marble foyer. *Let them be confused*, he decided, not caring what they thought anymore.

Adair could sense that Lanore's feelings for Luke were genuine; in a way, they were as strong as they had been for Jonathan, although they represented a different kind of love. It bothered him tremendously that he could lose Lanore to such an unremarkable man. It didn't take the sun god to steal her from him.

He kicked Luke as he lay on the ground, deep into his soft stomach, then a second time to his face. It felt good to hit someone, to exorcise his anger. "Why did you come here?" he asked when he'd finished working him over, his monumental rage finally subsiding. "Do you think you are more deserving of her than I, that you have any claim to her at all? What did you think you could possibly do for her by coming here?"

"I had to come," Luke managed to gasp out, arms clasped over his stomach, sputtering blood onto the blond wood floors. "I knew she was here. I couldn't abandon her. I'd rather die than live without her." Adair wanted to despise the man on the floor before him but couldn't; they were too much alike, both helpless in their love for her.

If he couldn't make himself kill this man, he wanted the lovesick fool to be gone from his sight. He pushed his sweat-soaked hair back from his face, then leaned over Luke. "I'm done with you—for now," Adair said, lifting him from the ground with one hand. "While I am gone, I want you to think about the hopelessness of your position. Give up. Just give up. You will never be with her again; I won't allow it." He took some comfort from saying these things, as though he could will the future into being merely by wanting it.

He nudged Luke down the hall. "Listen to me. Accept what I'm telling you and I might not kill you. I will send you back to your family, your daughters. I'm sure they still need you. Think about your obligation to them. There is no shame in giving up on her to go back to them. In fact, it is honorable." Adair reached into Luke's pocket and plucked out a cell phone. "Now, I'm going to put you somewhere quiet, by yourself, so you can think about what I've said. Remember, I don't want to kill you, so don't force my hand."

THIRTY-ONE

Adair knew of only one place where he could hide Luke: the garage, a cavernous space with bays for four vehicles. He secured Luke to a pillar, his hands tied behind his back. No need to worry about leaving his prisoner unguarded, since the garage was removed from the comings and goings of the household. Besides, the man was drifting on the edge of consciousness, dripping blood on the oil-stained concrete floor. He wasn't likely to make trouble.

After taking care of this unexpected visitor, it was time to move on to the matter weighing most heavily on his mind at the moment: Jonathan. His discomfort in Jonathan's presence was now nearly unbearable. Most of it was guilt, Adair figured, guilt for what he'd done to Lanore, and for robbing Jonathan of his peace. But partly, it was because Adair no longer knew what Jonathan *was* anymore. Despite appearances, he was not a product of this world alone. At times he seemed to be an oracle, given the gift of future sight. Perhaps he had been made into a portal between the two worlds, a conduit for messages from these greater beings. And yet, at other times Jonathan seemed merely to be a spy of this queen he spoke of so cryptically.

The idea of a queen filled Adair with surprising dread. A queen implied that there might be a king, too, a man who might feel betrayed by his queen's interest in Jonathan. Most distressing was the vague feeling Adair had that he must avoid this woman and that under no circumstances should he ever meet her. He had no idea why this should be, but he'd come to trust his instincts.

All this uncertainty left Adair queasy and off balance. He'd spent his life figuring out the unknown. However, it appeared that in order to understand this mystery he'd have to leave this world—a step he wasn't yet ready to take. If Jonathan was a connection to the afterlife or to the queen, Adair saw that he needed to shut this channel down.

Adair went to the kitchen and selected a knife, one that was heavy and broad, a serious piece of steel, and hefted it once in his hand. He then went upstairs, searching from room to room until he found Jonathan.

Jonathan looked at what Adair had brought, but didn't seem alarmed. He seemed to expect this development: the two of them alone, the butcher's knife. He spoke first, taking advantage of Adair's hesitation. "You didn't keep your promise about Lanny."

The air between them suddenly felt close and prickly hot to Adair. How could Jonathan know what had transpired in that room if a voice from the other world hadn't whispered in his ear?

"Don't bother to deny it. I can tell by the look on your face."

Adair turned away from Jonathan. "Then you should also be able to tell that I am in hell. The last thing I wanted to do was to hurt her. But I'd been waiting for this day for too long. . . . I couldn't help myself. My nature would not be denied."

"Excuses are useless," Jonathan answered. "Do you think it matters *why*? All that matters is *what* you did."

"You expected too much of me," Adair bellowed, angry at being taken to task.

"We're talking about Lanny's expectations, not mine."

"What happened . . . could not have happened any other way. A man cannot change his nature."

"We all have our natures to overcome. And if you couldn't overcome yours, that means you are too weak, Adair. You aren't deserving of her love. You've ruined whatever chance you had. Do you think she'll ever be able to forget or to forgive you now?"

Anger and despair flared inside Adair at these words. Lanore was his destiny, but the very thought of her plunged him into emotional chaos. It maddened him that he couldn't control her. He'd been able to force everyone else to bend to his will, because ultimately he was willing to sacrifice whatever feeling they might have for him in exchange for obedience. With Lanore it was different. It felt good, strangely, to surrender to his need for her. And she was the only one to whom he *could* surrender. Only when he was with her could he forget—could he let go of—everything else that had seemed important.

But he had underestimated the strength of his desire. Jonathan had warned him, after all. How stupid he had been to think he could change his nature so easily. It was not starting fresh and new between them; he'd seen to that, hadn't he? Destroyed any chance before it could even begin.

Still, he was only a man. He had limitations, he could not change completely in a day. He had expected too much, promised Jonathan too much. Damn Jonathan. Damn him back to hell. Adair would do things *his* way. Starting with Jonathan.

It was time to send him back to the afterlife. His place was no longer on this side of the veil. He was a shade, an apparition clothed in flesh, maybe a spy or trickster, meant to lead Adair astray. Besides, Adair felt in his marrow that Lanore mustn't see Jonathan again, that somehow this would lead to a great undoing. Even thinking of such an occurrence made Adair shiver.

Too, Lanore would take one look at Jonathan's ruined face and blame Adair. Know Adair was responsible, maybe even think he'd done it out of spite. He felt a sour, sinking sensation in his stomach at the thought of her disappointment. He seemed destined to disappoint her.

Damn it all. Damn Jonathan. Damn her, too. She'd brought this on herself, he thought bitterly.

A wave of shame washed over Adair, hot as boiling oil—shame that he couldn't control himself, nor could he hide this from Jonathan. Ashamed that Jonathan seemed to know more about him than he himself knew. And he burned with jealousy, too. "You needn't concern yourself about Lanore anymore, Jonathan. She's mine now." He thumbed the edge of the knife. "And since I have Lanore once again, I have no more need of you. It's time you go back to this queen of yours."

"You might lie to yourself but you can't lie to me. I know why you're sending me back, Adair. You fear her, the queen I've told you about, and you're right to be fearful. Trust me, you don't want her to come looking for you. But that's not why you're going to kill me now." Jonathan's dark eyes studied him in an unnerving way. "It's because you don't want Lanny to see me. As ruined as I am, you're afraid she'll still prefer me to you. And that would destroy you."

His guess hit its mark. Adair flinched as though an arrow had pierced his chest. Jonathan was right: it would *destroy* him to see Lanore's face light up with love for Jonathan. He couldn't bear it. He would rather be cowardly and petty than allow the lovers to be reunited. But this was a fitting part of Lanore's punishment, he insisted, if only to himself. For what she'd done to him, she should never see Jonathan again. If he must suffer, they would both suffer, too. If he couldn't be happy, no one would be happy.

"I don't care what you think, Jonathan," he said, bringing out the knife. "I will send you back to the world from which you came, back into the arms of your new mistress."

Jonathan held up a hand to stay the knife. "My last word of advice to you, Adair. You want Lanny's love—I know you do, and it's right that you should. For no one has ever loved you, Adair. Not your so-called friends, not your family. Not your minions. You might be the only soul in all of creation who has never been loved. The only unloved soul in the history of the world. Lanny is your last chance, Adair."

The revelation was too much for Adair. Flooded with shame, he drew the knife across Jonathan's throat in one fluid motion. He didn't flatter himself to think that he had moved too adroitly for Jonathan to defend himself: the dead man offered no resistance, wanting to return to the realm he had come from. Adair expected Jonathan's neck would be gristly and tough to sever, but bone and tendon parted like butter before the knife, the head sliced off cleanly. There was no fountain of blood, only an oozing of a black, sticky sap. The body remained upright, suspended by the contraction of muscles for as long as it took to exhale, and then fell in a heap to the floor like a marionette whose strings had been cut. It was as though he'd been keeping company with a shade, a golem, and not a real man at all. Looking down on Jonathan, Adair felt a chill pass through him.

Pendleton was the first one to come across Adair, standing outside Jonathan's room. Adair handed him the bloody knife. "Tell Tilde we will need some paid man to come for the body. I want it dumped in water—somewhere deep, where it can never be recovered." He continued down the hall before Pendleton could even acknowledge his instructions, so stunned was he at the sight of Jonathan's decapitated body crumpled on the Persian rug.

THIRTY-TWO

fter Adair left, I lay immobilized on the bed, curled on
my side with my knees tucked close to my chest. I must've
clenched every muscle in my body during the rape, because
now I hurt with every breath. My jaw, my ribs, my hips—all ached.
I felt this pain because he had willed it. He wanted me to suffer. Remembering what Adair had done, I pulled my knees in tighter and
cried in fear and frustration, knowing this—and worse—was to be
my future.

It was a miracle that it hadn't been worse. Adair hadn't hit me,
hadn't put a hand on me in any way. There had been no threats, no
taunts, no gloating. As a matter of fact, if I remembered correctly—
the episode was a blur of terror—he'd even tried to kiss me. And
after he climaxed, he rushed off as though ashamed. Not exactly
what I thought would happen if he caught me. It made no sense.

Someone was coming: I heard the rattling of the doorknob. The
door swung open and there stood Tilde's stepson Mika, spindly as
a colt. He was so pale that he glowed like a ghost. With those furtive eyes, he stared not at my face or at my bound hands but lower,
drawn to the unexpected sight of a half-naked torso: my skirt was

still twisted around my waist. I tugged at it awkwardly and he didn't move to help me, didn't cry out in alarm, didn't seem empathetic or outraged or frightened in the least. He just stared at me.

"Help me, please," I said, hoping to move him to pity.

He continued to stare for a beat or two and then shook his head. "That man—he told me to untie your hands so you can clean up." Of course, he didn't need to explain who sent him: no one else would've dared. Mika came over and studied the cord but I'd struggled against it so furiously that the knot had seized tight. He drew out a little pocketknife and sawed at it until it fell away. "Tell me, who is this man who has come to see Birgit?" he asked as he worked. He was plainly rattled by jealousy. "Why is he here?"

My instinct was to protect Mika from what was going on around him, thinking he was still a child. "He's dangerous. Stay away from him. Don't trust him." I rubbed at abrasions on my wrists, knowing they would disappear soon enough, though in the unlit room this tiny miracle was sure to escape his notice.

A faint smile turned up the corners of his mouth. "He said the same about you. He called you a siren and told me not to listen to your song."

"You're practically an adult. You can decide for yourself which of us to trust." You'd think it was plain enough whom he should believe, but I could tell by the distant expression on his face that he didn't care who I was or what had happened to me. He lived in his own world and, at that moment, had only one thing on his mind.

"Were they lovers?" he asked.

I hesitated. "Look, there are things about your stepmother that you don't know. . . ."

"I know more about her than you might think," he said almost proudly. He started to unbutton his shirt. I jerked back, thinking that he was going to take advantage of the situation and attack me, too, but that wasn't the case. He slipped the shirt over his shoulder, revealing the pure white skin of his back—or almost pure, for it was covered in rows of small black hieroglyphics, a series of letters I'd never seen before, spelling words I couldn't read. It was likely an ancient script and a long-forgotten language. Of course, I knew who had done this to him: from the chains of black pinpricks that formed the letters, I knew that the same hand had made the tattoo on my arm with a set of needles and a bottle of india ink hundreds of years ago. Tilde.

He dropped the shirt completely from his back to show me that his body was covered with the tattooed writing: across both scrawny shoulder blades and up his neck to where a collar would rest, down both arms to where cuffs would ride. The letters marched over the knobs of his spine. They disappeared into his armpit. He wore the tattoos in secret under his clothes, and God only knew what she had written there, but I think I knew why she had done it: to mark him as hers and let him prove the lengths to which he'd go to please her. And, too, she was playacting, pretending to be Adair by mimicking his habits, and trying to create her own dynasty. But her men were not immortal, and no matter what she did to try to keep them with her, they were destined to fail her in the end.

He looked at the writing on his right forearm, enchanted, as though a wild bird had settled there. "She says these are spells that bind me to her, and talismans to protect me," he said, looking up at me, hopeful that I would confirm his illusions, but I could not. I knew she had no real magic. She was not Adair. These were nothing more than tattoos he'd carry with embarrassment for the rest of his life, proof of his youthful gullibility.

"Yes, you are bound to her now." True enough in its way, but I said it only to appease him, even though it sickened me.

He smiled with a child's satisfaction as he pulled the shirt back over his tattoos and buttoned it up. "That man who's come to see her, he seems . . . twisted. There's something wrong about him," he admitted reluctantly. "Will these protect me from him, too?"

Such hope in his face. He wanted to be Tilde's youthful savior.

"Listen to me," I said, trying to break through his enchantment. "Nothing can protect you from Adair—nothing. You stay out of his reach, do you understand? Don't be left alone with him under any circumstances, and for God's sake, don't pick a fight with him."

But he only smiled smugly, secure in his folly. "Don't worry about me. I can take care of myself." And he probably thought in his naïveté that he was supremely capable—chosen, even. After all, he had seduced his stepmother; wasn't that proof of how special he was? "Adair says you are to get cleaned up," he said as he left the room. "I think he's coming back for you soon."

Once Mika had left, I took to the tiny shower in the maid's bathroom and stood under the stinging stream of hot water, wishing it could wash away what Adair had done. The water could make me clean again but not whole, quiet me outwardly but not quiet my mind. I was frightened of Adair but there was nothing I could do to stop him. I was powerless to refuse him anything, as my life would now revolve around the ebb and flow of his moods. When he was peaceable toward me, life would be tolerable, but when he was of a vengeful mind or upset by another matter, it would be hell.

I heard the door open while I was showering and wasn't surprised to find Adair slumped on the bed, staring at the spot on the mattress where he'd pinned me down and raped me. When I opened the bathroom door, sending a cloud of steam into the room, he looked up at me standing damp and naked in the doorway. There was neither desire nor anger in his eyes. He seemed as unnerved as I by what had happened earlier.

He pulled the crumpled sheet free of the mattress and tossed it to me. "I told that boy to bring towels," he said. I wrapped the sheet around my body and kept my distance, though he seemed chastened and subdued, and not in the mood to attack me again. "Get dressed," he said. "I want to talk to you, but not in here." Both of us, it seemed, were uncomfortable remaining in that room, where his violence still hung in the air.

I started for my discarded clothes, now ripped and stained, but he held out another article of clothing. "I brought something clean for you to wear," he said. It was the banyan I'd seen hanging in Alejandro's room in Barcelona, the one that had once been Adair's. The ancient olive and gold striped silk was fragile from age and thin as mist, but when I slipped it on and cinched the waist, I remembered the times I'd worn it in Adair's bedroom in the Boston house, fresh from lying in his arms.

As we walked through the house, I noticed it seemed to be empty—none of Tilde's family were in the great room, nor was there the murmur of voices drifting in from unseen quarters—and Adair led the way to a small private library, every wall of the small room lined with bookcases. He took the armchair and I sat on a love seat, perched at the farthest end from him. In threadbare silk and with wet hair, I was cold and shivering. His eyes scanned me up and down, and from those eyes and the set of his mouth and the crease of his brow I could tell there was something on his mind.

"What happens next?" I asked, careful not to show how frightened I was by what his answer might be.

He raised his eyebrows. "That is what I wish to discuss with you: what happens next. . . . You will come with me, of course."

I didn't want to appear to acquiesce, so I said nothing.

"We'll find a place to live, and you will sleep in my bed and eat at my table," he continued. "As long as you behave, do as you're told, and don't try to run away, I won't lock you up. I'll give you the run of the house as long as you live by my rules."

I wanted him to be plain about what he wanted from me, what was to be between us. Would it be as it had been in Boston? Would he expect me to act as though I adored him, and would I have to watch my every word? Or did he not care if I abhorred him, as long as I wasn't openly rebellious? "I'm to be like Uzra, then? Am I to take her place?"

"I hope it will be better between us than it had been with Uzra."

"And if I don't do as you say?"

He sighed, disappointed. "Perhaps it would be best if you didn't pretend that you have a choice, Lanore." He waited until I'd absorbed his advice before continuing. "We will leave soon—tomorrow, perhaps. Pendleton is locating a place for us to live for now. I want to get away from the others. I want it to be just the two of us, so as not to be watched and gossiped about constantly." I wondered if that was a bad sign, if privacy meant he would feel less constrained in his actions. "And once we have resumed our life together, we can look for a place that suits you better. We can go anywhere you want: what do you say to that?"

He was so subdued, he took me by surprise. And his desire to please me—again, it seemed like a trick. In the middle of all this, I was wondering, too, about Jonathan: if Adair had brought him, if he was somewhere in this house. However, I couldn't think of a way to ask without running the risk of enraging Adair anew.

"Now, there is one thing left that you must help me with," he continued. "Your friend is here . . . the man you took up with . . . the doctor from Maine. He came looking for you."

Luke is here? Panic bloomed inside me. He'd done the most foolhardy thing possible by following me—and how did he find me, anyway? I hadn't told him where I was going or whom I'd planned to meet. For one minute I was blinded by fear. But despite that, beyond common sense and words, I was grateful and amazed that Luke loved me enough to come after me.

I edged closer to Adair. "Let him go. Please."

Adair ran a hand roughly through his hair. "That is exactly what I have been thinking but, judging from your reaction, perhaps I should reconsider? You seem to care a great deal for him. Having him around will come in handy, it seems."

"That's not necessary. I'll do anything you want, Adair, I promise, if you let him go."

He looked at me, sadly cynical.

Cautiously, I placed a hand atop his. "What have you got to lose? You already have me, and this way you'll have my gratitude, too. Adair, you hold all the cards, you can afford to be magnanimous. Please."

He cast a sly sideways glance at my hand. "You promise very prettily, Lanore, but you've promised in the past, and see where that got me. You love this man enough to give yourself away for his sake. First Jonathan, now him. Never me. So prove to me that you will give yourself to me. Prove that you are mine. Come, sit on my lap."

There was nothing else I could do, so I rose and crossed around to his chair and carefully lowered myself onto him. The banyan was sheer, so I might as well have been naked, every twitch of his thighs and his groin evident to me. Strength and want emanated from him, his desire alone strong enough to crush me even while his arms remained by his sides.

"Okay," he said throatily. "Kiss me, Lanore."

I was afraid to do this, afraid of what he might be able to detect from a kiss, but I obeyed. I held his face in my hands, his beard prickling my palms, my thumbs pressed to the hard ridge of his cheekbones. I brought my lips over his, and his warm breath was caught between us for a second. Then I kissed him with as much tenderness as I could muster. I was afraid that he would know all about me in that kiss—my fear of him, my concern for Luke, and worry for what had happened to Jonathan—and that, in anger and spite, he'd destroy the man to whom I owed so much. I had sealed Luke's fate the day I selfishly asked him to help me escape from St. Andrew. I wouldn't be able to live with that, so I kissed Adair deeply, too deeply not to feel something, God help me, a rumbling deep inside me like distant thunder.

Appeased, he kissed me back fiercely, a kiss from the old days when he would pour himself into me without reserve. And then his mouth was everywhere: my cheek, my earlobe, down the length of my throat, the banyan pulled open to give him access, his leonine head buried between my breasts, his hands feeding them to his hungry mouth. From there it was only minutes until I was on my back on the love seat and he was on top of me and in me. Being with him again like this re-ignited my old desire for him, I admit, made it flame a bit around the edges, reminding me that it was not completely gone. But I felt a strange mix of emotions; I imagine it was like being mounted by a lion, pinned by crushing strength and furious passion . . . and, too, the possibility that like a wild animal he could kill me at any minute, his love switching to hatred in an instant. When he came, he collapsed on top of me, resting his head on my chest like a child, as though soothed by my heartbeat. I lay underneath him, wondering if I had performed well enough to deceive him, well enough so that he no longer felt threatened by Luke and would therefore set him free.

When we'd descended from our frenzy, Adair helped me up from the love seat, adjusting his clothing as I smoothed and cinched the banyan once again. He took my hand and turned to me. "And so it is settled," he said, pleased, choosing to believe it was different between us now. "We will go see this man Luke and you will send him on his way."

Adair took me to the garage, where he'd left Luke like a dog on the oil-stained floor in an empty bay, arms tied behind his back. I gasped at the sight of his face, which was bruised and cut up, one eye swollen shut and his lips fat and cracked, the corners crusty with blood. He'd likely have scars for the rest of his life, and his broken bones might repair poorly. He might never be the same again, and it was all my fault. I couldn't cry out in alarm and had to smother the words that leapt to my mouth and stop my tears in their tracks.

I cradled his head in my hands and he woke up, squinting at me in confusion. In my state, I was embarrassed to be before him, for surely he could smell Adair on me, and could tell that I was naked under the banyan. He'd know what I'd done. I would have to use it to my benefit.

"Lanny?" he mumbled.

"Luke, you shouldn't have come after me."

"Couldn't let you face . . . on your own. . . ."

"How did you find me, anyway?"

He squinted in confusion at my question for a moment. "Your cell phone. . . . Remember that program we downloaded, the one with the maps of Paris that would show you my GPS location in case I ever got lost? Well, it shows me where *you* are, too. I used it to follow you. . . ."

"Luke . . . listen." I pressed a finger to his lips to stop him from speaking. "I'm afraid you don't understand. I came here voluntarily."

He shook his head, disbelieving.

"And I'm so lucky. Adair's forgiven me. He's willing to take me back."

Luke closed his eyes and swallowed hard.

"So, you see, I won't be going back with you. I'm with Adair now."

"You're trying to protect me, but it won't work. You can't send me away as though I'm a child," he said without hesitation.

I looked over my shoulder and saw Adair standing a few paces off, arms crossed, watching us with a peculiar look on his face, one of hurt and sadness, and—though it didn't seem possible—terrible vulnerability, too. And then, like a cloud passing over the sun, it was gone, replaced by something as unreadable as stone.

I crouched over Luke. "I'm not protecting you, Luke: I'm finally telling you the truth. You see, I made a mistake thinking I could settle down with you. That night in St. Andrew when we met, I only wanted to get away from the police. I took one look at you and I knew I could get you to help me. You're such a Boy Scout, Luke. *A good guy.* It's written all over your face. I figured I could trick you into helping me get over the border into Canada and then I'd give you the slip and that would be that."

He wheezed with pain. "You're making this up. . . . I don't believe you. . . ."

"No, this is the truth. My head was a mess after what I did to Jonathan. I was sick of my life and afraid of being on my own. I *thought* I was ready to change; I wanted things to be different. And I thought you— I mean, you're so straight and honest, I thought you would make it happen.

"You're a good man, Luke, you were so good to me. You really tried; I can't fault you at all. . . . But you could try from here to kingdom come and it wouldn't do any good. You're not right for me. I can't make myself love you the way   I should."

Luke bit his lower lip and shook his head involuntarily, but his hand went heavy and limp in mine. He no longer squeezed back.

I kept speaking, hoping he was listening. "I didn't intend to fool you. I didn't think I'd ever go back to Adair, not in a hundred years. I didn't think he'd ever forgive me. But being around my own kind again has reminded me how my life could be. How it *should* be. We understand each other. It's not a constant game of protecting your feelings, always reassuring you that it doesn't matter that you're getting older, slower, weaker." He winced. It hurt me, too, terribly, but I had to poison his thoughts of me so he would never look back with doubt. So he would break with me forever. And apparently something about my deceit rang true, because in his eyes there was the shadow of a doubt.

"Come on, Luke," I continued as evenly as I could, "I don't have an ordinary life and I shouldn't pretend that I do. I'm not meant to raise somebody's children. Can you see me being happy in your little house in St. Andrew, doing mountains of laundry, waiting for the girls to come home from school to bake cookies?"

He strained at the cord tying his hands. "I know it's not true," he muttered. "You'd never go with him. You're afraid of him."

"I don't expect you to understand. Being with him again, I came to see that . . . I missed being with him. I missed the *wildness* of giving in to my darkest impulses. I forgot what it was like." I stood up, leaning over him. "It isn't easy to tell you this, Luke. We could've just left you here, and you'd never know. But I thought you should know the truth. So you can go back to your daughters and forget about me."

I waited, looking for an indication that he knew I was lying to him. Had he seen a waver in my gaze, a split second of regret that I was causing him pain? No, I was a good liar. I'd fooled Adair once, hadn't I? It was easy to fool someone as guileless and honest, as trusting and honorable, as Luke.

Adair chimed in then. "Did you hear that, little man? She has chosen me. She does not want you anymore."

Luke looked over at his tormentor. "Fuck you."

I threw myself in front of Adair to keep him from kicking Luke and then pulled him aside so we could speak outside of Luke's earshot.

"You heard him in there, Adair. He doesn't believe me," I said.

"You are not trying hard enough to convince him," Adair growled.

"He'll never believe I'd go back to you willingly, not after everything he's heard about you."

He gave me that strange look again. "Is that all he knows of me: the bad? Is that the only way you have thought of me?"

I was taken aback. How did he expect me to think of him?

"Could he not believe that you have the tiniest bit of love for me?" When I didn't answer him right away, he went cold. "Then perhaps you should try a little harder with your acting skills, my dear. As I recall, you could be quite a convincing actress when it suited you."

I was at the end of my rope, exhausted. I couldn't stop my tears. "Do you have to be so cruel? I've tried to do as you asked. You have powers, don't you? Isn't there something you could do?"

"I could kill him," Adair said, and then softened as he ran a finger through the tears on my cheek. "But that will not do, will it?"

"Please, Adair. If you spare his life, I will be grateful to you forever."

He winced at "forever." He wiped at my tears again. "You love him, and you don't want him to suffer for having loved you. You want me to do something to ease his heartache. That is what you mean, isn't it?"

I hung my head. "Yes."

"All right. That, I can understand. Would that it were so easy for all of us to ease our heartache. For this man, there is something I can do." He looked at Luke over my shoulder. "I will make him forget that he ever knew you. I will go into his mind and pluck out every memory he has of you. You must go to your room and wait for me. Don't come out of the room; don't try to steal a last look at him through the windows. He mustn't see you again before he leaves here or it could undo the spell."

This would be the last time I'd see Luke, I realized. He was streaked with blood and half-unconscious, and it was all my fault. Yes, it seemed it was in his best interest that he would never think of me again.

"Thank you, Adair. Thank you for . . . this kindness." I paused for a long moment, and with this last thought, I was unable to move from where I stood, feet firmly planted on the concrete garage floor. "But . . . how will I know you've done as you promised? How will I know you haven't killed him?" I asked, the thought just occurring to me.

Adair beheld me with those frightening eyes, as cold as the jewels they resembled, and said, "You won't."

THIRTY-THREE

LAKE GARDA, ITALY

The house Pendleton found for us turned out to be a château on the north end of Lake Garda, high in the Italian lake country and tucked on a switchback road to the Sarca Walls, the famously forbidding cliffs at the foothills in the Dolomites. Adair had known the region a long time ago, when it was populated by a straggly band of hardy, stubborn people who were able to survive on the demanding terrain. He had vivid memories of threadbare robbers who waylaid merchants in the mountain passes, and monks and priests who ran churches secreted high in the cliffs, strict old church stalwarts who commanded their parishes like despots.

Now the area attracted people who craved the difficult landscape for sport—rock climbers, windsurfers, and mountain bikers—but most of that activity took place in the valley, in medieval towns that bordered the lake, far from our sixteenth-century castle tucked behind an iron gate. Between the gate and the long, tricky descent into town it was impossible for me to leave the house, but there was one compensation for my isolation: a magnificent view of the mountain lake, its black surface hinting at its unfathomable depths.

I think Adair would've preferred that he and I move there alone, but in the end he brought Pendleton with us. Jude returned to Boston to make money, like a child delighted to return to his room to play video games; and Alejandro, despite much protesting that he wished to serve Adair again, was sent back to his photographer's studio in Barcelona. At least it hadn't been awkward leaving Tilde behind, as she told Adair she preferred to continue on as he'd found her. She'd done well for herself in some ways: she was wealthy, and completely independent. I think she wanted to be free to gather her own retinue of broken people who wanted someone to make them suffer for their sins. But if she modeled herself on Adair, she was the poor man's version at best; for although she had claws and fangs to sink into her victims, her only enticement was sexual humiliation, and there are only so many people who sought that kind of debasement.

In the castle, Adair spent much of his day with Pendleton, learning about the new world and the history and science that he'd missed. He left me alone for most of each day to read or watch television or shop online. I wasn't allowed to go down to the valley to actual stores, not even with a chaperone, but could have new clothing and sundries delivered to the château.

I trolled online news, too, and read all the stories I could find on Luke's return as a fugitive to St. Andrew. According to the news, he had no memory of me, and since he passed lie detector tests and brain scans, there was nothing the police could do and no charges were brought. After the news stories dried up, I tried to continue to follow him, but his name disappeared from the hospital's roster of physicians and shortly thereafter his farm appeared for sale on a real estate agent's website, even though I was sure my solicitor had completed the purchase as I'd asked. I couldn't blame him for leaving: his neighbors' curiosity had to be suffocating, and there were likely to be some who wouldn't believe that he had no recollection of me, what had happened in the hospital that night, or his months away. Despite it all, he'd managed to get out of St. Andrew, and I was happy for him.

As for the remains of my former life, I wanted to contact Henri, my lawyer, to consolidate my assets and settle my accounts, but Adair wouldn't allow it. The break had been made, he said. Burning the Paris house made it look like foul play and worked to his advantage, as he wanted it to look as though I'd disappeared off the face of the earth. He didn't want to leave a clue of any kind should someone try to find me. Besides, he said, it was fitting that I lose everything the way that he had.

The loss of all that money—though it was dwarfed by Adair's fortune—drove Pendleton mad, and he pleaded with Adair to think of it as my dowry, but Adair wouldn't change his mind. I didn't tell him about my last contact with Henri to purchase Luke's parents' farm, and to raise it to Adair would only put Henri in jeopardy. In the end, I think what Adair really wanted was to leave me penniless and make it even harder for me to escape.

As the weeks passed, I assumed no one in the surrounding villages knew of us or cared about us until I noticed that the housekeepers and gardener, who came up from town every morning, seemed strangely curious whenever our paths crossed. They never asked about who we were or where we'd come from—perhaps the hiring agency had instructed them to be discreet—and so one day I found one of the housekeepers who spoke a little English and asked her what the people in town said about us, thinking she might at least confirm that no one cared who'd rented the castle.

The maid smiled at being given permission to bring the subject up with her mysterious employers, and told me the villagers guessed we were movie people from Hollywood, here for relaxation and anonymity. Her dark eyes begged for me to confirm this, and I didn't have the heart to dissuade her. We were probably far more interesting to her this way; there are few earthly miracles that can compete with Hollywood, I've found.

Adair reserved evenings for us to spend together. I expected he would be eager to make up for two centuries of deprivation and revert to his old ways, and so I braced for a life of nightclubbing and other such diversions, such as dinners and parties and orgies with the sharply toned athletes who came to challenge the mountains; but to my surprise he seemed to have lost all taste for that and wanted to stay in. We sat in the darkened mezzanine on the second floor, looking through tall windows down the mountainside onto the lights of the city below and the stunning reflection of the moon on the inky lake.

I played Scheherazade as Adair had me tell him every detail of my life after Boston, from sailing to Europe, to being deserted by Jonathan in Morocco, to wandering through northern Africa and the Silk Road with Savva. He wanted to hear, too, about all the men who had loved me and whom I'd used subconsciously to mend the hole Jonathan had torn in my heart. Adair took it all in, rarely interrupting for a question or explanation, but making sure we touched the entire time, stroking my arm or holding my hand, or wrapping my hair around his fingers like golden threads on a spool.

I told him repeatedly that I found it embarrassing to talk so much about myself, and asked him to tell a story from his past, if only to spare me the sound of my own voice. He always demurred, saying he'd told me one chapter of his old life and look at what it had got him. I'd been the only one to figure out his deepest secret. The less I knew of him the better, he insisted. "Besides," he teased, "my stories would drive you mad with jealousy. I'd rather we make our own stories. Like the time . . . do you remember"—he pulled me on top of him—"when we went to hear that lecture on . . . oh, I can't remember what it was supposed to be about, because you were so irresistible that day that I had no patience for the lecturer. I whisked you from your seat and we went to the back of the lecture hall and we swived in the back of the auditorium. Do you remember? I can still see the faces of those shocked young men peeking over the partition, beguiled by the sight of you in such ecstasy. The rustling of your silk skirts crushed between us and the sound of your stifled cries still ringing in my ears. . . ."

"I remember," I answered, blushing.

"Tell me we will have this again, Lanore," he said suddenly, seriously. "Tell me you will thrill to be in my arms again."

I didn't know what to say; it was like being overtaken by a wave, knocked down, dragged under. All thought was squeezed from my head and I sputtered, unable to come up with a response I thought would please him, and he waved the moment aside, unhappy.

True to his word, he took me to his bed every night. I was anxious at first, unable to lose myself in the act of coupling. I couldn't stop thinking about Luke, wondering if he was all right and if he ever questioned why he couldn't remember the woman whom other people insisted he knew. Lying naked with Adair felt treasonous, but if it bothered Adair, he didn't show it. He tried to woo me most nights; other nights he seemed content to have my body to do with as he pleased. But mostly I wondered to myself about this strange situation, being treated as Adair's guest when by rights I should've been treated as his prisoner. I was grateful for having escaped the horrible punishment I'd expected to be waiting for me, but I lived in a state of continual suspense. I was afraid that perhaps I'd been living in a dream, and would awake to find the Adair from my past now lying in bed with me. I lived with the expectation that one day Adair's terrible temper would change abruptly and I'd be back in the hell I'd been dreading.

I was roaming the house by myself one afternoon, looking for fresh entertainment, when Pendleton came trotting down a staircase toward me. "There you are. I've been looking all over for you," he called out. "Adair wants to see you."

I knew I'd find him in the library, which was where they stayed most days. It was a magnificent room, probably the best in the whole château. Like the mezzanine, it had a wall of tall windows and unobstructed views of the lake, and in the afternoon, sunlight filled the room. The sun had lit up the dozens of shelves in the room so the walls were a bright mosaic of spines and different-colored leather, gilt trim sparkling.

Three round tables dominated the floor, each surrounded by armchairs, but Adair had set himself at the middle table, the one with the best view. His new laptop computer sat between stacks of books and sections from international newspapers the housekeepers brought up from town at his request. He was parked behind the laptop, staring at the screen, but he closed it when I came into the room. "Ah, Lanore. Please sit." He motioned to the chair next to his.

"What is it?" I was curious what could be on his mind; to call for me during the day was outside of his usual routine.

He studied me sharply for a moment but then seemed mindful of the severity of his appearance and softened his gaze. He'd been like this since Tilde's, a battle obviously being waged inside between brain, soul, and heart. "So, how long have we been here, two months? Are you enjoying our life here?"

"It's very nice," I answered.

"It is not quite the same as the accommodations you built for me, but it is secure, and it must be comfortable, since I must share your prison with you."

Had it begun this way with Uzra, too? I wondered. Had he been gentlemanly and courted her, encouraged her to talk about her childhood, her dreams? I could imagine how things started to go badly between them: another man catching her eye, perhaps, or maybe he began seducing other women again. Or maybe, unlike me, she had always hated him, always resented that he'd taken away her freedom.

Maybe they had had a conversation like the one we were about to have, and if I didn't tell him what he wanted to hear, my punishment would begin in earnest.

"Here we are again, Lanore, the two of us. I am pleased to see that, for your part, you are upholding your end of our agreement. You've tried neither to escape nor to contact anyone on the outside."

Our agreement. Such a deceptively harmless term implying a mutual decision. I thought of Luke, his face bruised by the beating he suffered, the last time I saw him. Do you have a moral obligation to fulfill a promise made by force? "We have a bargain," I responded.

"Correct. We have a bargain." A tense pause. "Now that two months have passed, I feel I can tell you, honestly, that I thought it would be different. You might find this naïve of me, but I thought we would reclaim what we had in Boston." I knew what he meant. There had been a period in Boston when I was taken with Adair, when I was amazed that someone as worldly as he could find me intriguing . . . when I would've been grateful for his love.

"You must understand: those days in Boston with you were the only happy times in my life. The only happy times I can remember. I am beginning to understand, however, that it may not be possible to have that time again," he continued. He seemed unable to look at me any longer and stared down at his hands. "I thought the problem between us, before, was Jonathan. He was so beautiful that I could at least understand why you loved him. Now that he is gone, I thought you would be happy with me. But there is this doctor, neither handsome nor rich, who has taken Jonathan's place in your heart. Again, there is no room for me. I cannot make sense of this, not at all."

His eyes flashed with anger for a second, and I cowered. I knew his fury too well. If that flash held for more than a second, things could go badly. It reminded me, too, that I had lived like this before, fear falling to the pit of my stomach, afraid of his black moods. I didn't want to live like that again. He saw me flinch and closed his eyes, the sight painful.

"You are well aware, I think," he went on, more calmly than before, "of my singular capabilities. In all the world, there is no one who can give you what I can. And there was a time when I would've done anything you asked. I would've made the sun shine for a full twenty-four hours or had the tides stand still on the shore. I would've made the world bloom, every field and plain, to worship you with flowers. I would've created a second moon to rise in the sky or made everyone disappear, every soul from here to the ends of the earth, so that we could have the world to ourselves, just you and I.

"There is only one man who can do these things for you, who can offer you the heavens and all of the earth, who can command the forces of nature. And yet" his eyes grew clouded, confused, and sad—"you won't have me. I could give you a potion and make you fall in love with me, but it would not be the same. That is not what I want from you. I had hoped that with time you would forgive me and come to love me, but I am beginning to understand that this will not happen as long as you love someone else in your heart. I have struggled to accept this but I find I cannot."

I held my breath and waited for his anger to break like a thunderstorm. The greater he professed his love to be, the more dangerous his disappointment. I cringed, waiting for him to dole out hellfire for my wayward heart, my intransigence. I couldn't help that I did not love him back as he loved me—exactly, it occurred to me, as I had once felt about Jonathan.

He was still speaking, even if in my panic I'd stopped listening. ". . . and it is destroying me to see that I make you so unhappy. So . . . I am letting you go."

I jerked my head up in surprise. Had I heard him correctly? I was sure I had misheard—that my ears were telling me only what they wanted to be true—but it was impossible to tell by the empty expression on his face. No, not empty: forlorn. His heart was breaking.

"What did you say?" I asked nervously.

"I release you. You are free to return to the man you love."

It was too much to comprehend at once, and I struggled to make sense of the facts as I knew them. Adair was letting me go to the man I loved—but Luke didn't even know me anymore. I'd been extracted from his memory.

Adair shook his head. "I know what you are thinking, Lanore, but there is still hope. It will be a challenge, but you must convince him that he does know you and that you shared a wonderful life together. Go find him, Lanore, and make him fall in love with you all over again. He will, if it is meant to be."

I sat stunned, afraid to move lest it break whatever spell had Adair in its grip. The lake below winked at me, and beside it the highway led to the greater world beyond. For whatever reason, a miracle had happened. Adair's stony heart was moved and I was free.

"I—I don't understand, Adair," I stuttered. "What has happened to make you change your mind?"

He ducked his head, searching for words that would explain the transformation he'd undergone. "When you fall in love, Lanore, you fall in love fiercely: we have both seen its power at work. That is the love that I want from you. Having seen it not once but twice, I cannot settle for less. I cannot be satisfied with the pallid, courtly companionship that is all you give me now. So I have resolved to make myself worthy of your love. I will figure out what it will take for you to give that love to me.

"I understand that everything must be different. Everything that's happened in the past did not work, so I must change. I plan to send Pendleton away and I'll go away myself, to a place where I can begin anew. I will teach myself to change. Such is the power of love," he said. "I can picture us having a magnificent life together one day—you smile in doubt, but eternity is a very long time, my dear—but it can never happen if I don't let you go now. I must take my chances. It would seem that there is one force of nature that I cannot command, and that is your will. Perhaps one day you will understand that, flawed as I am, no man will love you as I do, and you will search your heart and find that you love me, too."

I sat stunned and blinking for what seemed to be a long time. I was made dizzy by his speech and felt as though I'd been spun around in circles, happy and wary simultaneously. My heart leapt at the news: I was free! I could run to Luke, plead my case, try to restore his memories.

At the same time, however, I wondered if this could be a trap. Adair had given me as pretty a speech as any lover could hope for, promising eternal adoration, but at the same time he dangled freedom before my eyes, a key to the very cage he'd constructed so carefully around me. Was he testing to see which one I would choose, when there was really only one choice? If I asked for the front gates to be opened, would I be whisked away to the dungeon I suspected had been prepared in the castle depths? Would my body be fitted into the harness of straps? I began trembling at the thought.

You cannot live in fear of your beloved. Slaves cannot love their masters. I couldn't imagine staying with Adair and eternally twisting and ducking and wheedling to stay in his good graces. I drew myself up tall and looked him fully in the face. "I can hardly believe what you are telling me."

"Believe it. If you choose to leave, the car will depart in an hour to take you to the airport in Verona." His gaze remained fixed on my face, betraying no inner emotion.

"If that is so, then I choose . . ." I felt a fillip in my heart. "I choose to leave."

He tried to hide his disappointment, but a flicker in his eyes betrayed that he was crestfallen. He nodded and we rose together. I made no move when he leaned forward to kiss my cheek and then pressed our cheeks together. For that one second when our faces met,

I felt the fire from the old times just under the skin. Adair's special fire existed in no one else I'd ever met, and for a moment I almost regretted that I was about to lose it.

"The car will be waiting for you in front of the house," he said, his voice dry, not quite his own. And then he turned and left the room without giving me a chance to speak.

I packed hurriedly, still not believing my luck, half thinking that he would change his mind and come roaring down the hall with a length of cord to tie me up and whisk me away as Jonathan and I had done the night we bricked Adair up in the wall. As the suitcase filled, I became aware that the house had grown quiet, and it seemed that I was the only one in it.

There were two matters left for me to handle, and both required something from Adair, though I couldn't tempt fate a second time by asking him to his face. I sat at the desk in my room and composed a note. First, I asked him to release Savva, if that was what Savva truly wanted. *If you want me to love you,* I wrote, *you must be capable of compassion.* Second, I wrote that I hoped he would tell me someday about what had happened to Jonathan. I told him that I'd spent the past two months hoping to hear something about Jonathan's fate but that he'd chosen to keep this from me. I understood that my love for Jonathan was a painful subject for him, but I told him he had nothing to fear on this subject—not anymore—and that I hoped one day he would be able to tell me what I wanted to know.

Once the letter was finished and left on the desk, it was time to make my farewells. I rushed down the hall looking left and right through open doorways, hoping to see the housekeepers or Pendleton, but there was no one. No shadows in the golden late afternoon light, no muffled conversation floating up from the kitchen, no gardener visible on the lawn through the tall windows.

I paused outside the closed doors to Adair's bedroom and thought about seeing him, but realized the folly of it and hurried away. I passed the door to the library, too, where Pendleton normally spent his afternoons in Adair's company, but he wasn't there. I thought about searching him out to say my good-byes but decided against it. As I carried my suitcase over the open threshold—a black sedan was idling in the gravel courtyard—I felt like a princess in a fairy tale making her escape while the rest of the castle slept under an enchanted spell. For once, the enchantment worked in my favor.

The driver stepped out. I recognized him as the man who drove the van that transported the staff from town in the mornings and evenings. He put my suitcase in the trunk and held the door for me. As I settled into my seat, rummaging through my purse to make sure nothing had been left behind in haste, he leaned over the backseat to hand me a large envelope.

"The gentleman of the house asked me to give this to you," he said, smiling apologetically for his unsteady English before turning back to the steering wheel.

As we drove slowly through the open gates, I looked at the envelope, made of heavy-weight cream paper with a string-and-button closure, fat as an album of wedding photographs. While the sedan bounced over the rutted mountain road, I unspooled the long red thread, hands shaking with curiosity, and then slid the contents into my lap.

I recognized the larger of the two documents immediately, as I'd seen it before: it was one of Adair's old books of spells, just two scarred wooden covers and a collection of brittle loose sheets of paper and parchment. I sat weighing it in my hands for a moment, wondering why he'd chosen to give it to me. Maybe he meant that he'd renounced magic and alchemy, or thought it would give me some comfort, a sign that he wouldn't use his powers against me in the future.

The second object was an envelope made of the stiffest paper I'd ever felt. After first glancing at the rearview mirror to make sure the driver wasn't spying on me, I worked open the flap and slid out several folded pieces of paper. The sheets were covered with Adair's handwriting, ink dragged in sharp lines and dashes across a porous, thirsty page by a pen nib. The strangest thing, however, was that it was written in a language I didn't recognize and by all rights should not have understood, and yet, when I concentrated on it, I found it made sense. I could read it.

My dearest Lanore, he wrote:

> *Forgive my intrusion of your departure, but I ask for your indulgence in one last matter. In the hope that you may one day come back to me if you better understand me, I would like to share with you a few things that I have shared with no one else. I wish to trust you with this knowledge because I see that we must have nothing between us if you are to love me. No one else will be able to read these pages, only you. I am entrusting you with secret knowledge, my dear, and secret knowledge is the strongest knowledge. I will start at the beginning: 1038.*

My heart sped up. If his story began in 1038, it was much earlier than he'd previously confessed. The pages trembled in my hand.

Did I really want to know Adair's secrets? I was free of him now. I could put all that had happened behind me. But I wasn't sure that I could make it stick—that memories of him wouldn't visit me every night, beckoning, trying to coax me back.

One more time I glanced up at the rearview mirror. The driver's eyes remained on the road. In the last brilliant golden rays, I caught a fragment of the castle in the silvery mirror, a dark token jutting out of the brooding mountainside, receding quickly. The lake, lapping waves glittering in afternoon light, flashed from the valley ahead.

Cocooned in the silence of the car, I settled into the deep leather seat, smoothed the pages one more time, and began reading:

> *I was born in a stone fortress on the edge of the Ceahlău Massif mountain range in Romania, the castle clinging to the notoriously wild and dangerous rock face as fiercely as I, a sickly child, clung to life. . . .*

ACKNOWLEDGMENTS

I would like to thank my friends and family for the outpouring of support for my debut novel and the first book in this series, *The Taker*. Special thanks to Barbara and Joe, Margaret and Bruce, Geoff and Janis, Diana and Bob, Linda and Dennis, John and Joann, my in-laws Noralie and John, and Barbara Webster. Special thanks to Eileen McGervey and the wonderful women at One More Page Books: Terry and Lelia Nebeker, and Katie Fransen. Thanks to Michaela Hackner and Kathy Crewe for looking at early drafts of *The Reckoning*. Thank you to the many book bloggers who embraced *The Taker*, with a special thanks to Jennifer Lawrence and Swapna Krishna for the pep talks. Thank you, Janet Cadsawan, for being my shrink. Thanks to the Writer's Center and the Community of Writers at Squaw Valley for their support.

Heartfelt thanks to Jamie Ford, Danielle Trussoni, Scott Westerfeld, Kresley Cole, M. J. Rose, Meg Waite Clayton, Keith Donohue, C. W. Gortner, and Alexi Zentner for taking time from their busy schedules to provide kind words for *The Taker*.

"Thank you" doesn't begin to cover my gratitude to my editor at Gallery, Tricia Boczkowski, who poured a tremendous amount of time and thought into this novel. This book would not exist if not for Trish's boundless determination and clear-eyed vision. I am grateful for her good cheer throughout the entire process.

I am grateful to Louise Burke, Anthony Ziccardi, and Jen Bergstrom for their strong support of *The Taker* trilogy. My thanks to everyone at Gallery for being such a great group to work with: Alexandra Lewis, Kate Dresser, Mary McCue, Natalie Ebel, and Ed Schlesinger. Thanks also to Liz Perl, Jennifer Robinson, Wendy Sheanin, and Stuart Smith at Simon & Schuster for their generous support.

Thanks to Anna Jean Hughes for taking care of *The Taker* trilogy at Century Books/Random House UK, and to Ruth Waldram and Sarah Page. I am grateful for the work Intercontinental Literary Agency does on my behalf, especially Sam Edenborough, Nicki Kennedy, and Katherine West, and to Gray Tan of the Grayhawk Agency. My thanks, also, to Matthew Snyder at CAA.

My deepest gratitude goes to my agent, Peter Steinberg, for his incredible support throughout this past tumultuous year, and to his colleagues, Edward Graham and Lisa Kopel.

And lastly, I thank my husband, Bruce, for his love and support.

THE RECKONING

ALMA KATSU

INTRODUCTION

In the sequel to Alma Katsu's riveting debut novel, *The Taker*, *The Reckoning* opens with Lanore embarking on a new life—attending a museum exhibit showcasing a collection of her lost nineteenth-century treasures with Luke, who has fallen both into her immortal, hidden world and in love. She has seemingly outrun her past and has broken free from Adair's eternal power, imprisoning him over two hundred years ago. Yet when Adair breaks free from his cell, a treacherous hunt begins; one that will surely end in bloodshed. As Adair regains his strength and struggles to adapt to modernity, he vows vengeance against his once-beloved Lanny. Flashbacks to past centuries, dark magic, and wanton violence pepper *The Reckoning* as it swells to an intense showdown between Lanny and Adair. In the moment of truth, Adair must choose to put aside his feelings for Lanny in order to exact his revenge, or to forgive her betrayal and try to win back her love.

Topics & Questions for Discussion

1. In the beginning of *The Reckoning*, does Lanny seem to be living a happy life with Luke? What are her concerns and hesitations about Luke?

2. Consider the quote Lord Bryon inscribed on Lanny's fan: "Man's love is of man's life a thing apart, 'tis woman's whole existence." What does this quote mean to you? Do you think it foreshadows any future events in the novel?

3. Do you think Adair deserved to be locked away for two hundred years? Did Lanny have any other choice? Do you feel any sympathy toward Adair? Why or why not?

4. *The Taker* begins with Lanny confessing to murdering Jonathan, the eternal love of her life. Do you believe that she should be held to society's rules and tried for her crime? Or do you think the circumstances excuse her actions?

5. Do you think Luke made the right decision to follow his heart and run away with Lanny? What did he sacrifice? What would you have done if you were Luke?

6. When Lanny sensed Adair was pursuing her, do you think she made the right decision to leave Luke? What did this choice tell you about her character?

7. In your opinion, do you think Lanny is capable of ever really giving her heart to a mortal man, with the knowledge that the man will leave her behind by aging and dying? Do you think she can ever truly love anyone other than Jonathan? Do you think it is possible to be in love with different people at the same time?

8. If given the opportunity, would you choose to live for eternity? Would you consider it a blessing or a curse? How does Lanny view her immortality? Adair? Pendleton?

9. What does Lanny learn during her time with Savva in the Middle East? How does her ill-fated love affair with Abdul influence her perspective on relationships?

10. Which do you think would be a worse punishment for Lanny—to be possessed for eternity, like Uzra, or to die? Explain your answer.

11. Jonathan and Lanny do not spend any time together after his reincarnation. Were you surprised by this turn of events? Do you think they ever had a real chance at reconnecting romantically?

12. How was Jonathan changed by his death? How did his feelings for Lanny change in his reincarnated state?

13. Do you believe that people can genuinely change the way Adair seems to have changed by the end of *The Reckoning*? Compare Adair's and Tilde's capacity to change and evolve as characters.

14. Which characters are you most interested in learning more about in the next installment of *The Taker Trilogy*? Do you think Lanny is capable of forgiving Adair, as he hopes? Do you think they stand a chance at finding happiness together—for eternity?

ENHANCE YOUR BOOK CLUB

1. Consider serving a signature "elixir" at your book club discussion by adding food coloring to an ordinary drink or by serving it in a unique bottle or glass. Before everyone drinks their "elixir," go around the group and have everyone state what they would mix a potion for if they had knowledge of alchemy.

2. Create a "reverse" bucket list with your book club. Go around the group and ask: What would you do if you were *never* going to kick the bucket? What would you want to accomplish if you literally had all the time in the world?

3. *The Reckoning* takes place all over the world—from Casablanca, to Venice, to Boston, to London. Print out a map of the world and chart Lanny's and Adair's travels. Discuss with your group how each new setting impacted the narrative action and tone of the story. For maps available to print, visit www.english.freemap. jp/world_e/6.html.

4. Do you have a question for author Alma Katsu? Consider inviting her to your book club discussion of *The Reckoning*! Find out more about *The Taker Trilogy* and about how to contact Alma by visiting www.almakatsu.com/books.php.

A Conversation with Alma Katsu

How did the process of writing *The Reckoning* differ from writing your first novel, *The Taker*?

It was completely different. Okay, aside from a laptop computer being involved and getting to work with the same editor, Tricia Boczkowski, it was completely different. It took ten years to write *The Taker* on my own, wandering in the wilderness, as it were, whereas with *The Reckoning* I had about twenty months and a very clear idea of the story, and the process *still* didn't go as I expected. Add the usual angst associated with a sophomore book—you've pulled a rabbit out of a hat once, but can you do it again?—and all these voices that you now have in your head, the less-than-stellar reviews and criticisms (which every writer gets) of the first book to deal with. Luckily, I have several friends who were also working on second books and we'd get together for lunch and have a good cry. It helps to know other people find it as maddening as you.

In *The Reckoning*, your second book in the trilogy, you delve deeper into the sources and extent of Adair's alchemical power. How does alchemy's real history compare to Adair's life experience?

The practice of alchemy can be seen as the transition between the time when man used solely philosophy/theology to make sense of the world and the beginnings of modern science. It's chemistry and physics, but intertwined with religion and spirituality, or—another way to think of it—looking to the natural world for evidence of the divine. Alchemy was practiced for a long time and by many cultures, so—to address the question directly—I think its "real history" covers a wide range of experience. In other words, I don't think there is only one valid "experience" of alchemy. In classical Greek times, practitioners were more apt to look for evidence of the divine in their experiments than, say, a later Western practitioner like Sir Isaac Newton. Unlike Newton, however, Adair studied alchemy over *centuries*. He started in the flat-earth days, when some worried that attempts to understand the physical world would be an affront to God, and became more inclined over time to see his experiments as purely scientific.

Is alchemy truly magic, or just mastery of natural resources and processes? Would you consider modern-day medicines and procedures comparable to ancient alchemy?

Alchemy is an attempt to understand the world through both the natural/physical *and* the philosophical. The two are fused; you can't say alchemy is one or the other, and it's a reflection of our times (or perhaps Western thought) to think that alchemy can be defined in these terms. The best way to think of it might be as a sliding scale, with pure spirituality on one end (think Paul Coelho's novel *The Alchemist*) and pure science (Sir Isaac Newton) on the other. Even the "holy grails" of alchemy, the Philosopher's Stone and the Elixir of Life, have metaphysical properties that can't be derived solely from the physical world.

Which is why people don't practice alchemy these days: because we in the West tend to separate modern science and spirituality into two different realms. The scientific and the spiritual have each been banished to its own corner, and we look to science alone to explain the unknowns of the physical world. We know through chemistry that you can't turn lead into gold, case closed. Or is it? Look at quantum physics: latest research only goes to show that our understanding of the universe is incomplete, and new properties are being uncovered that, at this early stage, look an awful lot like magic.

What the reader should notice in *The Reckoning* is that while Adair professes to be a man of science, the feats he performs are more in the realm of magic, even if he doesn't acknowledge this. There's a reason, and it will be explained—all will be explained—in the next book, *The Descent*.

In *The Reckoning*, Lanny donates belongings acquired over several lifetimes. What was your inspiration when you described these items, including the fan signed by Lord Byron?

Part of my inspiration comes from a childhood experience. When I was young, we lived next door to an elderly woman, once socially prominent but long a widow, childless, pretty much living in seclusion. Her house was one of the fanciest in town, but inside, it was dark and formal, and seemed very exotic to me, since I'd lived only in military housing up to that point. It was filled with nice but odd things from earlier eras. One thing that stands out in my memory—to give you an example—was a pair of ornate wall hangings made with dead birds, stuffed and posed under glass, very Victorian, fancy and creepy at the same time. I suppose some people grew up surrounded by Grandma's "things," but to me, it was like visiting another planet. My mother sent me over to clean her house occasionally, so I got a good look at stuff as I dusted and vacuumed. I guess it made more of an impression on me than I realized.

The exhibit in the first chapter of *The Reckoning* was inspired by a show held at the Smithsonian in the 1980s, *Treasure Houses of Britain: 500 Years of Private Patronage and Art Collecting*. It was an exhibition of art objects from 200 country homes in England, Scotland, Wales, and Ireland, meant to illustrate the scope of British private collections from the fifteenth century to the present. It was jaw-dropping to think that these beautiful things normally graced someone's actual house (granted, the "house" was a grand manor home), that there were people who lived surrounded by priceless masterworks every day.

You write beautifully about several very different eras and geographic locations in *The Reckoning*. What era and location most intrigued you? What kind of research did you do before writing these scenes?

Like most writers, I tend to draw on places and periods in time with which I'm already familiar. This is where being a former intelligence analyst pays off, because you amass a huge amount of random knowledge, especially of geography and history. For instance, when I was with the Defense Department, I spent a lot of time working on Afghanistan—no surprise there—and came to learn a lot about the country and the people. That, combined with a fondness for Kipling, led to the idea of Lanny and Savva running guns in the Hindu Kush. For the character of Savva, the perpetual expat on the run from his inner demons, I drew on the lives of two famous Brits who also fell in love with the desert: Paul Bowles, author of *The Sheltering Sky*, and T. E. Lawrence, more widely known as Lawrence of Arabia.

In some ways, flashy technical devices seem magical, but Adair is not impressed; he dismisses them as distractions. Do you identify with Adair's critique of modern technology—and society's addiction to technological devices?

Not at all: Having grown up in the age before computers, I have a strong appreciation for technology. I meant for Adair's disdain of modern technology to show not so much that he didn't value technological change as that he was tired of having to keep up with the times. That even an immortal being will act like a crotchety old man sometimes. It's fairly universal as we age, I think, to be frustrated not so much by technology but by constant change. And these days, nothing exemplifies change like technology. It was interesting to put myself in Adair's position and think about how much life had changed between the nineteenth and twenty-first centuries, and to imagine how someone would leapfrog from the Industrial Revolution to the present day.

How do you approach writing female characters, like Tilde, Lanny, and Trish?

I don't think I approach female characters any differently from the way I approach male characters. I try to give all my characters depth, even minor characters. Not to harp on my past life, but analyzing behavior and evaluating people is a big part of intelligence work. You need to figure out what makes a person tick, if they're being truthful with you, what their motives are, that sort of thing. I try to utilize this experience and understanding of human nature when developing characters. Readers may not see themselves behaving the same way as one of the characters, but hopefully, because they understand what drives the characters, their actions will seem natural—inevitable, even. And that's why we read novels, isn't it, to step into someone else's head for the duration of a few pages?

Do you believe that anyone is capable of the kind of forgiveness Adair is asking of Lanny?

Sure—you see it every day. You see wives go back to philandering or abusive husbands, children nurse elderly parents who once belittled and tormented them, friends stand by each other despite the hurts they've inflicted on each other. Sometimes it's done consciously, but sometimes it's done because the person has been so shaped by his experiences that he's unable to function in a "normal" environment. Maybe he won't leave out of guilt or obligation, or because he fears if he leaves this person, no one else will love him. Lanny is trying to learn from past mistakes, to reach beyond her fears and insecurities—just as we all do—but only time will tell if she'll be successful.

Yes, Adair is a monster. He is as unfeeling as stone, and has done terrible things to innocent people. In *The Reckoning*, however, his stony heart begins to soften. He vows to change, and believes he can give Lanny the kind of devotion she has always wanted, if only she'll give him a chance. He's not unlike a felon who has committed a terrible crime but has gone to prison and done his time. He says he's reformed and only wants a chance to live a normal life. It's up to Lanny to decide whether it's in her heart to forgive him and whether she *wants* to be with him. There's one more waltz before the dance is over, and we see what Lanny decides in the third book, *The Descent*.

Do you think your characters are capable of experiencing true love?

Absolutely. You might ask, however, what I mean by true love.

To me, true love is the ideal state of love. True love is not conditional. It's not necessarily a two-way street. It may not be equitable, but you have decided that you can live with the terms. It's when you love someone so much that you'll do what's best for them, even if it's not going to get you what you want, even when it gets you nothing. It's not romance. It's not about what the other person can or will do for you but about what he or she brings to your world, how he makes you want to be a better person. True love works best if the person you love loves you in the same way. Really selfish people cannot know true love. Lots of people experience true love but can't sustain it. (There are a lot of broken people out there. They don't exist only within the pages of my books.)

Redemption is a continuing theme in *The Taker Trilogy* and the driving force behind Lanny, Adair, and Jonathan's actions. Is it a theme you identify with in other great works of literature?

I think I identify more with the *lack* of redemption in literature. It seems a recent trend—and by recent, I mean the past thirty years or so—that any character who has fallen from grace must learn his lesson and change his ways by the end of the book. Look at *Madame Bovary* or *Wuthering Heights*, look at Thomas Hardy. To require happy endings is understandable in a children's book, but in adult literature it seems disingenuous, because in life, most people don't redeem themselves. They continue through life nursing their shortcomings, the low-grade alcoholism, the occasional extramarital fling. Of course, most people aren't as flawed as Lanny and Jonathan, let alone Adair. But that's the reason for immortality in the story: when you're *this* bad, you need a very long time to straighten yourself out.

Continue reading for an exclusive excerpt from
the thrilling final installment of *The Taker Trilogy*

THE DESCENT

by Alma Katsu
Spring 2013 from Gallery Books

CHAPTER 1

The sunlight glinting off the Mediterranean that afternoon was bright enough to blind, and the boat bounced hard off the waves like a broken-down carnival ride. I'd come halfway around the world to find someone who was very important to me, and I wasn't about to let a little rough weather keep me from finishing my journey. I squinted against the headwind to the horizon, trying to will a rocky shoreline to appear out of nowhere.

"Is it much farther?" I asked the captain.

"Signorina, until I met you this morning, I never knew this island even existed, and I have lived on Sardegna my entire life." He was in his fifties if he was a day. "We must wait until we get to the coordinates, and then we will see what we shall see."

My stomach floated unsteadily, due to nerves and not the waves. I had to trust that the island would be where it was supposed to be. I'd seen strange things in my lifetime—my *long* lifetime—many of them stranger than the sudden appearance of an island that heretofore had not existed.

That would be a relatively minor miracle, on the scale of such things. Among the major miracles was the fact that I was destined to live forever. I'd already lived for more than two hundred years, but I was a mere babe compared to the man I was going to see, Adair, the man who had gifted me—or burdened me, depending on your point of view—with eternal life. His age was inestimable. He could be a thousand years old, or older. He'd given differing stories every time we met, including when we last parted four years ago. Had he been a student of medicine in medieval times, devoted to science and caught in the thrall of alchemy, intent on discovering new worlds? Or was he a heartless manipulator of lives and souls, a man without a conscience who was interested only in extending his life for the pursuit of pleasure? I didn't think I'd gotten the truth yet.

We had a tangled history, Adair and I. He had been my lover and my teacher, master to my slave. We had literally been prisoners to each other. Somewhere along the way he fell in love with me, but I was too afraid to love him in return. Afraid of his unexplainable powers, and his furious temper. Afraid of what I knew he was capable of and afraid to learn he was already guilty of committing far worse. I ran away to follow a safer path with a man I could understand. I always knew, however, that my path would one day lead me back to Adair.

Which is how I came to be in a small fishing boat far off the Italian coast. I wrapped my sweater more tightly around my shoulders and rode along with the ship's rocking, and closed my eyes for a moment's rest from the glare. I had shown up at the harbor in Olbia, looking to hire a boat to take me to an island everyone said didn't exist. "Name your price," I'd said when I'd gotten tired of being ridiculed. Of the boat owners who were suddenly interested, this captain seemed the kindest.

"Have you been to this area before? Corsica, perhaps?" he asked, trying either to make small talk or to figure out what I expected to find at this empty spot in the Mediterranean Sea.

"Never," I answered. The wind tossed my blond curls into my face.

"And your friend?" He meant Adair. Whether he was my *friend* or not, I didn't know. We'd parted on good terms, but he could be mercurial. There was no telling what mood he'd be in the next time we met.

"I think he's lived here for a few years," I answered.

Even though it appeared that I'd piqued the captain's interest, there was nothing more to say, and so he busied himself with the GPS and the ship's controls, and I went back to staring over the water. We had cleared La Maddalena Island and now faced open sea.

Before long, a black speck appeared on the horizon. "Santa Maria," the captain muttered under his breath as he checked the GPS again. "I tell you, signorina, I sail through this area every day and I have never seen that"—he pointed at the land mass, growing in size as we approached—"before in my life."

As we got closer, the island took shape, forming a square rock that jutted out of the sea like a pedestal. Waves crashed against it on all sides. From this distance, there didn't appear to be a house on the island, nor any people.

"Where is the dock?" the captain asked me, as if I'd know. "There is no way to put you ashore if there is no dock."

"Sail all the way around," I suggested. "Perhaps there's something on the other side."

He brought his little boat around and we circled slowly. On the second side was another cliff, and on the third, a steep slope dropped precipitously to a stony and unwelcoming beach. On the fourth side, however, there was a tiny floating dock tethered to a rock outcropping, and a rickety set of sunburnt stairs leading to a vacant-looking stone house.

"Can you get close to the dock?" I shouted into the captain's ear to be heard above the wind. He gave me an incredulous look, as though only a crazy person would consider climbing onto the floating platform.

"Would you like me to wait for you?" he asked as I prepared to climb over the side of the boat. When I shook my head, he protested,

"Signorina, I cannot leave you here! We don't know if it is safe. The island could be deserted . . ."

"I have faith in my . . . friend. I'll be fine. Thank you, Captain," I said, and leapt onto the weatherworn wooden dock, which bucked against the waves. He looked absolutely apoplectic, his eyes bulging as I climbed the staircase, gripping the railing as I struggled against the wind. When I got to the top, I waved to him, signaling that he should go, and watched as his boat turned back the way we had come.

The island was exactly as it had appeared from the sea, as if carved from one lump of black stone that had emerged directly from the ocean floor. There was no vegetation except for a stand of scraggy pines and a bright chartreuse carpet of moss spread at their roots. A few goats ran by and seemed to regard me with an amused, knowing air before scampering out of sight. They had long, silky coats of many colors, and one had a pair of twisted horns, wicked-looking enough to be worn by the devil.

I turned to the house, so ancient and solid that it seemed to have grown straight from the bedrock of the island. The house was a curious thing, its stone walls so sandblasted by weather that it was impossible to tell much about it, including when it might've been built, though it resembled a medieval fortress—small and compact yet just as imposing. The walls were pocked with small windows, and these were covered with iron bars, as though the occupants thought an attack by pirates was still possible. The front door was a big slab of wood that had been thoroughly dried and bleached by the sun. It had elaborate ironwork hinges and was decorated with iron studs in the Moorish style, and gave the impression that even a battering ram wouldn't be able to break it open. I lifted the knocker and brought it down once, twice, three times.

When I heard nothing from the other side of the door, however, I started to wonder if maybe I'd made a mistake. What if the captain had misread his charts and left me on the wrong island—what if Adair had moved back to civilization on the mainland by now?

I'd tracked him down through a man named Pendleton who acted as Adair's servant until Adair chose to go into seclusion, refusing all company. While Pendleton wasn't sure what had caused Adair to withdraw from the world, he gave me coordinates to the island, which he admitted was so small that it appeared on no maps. He had warned me there was no easy way to get in touch with Adair: he didn't use email and didn't seem to have a phone. I had no intention of alerting him to my arrival anyway—force of habit made me wary of Adair still—but I also didn't want to be put off, or dissuaded from coming, which Adair might conceivably try to do if he was of the mood.

I knew Adair was somewhere in the area, though, because I felt his presence, the unceasing signal that connected him to each of the people he'd gifted with eternal life. The presence felt like an electronic droning in your consciousness that you couldn't stop. It would fall when he was far away—as it had the last four years—or grow stronger when he was close. This was the strongest it had been in a while, but I couldn't tell if it meant he was on the island—and at the moment it was competing with the butterflies in my stomach in anticipation of seeing him again.

I had been distressed to hear that Adair was living by himself, particularly because it was such a remote location. Now that I saw the island, I was more worried still. The house looked as though it had no electricity or running water, not unlike where he might've lived in the eighteenth century. I wondered if this return to a way of life that was familiar to him could be a sign that he was overwhelmed by the present and couldn't cope with the never-ending onslaught of the new. And for our kind, retreating into the past was never a good idea.

I sought Adair out now after four years apart only because I'd been seized by an idea and wanted to put it into action, and I needed his help to make it work. I had no notion, however, if he still cared for me enough to help me, or if his love had dried up when it went unreciprocated. It would be harder for him to deny me to my face, though, so I'd decided to make my request in person.

I knocked again, louder. If worse came to worse, I could find a way into his house and wait for Adair to return. It seemed an arduous trip to make for nothing. Given my condition, it wasn't as though I needed anything to live on, food or water, or that I couldn't deal with the cold (though there was split wood stacked against the side of the house and three chimneys visible on the roof). If he didn't return after a reasonable length of time, I had my cell phone and the harbormaster's number, though the captain had warned me that reception was nearly impossible to get this far off the coast, though if I was lucky, I might be able to flag down a passing boat . . .

The door flung back at that instant and, to my surprise, a thin woman with brassy blond hair stood before me. She was in her late twenties, I would guess, and though pretty, she was worn around the edges in a way that made me think she'd worked hard at enjoying life. She had on a wrinkled sundress and sandals, and hoop earrings that were big enough to wear as bracelets. Unsurprisingly, she regarded me with suspicion.

"Oh! I'm sorry—I hope I'm not on the wrong island," I said, regaining my wits in time to remember to be charming, all the while thinking: *In seclusion, my ass, Pendleton.* "I'm looking for a man by the name of Adair. I don't suppose there's anyone here by that name?"

She cut me off so sharply that I almost didn't get the last word out. "Is he expecting you?" She spoke with a working-class British accent. Over her shoulder, a second woman stepped into view at the other end of the hall, a full-figured woman with long dark-brown hair. Her skirt came down to her ankles, and she wore embroidered Turkish slippers on her feet. Aside from their shared displeasure at seeing me, the pair of young women were physically as dissimilar as two women could be.

"No, he doesn't know I was coming, but we're old friends and—"

The two of them crowded the doorway now, shoulder to shoulder, a barricade of crossed arms and frowns set on lipsticked mouths. Up close like this, I could see how attractive they were. The blonde was like a model, thin and boyish, while the brunette was lush and womanly, and a picture of them in bed with Adair came to my mind unbidden, the three in a tangle of bare arms and legs, heavy breasts and silken flanks. Their lips on his chest and groin, and his head thrown back in pleasure. A wave of hurt passed over me, tinged with that particular sense of belittlement rarely felt out of adolescence. I fought the urge to turn around and flee.

Had I been wrong to come here? No, knowing Adair hadn't changed and had returned to his sybaritic ways made my task easier. There would be no strings, no possibility of reconciliation. I could forget about everything except asking for Adair's help.

"Look, girls," I started, shifting the weight of the knapsack in my hands. "Would you mind if I come inside to get out of this wind before I'm blown off a cliff? And if you would be so kind as to let Adair know that he has a visitor? My name is—"

"Lanore." His voice rang in my ear, rushing to fill a space left empty. And then he appeared at the end of the hall, a shadowy figure backlit by the sun. My heart raced, being in his presence once again. Adair, the man who'd hurt and deceived me, loved and exalted me, brought a man back from the dead for me, given me eternal life in the hope I would share it with him. Did he still love me enough to help me?

As I stood in Adair's magnetic presence, everything that had happened between us in the past rushed back to me in a tumult, all that passion and anger and hurt. The chaos of the strange world I had known when I'd lived with him tugged at me. I stood at his door ready to ask him to take a journey with me—a journey that wasn't without risk. The bond between us might be ruined forever. Still, I had no choice. No one else could help me.

A new chapter in our history was about to begin.